◆ FriesenPress

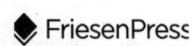

Suite 300 - 990 Fort St
Victoria, BC, V8V 3K2
Canada

www.friesenpress.com

Copyright © 2020 by Keara Gerda
First Edition — 2020

All rights reserved.

No part of this publication may be reproduced in any form, or by any means, electronic or mechanical, including photocopying, recording, or any information browsing, storage, or retrieval system, without permission in writing from FriesenPress.

ISBN
978-1-5255-7570-9 (Hardcover)
978-1-5255-7571-6 (Paperback)
978-1-5255-7572-3 (eBook)

1. FICTION, GAY

Distributed to the trade by The Ingram Book Company

ANGEL

KEARA GERDA

First, Heather, thank you for being one of the few people genuinely excited for me when I shared my progress on my novel and helping me grow over the years we worked together, and also thanks to my publishing team.

I wouldn't have been able to do this without them.

This novel was written with the hopes of broadening the LGBT+ romance section and some basic knowledge on a very different lifestyle than many people live. The story is vanilla compared to the depths of the BDSM world, and I encourage you, whether you are new, seasoned, have many partners, or have none, to (safely and personally) learn more about it.

CHAPTER ONE

I WHIMPERED AS I cleaned myself with slow, twitching digits. The only thing that kept me from crying was the small wad of cash that sat in the back pocket of my shorts. No, this job wasn't pretty, especially when kneeling in a little alley with barely any grace. It wasn't always gentle or joyful. It was often rough and dirty, and if you put yourself in a bad situation, it was up to you to get yourself out of it. People died in this job. People were kidnapped, raped, and beaten in this job.

But it was a job that paid just enough to get us to the end of the month... barely. The number of customers I was able to rope in varied; they were mostly older men who had nothing else to do other than pay for sex and cheat on their wives for a night. Some were women just looking for a good time, a friend. Some nights, all I earned was a long walk around town and not a second glance. There were a few regulars in between.

My walk home was, and always would be, agonizing. This night had been a particularly bad one; my insides felt as if they had been ripped apart, and I could feel the hot blood that trickled and seeped into my boxers. I shivered against the cool breeze that travelled throughout the darkness of night in Los Angeles. I wrapped my arms around myself to shield the chill and darted home, knowing the hot sun would soon be rising. The world was oblivious to the little boy who made his money by selling himself.

My mother hadn't risen yet, and I was thankful for the few hours of sleep she was able to get. Her over-time shifts at the diner left her exhausted, not to mention the constant fretting over the overdue bills and her own son. Sometimes the pay wasn't horrible when she worked extra hours. I told her not to worry about me. I told her that I had a job at Shopmart. I did have a job at Shopmart... until I began arriving late to work. Even running to the other side of Santa Monica wasn't enough for me to keep my job.

The decrepit house I lived in was warmer than the outdoors, but it would probably be a lot warmer if we had paid for the heating bill within the last few weeks. But it was... home. Almost. The building had always felt a little lonelier than all the others on the street. It had always given my mother and I a sense of alienation from the world. We weren't sure if it was the flaking paint or stained carpet.

My bathroom was the only place that came to mind when I entered my home. I was anxious to clean the dried seed and blood from my thighs because napkins and paper towels could only go so far. I paused to listen for my mother's snores, proving she was asleep, before locking the bathroom door and turning on the tap.

Nothing happened. I grimaced at the mirror.

Great. Just my luck.

Then I tried again, twisting the handle for a second time. The only reply I received was a muted squeak of complaint from the aggravated metal. My defeated expression stared back at me in the mirror. Long tufts of dark hair stood straight while my cheeks, elongated by high cheekbones, looked rather hollow. My lips, full, resembling my father's more than my mother's thin lips, were pulled taught with distaste. A little red mark that would soon turn into a bruise sat just under my thin, square jaw.

ANGEL

I had forgotten that we weren't able to get the water bill paid that month. We had been using the neighbour's hose outside.

I grudgingly cleaned myself in the shade of the ancient apple tree that stood tall just beside my mother's bedroom window. I believed the tree was one of the last pure things in the city, growing slowly, but surely. I could remember the times when I couldn't reach the apples that hung from those low branches, no matter how high I jumped or how far I reached. Now, I left them alone altogether. The birds would enjoy the fruit more than I would.

I changed hastily—shivering from the outside chill—clambered up the small tree, and snuck back into my bedroom window to curl into bed, seeking any form of warmth from my tattered sheets. I could feel my boxers scratch against cuts and bruises created by one man and his filthy hands, igniting flaming images that burned behind my lids when I closed them.

....

I was awakened by the slamming of our front door: Teressa Roggy, my mother, leaving for work.

During the day, I usually slept. Very few customers revealed themselves in daylight, and I decided that I should practice their rituals.

I rolled to my side while fiddling absently at the blinds covering my window, and began humming to myself-a tune I had felt vibrating the sidewalk as I passed a local gentlemen's club close to my home. Some of my favourite activities were singing and humming; often, I did it during sex to pull my mind away from the pain. I adored music in all its forms. But I didn't recognize most songs, as I had never been blessed with any kind of radio or cell phone, nor did I care about names or artists. I didn't need a phone to hear music. My voice was cracked and broken, but I managed to croak out the one line before being forced to clear my throat, swallow hard, and try again into my pillow. I fell asleep again, wishing I could one day meet one of the most famous pop stars that often roam Los Angeles. They never visited my part of the city.

I slept on and off that day, only leaving the attic to use the washroom and curl up on the couch in a broken heap. I had eaten the last of our cereal the evening before and hadn't eaten since. All that was left in the fridge was half a litre of milk and a mini bottle of ketchup. Maybe, if I searched hard enough, I would find the block of butter hidden in the bottom drawer. My stomach had been growling since yesterday, and I hoped that Mom would bring home some leftovers from the diner.

Eventually, after much moping around on my part, she did. I could smell it the second her feet hit our front porch. The smell of the diner stuck to her old jean jacket and long, blond hair and followed her through the front door. Once we had joined at the dining table, I ate a total of eighteen fries and half a caesar salad. After that, I left for "work," just as the sun began playing its game of tag with the mountaintops.

The air was just as cold as last night. During the midnight hours, Los Angeles stayed alive. My part of the city remained lifeless and eerie. Only the strip clubs and bars lit up the few blocks that were well-known for the dealers and workers like myself. "Looking for a fun night?" I asked, smiling at a passing man. Frumps like him weren't hard to find; I had only been walking for twenty minutes. He hummed in agreement but continued walking. I kept a seductive look glued to my face, refusing to be deterred by a lack of attention, as much as I loved it. I had a job to do, and if I didn't get to people before another girl or guy snatched them up, I would be out of a job. So, I usually found myself hovering outside clubs or nodding along to a new soundtrack in the back of a bar.

ANGEL

"How much do you charge?" A voice beside me pushed me from my focus on the group of men who had begun exiting the brightly-lit bar across the street. I had only been standing to the side, testing the waters and half-expecting a customer to come to me. On some occasions, they do, like right then. "Depends what you want," I replied with a pearl-white grin, glancing up at the tall, bulky man from under my lashes. He was like any other bloke from around here, weathered and accustomed to druggies asking them for cash. "I have sixty bucks on me. What does that get me?" he asked, his voice low and gravely. "BJ," I answered immediately.

He smiled and pulled his arm around my shoulders. I froze as he spoke again, his voice sending chills of unease through me.

"Great... let's go somewhere more private, hm?"

I nodded jerkily and let him lead me into an alley on shaky legs. A stray cat grew disturbed by our approach and darted out onto the sidewalk. It was the same routine most nights: lure them in, give them what they pay for, and clean up their mess. No questions, no strings, and definitely no paying less than the initial price. It had been easy to get started, and even if it wouldn't be a permanent job, it was always something that I could fall back on.

I only had time to gasp when rough hands pushed me against the wall, my cheek pressing against the cold brick. If I hadn't been trembling from the cold already, the sudden fear coursing through my veins would make me. "No screaming and you'll be fine," he growled, his breath tickling the inside of my ear. I whimpered. This wasn't the first time someone had told me they wanted a blowjob and decided they wanted my body instead. Hopefully, he would leave me alone once he was finished. Men like him didn't want to stick around long afterwards.

Tears began to gather in my eyes, a normal appearance at times like these, as he ripped away my shorts, his hand then spreading over my cheeks. I could feel those disgusting fingers igniting spark-like chills and raising goosebumps. His fingers were cold on my skin. He spread my flesh with a smile as I began to hum lowly to myself. My panting made the wall damp. The tune was sad.

....

"Keep the change," he told me, zipping his pants and walking away with haste after dropping a twenty at my feet. Once I was satisfied that the shadows had swallowed him, I sobbed and fell to the ground, a small puddle of water soaking my knees. Bruised handprints covered my thighs and hips, but I didn't find myself caring at that moment. I was too tired to care, too *hurt*.

I reached out to grab the money slowly, revelling in the feeling of the soft paper on my scraped fingers. That brick wall had been rough, and digging my hands into it was a better option than fighting back and knowing I wouldn't be able to stand his strength. Without the ability to see through my tears, I relied on my ears to tell me that I was alone in the alleyway. It was almost comforting. The sirens in the distance made my chest just a little less hollow.

"Are you okay?"

I nearly jumped from my skin at the voice, expecting the man to have returned for round two. I hadn't heard him, but if I had, I would probably have taken my chances with running. Now, that hole that was suddenly gaping open in my throat didn't allow me to move much at all.

I arched my neck to look up at him, my eyes widening at his height and build. This certainly wasn't the man who had used me moments before. His shoulders were broader and he was well-muscled, obviously someone who visited the gym regularly, but surely didn't make it a lifestyle. His raven-black, undercut hair seemed to shine in the dim light, much like his dark, blemishless skin. My gaze

ANGEL

was drawn to his razor-like jawline and narrow eyes that made black holes jealous before I followed them down to his sharp, eagle-like beak of a nose. He certainly wasn't that bad looking of a guy, but at that moment, I didn't want to see *anyone*.

I sniffed. "Y-Yeah," I croaked, standing frantically on legs that felt like jelly. They proved themselves as worthless as I stumbled and braced myself on the wall. I winced at the burn against my fingertips.

His eyes were glowing as they stared me down with... worry? He was concerned for me? I was sure I was imagining the way those thick, straight eyebrows pulled together.

"You here for a blow job? I... I don't charge as much as a lot of other people," I said, tears dripping off my chin before I hurried to wipe them away. He only scoffed and shook his head, almost as if he had become impatient with me. "Here," he said, drawing a napkin from his back jeans pocket. He held it to my cheeks and wiped the tears away gently. Then he handed it to me. I could only watch him with wide, incredulous eyes. The arm that he held out glittered; his skin was a smooth, tawny shade.

"I was just making sure you were okay. That guy looked kinda... sketchy," he shrugged. "So, if you're okay, have a good night," he smiled. The indents of his clean-shaven cheeks caught the shadows. They made his face look even squarer. The man's Cupid's bow was high, too; it copied his cheeks.

Once, a few months ago, I'd had a homeless woman approached me and offer me an extra blanket. Being in skimpy clothing (normally a pair of shorts and a t-shirt) in the middle of the night obviously wasn't something either of us were comfortable with, and although I refused to take her personal item, she sent me on my way with a few encouraging, heartfelt words. Very few people were empathetic for people in my position. More sympathetic, like this man seemed. He was dressed nicely in jeans and a grey cotton shirt; his attire didn't match the writing on the side of the duffle bag he was carrying over his shoulder. The words, along with the logo, informed me that he had been spending a lot of the night at the gym two miles up the road.

I expected him to be gone by the time I looked up, but the gaze that met mine didn't seem like it *wanted* to move. He was trying to decide something internally.

"I'm wondering if you want to spend awhile with me tomorrow night. I can pay you whatever you want, within reason," he said eventually. I felt cheated instantly; the man only saw me for my body, never with any concern for myself. But what could I say? I surely couldn't refuse if he really meant '*whatever I want*'.

"Whatever I want?" At my question, one corner of his mouth twitched up.

"Within reason." He had pulled a slip of paper from his gym bag and was then writing on it. I could tell by his hand's jerky, tired movements that he had very messy writing; I wondered if I would even be able to read his note. Once he passed it to me, I realized that it was his address. He lived in a nice part of town. I wondered what he was doing visiting a gym around my location.

I didn't allow my thoughts to deter me. "It's a deal," I replied to him. He nodded. I glanced back down at his address.

Then he was gone, leaving me to clutch the forgotten napkin and the note I couldn't stop analyzing between my fingers in a grip tight enough to bend metal.

CHAPTER TWO

I WENT HOME AND sobbed into my bed sheets, slept for a few hours, and then cried some more as the sun rose in the sky to welcome a new day. I cried until there seemed to be no liquid left in my body. My experience with that man hadn't exactly been consensual. It was my job. But what that man had done... I was caught off-guard, scared, and alone in an alley with a man who had been rougher than anyone before him. His nails had scratched deep into my skin, leaving purple, bleeding marks and raised welts. The next night, once I had replenished my fluids and swallowed my fear, I was still hesitant to put myself on the street again.

My mother was getting onto me, too, wondering why I had marks across my arms. She only frowned at them, her motherly instincts delayed after years of surviving instead of living. Those glowing blue eyes that were quite honestly the complete opposite of my sable ones, never shined anymore

I shrugged her off and left for "work" as my mind filled with images of the man who had come to my aid the night before. I couldn't deny that he was ruggedly handsome, his facial features angular and his actions quick and meaningful. A few stray locks had come loose from their gel confines and hung down to his lips. I wondered briefly what his exquisite-looking hair would feel like as I ran a shaky hand through my own. The texture of it helped calm me; I had washed it recently and was left with a shaggy mop of dark-brown layers. Again, they were the opposite of my mother's.

I was still sore from the night before. I didn't want to do my job anymore; I hadn't wanted to do it since the first time. I would rather die than do my job; I had been telling that to myself for days. Would my mother do better without me? Could I leave her? I had no work experience, phone number, email, friends, or hobbies, unless you counted the occasional tune I forced from my cracked windpipe. That was half of a resume gone, so what did I have left? We had been through the shelters, food banks, the free school lunches. When I grew up, they began to care less and less, and the both of us realized the hard way that people didn't care much unless they had a good motive to.

A woman gave a faint, tipsy smile as I passed. I flinched and continued on. She breathed a chuckle that faded off behind me on the street. Each new face that passed me would pose as a reminder of that man who had had his way with me. That was why I was suddenly so unwelcoming to new customers, I decided.

The direction I had been given to the city led me to parts I had never been to before. Rich parts, where the wealthy spent thousands on strippers and hookers nightly. Where I decided I would never have a place in society. That part of the city, I soon realized, was *warm*. It was alive with people, laughing with friends and family. With a nightlife unlike any other, I had no need to pull my hoodie tighter around me. Smells surrounded me from restaurants and street carts, more delicious than anything my mother had ever brought home. Did everyone eat like that? Was it always so joyous and loud at eleven at night on a Wednesday? Cars rushed past, free from the daily traffic jams, their paint jobs shining in the bright, glowing lights of the city. The city was alive even at night. It was...

ANGEL

stunning. I wished my mother could come to witness it.

I glanced back down at the note in my hand before looking up at the skyscrapers that towered high above the concrete jungle floor. At first I felt like I was in a cage, before I began to feel... better. The part of the city I was in wasn't so bad. Maybe it even felt freeing. I walked quickly down the sidewalk until I stood in front of one of the hundreds of skyscrapers in Los Angeles. It was thin, but tall nonetheless, with glass walls and very few lights on inside. Through the front glass doors, looking at the white leather couches and black reception desk, I could see that it was expensive to live there, very expensive.

I opened the glass door after checking the address once more and glanced around the spacious foyer nervously. "Can I help you?" A rough, deep voice pulled my gaze from the white leather sofa in the corner to a large man who sat behind a mammoth slab of black rock. The desk didn't belong with him; he looked more like a man who would enjoy a rougher decoration style. In front of him, a newspaper was folded, just beside his hands that flipped magazine pages. Still, I was deciding whether or not the African-American was part of security. Probably, I decided. His big, bald head shimmered dangerously in the light.

"I'm... I'm sure I'm in the wrong place. I was called here for a, um, a job offering from a... Mr. Arche?" I said nervously. I prayed that the name scribbled on the note was being pronounced correctly, as *arch-ee*. He nodded, a small, dark frown tainting the edges of his lips, and I immediately felt as if I had been wasting his time. I thanked him quietly, my eyes diverted, and stepped into the metal box that would carry me to what I expected would be a painful night. He was probably just an expensive version of the men I met nightly, I assumed, taking what wasn't theirs and leaving with smiles. A long time ago, I had learnt that looking on the bright side was hard, but not impossible. I wouldn't be forgetting the paycheck.

The elevator doors opened with a *ding* before I stepped out warily. A tall, blond man stood in front of me, grinning down with his freckled arms crossed over his wide, muscled chest. I could tell that he was the kind of guy who kept his body in good condition; he seemed more like security than a tenant. He was older than Mr. Arche. He also looked like he had a sense of humour that glittered in his steel-blue, deep-set eyes like a child.

"Hello. I'm Mason," he greeted with a thin smile. It was kinder than I expected, lighting his whole oblong face. Without another word, he turned and waved for me to follow him into the kitchen, a whole apartment in itself, and to the stairs that flooded into the room. The house was modern and expensive; I had goosebumps.

"Hi. I'm Luka."

He shook my hand firmly, a playful smile dancing on his face. The man kept his blond, greying facial and head hair short and neat. Mason certainly looked older than he was, but that took me at least a few minutes to decide. He was just too perky and passive to be older than fifty.

"How old are you, Luka?"

"Nineteen," I replied. I watched his feet move in front of mine. Was that it? Just my age and name and I was ready to become Mr. Arche's slut? I got the feeling that Mason and Arche had been through this before.

Mason led me down a small hallway leading from the elevator before he stopped in front of a tall mahogany door. It was stunning, with intricate carvings of swirls, branches and flowers. They looked like cherry blossoms, contorting around a shining gold, modern door handle. The man knocked lightly, the sound echoing around the hall ominously. It made my heart catch in my throat. "Come in," a deep voice sounded from the opposite side of the wood. So, he opened the door slowly, peeking his head between the gap first.

ANGEL

"Mr. Arche... this is Luka," he announced, his head held high as he motioned to me in the doorway behind him. I hadn't pronounced his name correctly; Arche was pronounced like '*Noah's ark*'. I felt naked when I was thrust into the bright light of Mr. Arche's office. My gaze first travelled around the room, absorbing the massive office space and ridiculously-high ceilings. The desk was the same colour as the door, centred on dark hardwood floors. Three glowing spheres hung from the ceiling, illuminating the room in bright, simulated daylight. I could see that the man kept his desk organized, with not a paper or pen out of place. I liked organized people; my mother was organized.

Then my eyes landed on the man who sat in the large, black, leather-padded chair behind the desk and I couldn't help but take a deep, necessary breath.

"Thanks, Mason... ." His voice was just as deep as the night before, just as moving. Something in his tone almost sounded surprised, though. My stomach quivered at the sound. "No problem... have fun, *Mr. Arche*," he replied with that frisky tone before leaving, closing the door behind him silently. I watched the handle return to its resting position.

The quiet was suddenly spread before us, cutting deep. He smiled at me from behind his sprawling desk. Meanwhile, his gaze swallowed me without chewing; I wondered if it was impatience or boredom which was poorly hidden inside those windows of black light. "It's nice to meet you again, Luka," he greeted. I stayed silent and stared at him. Was it too late to leave? Would he keep me there forcefully if I tried?

He sighed. "Strip."

I swallowed hard and nodded jerkily, removing my hoodie first. My reaction had been without thought; I felt like a trained mutt. Part of me knew that if we started sooner, we could be finished sooner. I removed my shoes. Yeah... just like the rest of them.

"Do you always pay for people like me? For... For boys?" I asked. He shook his head as I removed my shirt and shorts. I winced at the thought of him viewing my bruises and scratches. He would undoubtedly look down on me, I decided, unsurprised. I was like rust on a brand-new sports car. Everything else in the building was perfect, and I was the spec of dirt. But, instead of the unsatisfactory glance I expected, he stood and stepped around his desk, moving towards me until his chest nearly touched my own. I stared at him, taking in his full height. He loomed over my five-foot-eight frame.

"I said *strip*."

Those words made my eyes widen to saucers. His voice held a very authoritative edge to it that time. It was a *command*. My heart began to sputter against my rib cage, causing my breathing to become erratic. With a glance to my right, I decided that the walls of windows out into the city weren't facing another building directly, so any nudity hopefully wouldn't be noticed. I removed my underwear with nimble fingers, pushing it down my thighs before stepping out of the holes and leaving them in a pool on his floor. Then I looked back up at him, sure that what came next would be painful, just as always. "On the desk, hands and knees," he ordered, and I hurried to oblige. He scared me. To death. The wood was uncomfortable. I was sure my ass was reflected in the floor-to-ceiling windows that surrounded his office on two walls. I trembled in anticipation. In my haze of nervousness, I blurted, "You can be rough with me. I promise, I'm okay with it. Just... be prepared to pay more." I waited for him to say something; I didn't mean to make it sound that much like a threat. My gaze searched the wall for answers.

"Have you ever tried toys before?" he asked, sliding his long fingers through my hair as if he had any right to. I wanted to lean away from the soft, alien touch, but I fought the urge by shaking my head, yes. I had a few times, but it was nothing major. He hummed and moved around the desk. Right into it, then?

"What toys?" I asked, hoping to understand in hindsight what would go down between us, why I was in that situation. He hummed again, the sound emanating from deep within his wide chest. "You'll see."

I bit my lip when his hand came to rest on my left hip. His calmness made me uneasy. "So this is what you're into? Young boys like me... you have to be, what, thirty?" I trembled. I didn't mean to offend him, but curiosity had gotten the better of me, and my brain couldn't stop the onslaught of words from reaching my lips.

I yelped in surprise and pain when his other hand came down as a slap across my right butt cheek. It wasn't hard enough to really hurt, it was just enough to put me in my place. "Twenty-nine," he growled in reply.

I whimpered. Was he into BDSM, too? Was I in over my head worse than I had originally thought? I had heard of the horrors inflicted on subs, the rumours roaming the streets just like I did. On multiple occasions, I had joined groups or another person who wanted to get a little wilder; I actually got a lot of women who were Dommes searching for a slave for the night. I had enjoyed some of it, surprisingly. Other parts, not so much. But submitting to people who only wanted a one-night-stand was easy. I had no idea what Mr. Arche wanted. Most people accustomed to the lifestyle asked beforehand if their idea of fun matched mine.

I gasped when he pushed his thumb through my first ring of muscle abruptly, moving it slowly, even with the lube he had obviously coated his appendage with. It was an absolute relief, knowing we would be using *that*. Sometimes I would resort to carrying a bottle with me. At least I was *clean*.

"W-What are you doing?" I stuttered, whimpering against the

second finger he slid between my cheeks. It never entered me. Instead, it massaged the sensitive flesh just around my entrance. At least once or twice a week, men just stuck it in, orgasmed, and left me to clean up the mess. There was no prep, no pleasure. I was uncomfortable, and he seemed to know so. He seemed to be searching for something inside me, that tiny spot I loved the most, pressing his fingers against my soft, warm walls and rubbing them vigorously. I whimpered again before I released a susurration of a groan. Almost immediately, my muscles tensed and my fists curled. Only half the noise was for show.

"There it is," he chimed. I wanted to slap him madly; I felt like an animal.

Stars had exploded behind my eyelids, the sudden pleasure overtaking my body like a tsunami when he kneaded that spot harder. A hand encased my erection and pumped slowly, releasing the pressure. "Wh-What are-," but I had lost any ability to form coherent sentences as I began to fuck myself on his fingers shamelessly. But I *was* ashamed. I shouldn't have been taking so much carnal gratification. He shouldn't have been giving it. It wasn't how it worked. It was wrong on so many levels, yet I found that I couldn't care in the least what level we were on when I felt pressure coil in my gut. It had been far too long since I had felt that paralyzing haze. Once I found it, it was so hard to let it go again.

Behind me, he massaged my spine with his free hand, pushing it down and testing its flexibility limits. The pleasure pushed me into a spiral, the world swirling around me as I was lost in euphoria, my mind drifting as I was pushed off the edge by that second finger and his other hand that came to wrap around my cock. Semen splattered across his spotless wooden desk as I rode through my orgasm, my body tensing as my throat ran itself dry.

Even toys couldn't do *that* good of a job.

ANGEL

My front half collapsed, my cheek suddenly pressed against the cool wood, while my breath came in ragged gasps. It obviously wasn't the first time I had had gay sex, but it was the first time in a while I had ever felt anything that good on that particular spot.

"You've been a bad boy, Luka. I never said you could come." The man's growl sent a new jolt of fear through me, my orgasm forgotten. I suppose it was good while it lasted. I struggled into a sitting position in an attempt to apologize, but his hand around the back of my neck slammed my cheek against the desk again before I could utter anything resembling an apology. I whimpered as I heard his fly come undone, his firm fingers sticking to my neck like a ton of bricks. Then the rustling of a condom opening between his fingers and teeth came, an almost calming noise. I yelped when he filled me to the hilt with only a thrust-and-a-half, pain exploding inside me where we were connected. Tears gathered in my eyes as he twitched inside me. "Bad boys need punishment, Luka. Don't forget that," he whispered, leaning down as he gyrated his hips against mine. I whimpered and gasped before he drew himself away. There was never any gratification after the first orgasm; I had been drained. I wondered absently if he had torn me.

He only lasted a second before he pushed himself back inside my heat, the beginnings of a languid pace. I gasped with each thrust, unable to curse him out and praying for him to give me at least a moment to adjust. I realized, though, as my teeth dig into my lower lip, that he got off on my pain. Men like him were all the same. He was deep and powerful, but nowhere near as fast and rough as I thought he would be.

"Yeah, that's it."

I breathed a gentle sob at his words, my cock growing slightly hard once again. I was playing a dangerous game with him, and I knew it.

I felt my body beginning to move with his pace on its own, betraying me. But the desire and feelings had been bottled up, and I couldn't help but let them loose then. I was lost in internal explosions of light and rapture, and just the smallest twinge of pain, which hadn't even slightly diminished. I had only been distracted by the pleasure.

When I thought I was beginning to get used to our previous pace, his hips began to move with a furious, possessive motion. I sobbed, tears falling down my cheeks while his heavy balls slapped against my own. My voice was gone, only coming in abrupt gasps and moans while his own muffled groans faded and fell on deaf ears. My hand worked my erection rapidly, desperately.

It was too much. I couldn't take it. Could I contain my orgasm? I then realized I had been doing that already, scared of any other punishment he may be prepared to give. But the lid had almost popped, and when it did, I couldn't stop it.

"Come, Angel," he muttered, his hot breath tickling the shell of my ear. Thank god. I would have done so anyway.

I let the lid pop away with a muffled, short yelp, my body jolting as waves of my release washed through me, fireworks exploding within my body. I was once again thrust into an even more violent sea of churning waves, unable to distinguish up from down in the world around me. This feeling was usually a recurring reaction for the first few seconds after sex. As I clenched around him, he let out a grunt and came with a gasp. I could feel his hot seed fill the condom he wore before he quickly pulled away, removed it, and tied it off. It was then discarded into the trash bin beside his desk. I watched, panting.

I collapsed on his desk, completely spent. Again, a familiar feeling. I faintly felt strong arms coil around me, before the desk was replaced by something soft and comfortable, a sofa, a piece of furniture more relaxing than anything I had felt before. Under the

ANGEL

exhaustion that certainly showed on my features, I was somehow confused by this. He had never been forced to show me any comfort, pleasure, or benevolence. I also realized that I should have been getting dressed and preparing to walk home. There, I would take a shower and find sleep. My eyes opened wide suddenly; I could see over his shoulder. The desk faded behind us. It made me want to go home. I wanted to go to *bed*. My legs hurt from the trembling and hiking I had done recently; I wanted to *rest* them, not move to another room.

There was only one problem: the fucking sofa he had just laid me out on. It wasn't the bed I expected. With my face stuffed into the little satin pillow, I wondered how exactly I would ever get off it. For something so small, it was so soft and comforting, like a cloud.

Kai straightened, looming over me with an expression of disinterest. His gaze dismissed me. "Leave when you need to. I hope you have a good rest of the night."

CHAPTER
THREE

I WOKE SLOWLY, MY mind still foggy and slow.

Memories only flooded back when I struggled into a sitting position, my body aching from the night before. This was a very powerful but satisfying pain, something I was familiar with.

My eyes darted around the room with desperation, searching for any sign of him. He was gone. Taking advantage of his absence, I quickly found my discarded pile of clothes in the same place I had left them. The sun was also awake, pushed just above the sky scrapers across the city. *Shit.*

Despite the stunning view from his office, I knew my mother would be worried and confused as to why I wasn't sleeping soundly at home. So, I donned my hoodie and shorts and grabbed the small envelope on the once-again spotless desk before darting to the elevator, tearing open the envelope to see the gold inside. It was beautiful. I had never seen so much money in one place before. A kid on Christmas couldn't beat my excitement.

"See ya, kid," the doorman waved goodbye as I passed him, desperate to leave the main city and get as far away from wherever Mr. Arche was as possible. I realized with a twinge of regret then that I didn't even know his first name.

ANGEL

....

"Where were you?"

The dreaded question came quickly and quietly as Teressa Roggy set her plate in the sink. Her long, unkempt blond hair fell over her shoulders as she slouched over the kitchen counter. Our conversations only consisted of a few sentences these days. "I was working late. I got a little bit bigger paycheck, though," I replied, holding the envelope out to her.

Her brows furrowed as she took it tentatively.

She gasped when she counted its contents. "I-Is this fake?" she whispered. The woman's eyes were buggy. I shook my head.

The extremely rare smile that appeared across her lips made all the sex worth it, and, when I set out onto the streets that night, it was with new hopes. Sex wouldn't be that bad. I just endured it, hummed familiar tunes to myself, as always, and ignored the man or woman, played my part and acted out my scene, until he or she was done with me. I wanted to see that beautiful smile again. I ached for it.

As I wandered the lonely streets, the man drifted back into my mind: Mr. Arche. I had never had that kind of after care. I realized after waking that I had been cleaned, probably with some kind of cloth, and cocooned in soft blankets. He had decided to respect my exhaustion and leave me to rest; maybe he realized how badly I needed it.

With my thoughts, I was unaware of the three figures who had emerged from the shadows, following me closely. Their eyes were hungry and dark. I yelped when a hand clasped around my mouth, a strong arm snaking around my chest to pull me deep into a nearby alley. I was thrust onto my knees hard enough for them to crack loudly against the concrete, and my eyes widened with fear when

I felt something hard and cold press against my temple. My heart stopped as I stared up the barrel of a gun, fear turning the blood in my veins to ice. "You do what we say and no one has to get hurt," his voice was threatening and low, barely audible. I whimpered and gave a shaky nod.

"Open your mouth, slut," he growled, pushing the cold barrel through my hair as he unzipped his pants and let them hang loose around his waist. A woman chuckled as she pulled at my shorts. I shook my head, tears rocketing down my cheeks. I couldn't. Not *again*.

"Open your fucking mouth!" His order was loud, ringing through the alley. The fear it conjured made me want to vomit. The woman and man behind me finally ripped away my underwear and chuckled when I unconsciously tilted away from them. "Please... st-stop," I sobbed, shaking my head furiously. I began pushing away from him, and he let his lips pull over his teeth in a snarl. I didn't have any time to react before the muzzle of his gun came down across my forehead. Seconds later, once a massive, spiraling headache had bloomed within my skull, my world began to tilt. Blood dripped into my eyes and I released a shaky cry before my vision began to swirl. I was seeing double of everything; there was twice the fear. The colours that invaded my vision were almost pretty.

"Hey!" A deep, enraged voice pierced my ears before the world.

....

Sunlight filtered through a window to my left, blinding me effectively. I gave a subdued moan, my hand rising to shield my eyes from the harsh light. After a few attempts to sit up, I finally managed to crawl into a sitting position, my eyes widening as my gaze ventured around the room. I had been dropped in a massive king bed in the centre of a beautiful, large bedroom, decorated with

ANGEL

hardwood floors, beige walls, and intricately-detailed, dark ceilings. A gold chandelier hung from the centre beam. I lay on a mountain of fluffy pillows under a dark-brown duvet that was inevitably large enough to cover the floor space in my own bedroom.

I looked up when the door opened across the room, revealing a very amicable Mr. Arche, almost as if he *didn't* have an injured prostitute lying in his bed. "M-Mr. Arche?" I whispered, my fists curling into the sheets.

"Hello, Luka. Are you feeling better?" he asked, taking a seat in the small padded chair beside the bed fluidly.

"What happened?" I asked, looking around the room once more. He sighed. "Take these." He held out two pills and a small glass of water. "What are they for?" I replied, glancing at them warily. "Pain," he assured simply, motioning to them expectantly. I took them slowly, tilting my head back as I swallowed them with the water. I drank all of it, my thirst realized after the amount of time I had gone without any fluids.

"You're dehydrated and tired. That cut on your forehead won't heal if you don't sleep, so get some rest, Luka," he ordered, standing.

"W-Wait! What happened? How did I get here?" I winced at the memory of the firearm against my scalp. He frowned. "The police found that note I gave you in your pocket. That was all you had on you, so they called me. You're lucky some guy was passing by when you got attacked. He called the police for you. But I need to get back to talking to the police, Luka. Sleep," he ordered. How could I sleep knowing that I had come so close to losing my life? Kai had obviously told the paramedics, or the police, that he knew me, which wasn't exactly a lie, but… was it?

I swallowed hard as he closed the door quietly behind him, leaving me alone.

The next time I woke, it was because the sun was setting. I gasped and attempted to scramble off the bed. I needed to get home. My mother would be in hysterics. But the headache that had accumulated within my skull elicited a small moan from me. I could barely balance on my feet, let alone run home.

"Don't get up. Lie back down."

I jumped when Mr. Arche's voice sounded from the chair that had been pulled closer to the bed behind me. "You have a pretty nasty head wound. I shouldn't have let you sleep so long," he added, setting a hand on my shoulder and pushing me lightly back onto the pillows. I winced up at him. "Why are you doing this? Why couldn't you just pay me and leave me alone?" I mumbled, my hands moving to cover my face. The sun was too bright.

He frowned. "As far as I know, you would probably still be in the hospital, unable to contact your mother or leave, if that guy hadn't shown up." The man's voice was calm and soothing. It gave me chills. I stared at him silently. Then he sighed.

"Luka, I have a proposition for you, but I would rather speak to you about it when you're well-rested and fed. I'll get some food up here while you stay in bed," he told me, his black eyes watching me intently. I played with my fingers nervously in my lap. "But what about my mom? She's probably already really upset, and she could come looking-," but I was cut off by Mr. Arche raising his hand, silencing me. "It's fine. The police found yours and your mother's information when she went to the police station looking for you. She's worried, but she knows you're okay."

"What did you tell her?" I said in an accusing tone. My eyes were narrowed.

"I told her that you were with a friend. She was satisfied after talking on the phone with the police. She's expecting you home later."

As he said those words, he stood and pulled the duvet further around my chest. Then, as if he was a father tucking his kid into bed, he turned and left the room, allowing the door to stay open only a crack. I could only stare out the massive windows, deciding that watching the sun set would be my only form of entertainment for the next little while.

CHAPTER
FOUR

O N THE BEDSIDE table sat a set of neatly folded clothes and a wooden tray of scrumptious-looking fruits and meats. It filled the room with a beautiful, rich aroma, and my mouth watered simply at the sight. I ate the food quickly, finding that my body had no interest in savouring any of it as I scarfed the apples, cheese, and deli meats into my mouth. The first food I had eaten in days tasted better than heaven, but it was over almost as soon as I took my first bite. My stomach, after getting a taste of euphoria, decided it needed more. That's what I hated most about eating and sleeping. After a while, I become numb and ignorant of the treats. But once I finally got it, the pain of going so long without it hurt more than ever before.

I stood, slowly this time, testing the waters before setting my full weight on both feet. It was dark outside. I paused for a moment to gaze at the glowing city of Los Angeles. I could stare for hours and hours and never get bored, I decided. The blue jeans fit perfectly, although the t-shirt was rather baggy on my slim frame. But it was made of the finest cotton, so I welcomed it just as happily. Then I read the note that had been placed just between the clothes and tray of finished food. *"Come downstairs when you've dressed and rested sufficiently."* The note was written in barely-legible handwriting, so I highly doubted it was Mr. Arche's.

I soon found myself inside the hallway, hesitantly wandering past closed doorways. I managed to find the light at the end of the tunnel was greeted by a large living room and smiling Mason, his hands clasped tightly behind his back. "Are you feeling better, Mr. Roggy?" he asked kindly. I nodded. "You can call me Luka," I mumbled sheepishly. "Luka," he corrected himself as I stepped off the last step. My shoes had been removed. The wooden floors were slippery under socks. Mason motioned me to follow him, and I found myself doing so immediately, turning into the small, dingy hallway hidden behind the stairwell. It didn't suit the rest of the apartment much at all, especially with the cobwebs hanging from the ceiling and the outdated door handles. My house had the same ones. They made me feel just a little calmer.

"I just have a few things to take care of. Mr. Arche is out talking to the police for the last time before they have to talk to you. He advised me not to let you out of my sight until he returned."

"Really?" I asked incredulously. I had decided that even God couldn't force me to speak to a police officer about what had happened to me. I hoped to be able to leave as soon as possible. Mason nodded as he turned us towards a small, cheap, wooden door to our left. I realized, after being given a small stool beside one of the two massive tables in the centre, that it was a laundry room of sorts. The appliances were top-of-the-line, with steaming and cleansing choices of all kinds. A few canned goods were stored in the corner.

"So are you, like, a butler?" I asked. I then realized that we were not alone, when a very short woman stood from behind the table with a large basket of dark laundry. She looked to me and smiled. "Is this Luka?" she asked, her eyes lighting up. I blushed, and she laughed before setting her basket on the table to shake my hand lightly. "My name is Rosa. It's a pleasure, Mr. Roggy," she smiled.

"Just Luka," I replied.

Rosa wore a black, messy bob, her long bangs pushed haphazardly to the sides. Her hair framed her oval face beautifully, but her round, dark glasses made everything inside the frames pop, especially those dark-brown eyes and big, round cheeks. They weren't as deep of a black as Mr. Arche's. She definitely had some eastern blood in her too. Chinese, maybe.

She went back to her work, beginning to fold clothes in the table to my right as Mason pulled more from a second machine. "Well, to answer your question, yes and no. Rosa is more of a maid, I... I don't know, I live here for emotional support, but I also help Rosa," Mason told me. They glanced at each other. "Honestly, we just help out so we don't have to pay rent," he snickered eventually. Mason seemed like a kind man. Not a person that looked all that welcoming, but kind nonetheless. The guy was bulkier than Kai; he seemed dedicated to his gym time.

"Why does Mr. Arche want to keep me here?" I asked finally. The question, along with many others, had been burning on my tongue for hours.

Mason and Rosa exchanged a glance before Mason sighed. "Luka, you're the only boy I've seen who has stayed this long. You're just here until you're ready to go back home and to the police station. He's probably just making sure that you're okay... but I'm sure you know that Mr. Arche likes to make a habit of people like you." Mason obviously wanted to say it in the best of words, but it didn't make sense to me in the least.

"But why? He paid for me and I left, I thought that was how far anything was going to go."

Mason shook his head. "Truthfully? You should just let him do his thing. You can leave soon, you know?"

I huffed and crossed my arms. Rosa chuckled and pushed her

glasses up her nose with her knuckle.

I followed Mason closely for the next ten minutes.

"L-Look, Mason, I know I was supposed to stay with you and all, but I need to get home." I stood in the middle of the hallway where I waited for Mason to finish putting clean towels on the racks in the bathroom beside me. "I-I have a job. I need the money, and I'm not-," but I was cut off by a familiar, deep voice behind me. "Thank you, Mason." I whirled as Mason left the bathroom. He nodded his reply, on his way out, leaving Mr. Arche and I alone. I cowered against the wall. He pretended not to notice. "You won't have to deal with the police if you don't want to. They'll want a statement, but I've insisted that it won't be needed until you're ready. They seem satisfied, as long as they get to talk to you sometime later," he told me evenly. I nodded, unsure.

"Come with me." His hand was waving me forward before I could object, dragging me quickly into the elevator and up to his office. The stairs seemed much taller going up. The hallway was so much darker too. He took a seat behind his desk, letting me stand uncomfortably in the centre of his office.

"I don't want to make you stand in front of me for too long, so I'm just going to come out and say this. I want a sub. And, Luka, I believe that you would be perfect for that."

I blanched. The words had come so suddenly, and I nearly gasped. It took a few seconds to recover from the blow while my head spun. A sub? I barely knew the basics of submission. Not only was it considerably new to me, but the people I *did* have experience with weren't exactly seasoned, either. It could be worse than my street job if I even considered it. "You would only spend a few nights with me a week... and if you have no idea what I'm talking about, then I would rather you go home, rest, and we can never see each other again," he promised. I listened, frozen to his office floor.

"Last night... was that a sub and Dom thing?" I asked wearily. He raised an eyebrow and leaned back in his chair.

"So you've had experience, right?"

I nodded sheepishly while he leaned over the wood table. BDSM wasn't always about sex. It was about trust and empowerment for both partners. It was about pleasure, a rather fun way to unwind and find acceptance. Once, after meeting up with a new customer, I was shocked to find that he didn't actually want sex. He spent almost an hour simply kneeling at my feet, reveling in the feeling of someone above him, ruling him, allowing him to earn a kind of rare satisfaction. Afterwards, he gave me a blowjob. The experience was backwards and unfamiliar, but it also gave me a rare view of how incredible this kind of relationship could be. "Luka, a relationship between a submissive and Dominant is about gratification, trust, consent. It's about a power exchange. You need to understand that you'd be giving yourself to me completely, even if it only lasted half an hour. You don't need to sign any waiver or contract. This is your decision; you control this." He seemed to know how to keep a partner safe; it allowed me to trust him just that little bit more.

He could see that I still wasn't sold. I was scared of the deep waters; I was just barely able to swim. But that idea of bliss and pleasure was tempting. "I'm sorry, Mr. Arche, but I can't accept your offer. I... need to make money. I have a job." My voice was small, fearful. I never intended to refuse him, even after his hospitality, but money trumped 'pleasure'. It always would. Submitting to a stranger for one night was easy for me; I had done it for countless people. But submitting to someone I would be spending so much time with? That didn't sound like as much of a fun time. He made it sound so much more official. I realized that if I decided to follow him, it would be difficult for me to submit myself to him.

He frowned deeply. My fear escalated. He seemed disappointed.

ANGEL

His expression was more than just frustrated. But then, with a deep sigh, he seemed to relax. He folded his hands on his desk and straightened his back formally. "What's your price, Luka?" His question caught me off-guard. Price? Was I an object to him? I wasn't surprised.

"You mean... like what's the lowest I'll take?" I winced as the words left my mouth. I felt like a piece of furniture, a worthless piece of junk at a garage sale. He was just another interested customer, and I decided that I would be discarded after a few nights together anyway. "More like what do you think your time is worth." Again, I hesitated, thought.

Once I had decided, the cash I had imagined was the only thought that stuck in my mind. "The seven-hundred was enough," I told him finally.

Kaia didn't hesitate. He nodded and wrote a message down on a small slip of paper beside him. "You seem better. Mason will drive you home once you're ready. You can keep the clothes, and I'll see you... this Friday? We'll talk about it more?"

The sweat was beginning to bubble from my flesh. The feeling that I had just signed my life away, although it was only a few nights, made me queasy. I nodded and gave him the smallest of smiles.

"You're allowed to say no, Luka. This needs to be consensual."

There was silent, dead air between us for too long. The wooden floors seemed impossibly far away.

"Have a good night, Mr. Arche. I'll... see you Friday," I whispered, turning on my heel. The entrance felt small, made me feel trapped and claustrophobic.

"Luka?"

I froze, my hand on the gold doorknob. It was cold. After a second, the nervous heat that radiated from my hand warmed it.

"Call me Kai," he said, a small, kind smile playing on his lips.

"Kai?" When he nodded, I turned out the door, careful to close it silently and firmly behind me.

The slow drive back into my part of town was furtively after I had told Mason my address. The only sound was the hum of the engine and the wailing of car car horns around us. "You act like you've known Kai for a long time," I said finally. Normally, I was never the one to initiate conversation. In fact, I couldn't remember the last time I had attempted to start one. "So you're on a first name basis now?" Mason replied, ignoring my question. He must have known that Mr. Arche planned to make me into a sub. I shrugged. "You know that Kai isn't actually his name? I mean, it's his nickname, but his full name is Kaia. He hates it," Mason told me with a small chuckle.

"That sounds like a girl's name...," I said, playing with my fingers in my lap once again. I realized it was beginning to become a habit when I was uncomfortable. Mason nodded. "It is. His mother wanted a girl more than anything. So when Kai was born, she gave him a girl's name anyway. His dad wasn't a happy camper."

I thought about my own name. Luka was what everyone I had ever known called me. Most people didn't even know my full name. Lucika was just a peculiar title compared to 'Luka', and I supposed 'Luka' was easier to pronounce. My mother wanted a unique name.

"So... you've lived with him for a long time?" I wasn't prepared to let the burning question go. Mason seemed so much different than Kai, yet they worked together so closely. Mason was like... a head butler. The looks they exchanged had been so quick, but each time I had glimpsed just the tiniest flash of understanding in their gazes. Like they knew what the other was thinking without speaking their minds. Mason nodded. "I guess... we grew up together, but I didn't start working for him until a few years ago."

I nodded, realizing they must have been best of friends. They probably still were.

ANGEL

Mason still didn't seem like someone who was very compatible with Mr. Arche, though. Mason was more lain-back. I watched him, even in the apartment, and realized that his eyes were everywhere. His gaze never stayed on one thing, he seemed to constantly be searching for something. He missed nothing and refused to look anyone in the eye for more than a second. If he did, the twitch in his eye forced his gaze somewhere else. Kai was much the opposite. He seemed on edge, as if he was constantly holding his breath for something. Kai also obviously wasn't interested in much. His eyes didn't wander from what he was focused on, as if he simply didn't care about anything else.

"We're here, I think. This is it, right?" Mason's declaration broke me from my thoughts. I unbuckled my seatbelt and opened the *Bentley's* door. It shone bright in my dirty part of the city. I felt alienated when I sat inside it. "I'll be here at eight on Friday night," Mason told me, his shining green gaze burning a trail around my block. I nodded and thanked him quietly, preparing to close the door.

"Oh, and Luka?" Mason stopped me. I froze, the door already closed halfway. I looked to him expectantly. There was a moment of silence as he stared at me, his eyes burning with obvious desire to speak his mind.

"Never mind."

And with that, I gave him a flash of a smile and closed the car door behind me.

CHAPTER
FIVE

WHEN I OPENED my front door, a wave of cigarette smoke hit me like a wall. I was accustomed to my mother's smoking habit, but I had never smelled anything so potent before. So I closed the door slowly, catching a glimpse of my mother seated at the small dining room table, a long puff of smoke escaping her lips. Her flushed cheeks seemed sunken.

My mother was a woman of few words. She seldom spoke her mind, something I had clearly inherited from her, and often spoke in one or two-word sentences, only enough to get her message across. "Are you good?" Her monotone words broke the silence like a knife. She never even made eye contact, just stared into space with glazed eyes. But the words had so much more meaning than many would think. She was asking if I was okay, if I was going to go to my room and cry after this, if I needed space. She was asking how long it had been since I had eaten last. She was asking if I had lost a paycheck in the last few days I hadn't been at "work". She was letting her motherly instincts reveal themselves in one, three-word question.

"I'm okay," I replied in a whisper. And with that, I darted up to my room to curl into bed as she finished her last cigarette.

The rest of that night and most of the next day was filled with sleeping and sudden bursts of energy, when I could sing and hum

ANGEL

to myself as I slowly swayed around my bedroom. I fell asleep again around three in the afternoon, realizing that I was absolutely exhausted.

I was awakened that evening by my mother, who stood at the top of the stairs to my room. I looked up to her groggily, mostly confused as to why she had climbed those stairs for the first time in years. "Are you going to work tonight?" she asked in a monotone voice. I nodded slowly, although I didn't want to. I never wanted to go out onto the street again, but I had to. "There's a hamburger downstairs. Eat it before you leave." She didn't wait for me to reply before trudging slowly back down the stairs, the old wood creaking quietly under her weight.

Downstairs, my dinner welcomed me with open arms. It was like gold. A jewel. A rare and exotic treasure. Any food, lately, tasted as if it had been sent by the gods. But I was still dreading my midnight job. I wasn't sure how much more of it I could take. I pulled at the hem of my t-shirt that I had gotten from Kai, worrying it vigorously. Would he take me as a full-time sub if I asked? Maybe he would pay me the same every night. I would gladly give up my job on the streets for the position of being his sub—

I shook my head, attempting to quickly clear the horrifying thoughts as my last bite of dinner was swallowed. Yes, that night had been... a nice change. I never realized that I could feel that way, that my body could be wound up so tight and let loose just as savagely. The pleasure was unbelievable, but it scared me. It scared me how much control Kai had claimed over my body. It scared me that I had bent so willingly to him. Could I manage to do it again?

I took a shower in the house for the next two nights. With my new paycheck, we were able to turn the water back on and make a much-needed shopping trip. I felt clean for once, free of the blood, sweat, and semen that had dried and adorned my body. While I cleaned both the outside and inside of my body, I thought of the food my mother had brought home: a leftover salad and fries from the diner, and I was still full from our feast. It had been finished off by a bowl of cereal. As I let the hot water unravel my tense muscles, I thought about Kai too. He, for the first time, made me feel respected.

No less of a slut, but respected nonetheless.

But could he be asking too much of me? Could I be a sub for someone I had only just met? Would I disappoint him? I didn't know the first thing about sexually pleasing a Dominant. Submitting to someone simply wasn't that easy.

I only knew that I needed to make the money, somehow.

....

My mother hadn't come home by the time Mason pulled his car up beside my small house on Friday night. I was lucky to have had kind customers the previous nights; I had spent a few hours with some people I even caught myself considering friends. I locked the door securely behind me before darting across the dead lawn and entering the car, flashing Mason a small, grateful smile. He smiled back at me kindly. "How are you doing tonight, Mr. Luka?" he asked, sounding genuinely interested. I shrugged and looked out the window as rows of decrepit houses passed us. Some were dumps. Some were boarded up. Most looked dark and lifeless.

"I'm alright, I guess." My voice was small and monotonous as my anxiety increased. I couldn't be a sub. What the hell was Kai thinking? "Are you nervous?" Mason asked. I looked back at him as his gazed switched quickly between the road and my hands in my lap. I didn't want to admit to his question. My fingers were tangled together, worrying the skin around my nails and pulling at my knuckles vigorously.

"Mr. Luka, you're going to dislocate your fingers if you keep doing that. Kai will treat you fine."

Could the man read minds? I stared at him in shock before I could conceal my expression.

"You don't miss a lot, do you?" I could tell he was about to say something else before I had hit him with a question of my own.

"It's my job." His only reply was short and simple.

I sighed and looked back out the window, my eyebrows pulled together a little. "How long is this ride going to be?" I asked him. He shrugged. "You live more north-west of downtown, so it'll take us a good half-hour... although Mr. Arche ordered me to get you there as soon as possible."

I blanched. "Why?"

A small smirk played on his lips. "Isn't a guy allowed to be excited?"

My lip stuck out a little as my brain began to work. Excited. The way Mason spoke of Mr. Arche made him sound like a child who had found a new toy. I suppose I *was* a new toy for him. "Mr. Luka, being with Mr. Arche allows you to ask questions if you want to. He may be scary, but if you can look past his exterior...," his sentence faded off.

My mouth fell open. "Y-You know about all the sex stuff he gets up to, huh?" I realized that stuttering was another 'nervous habit' of mine, something that usually happened when I was too overwhelmed to create coherent thoughts.

Mason nodded. "You're not the first sub he's ever had, Luka. But you are the first sub I've ever seen him wanna bang so bad."

"What...?" I was confused.

Mason shook his head, signaling the conversation's end. I assumed that he couldn't find any words to explain himself. "So, do you have any food preferences?" These people knew how to change moods and subjects like they knew how to breathe air. I shook my head, my stomach rumbling embarrassingly at the thought of food. *"I just fed you! That was the biggest meal you've had in weeks,"* I mentally scolded my stomach.

"Kai has ordered me to keep you fed when you visit him, just like it's my responsibility to keep *him* fed. I help Rosa in the kitchen often, so I'll get you food if you ever get hungry."

"You don't need to do that... I'm kind of used to it. I don't get hungry very often." I didn't think I would be able to pig out on trays of food while my mother slaved in a diner. But when he raised an eyebrow at me, my stomach made a truly embarrassing sound. "You're skin and bone. Mr. Arche despises the feel of bones through skin. He likes to feel some give. Just saying."

I was like fucking livestock to him. I wasn't surprised, hearing that he would reject me if I didn't gain any weight. I wanted food, although I didn't want to gain too much weight. I learnt long ago that men didn't like fat boys. They liked boys with long, muscular legs and hard stomachs. But I wanted food. I wanted piles of meats and cheeses and pastas that I could sit and devour with my mother. I wanted to see her smile as she ate plates of spaghetti, pizza, and wraps. "Kai will pick up on your anxiety habits soon, too, so stop worrying. Your fingers are already red." I hadn't realized that I was pulling at my knuckles again until he pointed it out. How was I supposed to stop something I was subconsciously doing? I mentally added it to the growing list and pondered the thought of demanding that Mason just drop me off on the corner. I could walk the fuck home.

I realized then that we were close to the apartment.

"Do you have anything that can help me?" I asked suddenly. My voice cracked nervously and he looked at me in confusion. "L-Like words of advice... I've never done this kind of thing before." I had done it a few times. But for Kai Arche? My conscience made me feel like I was being led to the lion's den.

Mason didn't answer until we pulled through the gated underground parking and stopped the vehicle beside a large, sleek, black motorbike. It looked ridiculously expensive, but not as expensive as the shining, red convertible on its other side. I realized that the entire garage was filled with sports cars and vehicles I had never seen before, all probably mostly owned by Mr. Arche and the rest of the inhabitants of his apartment building.

"You'll be okay, Mr. Luka," were his only words as he stepped out of the car. But I didn't miss the small gleam of mischief in his eyes.

CHAPTER
SIX

"THANK YOU, MASON," Kai smiled. Mason nodded and turned to leave the office. "I'll be back in a moment," he replied before closing the door quietly behind him, leaving Kai and I alone in his office. For a moment, the two of us stared at each other. "There'll be food here soon. Did you eat dinner?" he asked finally. But the look in his eyes told me that he had no interest in waiting for food. His eyes were dark and hungry, but most-likely not for food. He was on me in a moment, attacking my neck and shoulders. I gasped at his ferocity as my legs nearly collapsed. His arms wrapped around my waist. I moaned, half fake and half real, as he sucked on my neck, undoubtedly leaving little raised red patches. I gave a breathy yelp when his teeth dug into the pale flesh of my collar bone, just before his feather-soft tongue licked away the pain. His fingers kneaded my hips, seeming to search for something, before they went still, and I couldn't stop the desire that coiled in my stomach. "We'll have safe-words." His voice just barely broke through the haze in my mind.

"S-Safe-words?"

He nodded and sucked a searing trail of kisses from the base of my ear to the point where my neck connected with my shoulder. They weren't endearing. The kisses were territorial. "Choose something to mean "Stop", Luka. First thing that comes to mind and something you'll remember." His breath burned the inside of his ear as he pushed his fingers against my ass. "Green will mean 'Go' and Yellow just lets me know that you need some kind of break or a check-in. It'll get easier to remember as time goes on." I glanced around the room over his shoulder, searching for anything I could make into a safe-word. I wasn't new to safe-words; I knew customers that used them with me. My mind was having trouble forming a lot of thought at that moment, though, as my hands curled into fists against his shirt.

Before I could think of a word, just as my mind began to overload with anxiety, I was saved by a knock at the door. Kai immediately left me standing alone on shaky legs, acting as if I hadn't just been turned speechless by his mouth and ferocity. I shivered and looked to the door as Mason entered and set a tray on Kai's desk. "Thanks, Mason," Kai said quietly. Mason simply smiled at him, then at me, before leaving just as quickly as he came. Kai motioned me forward, and it took me a moment to gain feeling in my legs once again. Once I did, I walked toward him slowly, where he sat on the edge of his desk comfortably. Then he pointed to a small sofa-like piece of furniture that sat just in front of his desk. It was nearly as big as the massive hunk of wood.

"Eat."

I sat immediately on the dark leather of the furniture, feeling very little give when I sat. It looked a little bit like a wave, a curve that rose and fell from the floor fluidly. It looked ridiculously expensive, with gold tacks and seams holding it together. "You like it?" he asked. The man didn't sound interested. I nodded slowly as I reached up to grab a slice of ham from the tray. Mason had brought us an assortment of cheeses, meats, and crackers to eat, and it looked absolutely scrumptious. Easy to make and light on the stomach.

I realized then that the room held two other pieces of furniture that looked similar. It was all over his house; I could remember seeing two in the living room. These artistic curves rose from the ground, different shapes and sizes everywhere, as if he decided to buy the sculptures instead of chairs. "Is it comfortable?" he asked, a small conspiratorial glint in his eyes. I shrugged. "It doesn't have a lot of cushion. Do you sit on it? Or lie on it?" They looked like chairs... but they also looked like terribly distorted beds. He smirked and shook his head. "That's not necessarily what they're made for, but yes, you can sit. Feel free."

He waited patiently for me to finish eating, but after a few moments, I was beginning to bore myself by glancing around the room. I stuck another cracker in my mouth. "Why not just make 'Red' the final safe-word?" I asked suddenly. He shrugged. "I find that subs don't take it as seriously when it's just a colour. If you say 'Red', then I'll stop everything. I told you that this relationship will be about pleasure, however long it lasts. If I'm doing something that makes you too uncomfortable, it's my job to make sure you aren't in any distress."

I nodded. He seemed so sincere. I realized then that he took this absolutely seriously. It was a lifestyle for him, and I wasn't sure how I felt about that.

"I just want it to be 'Red'. Can I do that?"

He nodded. "Of course... but you have to understand that I have safe-words, too, right?" When he had asked me if I had experience, he assumed that I knew that safe-words were for Dominants too. I expected that he wouldn't be putting himself in a situation that needed one anytime soon, though.

I stuck another chunk of cheese between my lips. "Of course. I'm done eating," I mumbled, pushing the tray away from my chest. He frowned and nodded; my answer was satisfactory. "You're sure?"

ANGEL

My brows pulled together. "Yeah."

Kai nodded, folding his hands on his knees. "Are you having any?" I asked. He looked down at me for a moment, his gaze switching from my face and the small piece of ham I held out to him. I set it on a cracker, before placing a small chunk of cheese on top. "Here." I assumed he had already had dinner. I just didn't want to be eating alone. But he shook his head and looked away, and my face fell.

"You're not hungry?" He shook his head once again, and I left it at that. He looked like the kind of man who ate large amounts often, before working the calories off at the gym for hours at a time.

But I was still done with eating crackers and cheese, so I figured I would start on something else. Maybe something that could earn me an extra bit of money... I leaned towards him and snapped his belt buckle loose. I knew how to get things like that done quickly after years of BJ's and sex. He leaned back to welcome me. I didn't make eye contact.

Kai snapped his teeth together and stood suddenly as he wrapped an arm around my waist. I could feel the hunger and lust. "You want to suck me off, huh?" he growled. I was the one who stared up at him that time, with wide, surprised eyes. I was about to reply, hoping he wouldn't be too mad. Had I gotten the wrong mood from him? I thought it would be okay, since I was there for sex in the first place. But instead, he thrust me to the ground, so hard that my knees gave a sharp crack when they hit the solid hardwood floors.

The man unzipped his fly and pulled his half-hard cock from his black boxers. "Suck it then." It was a command that sent my groin into overdrive, as much as I hated it. Without a second thought, I wrapped my jaws around him and attempted to take his full length. I choked and gagged before pulling away a little further to pull air into my lungs. Too much too fast. *Silly Luka.*

He rumbled deeply, a gruff sound emanating from his chest, the only indication that I felt relatively-good, when I licked a trail from his base to his tip, before stopping to suck on the pink, bulbous head. My tongue lapped around him, conforming to every ridge and indent of the appendage while reveling in the salty taste of him. His hand suddenly curled into my hair, pulling lightly at my dark locks. "Damn...," he mumbled as I took in as much as I could without gagging and sucked, hard enough to hollow my cheeks. I could feel his length pulsing against my tongue, and I gave a small moan. "Yes, Luka."

Both hands came to rest on the sides of my head, and I knew enough about men to know where he was going. So, I stopped sucking and waited for him to begin his thrusts, which came less than a second later. He was like an animal, vicious and unforgiving. He scratched against the back of my throat until I gagged and tears began to swell in my eyes. I could only take it, my fingers digging into his black dress pants as I choked for air. When he came, I nearly threw up. It was hot and messy, and there was so much, I could barely keep it in my mouth when he pulled away, his hair dishevelled and small glints of light flying off his skin with perspiration.

"Swallow it," he hissed. I swallowed it quickly, the salty taste embedded in my taste buds. The thickness of it made my throat tighten painfully. "Good boy, Angel," he said quietly, running his thumb over my cheek bone. I whimpered, desperate to sooth my own arousal. "See? When you're good, I give rewards." His voice was husky, promising something much more than just a 'reward'.

He took my upper arm in a bruising grip and helped me easily back onto the oddly-shaped sofa. He then turned me onto my stomach roughly, until my knees were positioned on the edges of the largest hump, with my arms holding my chest above the smaller one. I gasped when my shorts and underwear were pulled away and pushed down my legs. I could feel his gaze burning into my skin where bruises and scratches still healed. But, instead of shying away from my body, his warm hands pried my cheeks apart, revealing my most private parts.

I wasn't at all prepared when his finger swept a long stripe across my entrance, leaving a trail of fire in its wake. I whimpered and subconsciously thrust back against his hand, although I never gained any contact. His fingers played with the ring of muscle vigorously, until I began to whimper. I bit my lip and focused my breathing. My world was beginning to go hazy, and I needed him. I needed release.

"Please... please." My words broke through my chapped lips as pathetic whimpers, but it seemed to be enough. He stopped and pulled his long digits from my wet heat. Then a condom was torn open behind me.

"What do you want, Angel?"

My body shivered at the sound of the nickname I had been given by him. "Y-You... please, I want you."

"What do you want me to do?"

"Ha.... I... I want you t-to fuck me!"

With that, he gave one hard thrust, filling me to the hilt. My eyes opened wide and my mouth fell open in a silent scream; I was barely given enough time to recover from his first entry before he started on a languid, rhythmic pace. "Damn.... like heaven, Angel." He released a curse every few thrusts as he began to gain speed. I gave a low cry when he found my prostate, sending waves of white-hot titillation and pain rocketing through my body. In some part of my mind, I was aware of how little time I had before I was done for; I was so close, I just needed a little more...

"You don't come until I say you can, Angel."

I bit my lip as a new kind of heat began to gather in my eyes, his thrusts becoming violent and irregular. No. *No.* I needed to come.

So badly. I just needed one hand on my cock and I'd be over the edge. I felt as if blood dripped down my chin from where I had my teeth firmly planted in the sensitive flesh of my bottom lip, although I was sure it was only saliva. Instead of wiping my face, I let it drop so I could rest my head between my arms. The leather of the cushion was musky and old. Beside my ears, my hands gripped the edges of the leather as tight as possible.

"Come, Angel, let it out." Then a hand wrapped around my arousal and gave four solid strokes, his pinky doing a dance on my sensitive head. I submitted with a soft moan, nothing loud enough for him to really hear. Through the aftershocks, I could feel his own erection hardening even further and pulsing with need. My nails dug into the leather under me as he filled the condom with seed. if he had continued for another few seconds, I didn't think I would have lasted through the sensitivity.

My head lulled onto the sofa as he pulled out and away, his strong grip on my shirt the only support holding me up at the moment. The spinning of the room was definitely worth it, I decided. The aftershocks of my orgasm made his touch feel like fire.

"Good boy, Angel."

CHAPTER
SEVEN

MY MIND HAD disconnected itself from my body. I could vaguely feel myself shaking, before I collapsed, only to be held in place by a long, thick arm. I knew that the world would return to me soon. My vision was slightly distorted, but I managed to look up at him when he squatted in front of me, not a hair out of place. I watched with glazed eyes as he lifted the towel to my face and gently wiped away the saliva on my lip and what dripped down my chin. I winced when it stung a little. Finally, my lungs were getting air. The clarity came quick.

"You... didn't use any chains... or whips... or... or-," my sentence drifted off. He raised an eyebrow. "No, Luka. We haven't come to any agreements yet. Until we can sit down and talk about that, I can't do what I really want to with you." As he spoke, Kai allowed me to pull my boxers back up before pulling me into a sitting position on the bench. I nodded jerkily. "I-I should go home, unless you want round two," I said, my voice cracking embarrassingly. His brows knit together. "No. It's fine. I'd rather you take a bath." the man turned suddenly to the glass door on the other side of the room. A bathroom, probably. I heard water running a moment later. Then he reappeared. "You should leave once you've cleaned yourself better. Mason will never drive you home in this state." I nodded and gave a huff when I had to pull myself to my feet. I wasn't sore yet. My heartbeat still ran like a waterfall in my ears.

Kaia stopped at the entrance to the bathroom. "Do you need any help? The taps can be confusing."

"Taps? As in more than one?" We only had a small, stand-up shower in our house. The feeling of having hot water surrounding one so completely in a massive soaking tub sounded next to heaven. Before undressing, I did my best to turn it on. The hot water took a moment, and I wasn't sure if the glass knob was even supposed to turn. I worried that I had broken it for a good three seconds. Eventually, it was running quietly with steaming water. I looked back at the man who stood in the doorway. He averted his eyes, not in shame, but simply to give me privacy, and shut the door. For a moment, I listened to his receding footsteps, watching his shadow move away from the door. Then my gaze fell on the rack of fluffy white towels that sat next to the door. A candle flitted in the corner. The floor was white tile; the three glowing spheres that hung above my head glowed too. The room was plain. The only colour I could see was Kai's toothbrush, his five-in-one soap, and the other door that I assumed attached to his bedroom. I didn't want to spend too much time on cleaning myself, although it was almost impossible to move once the back of my legs hit the bottom of the tub. I gripped the edges of the basin tightly with a sigh, realizing my sudden predicament.

....

"Do you give all your subs baths?" I asked, not meeting his gaze when I exited the bathroom. No one had ever shown me such excellent hospitality. Sure, I had been invited to have a coffee after a night alone with a customer, but never a spa. But Kaia didn't seem fazed; he shrugged. "I try to make sure they're comfortable. Can I talk to you for a while or do you have somewhere to be?" Unsure of how to reply, I motioned for him to continue, half nodded, half bit my lip. He then set a sheet of paper on his desk. My fingers shook as I took two steps forward and picked it up, knowing he watched me intently from the corner of my eye. And suddenly, once again, I was very, very nervous. I had heard of all the items on his scribbled list, but was I ever prepared to actually *do* them?.

Liberator benches? Spread-bars? 'Extreme' bondage?

The rest seemed respectable. Whips. Canes. Cuffs. Anal beads and plugs. Vibrators.

"What are Liberator benches?" I asked, my utter nervousness and fear seeping through my voice.

"What I just screwed you on." His voice was smug. I was just barely able to contain my grimace. I blanched, glancing over his shoulder to the sofa that I could see in front of his desk. "Oh." Did people not know he had sex toys sitting out in the open like that, for everyone to see?

"If you aren't sure if you want to do something, we can try it first. That's why we have colours," Kai added. I nodded and set the paper back onto the corner of the desk, pretending to read it as my hands dropped below my waist and I began to worry my knuckles. The desk was suddenly miles below me. I almost lost my balance. "Luka...." I looked up to him when he said my name, trailing off in confusion. I didn't expect his gaze to be so crestfallen. Not disappointed in me, per-say, but upset. I was sure that he would be sad, rejected, when he noticed my sudden panic, but the question that escaped his lips sobered me immediately. "Why do you make a living on the streets?"

My mouth fell slack a little bit. "I... um, I guess I just do it for a night job."

He looked at me incredulously. "You risk the transmittance of

STD's and your safety for a night job?"

I bit my lip and looked away, wincing as I pulled hard at my middle finger. He frowned. "Stop doing that to your fingers." I stopped without hesitation.

"Take the papers home. Look over them. Show it to me tomorrow."

"Will Mason pick me up again tomorrow? At the same time?" I asked. He nodded. I decided that that was the only reply I would get. Kai called for Mason with an authoritative edge in his voice; the man seemed to be getting agitated. "Kai?" Mason appeared, opening the door a crack. Kai looked up expectantly, and I immediately hated the way his gaze regarded Mason with pure distaste. The man looked ready to have a tantrum; he was obviously tired. "The car is warmed up. Would you like me to take him home now?" Kaia only nodded.

"Come with me, Luka," Mason smiled as he held an arm out to me. I gave one final glance at Kai, who, despite his previous expression, seemed to take a deep breath and relax slightly.

But the door was closed behind us before I could decide if I had imagined his mood or not.

We passed Rosa in the hallway, and the doorman downstairs, who I eventually knew as Abraham, on our way to the garage. Neither seemed surprised after seeing me for the second time. "Which car would you like to take?" Mason asked, stopping in the centre of the garage. I nearly ran into him, confusion consuming my features. "I thought you said you already had the car warmed up." He shrugged and turned to me with a kind, mischievous smirk. "I thought you would like to choose a car to ride in tonight. The last one wasn't a very pretty car, if I do say so myself."

"So you like cars?" I asked, glancing around the garage thoughtfully. He nodded. "I've been driving since I could reach the pedals and fixing them since before that."

"I like that one," I declared, pointing a thin finger at a beautiful, shining Harley Davidson in the corner. I hadn't paid his reply any mind, save for the small nod. The bike stood in the centre of a small row of them. Mason snorted, and I turned to him questioningly. "Of course you choose a bike. The exact thing Kai told me never to let you ride on with me. He doesn't even let *me* drive it."

My brows knit together. "Why can't I ride a bike with you?"

"Because you're twice as likely to get hurt than if you were in a car, and Kai doesn't like the idea of that. That's his baby, anyway. Why don't we take the Spider?" When I turned to Mason, he stood beside a baby-blue *Ferrari*. It was... stunning. I had never gotten so close to anything so expensive. "I only use it at night. I like how the lights of the city reflect on the blue. Get in."

I blanched. "W-We're... taking that?"

"Mhm. Let's go, Mr. Luka."

I bit my lip and simultaneously pulled at my knuckles as I stepped down into the shotgun seat.

CHAPTER EIGHT

I WAS EMBARRASSED TO be in a car with Mason after what he had probably heard. I looked away in shame as he started the engine. It purred under us, sending the most comfortable vibrations up through the spotless leather seats. I could easily fall asleep in this car. "Mr. Luka, I don't want to harp on you, but you really must stop the hand and lip worrying. Is that a thing you do often?" I shrugged and looked out the window as cars slid past us, slowing with the traffic. Was it always so busy, even so close to midnight?

I could feel his sharp gaze on me, taking in my hands and bloodied lip, yet he stayed silent. "Are you hungry?"

My gaze snapped to his at the mention of food, and I was about to confirm his suspicions, but thought better of it. "No... I ate earlier."

He rolled his eyes. "I know, Mr. Luka. I helped Rosa make the food and brought the tray."

I nibbled at my lip and nodded. "I'm fine. I don't need fo-," but I was cut off when the car suddenly swerved through two lanes of oncoming traffic, narrowly missing the vehicles that raced toward us. My head collided with the window before the dashboard flew towards my face when, just in time, he slammed his foot on the brake, and suddenly, we had pulled safely into the parking lot of a local fast food chain

ANGEL

"Don't tell Kai I did that. He would be enraged."

I gripped onto the door handle tightly as I attempted to calm my heartbeat. My body was numb from shock, but Mason didn't seem to mind as he grabbed his wallet from the cup tray between us and swerved into the drive-through. "M-Mason, I'm not hungry. I'm okay. I ate." The words came out a little muffled. He ignored my persistent objections and looked to the ordering machine beside him. It made an annoying squeaking noise before a worker welcomed us to the restaurant.

"Yeah, just a minute, please." Then he turned to me. "What do you want?"

I stared at him, then at the menu. "I'm not... hungry." He frowned and sighed, turning back to the speaker. "I'll get a medium milkshake, please, and... the biggest, greasiest burger you got."

"Will that be all?"

"Yep."

"Alright, that'll be ten-forty-six at the window."

"Thanks."

He pulled through to the window where he paid silently. He replied with a wink when she wished him a good night. We then sat and waited behind the three cars who had ordered before us, allowing the cool night air flow through the open roof of the car.

"Is it too cold for you?"

I shook my head.

"Mr. Luka, if you're going to take this job offering, then you're going to have to get used to people buying things for you. That's just the kind of guy he is. He won't show it, but he loves to see the faces of people who get things they really deserve."

"So... he's like a teddy bear inside?"

He snorted. "Was he a teddy bear tonight?"

I paused before shaking my head, no, quickly.

"Well, there's your answer, Mr. Luka."

I sighed. "Mason, I really hate the Mr. in front of my name. You can call me Lucika if you want."

His curious gaze then fell on mine. "Lucika? Is that your full name?" I nodded before he released a genuine, caring smile. "I like it. It sounds very... Spanish, almost. Or Italian."

I rolled my eyes playfully. "My mother just calls me Luka, though."

"Where does your mother work?"

My smile vanished. *Fuck.*

Could I tell him? Really, it probably wouldn't make much difference to him, so I decided to shrug and say, "She works at a diner. Hopefully she'll be in bed by the time I get home."

"By midnight? Does she have a night shift?" I nodded. "She, um... She works most nights. And days."

Mason nodded as he pulled the car forward.

"What about your mother?"

I was hoping to get a small conversation started, away from the subject of my own mother. But his reaction was not the one I desired. He paused, his hand halfway up the steering wheel. I watched his hand begin to tremble. He shrugged his shoulders and shook his head as if he was trying to shake my question away. Had I offended him? Was his mother deceased? He seemed... angry at my question. "Don't ask me that question. How's your milkshake, Lucika?" His nostrils flared as he kept his rattled gaze on the road ahead. I got the feeling that he couldn't even process my question, much less answer it. His reply certainly didn't match his facial expression; his words were kept calm and playful while his eyes were withdrawn. I could tell that he knew how to lie but was rusty on his body language suppression. In a second, the light air around us seemed to grow thicker than molasses. I was panicking, mentally screaming at my stupidity. The rest of our drive through downtown and to my home

ANGEL

was sickeningly silent, save for the sound of Mason's burger wrapper crinkling as he ate. At least he wasn't so distraught that he had lost his appetite.

Upon arrival at my house, I had counted a good ten minutes since Mason had fallen silent. He had slipped a small envelope which contained my payments for the night into the drive-through bag and made sure I took it with me when I exited the car. This time, he didn't wait until I had my hand on my front door before he sped away, roaring the engine violently. It probably woke most people in the neighbourhood.

That night, my mother hadn't stayed up to wait for me. After telling her that some nights I would be 'working overtime', she understood my absences. But I knew I couldn't sleep with the constant regret of how my night ended. Was Mason angry with me? Why was he so sensitive to the particular question about his mother? I undressed until I stood shivering in my boxers before I crawled into my bed, pulling the covers up to my chin. For a moment, just a second, I wondered what it would feel like to have Kai's warm body next to my own.

But I was asleep before I could even shake the thought from my mind.

....

I had one more night with Kai until next week and a total of twenty minutes before I was picked up. Mom would be home within thirty. I couldn't shake the feeling that the list that burned my palm, crumpled and folded, only scratched the surface of what Kai would really dare to do to me. Whips, chains, bondage. It sounded like the opposite of "pleasure". It sounded... very painful. Violent. Scary. How well could I trust him? I felt as if I had already ruined the small friendship I had made with Mason. Kai was the deep end of the pool, and I was only just learning to swim. This relationship had the power to thrust me into the deep end and watch me drown. Or, I would learn to tread water. Was I willing to take the chance?

The answer was yes. Of course I was. The smile I wanted to see on my mother's face would be worth it, and I knew that the money could get me what I yearned for. I would be able to buy us meals. She would be overjoyed. A massive roar pulled me from my thoughts, vibrating the house around me. Mason sat in the driveway in the same blue *Ferrari*. He had come back to get me? Was I forgiven? A quick glance out my window sent me rocketing down the stairs, and my hand was on the door handle when I froze.

I needed to make a decision about Kaia then. Not when I got to his home, not when I was standing in front of him, not before I slid into the car that would take me to him. He would pay me if I stayed, but there was nothing stopping me from telling his roommate to get the fuck off my lawn. I could go back to my old job seven nights a week...

And with a loud groan, I made my decision. I was stupid to have pondered over it so long. I locked my door behind me before trotting around the front of the car and getting in the shotgun side. My heart nearly stopped when I turned my head and noticed that Mason wasn't sitting at his usual post.

"M-Mr. Arche!"

He looked to me with a deadpan expression. "Angel."

There was a moment of silence as the *Ferrari* purred quietly under us. "Do you have the papers?" he asked. I bit my lip and nodded. "I'll circle what I don't want to do... but I don't have a pen." I didn't miss the small smirk that graced his face before he snatched a pen from the small storage compartment between us. "Well, I do."

He handed it to me. I refused to let him see my trembling hand.

We drove in silence to Kai's apartment. It wasn't too awkward,

ANGEL

but my knuckles were red by the time we were within a mile of his home. "Is Mason okay? I think... I think I said something wrong when he dropped me off last night," I said quietly.

Kai sighed. The sound made me despise myself more.

"Angel, Mason has some mental issues that he doesn't like to talk about. The mention of his mother just triggered him, but he's still working at the apartment now. Couldn't pick you up because he decided to spill chocolate milk all over my freaking floors. He doesn't blame you though, Luka. You didn't know." I was stunned at the gentleness of his words. He had gone from a sex-crazed playboy to a kind, caring man in seconds.

"Oh... that's good, I guess." I wasn't sure what to say. At least he wasn't crying over his spilt milk.

"What do you want to eat tonight? I haven't asked for anything specific yet," Kai added. I shrugged, and he sighed. We were going too fast, twenty miles over the limit in an area where that behaviour was strictly prohibited. Soon, we would be in his garage.

"I'll tell him to make you something hot."

As we pulled up past his apartment building, my brows furrowed. I glimpsed half a dozen men and women crowded around the front doors of Kai's apartment. Were they... paparazzi? I was sure that Kai wasn't *that* popular.

"Mr. Arche, I don't know why I haven't asked you before, but... why are you so important?" To my relief, he didn't seem offended by the question. "If I can get us inside without being suffocated by paparazzi, then I'll tell you," he scoffed as he pulled behind the building and down into the garage. The massive iron gates closed and locked behind us. From where we sat, the paparazzi couldn't see us, and we could slip into the building undetected.

"Sorry, Arche. I did tell them to stay away earlier today. They're looking for that young lady that lives below you. Apparently she's dating another famous singer," Abraham apologized in a gruff voice as we made our way to the elevator. Kai waved his hand. "It's fine, Abraham. They're just annoying. I'm sure they're probably here for the Dusk family too." Something in his voice was dark. A brief flash of understanding illuminated Abraham's eyes. It made sense that Kai lived between famous Americans. He *belonged*.

When Kai spoke next, he didn't make eye contact with me. "I'm not important because of the work I do. I'm famous because of my parents; they're the ones who are important. In all honesty, this is their money. I'm happy to take it and they're happy to give it," he informed me, keeping his gaze straight ahead. He seemed to be waiting very impatiently for the elevator doors to open. I was happy to finally understand him a little better. "I work for my own paycheck for personal use, though. We're going to the kitchen first," he told me as the doors opened and he grabbed my wrist to pull me from the metal box.

I bit my lip, my hand wrapped tightly around the papers, as I followed him into the state-of-the-art kitchen.

CHAPTER
NINE

"**G**OOD AFTERNOON, KAI!" Rosa greeted us. "And you, Mr. Luka." I gave a sheepish smile in reply, diverting my eyes nervously as Kai took a seat at the twelve-foot-long island in the kitchen. The appliances were, of course, stainless steel, and the granite countertops and cupboards were white. It would be blinding, if not for the grey backsplash and black and brown decor of the sprawling living room behind us. To our left stood a longtable suitable for at least ten people.

"Do you have anything warm cooking tonight?" Kai asked Rosa. Her eyes lit up. "No, but I'll get on that now."

Kai nodded. I set the papers in front of him before he took them in his own hands. My lungs tightened, knowing that Rosa could probably read them from just across the counter. I glued my gaze to the granite to distract myself from the man sitting just beside me, absorbing my secret kinks silently. Neither Kai nor I turned to look at who it was when the elevator *dinged* behind us, but my eyes brightened with joy when Mason strolled around the island. "Good evening, Kai. Lucika." He looked... good, much better than I expected. He was well-rested and seemed to have forgotten our incident. Kai looked up at him, then to me. I turned my gaze back down to the island. "Lucika?" The mention of my name made my heart valves clamp closed in a second.

"Your full name is Lucika?" I nodded, finally meeting his eyes bravely. "I thought you already knew it. Sorry," Mason mumbled with a nonchalant shrug. Kaia didn't seem bothered in the least and mirrored his shrug. "Now I know."

"What would you like to eat, Mr. Luka?" Rosa asked. She didn't pay the men any mind. I shrugged. "I don't want to be a burden or anything, I'll have whatever you want to make." I rubbed the back of my neck nervously. She, instead of giving another kind reply, looked to Kai. "He'll have spaghetti," he declared for me, folding the paper in his hands with a shake. I blanched and looked at him, then to Rosa, but she was already bustling around the kitchen to prepare my meal. "You like spaghetti, don't you?" Mr. Arche asked as if he was asking more out of politeness than actual interest. I wanted to glare, although the thought of spaghetti made my stomach roll with excitement. Saliva burnt my mouth.

Rosa acted a lot younger than she looked, and I wondered how old she really was. Maybe it was the cherry-red lipstick she had applied to her lips every hour that made her look a little bit younger. Or maybe it was her litheness in the kitchen as she flirted between the stove and the countertop. Rosa already had noodles, although they weren't spaghetti, prepared, and an assortment of sauteed vegetables. All that was left for her to do was pull a large container of tomato sauce from the fridge.

"I circled things where I needed to... right?" I asked quietly. Rosa ignored us. Kai nodded quickly. "Yes, I'm just... never mind." His brows were pulled together, causing a twinge of hesitance in my gut. Did I circle the things he liked to do? Did I have too many limits? "Here you go, Mr. Luka," Rosa smiled and slid the bowl across the counter to me once the microwave had cried out. "Next time, it won't be microwaved. I'll make a full three courses next week," Rosa promised Kai as she began to wipe sauce and grease

ANGEL

from the countertop. My eyes widened when I grabbed the awaiting fork and took my first bite. "Oh my god! This is so good!" Rosa's lips turned up into a massive smile. She obviously loved praise for her food. "I'm glad you like it, Luka."

I couldn't stop myself from shovelling it into my mouth greedily. "I can't remember the last time I had tomatoes." Rosa gave a small, humorless chuckle as Mason and Kai watched our interactions intently. "Oh, I'm sure you eat tomatoes all the time. I don't always eat them because they're too acidic for me," Mason replied. I shrugged as I swallowed a large mouthful of noodles and chunky, flavourful sauce. "This is a treat. Thank you."

"Don't you eat relatively-healthy at home? You look like you've never seen a vegetable before." Mason smirked, leaning his elbows against the counter on my side opposite Kai. "Mom just kinda brings food home for us, you know? Usually we share a burger or something." My palms began to sweat, so I wiped them quickly against my thighs diffidently. Rosa nodded and looked to Kai before smiling back at me once again, as if she hadn't realized that I didn't eat because I *couldn't* eat.

"Well, I hope you have a nice night, Mr. Luka," she said, before disappearing into the little hallway behind the stairs quickly and quietly. I could barely reply with a 'You, too'.

"I can clean this up. I'll be here if you need anything," Mason told us, but his eyes lingered on Kai's for a moment. "Do you want anything to eat, Kai?" Something in his words made me uneasy. It was almost like... a warning? Was Mason scolding Mr. Arche? I became confused with a phrase I expected from a parent.

"No, Mason. Thank you." Kai's words were curt and low, sending shivers up my spine. No longer was he kind. His eyes had turned dark and his voice was obviously a warning, against something that was between Mason and him. "We can talk upstairs. Come on, Lucika," he ordered, standing quickly. But his gaze never left Mason's until he reached the first step. Then we both turned away to climb them, and mason returned to his duties. I played with the edge of my shirt nervously as Kai stared straight ahead, his face expressionless. His shoulders were tense and rigid, and I wondered why asking him if he wanted food triggered him so much. "Hey, Kai, can I ask you a question?" I asked once we had made it to the first landing. Five more steps transported us to the hallway. My voice was quiet and diffident.

"Of course, Angel."

I nibbled at my lip lightly before continuing. "Do you... have trouble eating? Weird question, I know, but Mason just kinda-," but I stopped short when he released a deep sigh. Kai stopped and turned to me at the top step. Finally, his eyes met mine. I could tell that he had explained the answer to my question far too many times.

"I have ageusia."

My brows furrowed together in confusion. Was I supposed to know what that meant? Was it some kind of disease that impacted his eating? A disorder?

"It means I can't taste my food. My tastebuds are shot. I rely on scent to taste."

My mouth formed into an "O" shape and I nodded my head in understanding. He couldn't taste... anything? No Chinese food? No alcohol? No burgers? None of Rosa's food?

"Without the ability to taste anything, eating becomes... a boring practice, especially if things don't smell very good." I nodded again. "So, you don't like eating. How do you... you must eat a lot. You look like the kind of guy who would eat a lot and then work it off at the gym." He licked his lips, thinking about his next words. Had I gone too far? Maybe conversation making wasn't part of the deal. Just sex. Understood. Got it.

ANGEL

"I drink protein and calorie shakes in the morning. Normally, that gets me through the day if I snack just a few times. There are only a few foods I enjoy the texture and smell of," he deadpanned. I swallowed hard, scared to make any further conversation, and followed him into the hallway on shaky legs. My eyes widened when I realized that the door we swerved into wasn't the office I was expecting. Instead, we stood on the edge of an elegant, masculine bedroom. The walls were pure glass on two sides that granted a view of the neighboring apartments and another of a few shops from downtown Santa Monica

A kitchenette sat to our right, just beside a mini-bar. It was obviously stocked with a good selection of alcohol, completed with glasses and tools for the most elite of bartenders. Maybe he could taste alcohol? Could he feel the burn? In the middle of the room sat a ring of black leather couches and a single padded chair. The bed made up a large portion of the room. Beside our elevator sat a second, smaller elevator, its doors open, waiting. I wondered where that one would take me. Maybe a red room? Some kind of man cave?

"My bedroom," Kai announced, retrieving a bottle of water from the mini fridge in the corner and offering it to me. I shook my head, and Kai motioned to the ring of sofas in the centre of the room. We each took a seat across from each other before Kai spread the papers between us on the sleek coffee table. "And you've circled everything you're not okay with? The things that are hard limits for you? Anything, even if they're not on there. If you aren't comfortable with it, then it's totally off the table for now. I'm patient, but only if you're willing to safely explore things that you're not sure of," Kai said, turning the papers to me and setting a pen beside them in the case I had forgotten anything. My signature was scribbled in the bottom right corner, simply to indicate that I had read the list carefully.

I leaned forward and grasped the pen in a shaky hand, my brows pulling together slightly. There was nothing new to be circled, so I glanced at the red, messy rings around some of the words. Hematolagnia had been circled by both me and Kai. I assumed that the word made his skin crawl too.

I realized that he had his own list of practices he was strictly against on a new paper he had given me, play that involved things like feces and drugs. I was suddenly very happy that he wasn't completely insane with new partners. My eyes briefly scanned over the list of rules he had for me. I must take care of myself: hygiene, medication if needed, etcetera. No self-harm. I had to notify him of body modifications and medical procedures before I had any so he could know how to ensure my safety afterwards. No masturbation without permission during our time together. The papers also mentioned that, with a discussion with Kai, the points could be changed at any time. If I wasn't supportive of the relationship, then all ties could be severed, and if I wanted more rules, ones to be applied outside of the bedroom, we could discuss those too. I'd had that before once; a woman had given me a list of things to do before I saw her the night after, things like 'do a workout before visiting her' and 'do something that makes me happiest'. At the time, I was confused as to why the orders weren't sexual, before I learnt that that was what a Dom *did*.

"What can I expect for punishments? Titles?" Of course, I was bound to break a rule or two, and there surely was no end to what kinky names he wanted to be called. "I like to use impact play for punishments, mostly. It's quicker and allows me better control… although, that doesn't always work for subs. I've used things like edging and more sexual punishments instead. As for titles, anything regarding me as a male superior is fine. I've been called pretty much everything," he told me. Kai then scratched his scalp before asking,

ANGEL

"What about you?"

My answer locked itself in my throat for a moment. "I've been called pretty much everything too… whatever makes you happy."

"Thank you," he replied sincerely.

I was accustomed to most finger and cock play by then, so the basics on the sheets weren't too much of a worry. I *did* begin to worry over the fact that the papers simply said 'toys' multiple times. "What does it mean by 'toy play'? Is that dildos? Anal beads?" I asked. I expected him to have a hidden stash of foot-long dildos in his closet, just waiting to ambush me. Kai tilted his head back as he took a drink and nodded. He swallowed before setting the bottle on the table.

"Butt plugs. Vibrators. The works. I have favourites that I always end up coming back to. Before anything else goes inside you, though, I'll have learnt your limits. Until then, we'll talk about it. Have you used many toys before?" I nodded nervously. "Yeah. I've never done… you know, big ones before, though."

"Define big."

Suddenly, the only thing I wanted to do was stuff my head in my hands. "Like… bigger than your… I've never taken a fist before. I've come close, though," was all my mind could blurt. He obviously wasn't satisfied with my answer, but he thankfully brushed off the conversation for another time. He could see that I was hesitating then. The papers were filled out and handed back to him. So why was I hesitating? Why were my fingers suddenly frozen to the paper? Was I ready for the real Kai? Kai described his time as pleasure. I described it to myself as money, money that I needed, and I had been with people that described it as pleasure too. It had been everything but.

"Let me show you," Kai said suddenly. His dark gaze locked with mine, and I flinched. He must have noticed my lack of enthusiasm.

"Sh... Show me?"

"Let me show you tonight what my BDSM really is, if you haven't already learnt it from a decent person. And if you still don't want the money or this relationship, then you can personally watch me put the limits through the paper shredder. You can leave, no strings attached, like we planned." I watched him in silence for a moment, gauging his sincerity. Was he really willing to bet so much on the outcome of the relationship?

I locked my lips and let my hands slide back into my lap where I could easily pull at them.

"Okay." My voice didn't seem sure, so I tried again. It failed miserably. One of his eyes twitched.

"O-Okay. You can show me."

CHAPTER
TEN

I LET HIM STAND and pull me to my feet, his gaze catching mine. His eyes were blown wide with lust, but that was the only thing that gave his intentions away. He gently took my hand and led me around the sofa to the bed on the far side of the room. "Remember the safe-words, Angel. You're familiar with blindfolds and sensory deprivation, yes?" he asked as he pushed me lightly onto the bed. I sat, my hands coming to curl themselves together in my lap, as he stalked around the bed to kneel in front of one of the bedside tables. "Yes," I replied clearly. First, he extracted a small remote from the drawer, and with the light press of a button, the windows around the room were slowly swallowed by dark blinds that allowed no light to intrude. He flicked on the lamp at the bedside table. After the remote, he pulled a blindfold from the drawer and stood, his knees touching mine. "Green, yellow, and red," he reminded me again. He was giving me every chance to decide against this, I realized. A part of me did want to, but there was far too much at stake for me to harbor any of those thoughts.

I bit my lip and watched as he straightened the black blindfold and prepared to cover my eyes. My lips involuntarily locked together as he pulled it over my face, tying it in the back. My world wasn't filled with dim light anymore, and it almost made me sick.

The fabric almost made me excited, though, knowing that pleasure was to come. His fingers were so light, I wasn't sure if they were really there. Once the blindfold was on, I felt him removing my clothes; first my shirt, then my shoes, socks, and pants. My underwear stayed, and I wasn't sure if I was happy about that. What else was he planning?

My breathing quickened with the suspense. I couldn't see, only feel his movements, but there were no hands on me once I was nearly naked. I flinched at the softest blow of air across my body, the hair on the back of my neck and arms rising with goosebumps. I gasped when something small pushed against my left nipple, immediately raising the sensitive bud. A small vibrator moved over me while Kai tugged lightly at the opposite side of my chest. He rolled it between his thumb and forefinger before pushing down on it roughly. I gave a gentle, breathy sigh, my cock growing hard quickly when the sensations rushed straight for my groin.

"There are a lot of rules in this relationship. Ones that haven't been mentioned yet," Kai's voice was oddly soothing. He was being gentle; I could hear it in his voice, even with the constant stimulation at my chest. Another shiver rocked me when he switched the vibrator to the other nub. "There are also punishments if you disobey them. Like orgasming without permission, for example. That will stop now." I moaned when his hot tongue lapped across my skin, burning a line from my collar bone to my nipple, and combined the sensation with a heavy palm gyrating against my groin. "But there are many for me too. I'll get you anything you want for after our sessions. Or you could bring items from your own home, like blankets and pillows. My past subs have told me that they benefited from that greatly. Whatever you need to feel comfortable after a scene, do it."

If I hadn't been so aroused, I probably would have been more

ANGEL

hooked on the mention of his past relationships. How many like me had he roped in? What happened to them? Fluid dripped from my erection and seeped into my boxers, my mind just barely registering his words. I would remember them, but only because I was so sensitive to my surroundings. "I have limits, too, though. You won't be encroaching anywhere near them tonight, but later, it's only fair that you listen to them. I am also responsible for your physical health, if you'd like to take this to such extremes, like exercise and eating habits. My rules are different from a lot of other people." Kai kissed my jawline. I leaned towards the touch.

My back arched off the bed when the vibrator nudged my cock, just the slightest bit of mind-numbing pressure. I needed that pleasure. So badly. I ached for it.

"P-Please! I need... I...," but my words fell short when he hushed me gently. A bottle was opened and closed. I felt him toss it close to my head. "Patience, Angel," His voice was low and comforting, but failed to distract me from the hand that crept up my thigh. His hand dipped under the waistline of my briefs, between my legs, and gently rubbing against the rim of my entrance with well-oiled fingers. My last piece of clothing was pulled halfway down my thighs during his intrusion, but I had no complaints.

He flipped me suddenly onto my stomach, my hands gripping the sheets until the knuckles turned white. A single finger entered me quickly, massaging my inner walls gently. I wished desperately for him to add another finger or two. I needed him to reach that spot again, despite the pain that turned my brain to a fruit punch of electricity and haze.

Once he added a second one, I began gyrating my hips against his hand shamelessly. When he found that spot, he knew it immediately, and wrapped a firm palm around my erection that bobbed beneath me. The light moan of ecstasy I released was a dead giveaway. Then, suddenly, just as my body began sucking him in further, his fingers were gone. There was no more pressure on that spot, or anywhere else. I felt so empty, almost painfully. I wore a betrayed expression on my face. He couldn't see it well.

"Can't you... I need it!" I cried, waving my ass as if it was on fire and realizing that the burn in my eyes was from the disappointment and abandonment I had been left with. Then my left arm was disconnected from the sheets and bound by the wrist to the bed. It stretched me to the left uncomfortably. "Ah." I released soft sighs and gasps when he bound my other wrist to the other side of the bed. "Please...."

My chest heaved up and down with each gasp, my cock hanging free over the sheets. It dripped pre-cum onto them, staining them dark-brown. I let my hips down a little, seeking friction on my cock. "No playing with yourself without permission, Angel, remember? That's a punishment." Kai's words scared me just as much as they turned me on. I gave a yelp when his hand slapped across my left cheek. Even before the shock could reverberate around my body, he stopped to massage me gently. My spine quivered as the shockwave rattled it, and my waist nearly collapsed. "Count them," he growled. I whimpered, but I was able to mumble a broken "one." Surely, he could make his motions more aggressive and painful, but for now, as he mentioned, he was still learning my limits.

Another slap reverberated off the windows, and this time I released a loud moan, a mixture of agony and bliss. "Two." My voice was louder, more confident. He continued for five more times. After each one, my waist nearly crumbled under me, and I nearly came twice with his hand occasionally reaching below to pump me. The only thing that prevented me from coming was the fear of a greater punishment after ejaculating without permission. "Please, Kai, please... I need... I need to come."

ANGEL

Tears weren't only burning my eyes, but that also had begun to burn my cheeks. My wrists ached from how hard I pulled against the restraints. "You can come, Angel. It's okay." As he said the words, his hand left my ass to wrap firmly around my erection for the last time, and I let the dam break. Semen splattered across the sheets while drool threatened to drip onto the silky comforter. I rode through it eagerly, deciding to savor the emotions and sensations. Then I yelped when he added two more slaps, rubbing them away a moment later with his free hand. I could hardly believe how comforting the aftershocks were, accompanied by his hands on my body. The suddenly soft touch after such a draining experience had the same impact as an addict's fix.

I couldn't breathe. The darkness and the sensitivity, the pain and the utter ecstasy, threatened to envelope me like a cage and never let me free. My body still quivered, completely consumed. "Breathe, Angel," he said, creating a dip beside me on the bed where he knelt. His breath smelled like alcohol, expensive cigars, and an undertone of cigarettes when he leaned in close. I was accustomed to the disgusting, cheap cigarettes my mother bought. What he obviously smoked was so savoury and rich, my mouth was nearly watering. The smell *worked* with his natural scent.

I took in a deep breath, filling my aching lungs quickly. I could feel them expand, freeze for a moment, and then release the air hesitantly, as if I wasn't sure exactly *how* to breathe. The air burnt my dry throat, and I swallowed hard soon after. "There we go," Kai said gently. I repeated the process once more before feeling my left wrist fall from the restraints. I pulled it to my chest, my head still buried in the sheets. Then the other one was also released.

"Let me see them," Kai ordered. It was a command, but his voice was still quiet and gentle. The blindfold had yet to be removed; I didn't mind. He couldn't see my watery eyes when the blindfold was on, and I wasn't sure if I was ready to face him yet. Not after *that*. Apparently, my wishes of never removing the blindfold were not answered. He slipped it off slowly, allowing my eyes to grow accustomed to the bright light, and I looked up at him with wide eyes as he took my wrists in his hands. I winced as he held the tender flesh. It was red; we both knew the cuffs would leave bruises. They weren't the ones that I had used before; I enjoyed the expensive leather ones more. He would have to invest in better quality gear, I decided. Or maybe I would learn to enjoy the pain that followed.

"You did a very good job, Angel. Perfect."

I licked my lips. What was I supposed to say to that? I winced again when I shuffled against the sheets, my bottom sending bouts of pain up my back.

"Come on. I'll run you a bath," Kai told me, pushing an arm under my chest to help me to the edge of the bed. I was exhausted, too exhausted to reply, but he understood. I shuffled past the elevators and into a bathroom, the same one I had taken a bath in after our previous night together. Kai's apartment wasn't that big or excessively modern, really. It was only his cars that made him seem rich; I guessed that he didn't see the point in spending more when there were only a few people living there. There was no reason to have a private bathroom for an office, anyway.

He set me on a small bamboo stool beside the door as he bent to turn on the water for the soaking tub. I realized then that he hadn't ejaculated himself, and was still fully clothed. Was I expected to help him with that? Why hadn't he said anything?

As he turned around, I slipped off the low stool to my knees and began to unzip his pants. My muscles screamed in protest while my mind scolded them. But his hands grabbed mine and pulled them away before I could get his zipper more than halfway undone. "No, Luka. It's okay," he declared. My brows furrowed in confusion; I had never had anyone refuse a blowjob before. "But you didn't-," he cut me off. His orders were final, I realized. "I said it's okay. Relax."

I bit my lip and nodded, looking away at the floor. "Stand up, Angel. The bath is almost done."

I stood on very shaky legs, letting Kai support me as I stepped over the side of the bathtub and into the hot water. I let in a gasp when the water stung my buttocks, where I assumed handprints still lingered. "Sh. Just sit down. It'll pass," he promised. "Next time I'll have lotion on me. I left it in my office this time. I'm sorry."

I shrugged. "It's okay."

I pulled my knees up to my chin in the tub as Kai watched me, his eyes still as hungry as before. Maybe it was just the fact that they were so dark that made them look so full of lust. Either way, they were stunning, I decided.

"Do you think you would be willing to try this relationship now? Even if you want to end it in the future? You just have to name your price and all the money is yours," he said. I had nearly forgotten about the money. I had almost forgotten why I was here. I had forgotten my mother most-likely smoking her last pack of the day at the kitchen table right then. And the guilt was crippling. I had enjoyed it *too* much.

I bit at my lip, resisting the urge to pull on my fingers. What did I have to lose? I certainly had everything to gain. "Yes. I want to try this." My reply began as a shaky grumble and ended in a determined, full, proud sentence.

The grin that played on the edges of his lips made me just as scared as I was excited.

CHAPTER
ELEVEN

KAI LEFT ME for a few moments during my bath to speak with Mason in his bedroom. He returned with a bottle of water and a platter of fruit. "You're dehydrated and hungry. Help yourself," Kai said, pulling the stool beside the tub so he could set the tray on it. I took a swig of water before popping a strawberry between my lips. The juice burned my lips. "Those are delicious," I said simply, only pausing long enough to say that before eating another one.

He stayed silent, watching me. I realized how jealous he probably was. I would have starved myself if I couldn't taste anything. There would be no point in eating. "What kinds of foods do you like the texture of?" I asked. He shrugged. "Crunchy apples. Raisins. A few other things. Rosa makes the best dough balls. I love those."

I giggled at the thought of Kaia stuffing himself with pastry, and I almost smiled. Almost.

At the edge of my mind, a voice told me that this was wrong, that I shouldn't be giving my body away. I shouldn't be sitting in a bathtub beside a man I had met only a week or two ago. He was absolutely stunning, a sex god, in my eyes, even with his questionable sexual attractions. Did that make him any different?

"Is aftercare always like this? That's a thing you mentioned, right?"

ANGEL

I asked. He nodded. "A lot of subs, even well-trained ones, can get overwhelmed after a scene. After care, well, it's kind of in the name. It helps them calm down after scenes. Baths. Cartoons. Kisses. Whatever the sub prefers. Some people just like to be left alone too."

"Oh. So... do I get after care?"

His brows pulled together. "Of course. All subs get some kind of aftercare. Scenes can be just as exhausting and painful as they are pleasurable and exhilarating. Even doms need it sometimes."

I bit my lip and nodded, finding that my gaze was beginning to roam around the room instead of staying trained on Kai's.

"Now, I haven't ever paid a submissive before. I want to talk about price," Kai began, and my gaze snapped to his. As he spoke, the man fished a package of cigarettes from his back pocket, stuck one between his teeth, and lit it with a lighter. "Do you mind?" he asked. I shook my head. I almost expected him to offer me one. "I don't normally pay people for sex. But I went after you because I know that your only other job is selling your body on the streets. And I won't let you do that any longer. No one should ever have to do that." The man shook his head with a dreary glaze in his eyes.

He paused for a moment, letting me absorb his words. I nodded slowly, urging him to continue. Kai was the first person to ever show any sympathy for my lifestyle, as much as I hated to think of him as any different than my other customers. I still had to please him one way or another, but he *understood*.

"I want you to stop that job. I will not have my submissive on the streets at any time of night. Especially when their body is mine and mine only." My mouth fell open, unsure of how to reply. "Kai, I know that that's a big point for you, but I can't give up those five nights a week... I need the money." I looked down at my hands, which had begun to come together nervously again. I didn't dare meet his eyes. I could feel his frown.

"Then... I'll give you a job," Kai said after a moment of thought. With a glance, I saw that his eyes were dark, almost frustrated. But his voice didn't match his expression. I blanched. "A job? You'll hire me?" Briefly, images of my mother flashed through my mind. She was happy and we weren't struggling financially. We were well-fed. The idea seemed so unrealistic. "I've been looking for someone who can keep track of my bank accounts, keep what goes in and what goes out on the records. Someone I can trust. Until now, Rosa has done that." I nodded, my interest and excitement piqued. He could see that in my eyes. "And... you'll actually give me this job? How much does it pay?"

He gave a small, hopeful smirk. "A lot more than you're getting paid right now."

....

Thank you, Mason," Mr. Arche said as he followed us out of the elevator. We stood in the foyer where Abraham watched us from the corner at the large desk. "Have a good night, Luka," Kai replied, sending me a quick smile as he adjusted his collar. It seemed as though he never wore anything other than suits. He exchanged a glance with Mason, having an entire conversation in under a second, before turning away from us. Once we were safely in the garage, Mason unlocked the *Ferrari* and we both climbed in. This car would definitely be my favourite for a long time.

"The way Kai smiles at you is kinda creepy, you know," Mason told me suddenly as we pulled away from the apartment building. His gaze didn't leave the road.

"Huh?"

"The way he smiled at you just when we left. It was super creepy. Just saying."

"Maybe he's just happy that he has another sub now. I can see why it would be a drug to some people," I mumbled. He snorted. "Trust me, Lucika, you're different. Kaia Arche would never pay a submissive to have sex with him. Ever. Maybe he'd pay people off the street, like you, but he'd never go as far as chains or whips with them." Mason was acting like he had forgotten our issues earlier, so I figured that after what he had told me, I could apologize safely. Really, I didn't want to talk about Kai anymore. "Um, kind of off topic here, but I just want to apologize for last night. I didn't know."

"I know. It's fine." His reply was curt, and I could see that the smile he flashed me was forced. He seemed like such a kind man, someone you could trust your life with. I knew he was. But he was in pain. I could see it in his eyes and engrained in the small wrinkles around his smile. "You shouldn't feel bad. There was no way you could've known."

I was only slightly comforted by his words.

"So where does Kai want you to work?" Mason asked, sparking new conversation as we paused at a red light. The man's thumb tapped against the wheel rhythmically. "He says I can keep track of his bank accounts for him. Put everything that goes in and out on a record. I don't really know where I'll be working, though," I replied. I would probably be working during the day, so I would at least have something to do other than sleep. And I could give up my street job. The thought of that made me more excited than anything. I suppose, as long as I remained as his sub, I would be able to keep the job. Sounded easy enough.

"Sounds good. It's an easy job. You'll be fine."

We sped through the streets, probably faster than Kai would want Mason to drive. I could tell that he was the kind of guy who only followed the rules in the presence of his 'boss'. He was free when he was by himself.

"He also wanted you to have this," Mason said, grabbing a small black bag from underneath his seat. He dropped it in my lap. I felt its contents through the plastic before I opened it. It was a box of some sort. I opened the bag with nimble fingers, feeling the smallest twinges of fear. I just couldn't know what Kai had given me this time. He was too unpredictable, but I was sure I would discover something I enjoyed.

My mouth fell open when I pulled out the box, which was actually the container for a cellphone. It was an older model, but they weren't completely off the market yet.

"Oh my god." I was stunned. The box's smooth surface tickled my fingertips. Mason simply glanced at me, then back to the road.

"I... I... w-what the fuck?"

Mason's gaze snapped to me. "Kai hates that word. If he ever heard you say it, you'd be in a lot of trouble." My mind drifted back to when I had sworn during sex. He hadn't seemed too bothered by it. Maybe it was an 'in the moment' thing. I swallowed another f-bomb back and turned the heavy container in my hand. "I... I can't accept this!" I exclaimed. Mason shrugged. "I'm just gonna give you some words of advice. If Kai gives you gifts, you should accept them. He likes to give gifts. I thought I told you this. If you don't accept them, it's a personal offence to him."

"But this... this is a phone! These things are hundreds of dollars! He can't just drop money like that!" Mason only snorted. "He can. He's dropped more on things even less important. He says it will mostly be for communication through the week. He's already put numbers in that you might need, you know, if you have questions or something."

I could feel the tears burning the back of my eyes. Three month's worth of money for food was in the single little device. I didn't open it yet, though. I simply pushed it back into the bag and glanced at the other object. I realized that this one was wrapped in even smaller black plastic, and I wondered if this was going to be just as expensive. I didn't remove it from the larger bag when I opened it. With one glance, my cheeks were aflame and I had crumpled the plastic tightly closed. *Hell no*. Mason noticed my wide eyes and audible gasp, and glanced at me quickly before smirking back at the road. He fucking *knew*.

Inside the bag sat a neon-green dildo, shining brightly under the passing streetlights. I had briefly glimpsed a small note and my cash beside it before I had closed the bag.

A dildo? Really? As if I wasn't going to already get enough dick from him.

CHAPTER
TWELVE

"THANKS FOR THE ride, Mason," I smiled. He shook his head. "It's my job, Lucika. You're very welcome."

I closed the shotgun door and darted across my dead lawn, pausing to listen to the roaring engine fade down the street. I gripped the bag to my chest firmly and closed my front door behind me. Then I climbed the stairs to the attic faster than I ever had before. It was like Christmas morning. Immediately, I set a pop singer in my ancient radio and turned her up until I wasn't sure I wouldn't wake my mother. Once I was comfortable on my bed, I unwrapped the phone from its plastic wrap and slid the lid off with a satisfying whoosh of air. I gasped when the phone immediately fell onto my tattered bedsheets, bouncing a little to the beat of the woman's singing. With a tap, the phone screen lit up, sending a soft white glow across my awed features in the darkness of my bedroom. It was heavier and colder than I expected. The thin design nearly slipped from my hand.

What I noticed first was the message that Kaia had sent.

"*This is yours from now on, Angel. Glance through your contacts. Each one is labelled appropriately. Feel free to text me any time; I'll answer back as soon as possible. Text me once you've made it safely home.*" I immediately tapped on the messaging app and began to type. "*I'm home and very safe.*" It took less than thirty seconds for him to answer back. "*Wonderful. I'm sure you'll find the toy I gave you soon, if you haven't noticed it yet. We won't be able to meet together every single night, as much as I would like to, so that can help you if you miss me.*" A little winking face had been added to the message. Would I really be missing him that much? Did he expect me to? The urge to slap him through the phone for assuming I was such an eager slut was strong. But, hey, free sex toys.

"*Thank you so much, Kai. Are you sure you really want me to have this phone?*"

"*Of course. I don't ever take gifts back. I have to go. Go to sleep; you're probably exhausted. Text me when you wake up. I might have some work for you.*" I sighed and leaned back against my pillow, knowing I couldn't argue with his word. Not even over text.

"*Goodnight, Mr. Arche.*"

"*It's Kai. And goodnight, Angel.*"

Before going to sleep, I stuffed my pay into the top drawer of my dresser before removing the toy and the note from the plastic bag. It almost glittered against the light from the street lamp outside my house. The dildo was long, but not as thick as Kai. I knew this would never come close to- wait, no. No. *No.*

I couldn't deny my sexual and romantic attraction to him, as much as I wanted to. He was one of the few memorable sexual encounters I had had. He was gorgeous, stunning, beautiful. It hurt to know that I was only his pet, yet I understood completely. He was like a sugar daddy, especially after tonight. I shivered at the thought. Could I handle having a fucking sugar daddy? Would I like it? What were the downsides, honestly? I was about to shut the phone off after glancing at the three contacts left on the phone, Rosa, Mason, and Kai, but a sudden thought stopped me. This device had a video app, hidden in the bottom corner beside the camera. I tapped it quickly and scrolled through the suggestions until I found what sounded like it could be a song worth listening to. With another tap, a gentle beat filled the air, a new one I hadn't ever heard before, and I turned off my music player quickly to hear it.

It took me eight whole seconds of blasting that one song to decide that maybe I *could* handle having a sugar daddy.

....

When I woke, my mother had already left. I swallowed my grogginess and turned to the phone I had set on the nightstand. "*Good morning Mr. Arche,*" I texted. I didn't expect him to be awake at seven, but his reply came only a moment later.

"*Good morning, Angel. Did you sleep well?*"

"*Yes. Thank you so much. I slept amazing with the app.*"

"*App?*"

I bit my lip as I typed my reply; my fingers were rather slow. "*Music. There was a music video app.*"

"*Sounds nice. Mason is waiting outside your house at the moment. We'll discuss your new job at the apartment.*"

I gasped and jumped from my bed, warm sheets forgotten as I stared out the window. Mason leaned against the *Ferrari*, which reflected the overcast skies in its blue paint. He scrolled through his phone nonchalantly as he waited for me. How long had he been waiting there? Had my mother seen him? I dressed myself hastily in a pair of blue jeans and a t-shirt before bounding down the stairs and out the door, my new phone gripped tightly in my palm so I wouldn't drop it on the concrete steps while I locked the door. "Why didn't you knock on my door and wake me?!" I exclaimed, out of breath after running to the car. Mason smiled and slipped his phone into his jeans pocket. "G'morning, Lucika. I thought you'd want me to let you sleep," he replied. I gave an exasperated huff and climbed

ANGEL

into the car beside Mason. "Do you ever sleep? When did you even get to my house this morning?" I asked as the car gained speed and maneuvered away from my home. "I got here around eight-thirty. I don't have a bedtime, since Kai's schedule is mine, too, and his can get hectic. But I wake up around three-o'clock regardless of what time I went to sleep." I cringed when Mason suddenly sped to race through a yellow light. My hand shot to the door handle.

I stayed silent as the man drove us closer to the heart of town. I hoped that Rosa would have made some kind of breakfast. I was starving, and I wouldn't be able to last until lunch. When Mason pulled into the garage, he allowed me into the elevator first. Then he set his sunglasses in his back pocket as we rode the box to Kaia's apartment. We entered furtively. Rosa was asleep on the couch, so I made an effort not to wake her. "What time does she wake up?" I asked in a whisper. It was only eight-o'clock, but the woman didn't look even slightly prepared to face the day, and *I* even woke up in time to see the clock turn to its double digits. Mason shrugged and said, "Sometimes she doesn't. Maybe she'll do more laundry if she wakes up by noon. We'll see how many bottles of alcohol are left in her stash; that'll tell you."

"Oh... well at least she sleeps well."

"Whatever makes her happy." Mason climbed the stairway with more energy than any human should have in the morning. At the top of the hallway, I could already hear Kai's voice echoing quietly from his office. He sat behind his desk, occupied with a conference call. I could tell that he had been working hard that morning; his hair was unkempt and his eyes looked slightly bloodshot. He still wore his normal apparel, though, despite the ungodly time.

Mason and I took seats at the small ring of chairs in the corner of his office, and I was instantly thankful that he had at least a few proper chairs in his house. Not *everything* was sex furniture.

Mason pulled his feet up onto the seat and sat cross-legged childishly. "Perfect. Goodbye, Dad," he said, ending the conversation abruptly upon our entry, before hanging up his phone and standing. The smile he sent me was bright and wide. "Hi, Luka. How was your morning?"

"Good. Yours?"

"Exhausting. I woke up—," he checked the clock in his laptop, "— two hours ago."

I grimaced at his answer and watched Mason bounce his knees almost excitedly from the corner of my eye. "What's the plan today, Kai?" Mason asked. Kai stood quickly, smiled at me, and closed his laptop to signal the completion of his work. "I figured I would tell you a little bit about your job today. I want to get out of the house, though. I'm hoping that the shops won't be too busy this early in the morning. How does the mall sound?" Kai asked. He was gathering his items, shoving his computer into a messenger bag along with some files.

"Um... I don't really have any money on me. I'd love to hear about my job, though," I replied nervously.

Kai sighed. "No. I'm thinking of a certain place for breakfast. My treat."

"Does that mean I have to wake up Rosa? She's been in your Jägermeister all night," Mason whined.

"Well, I'm not doing it. I did it last weekend," Kai replied stubbornly. Mason's head lolled back against the leather couch as I silently submitted to Kai. How was I supposed to object to free breakfast? It was better than waking a drunk friend, anyway.

CHAPTER THIRTEEN

KAI LED ME quickly back down to the garage, where he, instead of the blue *Ferrari*, climbed onto that dark, sleek motorcycle. It didn't look like a retro gem that I expected most people with money to have. It was a brand-new bike with a beautiful black shine and polished leather that was obviously not faux. It looked as if it had just come straight out of a movie. "Get on," he said, holding out a helmet, which had been mounted on the wall, to me. "Mason said you'd be pissed if I got on a bike," I said as I slipped the black helmet over my head. It was a lot bulkier than I thought it would be. It was slightly too big for me too. He chuckled. "Yeah, I would be, if I wasn't driving. But I have no intentions of crashing, and I trust myself to drive a bike in Los Angeles."

I nodded as he grabbed a thick leather jacket that hung over the seat of another bike beside it. "Put this on."

"I thought we weren't going to crash," I said, taking it slowly. I trusted him not to wipe out. The smell of the jacket comforted me more; he had worn it many times.

"We aren't. But if we do, that will protect a little bit," he replied through a humorous snort. I couldn't help but give a small smile as he climbed onto the bike before motioning for me to join him. The man worked to apply thick gloves to his hands before he even touched the handles. "Hold on tight," he told me as I seated myself and wrapped my arms around his stomach. The seat was freezing. He wore black dress pants and a baby-blue dress shirt under his thick leather jacket that morning, which hugged his muscles in all the right places. I could feel his core, softened by that tiny little layer of fat that had never been worked off at the gym, rippling under my fingers as he pushed up the kickstand with his heel and drifted us out of the parking spot.

The only problem was that I had a new favourite vehicle.

I learnt quickly that there was nothing like being on a bike, hearing its noise rip through the streets from between Kai's strong thighs. The vibrations made my skin itch in the best way. The wind would have been much stronger and more freeing if we were going seventy-miles-per-hour down an empty freeway, but I took what I could get with the endings of the morning rush hour. Kai knew some back roads we could take and other alleys that cars couldn't fit through, so our route to his destination was cut shorter. I enjoyed it more than I ever thought I would. Parking was a lot easier to find with a bike, too, at Santa Monica Place. I realized that the mall he had chosen was massive, stretching on for what seemed like miles. I had only been there once or twice in my life, and memory hadn't done it justice.

We both set our helmets on the seats and took the short walk up to the mall. We entered through a back exit where we could enter into the main store centre. I couldn't contain the gasp that slipped through my lips when I finally had a moment to absorb my surroundings. There were people everywhere, despite the clock on Kai's wrist telling us that it was only just after ten-o'clock in the morning. Voices spoke in different tongues to people from around the world. Music played in the distance. The air was hot and comforting, thick with the smell of all kinds of food from the

ANGEL

food court. I stared in awe, turning slowly with massive, incredulous eyes. "It... It's amazing!" I exclaimed, bringing a hand to cover my mouth in excitement. "It's just a shopping mall, Angel. I come here all the time," he laughed. "B-but this! This is freaking awesome! How many stores are in here?!" Everywhere I turned, a new smell hit me like an energizing slap to the face: sweat, soap, freshly-cleaned clothes, deluxe hamburgers. Kai wrapped an arm around my waist; I paused. It was a small gesture, but sent shivers up my spine despite the heat around me.

"A lot. Dozens. Tens of dozens," he replied with a small smile. I gave a massive grin back to him. "Where do we start?"

We flitted in and out of shops throughout the next four hours. I quickly realized that Kai had very expensive tastes in clothing, and led me strictly towards the higher-end brands. I nearly choked when I dared to glance at the price of a t-shirt I had picked up. But whatever I didn't show maximum interest in was returned to the shelf. As we shopped, after glancing at him from over racks of clothes and guessing if the dip in his forehead meant he liked or disliked the piece he was currently holding, I quickly realized that I knew very little about Kai. Things like his hobbies, his dislikes and likes, were subjects I had been too scared to encroach on. I was now working for him, though, in more ways than one, so did I deserve to have a conversation with him? Did I want to learn more about him? "So do you have any hobbies?" I asked as I pushed through a rack of dress pants. My gaze instantly flew to my hands instead of meeting his; the question hadn't come out right. It sounded awkward on my lips. "Hobbies? I suppose I have a few," he began, holding up a white dress shirt. I nodded, telling him it looked good. I would wear it. He slung it over his arm and kept talking. "I play the drums," he shrugged. "And I also enjoy sports. I always have."

"The drums? Really?" I asked in surprise. He nodded. "Wow.

I would love to hear you play sometime!" I said, standing on my toes with excitement. He chuckled and refused to make eye contact. "Maybe sometime."

We continued in and out of dressing rooms, buying pieces of clothing at a few select stores. We were passing a lingerie store in silence when a sudden thought flashed through my mind.

"Do you have any fetishes?"

I couldn't stop the question before it bubbled off my lips, and my eyes widened. But he gave no indication that I had crossed any boundaries. Instead, he wound his hand around my waist tighter than before. It felt uncanny to have such a new relationship with him and have his arm wrapped around me so intimately. He also glanced at the lingerie store, a small smirk gracing his features. "I like heels," he said.

"Heels?"

He nodded. "High heels."

"Oh," was all I could manage. High heels. That was what got him off. We passed the lingerie store before I made a beeline for a popular soap and lotion shop. I smiled and closed my eyes, breathing in the scents that were so new to me. "I love the smell of this place," I said when he had caught up to me. He released a disgusted grunt from deep in his throat in reply before motioning me in through the doors reluctantly. It was busy and warm in the store, though, so I welcomed it.

"Choose something you might like for baths. One of my old subs loved her bath bombs," he told me. Deep in my gut, there was a twinge of anger. I didn't want to hear about his old relationships. I frowned in confusion. "What are bath bombs? They sound dangerous." Maybe they were another BDSM toy. Did they sell them at malls? Kai broke into laughter, low and controlled. But it was laughter. "They're like bath salts, I think. They dissolve in water, hence the name." I knew what bath salts were. My mother loved them.

ANGEL

The racks around us were filled with bottles of creams and liquids, like body lotion and soap. The entire store smelled heavenly. Beside the entrance sat a massive rack of hundreds of baseball-sized orbs, ranging in different colours and textures. "Are these bath bombs?" I asked, picking one up. It was heavier than I expected. Kai nodded. "Pick some. You can use one or two next time we spend a night together," he said, catching my eye. I thought his words held other meanings of what he planned to do *that* night, and I realized that it was going to be the norm now if I wanted to keep the job. I hadn't even *started* it yet and there was so much pressure.

"Okay. But you also have to pick one out for me," I replied, grabbing another one. I held it to my nose and took a deep inhale of peaches.

"Okay," he replied, and turned his attention to the balls.

After the bath bomb shop, we hit the closest food joint. The smell was almost as good as sex. There were so many kinds of food, some I hadn't even heard of before. Kai urged me to try a breakfast burrito from a taco joint in the corner. "Mason says they're pretty good," Kai told me after ordering our food. It *was* good, I decided, after we had received our meals and taken a seat to enjoy our breakfast in peace. I gave a low moan around the food stuffing my mouth as Kai watched me absently, one fist supporting his chin. He dipped a chip into salsa briefly and then popped it between his lips. "Holy shit! This is so good! It tastes kind of like the breakfast quesadillas that Mom makes at the diner!" I exclaimed, taking another bite and swallowing it greedily.

"Well, do you think you're done shopping? I've taken you to the stores that I usually visit. There's just one last shop I'd like to visit before we head back to the apartment," he told me. "Okay, lemme just-," but I shoved the rest of the burrito through my lips instead of finishing. I chewed the mammoth amount of food, ignoring the incredulous glances Kaia shot me. "At least you don't have a gag reflex. That's always good," Kai mumbled, and I thought I didn't hear him right. If I was sure I heard him correctly, I would have choked on my burrito.

He led us back to the parking lot once again, letting me straddle the bike first. I didn't think I would ever get bored of wrapping my arms around him or the purr of the engine. "Where are we going?" I yelled over the roar and wind around us as we sped out of the parking lot. I could tell that he was skilled on a bike, obviously having years of experience with them, as he swerved between cars expertly. "Our last stop. You'll see," he yelled back. We continued through the streets, passing shops and skyscrapers on every side, until he abruptly swerved down a side road and into a small, hidden parking lot. He shut down the bike with a flick of his wrist and jumped off, looking to me expectantly. "What is this place?" I asked nervously. It looked sketchy. The garbage beside the barred windows was overflowing. A homeless woman slept on the other side of the parking lot.

"You'll see. I promise, you'll be fine. Just remember the colours," he replied, taking my hand as I set my helmet and jacket beside his on the seat. "Okay...." He led me slowly through the few rows of parking spaces, which were empty, save for the occasional rust bucket parked between the faded yellow lines. My anxiety rose with each step as we neared a glass door, covered with a plain sheet of yellowed paper. The only reason I wasn't playing with my fingers was because Kai had one of my hands firmly set in his own, and I didn't know if he suspected my anxious urges and decided to stop it before I even started.

"It looks sketchy, but I think you're going to like it," he said, holding the door open for me.

When I entered, he released my hand and allowed me to stare around the room in shock.

It was an adult shop. A very, very, high-end adult shop.

CHAPTER
FOURTEEN

"COLOUR?" HE ASKED. I was too stunned to speak. I didn't think any store like it existed. Sex toys, bondage gear, and more sex toys ran on for as long as the eye could see. There were so many racks of outfits of the sluttiest kind, obviously used for role-play. I thought places resembling this one only existed in movies.

"Lucika... colour?" My wide gaze snapped to his. He was nervous; the emotion was a bizarre one to see in his eyes. "Um... green, I guess," I said quietly, playing with my fingers at my stomach and bending them back and forth. It was slightly overwhelming; I didn't have experience in romance shops. He put a comforting hand on my back; he didn't believe me. "Okay."

"Kaia?! Is that you?!" A shrill voice erupted from the corner of the shop before a short, pudgy girl bounded towards us. Her black hair was done up in two buns on the top of her head, and her clothing, ripped and dark, was just as skimpy as everything else in the store. Two apple-green eyes stared at us with excitement as she smiled wide, her plump cherry-coloured lips stretched over pearly-white teeth. She didn't look a day over fifteen. Her round, button features were adorable.

"You've brought someone new! You're his new little toy, hm?"

She wiggled her eyebrows at me, and I cringed away in dismay. "Luka's a little shy, Alice. He's *very* new," Kaia replied, letting me shrink behind him momentarily. Her excited smile turned kind; she waved at me from the other side of Kai. "Hey, Luka! What can I do for you two today?"

"Just a few things," Kai replied before looking to me. "Go look around. Find something you'd like to try. Trust me, it looks a lot scarier than it is." I bit my lip and walked away slowly, quickly finding myself lost on the tall rows of gear. A handful of different toys hung on racks beside the slappers and the canes. I cringed at the small selection of bullwhips that hung closer to the floor. I heard that those hurt more than anything, although a small part of me wanted more than anything to try it. The store wasn't very busy at all, with the exception of us and a couple who sorted through R-rated magazines in the corner. With a quick glance, the prices on most gear explained why. For a very sketchy, hidden exterior, the interior of this shop was sleek and modern, built and priced for the upper class and experienced kinksters. It also seemed to tailor towards submissive and Dominant supplies; puppy play wasn't a common theme, and neither was ageplay. I saw mostly leather, rope, metal, and a lot of sex toys. I ran my fingers lightly over a silky blindfold as I passed, remembering last night. I shivered at the thoughts that flooded back when the pads of my fingers memorized the texture of the fabric.

"Angel, can you try this on for me?" Kai seemed to appear from nowhere, and I was pulled from my thoughts quickly. He held a leather band in his hands. "What is it?" I asked, my voice only curious. "A collar. It's not permanent or anything; I'll explain later. Can I just see it on you?" he replied. I stood perfectly still as he wrapped the black, leather collar around my neck, strapping the ends together gently. The way his arms wrapped around my head made my skin crawl deliciously. Both he and Alice took a step back

ANGEL

to admire me. I blushed and pulled my hands behind my back, worrying my knuckles again. "Does it look okay?" I asked when I heard silence. "Perfect," Kai breathed, and Alice shot me a toothy smile. One of her canines was gold. There was another moment of silence as the two admired my new accessory, before Alice turned to Kaia. "So do you want to check out the plugs?" she asked him. Kai nodded and grasped my hand, pulling me to another part of the store. They hadn't removed the collar. Was I expected to keep it on? It was rather annoying; I never liked wearing jewelry.

The aisle that Alice led us through held plugs for all different body openings, with different sizes and colours, different textures, and ends festooned with jewels and glitter. "One of these. Choose one," Kaia ordered, motioning to a group of rather large ones. "But... won't they kind of... hurt? I've never tried one," I mumbled. They looked too big. Would they even fit? Could they? The ones to the left looked much more enjoyable.

Kai paused momentarily. "Then pick a smaller one first," he said finally. I nodded slowly and reached out to the first one that caught my attention. It wasn't too small, or textured. It was black, fading into an aquamarine at the tip and a massive aqua jewel at the base. "I like this one," I told him. I knew it would stretch me rather wide, but I hoped it would please him. He hummed in approval and handed it to Alice beside him. "One of these, and, um... this one," he told her, reaching up higher to grab one of the largest ones. My eyes widened at the size. There was no way that that could fit in *anybody*, I decided. I hoped the idiot planned to use it on himself, because it certainly wasn't going inside *me*.

Alice snatched the butt plugs from Kai's grasp without any hesitation. The girl was so forward and easily excited, it made me wonder how many coffees she'd had that day. It made me wonder if she knew that I could take the plug Kai had chosen.

Kai told me to hold the small bag of supplies as he mounted the motorcycle again. I followed suit, barely able to grab onto him in time to speed out of the parking lot. He bought me a milkshake on the way back to his house. Vanilla, my favourite. Kai sat across from me at the booth, gazing out the window with his chin supported by his fist as I slurped at my treat.

"Do you want to try some?" I asked.

"No, thank you," he replied, refusing to spare me a glance. I pouted a little. It felt uncomfortable to be enjoying food while someone sat there with no interest in it. How was he not starving? Surely, protein shakes in the morning weren't enough to get anyone through an entire day, especially for someone who exercised as often as he obviously did. "They actually have a good texture, though. I like the thickness. And this ice cream is a little bit grainy too. You might like it," I added, holding it out to him. It was overly-sweet, but he obviously wouldn't notice that. The man sighed and leaned forward to take a small sip, licking his dark lips when he leaned away again. Kai had crumbled much easier than I expected. He pondered the quality of the texture for a moment before shrugging. "I suppose it's alright. I don't usually eat out like this, though. Rosa makes everything for me," he said.

"Maybe Rosa can duplicate this for you," I suggested, sucking up air through my straw when I finished my shake. I licked my lips and set the empty cup on the table. "So why am I wearing this, um, collar?" I asked, tugging at it lightly with my index finger. He turned to me, giving me his full attention. "It's like... a form of protection. It tells other people, especially in clubs and such, that you're off limits."

"So... I don't need to wear it at home? It's only for when we're out together at a place we know we'll be hit on?" I asked. I didn't want to wear the collar much at all, especially at home. He nodded, glad that I understood. "If you don't want to wear it, then it's your choice. It looks good, though." A moment of silence hung between us. Was he actually allowing me a choice? When I sat down to talk about his actions with him, Kai didn't seem like such a cock-fueled bastard. He valued my decisions in the relationship.

"So are we ready to go?" he asked, certainly to avoid any further conversation. The man had taken my silence as an opportunity to escape. I decided to follow him, nodding and standing. I tossed my cup into the trash on our way out.

CHAPTER
FIFTEEN

"ARE YOU STILL sure you want to hire me?" I asked as we slipped our jackets off in Kai's bedroom. I knew I would never be able to overcome the size of the space. "You're already hired. I just need to tell you how to do the job," he replied, tossing his jacket onto a couch. He took a seat on one of the sofas and pushed the large black box that sat on the coffee table towards me. "Everything you'll need is in there, and you can pretty much work from anywhere: your house, my house, the park. As long as you're sure that no one will be able to see what you're doing, then I have no problems with it," he told me. I understood why his financial privacy was important to him.

I opened the box and gaped at the laptop in front of me, set on top of files and books. "It also has the software you need on it to help keep you organized. I would also suggest that you copy everything into a notebook, which I put under the computer, in case the device is compromised," he added. He had done this before. The computer was an old model with scuff marks and 'MASON WAS HERE' written in bold black ink in one corner. It made me want to laugh. Unable to contain it, I smiled.

"So I won't be working at an office or anything?" I asked. He shook his head. "No... unless you want to. I could give you a spare bedroom as an office."

"No, no, I don't. I like working at my home more."

"Perfect. You'll start on it tonight then."

....

Despite my previous suspicions, Mason brought me an early, delicious dinner of curry chicken and rice, and drove me home once I was finished. There was no sex or fellatio. Kai made sure to send me home with the outfit he'd bought me, the computer box, and an envelope of four-hundred-dollars. It would be my last pay before I started getting legitimate paychecks once every two weeks. I would make a budget with what I had at the time: a few hundred for bills and groceries... a fifty for Mom's cigarettes. I probably had enough money to take us out for dinner. When was the last time she had eaten anything other than diner food or macaroni? I was home early enough to be able to hide the clothes in my drawers and stuff the computer under my comforter before Mom stalked through the front door. She looked exhausted. When I realized that, when I really noticed the dark bags under her eyes and the lag in her steps, I deflated with guilt. I could see her standing in the doorway from the opposite end of the kitchen as she lit a cigarette in shaky fingers.

The fifty in my pocket burnt a hole in the fabric. After grabbing my grey sweater, I skipped down the centre of the kitchen tiles with a large smile, my heartbeat thrumming with excitement. Her eyebrows pulled together when I came to stand in front of her. She stared and waited for me to speak. She was too tired for my bullshit; her expression made that clear. "Mom, are you hungry?" I asked. My voice was louder than intended. "Yes...," she replied, trailing off in confusion.

"Then come on, I want to take you somewhere." I took her hand tightly and pulled her toward the door. She didn't struggle, and I realized that she probably didn't have the strength to. She simply followed, stumbling over her own feet when they hit the doorframe.

I could tell that she wanted to ask where the hell we were going. Such behaviour was abnormal for me; even I was surprising myself. Everything was changing. "Tacos or Chinese food?" I asked, locking the door behind us and bounding down the steps with her in tow. "Wait... Lucika," she said, digging her small heels into the sidewalk. I stopped and turned to her. "Where are we going? We can't go out to eat, Luka." It almost sounded as if she was scolding me, like I was seven instead of nineteen. I looked to the ground with a sigh. "Mom... I got a new job, okay? It pays better than my old one. A lot better. I just wanted you to have a good dinner. When was the last time we actually went out to eat?" I told her, my hands falling behind my back. I pulled at my middle finger knuckles.

I only looked up after a long moment of silence between us. Her eyes had softened, and she tilted her head to the side a little. Sometimes I couldn't tell what was on her mind. This expression was truly a rarity, so I had no experience with it. Love, maybe? Fondness? Was that pride in her eyes?

"Okay, Luka."

She pushed an arm around my slim waist as she finally caved in, and I pulled her close and let her rest her head on my shoulder as we began a slow stroll down the side of the darkening street.

"Okay."

Eventually, we decided on the taco joint that stood just between Mark's Barbershop and Ani's Pizza. I had only picked at my meal, as I was still full from Rosa's scrumptious chicken. I would definitely have to ask Rosa if she could package it up for me to take back to Mom when I saw the woman next. Meanwhile, Mom had just finished her second fish taco, and leaned back into the booth with her eyes closed gently. There was only one other couple sitting across

ANGEL

the room. I could smell their chicken fajitas from my seat.

"Thank you, Luka," she said quietly, tossing her used napkin onto her empty plate. "That was delicious." I couldn't stop the smile that spread across my face. The scene was perfect: she was happy, from the looks of it, and well-fed, like a mother should be. Like I always imagined her. The lines of exhaustion had faded slightly once she was off her feet.

We walked back home slowly, stuffed full from dinner, with her arm wrapped in mine.

"Where are you working now?" She asked quietly. I bit my lip. Could I tell her? I wouldn't dare tell her about the relationship I had gotten myself tangled in; I hadn't even come out of the closet to her yet. I didn't know if I ever would be comfortable enough to do that, and she would most-likely be curious as to how I went from a store employee to working in a prestigious man's bed.

"Um... I kind of keep bank records, I guess," I told her. It wasn't a lie.

"Really? You don't need any degrees or anything to work at a bank?" I knew what she was really asking. She probably assumed that to work in banking, I needed to at least have graduated high school. I dropped out in grade eleven when I realized that I needed to make money. Mom had been looking for work at the time, and our financial situation had been even more dire.

"Not for this job. I guess it's not very official yet... I haven't even started it."

She was about to say something else, I could tell, but a deep African accent interrupted us as we turned into our empty driveway. "It's been a while since I've seen you, Miss Roggy," Ms. Peach greeted from her porch. Our widowed neighbour, Ms. Peach, moved to the city from a tiny town somewhere in North Africa when she turned fifty. We could tell that she did her best to be kind, but sometimes that woman could be the nosiest, cruelest person on the block. We did our best to avoid her.

"Hello, Ms. Peach," my mother greeted with a kind smile. I could tell that it was taking a lot of her energy to keep it up. "You two have been busy lately! I swear I've seen ten different hot rods pass by this home!" she exclaimed, setting her knitting down on her lap as she rocked in her old, creaking rocking chair. My mother looked to me in confusion. I blanched.

Fuck.

"Yeah, I, um, have a friend that picks me up sometimes for work," I said, flashing my best fake smile. I just wanted to get back inside where it was warm and safe, where I could begin some work and, dare I say it, escape my mother and her scrutiny. "Hey, tell the boy to gimme a call sometime, eh? With that kinda money, how you think that dick is?!" She broke into a fit of wheezing laughter. My mother and I exchanged a glance. I pretended to act as if I had never seen a dick in my life with a shrug.

I also resisted the urge to inform Ms. Peach that the dick was actually amazing. Knock you off your feet, kind of dick. You never knew what hit you, kind of dick.

"Have a nice night, Ms. Peach," my mother waved, pushing us inside the house with haste before Ms. Peach could begin on one of her speeches. "So you don't walk to work?" Mom asked. I shook my head. "A guy who works with me picks me up," I replied, hanging my jacket over my arm. She nodded, silence consuming us once again. After a moment, I couldn't take the silence anymore. To escape it, I drew my eyes to the floor and licked my lips.

"Goodnight, Mom," I said quietly, my hands drawing together in front of me. I turned away from her slowly.

She nodded, surrendered, and slipped a cigarette package from her pocket. "G'night, Luka."

CHAPTER SIXTEEN

WORKING BETWEEN THE laptop and notebook was a lot easier than I expected. I was still an extremely slow typer, and there was almost a month's worth of deposits and withdrawals to copy down, but it kept me busy. So I worked hard into the night, only glancing at the clock when I went to turn off an old tune that had gotten boring. It was almost midnight. There was still work to be done, but I ached for a break. So, instead of turning off my computer and music, I searched for new tunes in the music app. After a moment, I found something promising. I stood, instantly feeling the beat through my newly energized body, and began to sway lightly. When I started dancing, there was no stopping me. I never did anything too crazy, but once I had found a rhythm, I was on cloud nine, even if I didn't know the words to sing along like I usually did. I raised my arms above my head, my lips moving slightly in an attempt to sing along at least a little bit. After listening once, I could probably remember most of the words for next time I heard it. I let the music guide my body for another half hour, smiling when a new song began and the beat changed.

I was interrupted when my phone notified me of a new text message. It could only be Mason or Kai, and I assumed it was the latter. I read it quickly, still nodding my head and bouncing on my toes to the beat.

"*You asleep yet?*" Kai messaged.

I stopped moving and stared at my phone with confusion and momentary fear.

"*... am I supposed to be??*"

"*No, no. But you won't be able to function properly tomorrow if you only decide to get two hours of sleep.*"

Kai didn't even say anything face-to-face, and I still could hear his voice ringing in my head as I read his message. I thought of how stern his text could be and how deadly his gaze would probably be if he were standing in front of me, challenging me to defy him. Or maybe he was saying this as a friend and not a Dominant; any person would believe that. Something so simple could be something very menacing with him. But he wasn't my mother. He shouldn't care when I went to bed and how long I stayed awake during the week.

"*I'll go to sleep soon. I'm going to stay up for a little while longer,*" I replied. It was so much easier to stand against his word when he wasn't here with me.

His reply was lightning-fast.

"*If you were here with me, you'd be over my lap this second. I'll let it slide this time, but don't think you can get away with self destruction. You're going to be exhausted.*"

I couldn't help but shiver at the text. Fuck. So that had been an order? I could receive a punishment just for refusing to take care of myself? How did that make any sense? How could he care so much for me?

Five minutes later, my teeth were brushed, the music and laptop were shut down, and I had undressed for bed. I shut off the phone, too, and set it on the nightstand at the head of my bed. I missed the music immediately, and tried to focus on that instead of the voice that told me Kai had way too much control in this relationship already. But that was the point of a BDSM relationship, wasn't it? Control was half the idea. He had more control than my *mother*.

So, instead of closing my eyes and listening to the unnerving silence in the house, accompanied by distant sirens and car horns, I looked up at the ceiling and hummed to myself. I had remembered as many songs as I could, playing them again and again until I knew every lyric. My head swam back and forth lightly on my pillow, creating a shuffling beat in my ears. Music helped me forget everything. When there was music, there was nothing else, no prostitutes, no hunger, no shady-ass people who held guns to my forehead, no Dominant threatening me with punishments so you could keep the job I desperately needed. The kind of comfort I got from the music was like a drug. I didn't think I would ever get enough.

....

The rest of my week consisted purely of music and work. Five minutes of document filing and downloading, then a twenty minute break of dancing and singing. I even neglected to come back down the stairs for dinner one night, completely forgetting the sandwich that sat at the table for me. Kai's threat of punishment loomed in the back of my mind constantly. Would he ever use whips? More bondage? Would he ever toss his talk of "baby steps" out the window and decide to use the larger butt plug on me, knowing I wouldn't be able to take it? The horrifying possibilities were endless.

Friday night would be the first of two that I would spend with him. Seeing Mason pull up in my driveway hit me with the reality I had nearly forgotten during my time away from Kai. I couldn't deny the fact that I was wary, but my desire to please my new boss was overwhelming.

"Good afternoon, Lucika," Mason greeted with his familiar

scandalous smirk once I had climbed into the car. "Hey, Mason," I replied quietly, diverting my eyes. "Are you hungry?" He asked. That question seemed to leave his lips at least three times a day. I nodded. "Can we go get milkshakes?" Mason nodded quickly and drove us away. He let me pull on my knuckles in the seat beside him. Once in the drive-through, Mason scrutinized my request for two medium milkshakes. He raised an eyebrow at me. "Why not a large?" Surely, I had never been so open and asking for food. I had probably caught him off-guard. I shook my head, prepared to answer, but not offer an explanation. "May I please get two?"

The woman at the drive-through gave Mason a free coffee; the person in front of us had decided to spread the love. He informed me that not only was he slightly allergic to caffeine, but the last time he'd had a cup of coffee, he hadn't slept for three consecutive days. Despite this, he drank half of it in three minutes. I didn't drink from one milkshake and finished the other in under five minutes. Horns honked behind and in front of us, judging Mason's driving habits harshly. I didn't ever want to learn to drive in Santa Monica, or anywhere in LA, for that matter. There were just too many people and too much traffic; too many hazards and targets to run over. Only when we were finally inside the garage did I feel better. The stress of his car ride was complete.

"So what did you do to make yourself so worried that you felt you needed to get a treat for Kai?" Mason asked me as he watched my form stumble out of the car. He refused to believe that I had gotten anything for Rosa.

"Mason, if I tell you that, you're just going to tell him. You guys really don't have any secrets, huh?" I mumbled, refusing to meet his eyes. I really didn't want to know what Kai was going to do to me if I messed this up. I was too scared. Mason shrugged. "Nope. I tell him my deepest secrets while we braid each other's hair every night.

But, seriously, worrying isn't going to help anything."

"Don't you think he's kinda oppressive? I mean, aren't you scared to mess up around him?" I asked with a hint of venom. Mason's smile fell quickly, his gaze spanning over me with hesitance, like he was pondering his next words, contemplating whether or not to give me all his hints and tips to keep myself safe from Mr. Arche. Eventually, he sighed and put a hand on his hip. "He's not that bad. I grew up with him, and sure, he's lost a lot, but that just means that he'll treat you like he's going to lose you too. You shouldn't be scared. You should trust him with your life, like I do. It's easier that way."

With that, he spun on his heel towards the elevator. In that same second, his mood seemed to lighten from somber to his usual cheery.

....

Mason knocked on the door to Kaia's office lightly before I was pushed inside. Kai stood leaning against his desk, facing away from me as he stared out at the beautiful setting sun beyond the Los Angeles skyline. I couldn't help but take a moment to stare in awe myself. The colours were magnificent, dousing us in bright yellows and oranges, as if the sun was setting ten miles away instead of ninety-three-million miles away. He was peaceful, quiet, especially with the relaxing lighting. "I... I brought you ice cream," I said finally, setting the cup on his desk with a tired, shaky hand. He looked to it slowly, before his dark gaze met mine. I couldn't help but shiver. His eyes were suddenly the most beautiful thing I had ever seen. I couldn't tell if they were impacted by the sun's colours, or if it was simply the light shining at the right angle, but they were no longer their shining black hue. They were like gold, glowing unbelievably bright, like the rare mineral that people worked so hard to extract from deep within the earth. My jaw went slack at the sight. Kai turned away momentarily, and my heart almost broke when I could no longer see his eyes. His steps were long and determined when he walked around his desk to stand in front of me, blocking the bright light. It sent dark lines of shadow across the hardwood floors behind us. Our chests almost touched, and his face sat so close to mine that I could feel his soft breath against my own lips. The air around him smelled like a delectable cup of over-sweetened coffee, mixed with the sharp tang of dark chocolate. He didn't even eat chocolate, as far as I was aware. How could he smell so delicious when he didn't even eat the food he smelled like?

"Why did you bring me ice cream?" I swallowed hard. Coming clean hadn't always been the easiest thing for me to do. "You… seemed grumpy last time we chatted. Something about putting me over your lap for something so small—"

"You think that getting me ice cream will get you out of some kind of punishment."

My hands trembled as I stared up at him. He didn't look angry. Frustrated, maybe, but in that calm, unnerving way. "Understand something, Luka," he murmured, leaning into me. I could feel his breath against my cheek, his tongue flicking against his teeth like a snake's.

"If I want to punish you when you're in my care, I will, and you won't *ever* have *any* control over that."

CHAPTER SEVENTEEN

HE MATERIALIZED A thick blindfold from his desk, wrapping it around my head and tying it tighter than before. His movements didn't seem angry; instead, they were slow and deliberate, instilling stronger fear within me by the second. "Get on the desk," he whispered against my neck, pushing me around until the back of my thighs hit the cold wood. I whimpered, half aroused and half terrified. So was he angry now? Was this a punishment? I told myself to stop fearing him, to trust that I would *know* when I was in trouble. Once he had removed my shirt, jeans, and boxers, I felt his hands ghost up and down my thighs lightly as I lie on my back against the desk, my nerves calming momentarily when I was exposed to the warm sunlight. But my relaxation dissipated when Kai squeezed my lower thigh particularly hard. "This isn't a punishment… you need to know that. None of this is. Not until I say," he said quietly. His voice was deadly, his words calming.

"Do you understand?" he asked, the tip of his finger burning a trail of ice down the centre of my chest and to my navel, before lightly scratching the underside of my hardening cock. I whimpered and nodded. My actions were met with a strong hand pushing my neck onto the wood roughly. The man's fingers curved against my ligaments, jugular, and windpipe like it was made for my body. "I said, do you understand?" he asked again.

"Y-Yes," I whispered.

He suddenly gripped my cock, squeezing it mercilessly as he dug his thumb into the sensitive tip. "Try that again," he hissed. I gave a small cry and threw my head back against the wood slab. "Yes! Yes… sir!" I yelped, my voice cracking multiple times. Finally, his grip around my throbbing erection loosened slightly. I whined.

"Good," He said, his silky voice dripping with malice as he began to stroke me slowly. I raised my bent knees slightly, aching to wrap them around his waist. It was so uncomfortable to let them simply hang. Tiny whimpers and moans escaped me as he jerked me, my eyes closed behind the blindfold in blinding pleasure. But my eyes shot open when I felt long, wet fingers working me open, searching for that spot again. I helped him by slightly writhing. I needed him to touch that spot again. I was so close to exploding, I thought I would scream. But before he could reach it, his hands disappeared altogether, and the fireworks that had been lit in my stomach were reduced to burnt-out fuses. I gave a few small moan-like whimpers, my arms reaching feebly for his hands again. I could hear his quiet footsteps as he walked around the desk. Then I heard chains rattling, disrupting the agonizing silence. "P-Please! Please let me come, I need it!" I cried. Instead of a reply, he grabbed my wrists tightly and pulled them above my head where I felt warm leather wrap them together. They were cuffs; this time they were padded. He had pushed them through one of his drawer handles to lock my arms above me.

A half-whimper, half-moan bubbled from my lips when his fingers rolled and pinched my nipples until they were a darker shade of rose, his fingers replaced soon after. I whimpered and arched my back against him, releasing a small cry when his actions were combined . Fuck, it felt so good. I could get high off the feeling. I already was. My mind was in the clouds; I could feel them clogging my ears and making my brain levitate. His fingers began to work me open again. Couldn't he just put it in and fuck me already? I cleaned myself beforehand at home for that purpose. How long was he going to wait? I would be happy if he fucked me as hard as he could, even if this *was* a punishment...

I almost screamed when he finally reached my prostate. Instead, I gave a loud moan. "Yes, please, yes," I mumbled repeatedly. I could feel my climax building, my muscles tensing in the most satisfying way, as he massaged my inner walls, adding a second finger and burying them to the knuckle. He jerked me quickly between three fingers. "I-I'm gonna... I'm gonna-," but I was cut off when his fingers left me for a third time, abandoning me when I was right on the edge. "No! Kai... K-Kai, ple... please," I sobbed. I grabbed the chains and pulled at them, giving a frustrated cry when they only rattled and remained secure. The coiling rapture in my gut dissipated painfully, and I could feel liquid dripping down the side of my stomach where my neglected cock lay. It was proof of my torture.

I quivered, my lungs fluttering and my back arching high and then relaxing a little as I was pulled violently away from the edge of my orgasm.

This pattern repeated three more times. I sobbed and begged for release, but I was simply met with silence and more merciless stimulation. My mind wasn't even capable of forming any coherent words. Using safe-words wasn't an option. Maybe that was what he wanted. Maybe that's what I wanted. After the three periods of denial, there was an extra moment of silence with no touches or caresses. I simply lain there, soft whimpers escaping my lips. My cock still sat achingly hard on my stomach, the tip surely a reddish-purple colour. "Luka, can you tell me what the safe-words are?" Kai asked suddenly.

Huh? Was he purposely trying to end the scene? ... could I conjure enough energy to say anything? My mind was too full of clouds, and they were spilling into my lungs and choking me. My tears almost turned happy when I felt him unbuckle the restraints, massaging my wrists lightly. They stung, but the padded leather was gentler than I imagined it would be. I weeped against the blindfold, wincing against the light when it was removed. I didn't dare touch myself.

"You did so good, Angel. Tell me what the safe-words are," Kai said softly. I whimpered as he sat me up on his desk and stood between my legs, wiping my hot tears from my cheeks with a gentler touch than I expected. The man allowed me to fall forward and bury my face in his neck. "R-Red and Yellow...," I mumbled. He nodded and smiled at me. I could see that he was proud from under my drooping lashes. "Good," he said as he rubbed soothing hands down my sides. I let out another sob that ended in a whine. For a good minute, he allowed me to sit and catch much-needed air. His hands didn't hurt when he touched me anymore.

Once I had gathered enough strength to wrap my arms around his neck, he leaned his forehead against mine and quietly watched me gasp when he wrapped an entire hand around my aching erection. My arousal hadn't softened at all. Half expecting him to leave me at the edge again, I grabbed for his shoulders and biceps, silently begging him to stay, to never stop. His mouth was dangerously close to mine, tasting the air that we exchanged. It was heated and musty. "Please, don-" he hushed me softly.

My body pulled taut when I came, my nails digging into his shoulders and my head slipping onto his shoulder. It was overwhelming when I fell from that highrise, succumbing to the swirl of light that trapped me. His hand didn't stop until I was finished, when the high was over and My brain had finally met my body. "So good… you took that so well." I could hear him muttering against my ear. We stayed linked for another minute, breathing hard. I tried to match my lungs to Kai's rhythm. He patiently waited. "Do you want a bath? A shower?" I shook my head, "No."

"Are you tired? You can rest now, I promise."

"Mhm…"

"Come on, then."

The man helped me to my feet. A tissue wiped away the mess we made. Then he helped me into my jeans, discarding my boxers. I gripped his shoulders harshly. Was he unbothered? Was he aroused? Was I still expected to do anything? Why did the relationship feel so one-sided? The jeans were followed by my shirt.

"Can you drink the milkshake?" I asked suddenly.

He looked up and allowed me to stand without assistance.

"What?"

Miraculously, the drink hadn't been knocked over. I shook it in front of him.

"It'll be a waste of Mason's money if you don't."

Kai scoffed and took it from me. With both hands free, I buttoned my fly.

We crossed the bathroom to his bedroom where he watched me collapse on one of the couches. I watched him with blood-shot eyes as he went about his small kitchen, retrieving a glass of water and handing it to me. Still, he held the milkshake. "Drink," he ordered. I frowned at it. "You should drink too." I could see his expression darken. But, to my surprise, he swallowed a quick sip of his gift. I watched him lick his lips, the little pink muscle darting out and returning to its lair before he shoved the water back to me. "Drink."

I couldn't argue this time, so I took a few small sips to make him happy. The dimming sun filtering through the windows around us was still warm, making my eyelids heavy with fatigue. "If you're tired, you can stay here tonight."

I woke right the fuck up at his words. "Stay here... tonight? Like sleep here? Overnight?" I asked incredulously. He nodded. "I let my subs sleep here all the time when they needed or wanted to. The spare bedrooms are always free, and I have clothes that would probably fit you. PJs, at least." My face fell slightly knowing that I wouldn't be sleeping in his bed. It was a stupid idea, I knew, but it hurt nonetheless. There were lines I couldn't step over, and some of them I still needed to learn. ASAP.

We sat in silence for the next few minutes, watching the sun set lazily. The yellows and oranges faded to blues and peaches. I hadn't given him an answer.

I wanted to smile at the fact that Kai had been taking sips from his milkshake. One point for team Lucika. The silence was comfortable, especially so on his beautiful sofas, but I would have rather had a playlist going in the background. The quiet was interrupted by the ping of a phone notification. Kai snatched his phone quickly from the coffee table and read the message before standing, his face contorted with thought. "Rosa has dinner ready. Are you hungry?"

I shrugged and stood with him, letting him lead us down the hallway and stairs. I still hadn't discovered where the bedroom elevator led to. The third door I had noticed on this wall was most-likely his closet, as there were no dressers or clothing items in sight, other than what he was wearing and a discarded tie he had forgotten on the floor beside his bed. We navigated the stairs in silence, entering the kitchen to meet Rosa with a wide smile on her innocent face. "Good afternoon, Kai! I hope you're ready for dinner, Mr. Luka. I made noodle stir-fry with pork and teriyaki sauce. Enjoy!" She pushed a bowl of steaming noodles toward me, and my mouth fell open in shock. If I wasn't careful, my saliva would begin to drip. "Thank you, Rosa. Really, you never have to go through the trouble if you're just cooking for me, though," I replied sheepishly as I sat beside Kai at the island. "Trust me, Mr. Luka. If I didn't want to make it, then I wouldn't have agreed to do this job... Kai would probably die from lack of nutrition if I wasn't here, anyway." I giggled quietly at her words.

I glanced at Mason, who leaned against the counter behind Rosa before picking up my fork and wrapping noodles around it. I blew on them lightly before stuffing them into my mouth. It was probably a bigger bite than I should have taken, but I was undeniably starving. "The sheets in the first spare bedroom will need to be changed before Luka sleeps," Kai reminded his roommates. "Sure," Rosa nodded, before Mason could reply, and left the dishes on the counter to change the bed sheets on the second-to-top floor of Kaia's apartment. Mason began doing the dishes himself, humming lightly as he worked a brush over a greasy bowl. I took another bite, savouring the delicious pork and unique spices. I was exhausted after today, but my hunger drove me to continue.

Kai had pulled his phone out once again and began scrolling silently through his emails. He had hundreds of unanswered and unread messages. Working in a business as big as his father's seemed like a lot of hassle for his money. Wouldn't he be happier if he found a smaller job he enjoyed for a smaller paycheck? Maybe he already enjoyed his job, although I couldn't begin to fathom how anyone could be happy in his hectic lifestyle.

The three of us sat silently, my mind only slightly comforted by Mason's hums and sighs. It made me happy that at least *someone* understood my urge to sing sometimes, even if he never truly let his songs evolve into any words.

When Rosa returned, I had finished my delicious meal and had given my bowl to Mason. "I changed the sheets, but I also found something else...," Rosa said, coming to stand beside Mason. She dropped a small box onto the table, the slap of rock on cardboard echoing through the large room. Kai didn't even glance up, but my lips turned up into a smile. "Since you're staying for the night, Luka, would you like to play a game of *Yahtzee* with me and Mason?"

Mason and Rosa exchanged an amused glance when I nodded eagerly. "I don't know how to play, but yeah, I'll try!"

"Don't worry. We'll teach you!" Rosa exclaimed, pulling me by the hand from my seat and towards the ring of couches in the living room excitedly. Kai ignored us from the island, continuing to stare at his phone with disinterest. His brows were knitted together and his lips were pulled taut over his teeth. The man seemed more worried about whatever he was reading than the prostitute in his living room.

CHAPTER
EIGHTEEN

"HA! FOUR OF a kind!" I smiled in victory as I scooped my four sixes and one back into the leather cup. I scribbled my winnings onto my score sheet and handed the cup to Mason, who sat beside Rosa across from me. The plastic cubes rattled loudly between his palms.

"I'm going out to the gym. I'll take the Viper. Tell me when you've finished the game," Kai declared, standing beside me when he was finished with scrolling through his phone. Rosa's car keys swung around his index finger. He hadn't moved for the last half-hour. I was happy. I had forgotten about my session with him earlier, and my stomach was satisfyingly full. It had been so perfect with him sitting quietly by us.

"No, you have to stay! It's so fun!" I replied excitedly. I didn't think to tone my excitement down around the guy who didn't have the longest patience at that moment. He frowned. Then his lip jutted out. "Luka, I-," he was in the process of objecting when my hand shot out to grab onto his wrist to pull him down to the couch with as much strength as I could muster. I had caught him off-balance, and he fell rather heavily into a sitting position beside me, his eyes slightly panicked. Obviously, he wasn't accustomed to people forcing him to do things. "Do you know how to play?" I asked with a toothy smile and not a thought of rejection. He glanced nervously up to Rosa and Mason, who smiled back encouragingly. He was way out of his comfort zone, I realized, which was rather sad. Maybe he didn't like board games. Maybe he was stressed.

"No... I don't know how to play any games like this," he replied hesitantly. I shrugged. "That's okay. I'll teach you," I promised, taking his hand and shoving the cup into his palm. I began to explain the rules to him, going through the motions as he watched me intently, so many emotions flashing through his black eyes.

Rosa and Mason looked to each other, exchanging more words than they were allowed to say. All I could distinguish was surprise. Kai and I ignored them. Throughout the game, he asked many questions, getting lost on the rules. Truthfully, it wasn't that difficult of a game, and he admitted that once he understood it better.

The four of us played on for a few hours. Eventually, we switched to a different board game. Mason had grown bored of our current one.

When I released my seventh yawn, which was much larger than one I could blame on being bored, Kai sighed. The clocks certainly didn't read as midnight; I refused to believe that we had been playing for so long. Kai had been quiet until then, watching with boredom as his housemates and I played. I wondered why he hadn't insisted on leaving us. "You should go to bed," the man told me. I shook my head and yawned again, my eyelids warm and heavy as my lungs filled with that wicked potion of sedatives. My mind didn't register the fact that I was susceptible to any form of punishment by refusing to go to bed again. Maybe he didn't care.

I leaned into his shoulder slightly, the world blurring around me for just a moment with the hot tears that had gathered with my yawn. He was hot and his muscles were pliant, so I found myself welcoming him. Mason leaned back against the couch, rubbing his

ANGEL

hands over his face. The man was also fighting sleep.

"Yes. You're going to bed. Have a good night, Rosa," Kaia replied before standing and slipping his arms under me. I didn't even object to his actions, instead leaning into his chest. God, he was warm. He was comforting. He smelt like home when he carried me across his kitchen and up the stairs. In the back of my mind, I was faintly aware of the danger of being dropped. I was lighter than him, but I wasn't *that* light.

I wrapped my arms loosely around his neck and tucked my head under his chin. He didn't push me away or loosen his hold on my body as he carried me, to my surprise. When we made it down the hall and to the spare bedroom I would be staying in, I was already mostly asleep, and the car horns downstairs were beginning to fade. Truthfully, all I wanted at that moment was a bed, despite the fact that I hadn't changed into any pyjamas. I wasn't thinking about my mother who probably waited for my return home. I could barely even hear the quiet "Goodnight, Lucika" that Kai whispered to me before pressing a small kiss to my cheek. His scent lingered for a moment, but once he left the room, it had dissolved and left me to face any incoming nightmares by myself.

....

The next morning, I strolled into Kai's kitchen groggily, my hair disheveled and my eyes clouded. Most mornings were like that; I loathed the thought of waking before ten-o'clock. "G'morning, Luka. What would you like for breakfast?" Mason greeted me. I took a seat at the island and balanced my chin on my fist. "Is Kai still sleeping?" I didn't bother to reply to his question. Mason shook his head. "No. He left an hour ago to talk with some people across town. But I'll make you breakfast. Do you want an omelette?" I nodded and rubbed my cloudy, itchy eyes again. My sleep had been satisfying; I had earned myself a good night's rest.

"That was a fun game last night. Thanks for playing with me," I told the man while taking a seat in front of him. He smiled. "No problem. It's been a while since Kai has sat down for a game like that. I think he had fun." I giggled. "Yeah, he doesn't seem like the kind of person to ever play games like that." He shook his head silently and poured eggs into a waiting skillet. Mason chopped onion and tomato to add to my breakfast. Bread cooked in the toaster. We both jumped when it popped.

Mason eventually drove me home once I had finished my breakfast. He was exceptional at cooking; I wondered if he had learnt his skills from Rosa or some other source. Instead of staying at my house like I should have done to work on the computer, I decided to walk to my mother's diner. I made sure my hoodie was not left at home, hoping it would cover the already-faded marks left by Kai's ravenous appetite for boy flesh.

My mother was absolutely shocked that I had made the one-mile journey, but I knew she was happy to see me too. Once inside the diner, her face lit up. *That* never got old. "Where did you sleep over last night?" she asked rather brightly as she filled the cash register with change. I stood opposite her and shrugged with my hands stuffed into my pockets nonchalantly. "I just stayed at a friend's house."

She seemed to believe me—I mean, I didn't lie, did I?

After my answer, the quiet between us was briefly uncomfortable. Was she mad? I thought 'staying at a friend's house' was a good fib. I had begun to think of Mason and Rosa as friends, even if they were old enough to be my parents. And Kai, well, Kai was in a category all by himself.

I waited for thirty minutes until my mother's lunch break to walk her down the street to a small bistro on the corner. It wasn't popular,

ANGEL

but it was cheap with considerably better food than the diner.

"You keep bringing me to places to eat. How much money do you really make, now, Luka?"

I shrugged as we sat down at a booth. We were greeted by a smiling waiter who took our drink and food orders. "A lot more, I guess. It'll be more... regular, now." There would be no more coming home with paychecks that never had the same numbers written on them. Working at the diner, Mom only made minimum wage. It was unfair, the amount she had to work and the amount she got in return. But it was one of the few places she had found as a job, and hadn't been able to find another one. She didn't have good transportation, and I knew that she was scared to find a new job too. She had been living in her comfort zone for so long, it would take a miracle for her to break from it.

I smiled sheepishly, a blush rising to my ears as her gaze scrutinized me. But she didn't question me further.

"I thought maybe we could eat out like this a little more often instead of bringing home dinner from the diner every night. You know, like visit the food bank and grocery store a little more often," I mumbled. In my lap, I tugged at my knuckles. She nodded with a small, distant smile. "That sounds nice." The two of us began to eat, savoring our food that we had *earned*. She picked at her chicken while I twirled noodles onto my fork. She watched me; I wondered what was so intriguing to her. We stayed in a constant circle of chewing and chatting, straying from the topic of our questionable careers. We may have been doing dirty work, but it took guts. A lot of people couldn't do my job, and being a waitress took a certain personality that a lot of people just didn't have.

After we had finished and I escorted my mother back to her work, my slow walk home was hot. I loved the sun in Santa Monica. I loved the beaches. I loved the warmth. I loved the sunsets. But I did *not* like when the temperature exceeded one-hundred degrees, which was what it did a lot of the time during the end of the summer. I ached for the winter, one of my favourite times of the year. I had only seen snow once in my life, and seeing it again would be a dream-come-true for me.

Once safe and curled into my blankets at home, I opened my laptop and began to work, turning the music up as loud as it would go.

"*Mason told me that he dropped you off a long time ago. You're safe at home now?*"

I read Kai's text as soon as it was delivered, notified by the vibrating against my thigh.

"*Yep.*"

I didn't know exactly what to say in reply. Instead of looking back to my computer, I set it aside and hopped off my bed, scrolling through my music. My body began to jerk and sway again. I could feel the energy in my toes and sending shocks up my spine as a popular band began to play a slow guitar solo, accompanied by soft bass and a beautiful piano piece. I wasn't sure if the jittery thrums in my belly were in anticipation of Kaia's reply or the music. My arms rose above my head as I closed my eyes, letting the beat of the drums move me with excitement.

Soon, Kaia's reply didn't even matter.

....

"Kai won't be home for a while. Rosa is making you dinner, though," Mason told me as he led us into the house that night. Rosa smiled at me from the couch. "Good afternoon, Mr. Lucika!"

"Hey, Rosa."

"Do you like chicken fingers, Luka?" She asked. I nodded enthusiastically. "Yeah! Who doesn't?"

ANGEL

Mason chuckled at my reply and sank into the couch where Kai had sat the night before. Rosa glared at him when he jostled her, nearly causing her to spill her glass of bloody-red wine across the expensive leather. "I'm thinking we have about half an hour before dinner and Kai is ready to finish up his work. Do you have any game consoles at your house, Luka? Are you up for a game of *Mario Kart* with me?" I shrugged. "I've never played. But, sure, if you can teach me," I replied, snatching a controller from the table. Neither Mason nor Rosa looked like people who enjoyed video games, but I knew all too well how looks could be so deceiving. Mason smirked. "I promise you'll be able to beat Rosa by the time dinner is ready."

We had made a meal of chicken strips and potato wedges, handmade by Rosa herself. She was a truly gifted cook, and I understood why she had probably seemed so appealing to Kaia. As we played, crumbs were spilt, wine was splattered and downed by distracted gulps, and all three participants had grown extremely competitive.

I ended up winning only two races, but Mason also mentioned that he had only met two other people who could beat Rosa at *Mario Kart*. She sat silently, her eyes never leaving the screen, as her fingers worked magic in a mystifying blur.

"Kai wants you in his office. Are you finished with dinner, Luka?" Mason asked suddenly. He had gotten a notification on his device, but Rosa and I disregarded it. I nodded. "Yep. I can probably find my way up there myself. Beat Rosa for me," I told him. Mason smiled widely and took the controller from my hands.

I gave a cheerful wave towards Rosa before finding the first step to the stairway. After scaling the flight of wooden stairs and following my memory down the narrow hallway, I stepped up to Kai's office. I didn't knock until I had taken a very quick picture of the swirls of cherry blossoms on the door. Such detail must have taken months to produce.

"Come in," Kai's voice echoed from within the office. I entered quickly. No, I wasn't too eager to discover what he had planned for me, but I wasn't scared, either. I was becoming comfortable with his intentions. Kai sat behind his desk, papers scattered uncharacteristically across the hardwood. "Did you have a good day, Luka?" He asked, leaving no room for a greeting and pushing his papers to the side slightly in an attempt at making them appear tidier. I nodded. "Yeah, I hung out with my mom a little bit. That was nice."

He nodded, gave me a genuinely happy smile, stood, and crossed the space between us in three equal steps. "That sounds fun," he replied as he removed my shirt. My heartbeat began to sputter and quicken as he attached his lips to my neck.

CHAPTER
NINETEEN

I MOANED SLIGHTLY AS his tongue lapped across my collar bone, working magic against my sensitive nerve endings as I knelt on his desk, careful to keep the papers as wrinkle-free as possible. God, I enamored that tongue. His fingers worked me open, pressing against my prostate with each little thrust. Thank Jesus I had cleaned out properly that day. "M-More!" I exclaimed, pushing down onto his digits forcefully. He gave it gladly. "Come on, Angel, come for me," he growled, gripping my erection and giving it a few satisfying strokes. My seed bubbled over his fingers as I came undone, a small cry leaving my lips as my body stiffened. My world fell away as I succumbed to the blinding, crippling pleasure. He seemed to be making up for the orgasms I lost last night, and I was thankful for that. I had been too tired to cash in on his promise. "Good boy, Angel," he whispered against the nape of my neck, leaving a small purple mark in his wake, just over my pounding carotid. Then his burning mouth moved lower and printed a little red mark on my chest. I could cover the one on my neck with my hair, but I also knew it would become increasingly hard to hide the other ones from my mother. Hoodies and scarves weren't going to last, even if they only lasted a day.

I was still quivering from my release when Kai pushed my back onto the desk and slid inside me slowly, deeming me stretched. The first ring of muscle was always the hardest, and the further it was stretched, the more I wanted to go home. But soon, I would begin to enjoy my time there on his desk. He was wearing a condom again; the sound the wrapper made had been engraved in my memory long ago. "God," he breathed, working through my rings of muscle until his dark pubic hairs hit my flaccid cock. I had shaved what little hair I had away the night the water was finally turned back on in my house, and he seemed to prefer that. But all his hair was hot. I would be sad if he shaved any of it.

He started off with a slow pace, hitting my favourite spots with almost surprising accuracy. I clenched around him, earning a groan from deep within his vast chest. I liked his playtime, but it seemed so... *vanilla*. I had a feeling that it wasn't going to last long, though. His were merciless, turning my brain to mush. I could barely think straight enough to tell myself to breathe regularly. My spinning world didn't give any room for air, only occasional whimpers and grunts.

When he stiffened and went slack above me, there was nothing but the sound of his heavy, controlled panting. The sounds of wet skin slapping together left the room with my conscience. His right hand supported him when he placed it just beside my head on the desk.

"Breathe, Angel," he told me softly, his free hand ghosting down my stomach. The muscles fluttered under the pads of his digits. Cool air filled my lungs, and my eyes opened to meet his even gaze. Perspiration coated his forehead in a thin sheen, his thick hair falling into his eyes and down his cheeks. If I had the energy, I probably would have come for a second time just from looking at him. I knew it was wrong to get attached like I was, but could I help myself? I was a sex toy to him, someone he could use over the weekend for his own pleasure. Was I really as different as I wanted to be? How could I not be attracted to the image above me?

He slid out, slipping the condom off his softening length and tying it closed before tossing it in the trash bin beside his desk. Maybe he just wasn't willing to clean up the mess. Whatever the reason, I was the slightest bit happy. He sat me up on the edge of his desk, massaging my thighs lightly as he pulled a cloth from one of his drawers and wiped away the seed on my stomach. I was still gasping for air quietly, yet he looked as relaxed as always. "Good boy, Luka."

I shot him the smallest hopeful smile, and he helped me dress myself again in return. "Are you hungry?" he asked. I shook my head. "Rosa made dinner." He pulled me to my feet lightly. No matter how rough he was during sex, the way he treated me afterwards made everything better.

"Would you like to stay the night, then?"

"Tonight? Again?"

Kai simply nodded, his gaze wandering to the skyscraper beside his. It reflected the fading skyline beautifully.

"Is that it, then? Are we gonna visit a red room or something? We could play more board games." My question even surprised myself.

"We could, but Mason usually leaves around this time. It's not that much fun without him."

"Where does he go?"

"He goes out to see his daughter, usually. From what I heard, her mother isn't very happy with Mason."

I frowned. "Mason has a daughter?"

Kai sat on the desk where I had been taking dick not ten minutes ago. He crossed his arms over his chest. "Before he got a divorce, he had a child. But he doesn't see her very much anymore."

"Oh...." Mason didn't seem like the kind of man to settle down or even attempt to make a family. But I could see him with a daughter. It seemed right, somehow. Mason could be happy for just a few more hours, I decided. I wouldn't dare call him to come back and play. It was already eight-o'clock, so I assumed that he would be home shortly.

Instead of waiting, I decided to challenge both Kai and Rosa to a *Mario Kart* duel in which we were sorely beaten by Rosa. Mason joined us after an hour of losing looking refreshed and gleeful. He finally put her in her place once he had grabbed himself a beer and controller, pushing her into second and myself into third. Kai was too far behind to be seen on the scoreboard.

Kai visibly relaxed when Mason had entered the building. I could relax, too, when I didn't have his eyes constantly on me or watching the game over my shoulder. Once Mason was comfortable and our attention was completely captured by our competition, Kai bid everyone goodnight. His brief smile was sincere, promising a good day tomorrow. After a few moments, we could hear his footsteps cross his bedroom.

It was eleven-o'clock by the time Rosa yawned. I followed suit, tilting my head away slightly. The tears that had accumulated in the corners of my eyes from the yawn were wiped and I set down my controller. "If I'm staying the night, can I go to bed, too? You guys won't be upset if I leave you now, right?" I asked. Mason shook his head. "Of course not. You can stay in the same room as last night." Again, I yawned. Then I smiled at them and stood, clasping my hands together behind my back. If this continued, I would need to start packing an overnight bag.

"Goodnight, Luka," Rosa dismissed me. I waved goodbye as I climbed the stairs. The spare bedroom sat just beside Kai's, so I paused at his door; it was only open a crack. The light was off. I could see the outline of his body under the sheets, which shook me

ANGEL

from my daze and urged me to move on. No one enjoyed being watched while they slept, so I turned my attention to the next room. The spare bedroom I had been staying in was beautiful. Nothing compared to Kai's bedroom, but the little things that I loved so much made it so different from the other rooms I had stayed in before. The browns, blacks, and golds made the room warm and comforting, while the floor-to-ceiling windows on one wall made one feel as if they could step out onto the clouds. A hundred feet below, though, sat the street, busy and waiting for anyone eager enough to walk the plank from that high. Two padded chairs sat in the corner on each side of a dark wood desk. A small bookshelf sat to the right, but it was empty, making that end of the room feel slightly lonely. What were you supposed to do when you sat in the chairs? Of course, the view could probably stay on par with reading any day.

The bed was the most beautiful object in the room. It was obviously the focal point. Under a thick, dark-brown feather duvet sat a king-sized mattress. Pillows wrapped in gold silk and leopard-print faux fur promised a comfortable night's sleep. A black, fluffy blanket hung off the foot of the bed and onto the white rug below.

I wondered if I should call the fur room from then on. Comfortable. Warm. Soft. Home.

I fell into a deep, exhausted trance after changing into a pair of pyjama pants and a thick t-shirt. They had been hidden in a small bag that had been tucked away at the edge of the bed, so I assumed that they were there for my own use. The only things I didn't change were the pair of boxers around my waist. The mattress swallowed me like an anchor had literally been strapped to my waist and dropped onto the sheets. If I was allowed, I would stay there forever. It was like being engulfed in clouds that smelt like dark chocolate. What was with the chocolate smell everywhere? Had Kai slept in the bed?

Horns honked far below me, and I was oddly comforted by them. If I ever left the city, I would most-likely feel nervous with the silence; I would undoubtedly go insane without the sounds of curses, sirens, and car engines falling on ears that had long-since grown accustomed to the noise. My knees curled up against my chest so I could tuck the blanket under my feet and snuggly around my shoulders, ensuring there was no crack for heat to escape. My eyes closed. I drifted.

But, even with the comforting sounds that wafted around me and the slowing of my lungs, my heart came to a halt under my ribs when a scream pierced the air. I had been sleeping, or almost sleeping, soundly. Even from the end of the hallway, the voice travelled easily through the vents and hit every eardrum on that floor—probably ones below it too.

It was deep. It wasn't a female's scream. The sound was so full of agony and fear, my own heart broke upon hearing it.

But the thing that scared me most was the fact that I knew immediately who it belonged to: Kai.

CHAPTER
TWENTY

I WAS FROZEN FOR a good thirty seconds after silence had returned to the house.

But, once my mind had partially regained its composure, I tore myself from the sheets and my feet burned a trail to the door. I couldn't get it open fast enough. Why did it take so fucking long? By the time I stood in the hallway, Mason had already disappeared inside Kai's bedroom. His footsteps weren't frantic like mine, though. If I had heard something crash or someone yelling, I probably wouldn't have been so alarmed. But that scream... it wasn't even a shout or a yell. It was built from terror and guilt, rolled into a horrifying reality.

My fingers ached by the time I had walked down the hall and come to stand in front of the thick, wooden door. When I had finally gathered enough courage to put a shaky hand on the handle and open it, I realized that I probably didn't prepare myself very sufficiently for what I may see. The lights in the small kitchenette and a light beside the king-sized bed were turned on, illuminating Kai who sat up in the sheets. My breath caught in my throat, refusing to give my lungs any relief, and the comforting smell of Kai's home around me turned sour. Sweat dripped down Kai's chiseled body and soaked into the sheets, staining the beige a chocolate-brown colour.

I could see his body quivering from across the spacious room.

Kai's eyes were wide and glazed with fear. He didn't look... awake. His eyes were distant and unfocused, staring blankly at Mason, who had taken a seat beside him on the bed and held Kai's head between his hands. It seemed so intimate, the way Mason attempted to comfort Kaia with low words and soft caresses. I wished for that kind of relationship with someone.

Kaia mumbled words to himself too. I couldn't determine whether he was repeating Mason's comforts or if he was talking about his own reason for waking. It looked like a nightmare, if I ever saw one. Rosa appeared behind me, careful to not startle anyone. Her narrowed eyes softened when she noticed me nervously pulling at my knuckles.

"Come on," she briefly glanced past me to get a view of the scene. Then she pulled me by the shoulder back into the hallway, shielding me slightly until the door was closed. But I didn't miss Kai's broken voice, uttering words that dripped utter sadness.

"She... she's g-gone."

"What happened to him?" I asked once we were hidden by the closed door. I wanted to comfort him. I wanted to be Mason. Even *I* had never been that broken. Even I had nightmares, but nothing compared to this.

"Nightmare," she replied quietly, confirming my suspicions.

"Is he okay?"

She looked away. What haunted someone so deeply for them to wake screaming in the night? "He's just shaken. It happens sometimes. If you plan to stay over during the weekends then you should get used to it." I could just barely distinguish a flash of sadness in her diverted eyes. It surprised me that her words held acceptance, as if she knew that this would never change. "Why? Can't he see a therapist or something?" I asked hopefully. Rosa tilted her head to the side a little and finally dragged her gaze back to mine. The woman didn't want to go into detail about him, I could tell. "He is, Luka, but it takes time to heal things like this. There is only so much a therapist can do, although Kai still speaks with one regularly. Even mixed with medication, nightmares can be a struggle."

"Oh." At least he was getting help.

Rosa led me into the kitchen, *Mario Kart* sat on the television screen across the room, waiting patiently for one of us to continue the race that had been cut short. The woman across from me pulled the edges of her white tank-top down her thighs over her navy-blue cotton shorts. Beneath them, a pattern of tattoos adorned her flesh. Some were actual pictures, like the bird sitting just above her knee. Others were just swirls of colour and words. Most were in inscrutable languages. I recognized a few as Russian. I searched for other tattoos on her, but I only found one on her wrist: a shockingly realistic black widow spider. "I'll make us a midnight snack. How does that sound?" Her voice was groggy, the adrenaline fading as we moved away from the commotion. I nodded and took a heavy seat across from her workstation.

"Does he have nightmares about the same thing? Or is it like a nightmare disorder?" I asked. Did I want to know? She shook her head, making it clear that she had no intention of passing on any further information, so I set my chin on my hands and watched, memorizing how her wrist flicked delicately over a slice of bread when she slathered peanut butter on it. She did the same with the jam until she had two sandwiches made. I sighed as I picked at mine, tearing off small chunks of bread. For once in my life, I wasn't all that hungry.

"When was the last time you cut your hair?"

Rosa's question was sudden and random, but I assumed that it was an attempt to distract me. I shrugged. "Last year, maybe? I don't cut it, really."

"Do you want me to cut it sometime? It's pretty long."

I nodded, suddenly eager to get it off. It was hot and annoying, and I was constantly pushing it out of my eyes. "Yeah! Are you a hairdresser, too?" She gave a small chuckle. "No, no. I just cut Mason's and Kai's hair. Abraham shaves his own head now, but I used to cut his hair too."

"Who's Abraham?"

"Our doorman. You've met him, right?"

I nodded. How could I forget him?

"He's okay," Mason said suddenly. Both our gazes snapped to his as we heard those heavy, exhausted footsteps nearly slide down the stair steps. He appeared refreshed and awake, despite the lag in his motions, probably because he was accustomed to waking this early, even though his hair was disheveled and his clothing consisted of a pair of sweatpants and a white t-shirt.

"Is he sleeping again?" I asked. Mason shook his head. "No. Hopefully he'll get some sleep tomorrow night. He's in the studio now."

"Studio...," I wracked my brain for an explanation. "You mean playing the drums?" He nodded, taking a seat beside me. "Here, Mason," Rosa said quietly, pushing her plate of a half-eaten sandwich towards him. Mason thanked her, which sent us into a depressing silence. I felt helpless with the knowledge that Kai was losing sleep with such terrifying dreams. He must be in the studio to forget about it. I understood that, at least. How bad did Mason and Rosa feel after knowing him for so long and seeing him struggle like that?

"Does anyone go and talk to him when he's playing the drums?" I asked, finishing my sandwich by pushing it away from me. The pair exchanged a glance before they both shook their heads. "No. He doesn't like to be bothered. That's probably why he put his studio close to his office. It's better to just leave him alone." Mason's

ANGEL

word seemed final. I bit my lip. Hard. "I think I'm gonna go back to bed. You two will go to bed, too, right? Soon?" Mason and Rosa nodded as she set the dishes in the sink. Mason licked his lips and brushed the crumbs off his hands. "G'night, Lucika," Mason gave a small smile. "Sleep well, Mr. Luka," Rosa added.

I squinted slightly from the bright light that filtered from the upstairs hallway.

Fuck, I was going to regret this.

I took a deep breath before climbing the stairs, knowing that I wouldn't be going straight to my guest room. Instead, I would search for the music studio. I could already hear the drums beating loudly; it was a hollow, empty sound when I knew that the inspiration was coming from the wrong place. When I was even halfway down the hall, I almost covered my ears. It was so loud. I wasn't complaining, but he had to obviously be wearing some kind of headphones to lower the noise. I could even hear it through the tall wall that divided us. The cymbals and drum beats vibrated the floor under my bare feet, making me want to dance more than anything as I worked my way toward the beautifully designed entrance to his office. There was a second door beside it. Even if I could hear Kai playing to a heavy metal band, music was music. I would find a way to move my body to any rhythm.

Around me, once I had swerved into a second entrance, was nothing more than a square of black walls, littered with dozens of band posters and enlarged album covers. *Guns and Roses. Skillet. Iron Maiden. Three Days Grace. Metallica.* The list went on and on, some of the posters covered by extra sound gear like speakers and cymbals. I set my hand on the silver door handle, the one that stood just in front of the original one that led to the hallway, hesitating for a moment. Would he yell at me? Would he find comfort in someone like me? Maybe he was relatively relaxed by then.

I opened the door, immediately slammed by a wall of sound. The room was painted black and dimly lit by thin lights lining the upper corners of the walls. More posters. The room reeked of sweat and loneliness. I hated it; it didn't feel like a studio should. I imagined it more like an imagination outlet where one could have fun creating new, moving sounds. There really was nothing in his massive space, save for a mini fridge in the corner, a black leather sofa, and a mammoth drum set that sat across from the couch. The drums sat between two speakers and a few other appliances I had no hope of naming. The only thing I really noticed, though, was Kai.

He sat behind his drums with a pair of massive black headphones perched on his head, a white tank, and black sweats. I had never seen him in clothing that casual before, but he had probably picked something off the floor instead of staying shirtless and sweaty. His body was shiny with sweat, his eyes closed lightly, and his thick, dark brows pulled together as his knee and head bounced. His sturdy arms worked with the beat, completely immersed in the music. The man seemed oblivious to everything around him. I knew what that feeling was like. He was on his cloud nine.

I stepped into the room and closed the door behind me without him noticing my presence.

God, he was hot. He didn't look like anyone haunted by nightmares when he was there. He looked free. I stopped in front of his setup, never daring to stray any further. I was frozen, torn between running to him and staying to comfort him as best I could.

But I had no time left to decide.

My heart sputtered against my rib cage when his black eyes slowly opened, the pupils blown wide in the limited lighting. His expression didn't change, but he slowly stopped moving. He looked confused. Sad. Guilty. Scared. So many emotions were shown to me in just a second, played like a movie projected from his eyes before it was all shielded. With a flick of a switch, the speakers were turned off.

"Are you okay, Kai?"

The question hung between us for a moment. I had whirled so many questions into one simple inquiry. The man only stared at me, his eyes burning holes into my own. I could feel a soft blush creeping along my high cheekbones, and I didn't know exactly what I would do if he didn't reply and the silence continued for any longer.

Then his long arm rose to motion me towards him after he set down his sticks, his eyes lowering as I bounced around the intricate drum setup and stood in front of him. He pushed his headphones carefully onto his neck. I wasn't expecting his arms to wrap around me tightly, his face pushed against my stomach with his sitting position. I felt his strong fists grip the back of my shirt as if it was the only thing tethering him to earth. He panted against the front of my shirt and I could feel the heat of his body soaking through it.

"God...you even smell like her...."

His broken voice trailed off after cracking a few times.

"K-Kai...?"

He sighed and leaned back to look at me. The man's eyes held something akin to grief. It ran deeper than that, though, something that twisted his soul and was slowly breaking it.

"Who's 'Her'?"

I wasn't sure what I expected as an answer. I only hoped that I wouldn't get silence.

He shook his head and looked away. "I'm sorry... I don't know why I said that. She's no one." The man's reply shocked me. How could he lose sleep over someone that didn't matter?

"Are you sure you're okay?"

His gaze snapped to mine then, and I shivered. He was upset again, although I didn't believe he was angry. More... sad. Hesitant.

The air around us had changed, darkened. Thickened. Shit.

He stood quickly and pushed past me. "Go to bed, Lucika."

I could only watch as he stomped away, slamming his bedroom door behind him. I followed him out into the hall, but by the time I hit the second door frame, he had locked himself in his office.

I gave up.

The rest of my sleep that night was rough. Every time I closed my eyes and listened to the city, the sirens turned into Kai's screams, the horns into wails of agony.

I pulled out my phone and the earbuds that came with it, eager to drown out the sounds with music. I was soon able to find the perfect tune to calm my mind, although I knew it wasn't a permanent solution. It wouldn't fix Kai's hurting.

CHAPTER
TWENTY-ONE

I WOKE AT DAWN and met Rosa in the kitchen. I had decided to take a shower, and I still wasn't sure if jacking off had been a good idea. Kaia wouldn't know, how could he, but the guilt I felt both confused and angered me. "Mason and Kai went out. I'll drive you home today whenever you want," she told me. I nodded and joined her in front of the oven instead of taking my usual post across from her. "Do you think I could help you make something for breakfast? If you don't like working in the kitchen with others, I understand...," my voice trailed off as I scratched my cheek nervously.

"Of course! What would you like to make?"

I thought for a moment. "Pancakes."

She moved into action, setting a pan and bowls on the counter. "You'll need two cups of flour. Start by measuring that into the big bowl with the cups in that drawer over there-," she pointed to the drawer closest to the fridge, "and then you'll need the milk and two eggs."

Soon, after slight bickering and a flour catastrophe, we had a total of twelve pancakes cooked and a pack of bacon fried. Rosa sat beside me as we both ate ravenously.

"So where is Kaia now?" I asked after swallowing the last of my second pancake. "He's in a meeting, I think. I'm not totally sure. He probably will be until around noon, when I know he'll probably be meeting someone important for lunch. But Mason usually accompanies him wherever he goes, so I guess it's just you and me," she replied, popping a strip of bacon between her painted rosy lips. Even so early in the morning, she valued her looks like gold.

"He has such a hectic schedule. No wonder he doesn't get any sleep.

She sighed. "Yeah, and with the nightmares too. Normally he uses the midnight hours for his late-night workouts. The gym down around where you live that he visits isn't usually open during the day. Really, he only plays the drums when he's upset. It calms him down."

"I know how he feels...."

Rosa didn't ask for clarification. We only sat in silence and ate with less hunger than before. Once finished, which didn't take long, I grabbed my belongings while Rosa did the few dishes. Then she followed me into the garage. Her heels clicked loudly on the cement.

....

"Have a good week, Rosa," I said as I stepped out of her canary-yellow *Dodge*. My house looked inviting; I missed it.

"You too, Luka! Don't work too hard!"

I snorted and waved to her as she faded down the street, the noise disappearing soon after she did. My mother wasn't home. I knew she wouldn't be, although she had left her pack of cigarettes sitting on the kitchen counter beside her bottle-green glass ashtray. Normally she brought them with her to ease the stress at work.

My work pile was piling up too. I had a few dozen new emails from the bank, showing me new activity in Kai's account. This, when I was alone, was the time perfect to blast new music and get some work done.

ANGEL

My week would be exhausting and lonely. Very lonely. Some of the time was used when I decided to walk three miles to the clinic and get an STI test. I got them regularly in my job; even if I asked beforehand, I knew that liars ran LA. The tests came back negative. Would Kai still want to use condoms, then? Personally, I preferred them.

Without Kai, Mason, or Rosa, I had no one to speak to. I had only spoken a maximum of ten words to my mother and a few short sentences to the woman at the checkout in the drugstore on the corner when I wasn't locked in my bedroom.

At least we had managed to buy enough food to last us comfortably to the end of the month. Between meals, I worked. I hadn't even texted Kai, as much as I wanted to. I missed him. And I hated myself for it. I didn't want to be a clingy submissive, but I still couldn't hide my arousal at home. I was cursing him from my bed, cocooned in a thick blanket, which I was sure I would be bringing back to Kai's house for an aftercare item, when my eyes widened suddenly. I had stuffed the dildo from Kai under my bed, hoping I would forget about it. But, to my horror, it was closest to the thing I wanted most right at that moment. Seeing Kai tomorrow was too far away. I reached for it slowly, feeling under the bed, but stopped short. Kai would probably want to give me permission before I used it. Would he know if I did? How could he, really?

Then I remembered my punishment and shivered with fear, deciding it would probably just be safer to ask.

"Can I use the dildo you gave me?"

My question was abnormally straightforward and ballsy. It didn't sound that way when I was typing, though, and reading it a few times over once it was sent made my stomach clench.

His reply was almost immediate.

"Yes."

I shuddered, my cock growing with his unexpected text. But what *was* I expecting? What was he supposed to say? What was I supposed to ask?

"*Thank you…?*"

"*But only if you send me a video.*"

I bit my lip as I typed, then deleted, then typed again, ignoring the music blasting from the laptop. I didn't know how to reply to that, and I really didn't want to send him a video. "*I'm kidding, Angel. I think you deserve it. Go ahead, baby boy.*"

'Baby boy' was a new one. But I loved it almost as much as "Angel".

I turned off my phone and pushed it towards the computer as I grasped the dildo and the bottle of lube I had hidden beside it. I was only in the grey boxers I had worn for the last two days, and I pushed down the thin fabric to let my cock spring free. I groaned and gave it a few slow strokes as my other hand traced the ring of muscle around my seizing entrance. It was hot; my fingers nearly burnt. Tissues were pulled close, I didn't bother cleaning myself, and the sensations made me miss Kai.

"Ah…," I gave a breathy moan when I pushed a single finger in to the knuckle, the dildo ready at the side.

God, I missed that feeling.

....

That night, mom came home with a terrifying aura around her. She was stressed, anxious, and she reeked of cigarettes. She must have bought more. Her hair was matted and thrown up into a hasty ponytail, and her dulled blue eyes no longer stood out against the grease and ketchup stains on her uniform. Alarms rang in my mind.

"Dinner is ready," I said quietly, mixing the pot of macaroni and hotdog slices slowly. She ignored me, a bad sign, and took a seat at

ANGEL

the table to light a smoke with quivering hands. Normally she at least attempted to smile and make even the smallest conversation with me before we both retreated to our bedrooms for the night. Would she ever be able to quit her job? Maybe we had enough money to get by with just my one paycheck.

"I'm not hungry... eat what you want," she mumbled, standing on stiff muscles and limping to her bedroom on the opposite side of the kitchen. I watched her leave with crippling sadness. She was suffering, and I didn't know what to do to help her. All I could do, I decided, was leave a sizable amount of macaroni for when she did get hungry, eat, and then head to bed. I would stay quiet until morning.

That night, music danced quietly in the air of my bedroom. I sat nearly nude in only a t-shirt and had curled myself into my favourite blanket. Maybe I was hungry. Maybe I was cold. Maybe I was lonely again. All I knew for sure was that I hadn't eaten as much as I had wanted; I had misjudged the amount of macaroni and didn't want to eat into my mother's portion, my mother was upset, and Kai would be rather angry if he knew I had decided to skip any meals of mac-and-cheese, even if it was partly because of the butterflies that left no room for nutrients.

When my phone gave an alert, I scrambled to read the text.

"*Mason will be there in ten minutes if you want. I'd like you to spend an extra night with me.*"

Was sleeping over at his house becoming the norm? I bit my lip and thought for a moment. Maybe I could sneak away without Mom noticing. She was probably already sawing logs, I knew, but I didn't want to leave her on one of my nights off. I could refuse his request, or order, or whatever it was.

"*Okay.*" My fingers made my reply for me.

I jumped off the bed and scrambled to get ready, throwing on a pair of light jeans before wrapping up my blanket and shoving it under my arm with a pair of clothes. I only had to wait a few minutes before Mason pulled into the driveway, wearing an unusual combination of brand-new blue jeans and a white dress shirt. Where was the hoodie? Where were the ketchup-stained sweatpants?

"Hey, Mason," I mumbled after I had just snuck down the stairs and out the door furtively.

He smiled. "Lucika."

Once my seatbelt was secured and my clothes and blanket were thrust into the backseat, we were speeding through my sketchy neighbourhood.

"So what message did you send Kaia earlier today?" I could hear the smirk in his voice, and I froze.

"I'm just asking for comedic reasons. He literally choked on his coffee in the middle of the restaurant. It was hilarious. You really are a special kid."

"I thought Kai didn't drink coffee," I replied, attempting to distract him. God, I didn't want to answer *that* question, but I had a feeling that Mason already had a hunch as to why I would text Kaia in the middle of the day. He just knew things like that. Mason shook his head. "He keeps up appearances when he meets other people for meals. Sometimes his father forces it into him. He doesn't, if he can help it."

There was a pause. "I was asking him if I could do something and I guess it surprised him." I really didn't think he was the kind of person to get flustered like myself. But I was becoming attached, it made me realize, and it scared me to death.

"Ah...," Mason hummed fondly. He knew exactly what I had asked Kai.

CHAPTER
TWENTY-TWO

IT WAS SIX-O'CLOCK by the time we pulled into the garage. Rosa was leaning against the side of the *Bentley*, her arms folded over her chest, wearing a beautiful black dress that flowed freely around her knees. It wasn't too formal, but I could tell that she was dressing up. Why was everyone wearing such nice clothes? She displayed a bored expression which returned after she flashed us a quick smile. "Kai is upstairs. Go meet him up there. Then we can leave," she told me. Despite her expression, her voice held no venom, only her usual politeness.

"We're going somewhere?" I asked, my brows pulling together. Kai didn't want an extra night of kinky sex? Mason and Rosa nodded, shooing me away with smiles.

I bit my lip and pulled my knuckle vigorously as I rode the elevator to his main floor. After a quick inspection, I realized he must be in his office or bedroom. When I entered the latter, he met me by wrapping his arms around my waist and pulling me towards him. "Kai?" He buried his nose against my neck, his soft, deep breaths tickling my collar bone. The air was hot and moist.

"Are you okay?"

He was silent for a moment, and I waited for him to lean away. I was sure he could feel my heavy heartbeat against his cheekbone.

"Fine," he said finally, leaning away and loosening his hold on me. I gave a nervous smile. "I-I brought a blanket...." I held it out slightly to show him the beautiful patterns of greys, whites, and a few mystery stains in one corner. He examined it with amusement. "Perfect. I forgot about that."

With a smile, I passed Kai and set it on the edge of a couch, watching him grab a small bag beside the door.

"Put this on."

I looked at him with utter confusion as he held the black paper bag out to me. "Um... what is it?" I asked, taking it slowly. "It's a suit for tonight. I'm taking you out to dinner." I suddenly regretted not leaving *all* the macaroni for my mother. She would need it much more than myself. Within thirty seconds, I was in the bathroom and emptying the contents of the bag onto the massive granite countertop. My shirt was changed, along with my jeans, replaced by a pair of light-grey dress pants, a white dress shirt, and a suit jacket that matched the pants.

"I've never worn a suit before," I mumbled as I stepped out of his bathroom. I felt *fancy*. He shrugged, his captivating gaze swallowing me whole. "That's okay. My mother always told me that it's never too late to start." His nonchalant reply made me feel more welcomed than it should have. Playfully, I took both sides of the blazer in my hands and executed an exaggerated spin. The man's grin widened. I giggled.

"Beautiful. I'm so glad it fits," he growled happily, pulling his arm around my waist once again. I could only let him guide me away. We met Mason and Rosa in the garage again, leading us both into the backseat of the *Bentley* before they slid into the front. Rosa was in shotgun. I shivered, fearful of the car crash Mason's driving would inevitably induce. "You know where to go," Kai directed. He leaned back against the leather and folded his hands together. Mason nodded and the car turned silent as we left Abraham to guard the fortress in which Kai lived. Wherever Mason was driving us was sure to be a one-of-a-kind experience.

During our ride, Kai was mostly interested in what I liked to eat and why. Rosa joined in after my reply of 'I don't really eat fish', claiming that she could have made us all a five-star chowder without even leaving the apartment. I wasn't a huge fan of meat, either. I hadn't been eating anything other than hotdogs and Spam before I fell into Kaia's life.

We pulled up to a restaurant that, truthfully, didn't look very high-end. It was another skyscraper. Was it even a restaurant? The only indication was the shine of bright lights at the top floor, all four of us craning our necks to see. Mason and Rosa opened our doors for us, which shocked me, and Rosa gave me an encouraging smile as I slid out of the car. I could see Mason mumbling soft words against Kai's ear as we walked towards the restaurant. Kai chuckled; Mason laughed. I ogled at the little smirk that remained on Kai's features. Mason was once again working his charismatic magic.

The restaurant was definitely high-end. Even the waitress who had taken our reservation and led us to our seats at the top of the building was a gentle beauty. Decorated with a modern, angled ceiling that showed intricate metalwork and geometry, dark hardwood floors, yellow wood tables, black metal chairs, and a breathtaking view on three sides of the Los Angeles skyline, this restaurant was infested with beautiful women and attractive men who obviously had money to splurge with. Anyone would splurge for the view, I decided. It even blew the view from Kai's bedroom out of the water.

"This is stunning!" I whispered in awe, staring out at the setting sun. God, it was beautiful. Amazing. Gorgeous. Yellows mixed with rich oranges and reds sat far away in the distance, uninterrupted by other buildings. It sent a glowing light across the floors, disrupted by harsh shadows made by the furniture.

Kai couldn't stop the smile that I saw when I looked back at him. Fuck, his eyes had turned golden once again with the sunlight too. We all picked up our menus after a moment of admiring the setting sun, our eyes roaming hungrily over the selections. I realized then that Kai hadn't taken me there for a hearty dinner. He took me here to experience what real food was supposed to taste like.

"I always get the 'Sugar Snap Peas' for the first course," Rosa told me quietly, leaning in towards my shoulder. "What about the other two? There's three, right?" I asked. She and Mason exchanged amused glances. "Mason and I get the 'Handkerchief Pasta' for the second course and the 'New York' for our third." I nodded slowly, looking to Kai for his answer. But he only stared into the sun, the light reflecting off his eyes like gold. "Kai... what are you planning to have?" He, who had been staring at the blinding sun, suddenly seemed to notice that he wasn't sitting alone. The man gave a small reassuring smile to hide that fact. "I always get what Mason gets."

I pouted slightly. He hadn't even looked at his menu.

Dinner was lively. Mason laughed with Rosa and I while Kai occasionally added to the conversation. There were so many flavours around us, shooting waves of electricity and excitement through our veins. A bite held so many different tastes and textures, from sugary-sweet, to juicy tang. Kai seemed... suddenly introverted, lost in his own thoughts as he watched the sun finish setting, a crystal glass of sparkling wine between his thumb and forefinger. I watched him trace the base of the wine glass with a slow digit. He couldn't even taste it. Maybe the carbonation gave him a rush like the flavours would have.

"I can't believe you haven't upgraded to a different apartment. Imagine the view that could all be yours," I told him quietly, attempting to start a new conversation as Rosa and Mason occupied themselves. Kai tilted his head to the side with a soft smile. "That is a good idea... isn't it?" I could see that his mind was working. Fuck, I had just given him the idea to literally buy the place, hadn't I? "He's not that rich," Mason chuckled. He was probably right; his *parents* were the rich benefactors.

"Did you enjoy your food, Angel?" he asked suddenly. I nodded and set my chin on my folded hands comfortably. We weren't necessarily full, but the haze around us was certainly satisfying. "That was amazing. I wish my mother could have tried that. She used to cook all the time, you know?"

"Oh?" Kai's interest was piqued. I wondered why I had never told him that much about Teressa Roggy. "She always told me that before I was born, my dad couldn't get her out of the kitchen. She had always been very experimental with her cooking. She loved it."

"Does she still have the same passions?"

My face fell slightly; I looked away. Not since she got pregnant and my father had walked out on the both of us. Being pregnant with me ruined her love of cooking. "Not really... she just got busy with other stuff, I guess."

Kai took that as an answer, to my surprise, and nodded encouragingly. "That happens to the best of us."

The sun had fully set by the time we were escorted back to the lobby. During the dinner, our energy had been exhausted by our laughter and conversation that went on long after we completed our meals and the sun had finished setting. Kai slipped into the back of the *Bentley* with me once again, but this time, I was pulled against his side. My mind fogged with grogginess. I could only lean into him, pressing my cheek against his shoulder. Jesus Christ, he smelt like melted dark chocolate and fresh-ground coffee beans, the perfect balance of sweet, savoury, and bitter. The man, who was quite tired, too, took my hand and rubbed a thumb over my knuckles. I wondered if his touch was laced with a sedative.

Then we were pulling into the garage. It seemed as though we had only just left the restaurant. I was too tired to care. My eyes had fluttered shut, and I found comfort in the warm arms that wrapped around my body to lead me into Kai's beautiful home. The bright lights and the fact that I was forced to use my legs woke me up. The elevator hummed under our sluggish feet for a moment; I opened my eyes to watch the numbers at the doors count each floor. Then we were walking over hardwood floors. Kaia paused long enough to remove my shoes once we were safe in his bedroom.

"I can do that," I mumbled as he knelt to untie them. Really, I wasn't sure if I actually could.

The couch he had dropped me on allowed me to sink and my mind to fade. Eventually, he managed to remove my footwear and suit. When I was finally allowed to sleep, I was only in socks and boxers.

I wasn't even awake long enough to feel Kai, through a yawn, slip me into the sheets of his bed.

CHAPTER
TWENTY-THREE

I WOKE WITH A heavy heat pressed against my bare waist. It was *hot*. I stirred lightly before I froze, my eyes widening when a sudden realization hit me in every body part at once. The scent of chocolate and coffee encased me like a cloud. His breath tickled the top of my head like a feather.

Kai wound his arm tighter around my waist.

I inhaled a deep breath and rolled over, my lungs quickening when his nose nearly touched mine. His smell was so strong, it almost burnt my nose. I noticed a tiny hint of a musk I could only detect when I was so close to him.

"Did you sleep well?"

I nearly jumped from the bed in surprise at his question. Conversation before sex this morning, then? "Y-Yeah," I stuttered, flustered. I felt long fingers digging into the hollow of my hip. "Good," he breathed, his nose grinding into his pillow. My brows immediately pulled together. People in a relationship did that. I never thought of us, as a Dominant and submissive, as people who would someday share an actual bed for anything other than sex. "Um- uh, y-yeah," I mumbled nervously, pushing him away slightly. It was wrong, I decided. Kai shouldn't ever be treating me like he was. There was nothing but business between us, even if I wanted more with all my heart.

"No...," he commanded, his fingers suddenly digging into my hip, pulling me flush against him. He was only wearing boxers; his morning erection pressed against the back of my thigh. "Stay." His voice was almost pleading the second time, as if he really, with all his heart, did want me there with him as the sun poured golden light onto us and the blankets.

"Why?"

My voice was tired and cracked, but that would change once I had brushed my teeth and taken a shot of water. Damnit, I didn't even have a toothbrush here.

"Just... don't leave."

Toothbrush forgotten, I suddenly realized the severity of the situation. Kai wasn't ordering me into bed, he was asking me. Right at that moment, I wasn't his slave, I was his friend. A lover, even. I stilled, my hands resting lightly against his firm chest, feeling the steady beat of his heart under his dark skin. Kaia had shaved his chest too. The skin was soft.

"Why?"

There was a silent pause. I could physically feel it, like the air between us had been sliced with a knife. "Why are you doing... this?" The thoughts I wanted to say couldn't be put into words. I could only do my best to make him understand that I felt like an alien in his life. I would never understand how he could want anyone like me in his bed for anything more than sex. I looked up to him with a searching gaze. He stared back, his cold orbs searching just the same. I wondered what he could be thinking about when his eyes looked so torn.

"I need to get up. I have a meeting in an hour," he said suddenly, the covers flying away from him as the heat left. I missed his warmth in a second. I was freezing in the massive bed alone, reeling from his sudden departure.

"B-but, wait, Kai!" I exclaimed. I needed an answer. For so long,

ANGEL

I had convinced myself that I was worthless, that we lived so far under the poverty line that we had no hope of ever earning a place in society. But that changed when I met Kaia. He made me feel safe and special. Important. Proud of who I was and hopeful for my future.

"Luka," he whispered, turning quickly with a knee supporting him on the bed. His words suddenly held a calming edge to them, softer than before. I watched with massive eyes as he put a warm, calming hand on my cheek. His thumb momentarily traced my cheek bone. "Sleep, Luka."

Then he was gone, picking his discarded shirt off the floor and darting into the bathroom, the door locking behind him.

....

Well-rested and lonely, the next time I woke, the digital clock beside Kai's bed told me that it was nearing noon. I had been unexpectedly tired, and I still was.

"Are you hungry, Mr. Lucika?" Rosa asked.

I swivelled my head around, the bright light perforating my vision as I attempted to smile at her. "G'morning, Rosa," I mumbled. Her noise must have woken me, I decided. She sighed and smiled back. "You've slept for a long time. Do you want any water? Breakfast or lunch, maybe?" I should have been getting up. I should have been going home and doing laundry for my mother. But, oh, it was just too hard to leave those sheets. "Can I get a glass of water?" I asked, motioning to the tray she had brought with her where a tall pitcher had been placed, the condensation dripping steadily down the sides. It promised a cold, refreshing glass. She nodded and immediately poured me my water before handing it to me, taking a seat on the bed beside my bundle of sheets and cross-crossing her legs.

"So where's Kai?" I asked, attempting to make conversation.

It must get boring working there alone with only Abraham and a few neighbours to entertain her while Kaia and Mason went out on the town. She probably never saw many new faces before me… or maybe there had been lots like me. Maybe there still was.

"He's at the office location downtown for about thirty minutes before he gets to a meeting across town and then spends a late lunch with an important guy from somewhere in Japan." She waved her arms as she spoke in a bored tone. I smiled as I listened intently. Rosa was a good listener and a good speaker. She was like a teenager and a ninety-year-old combined to create an empathetic, diligent, playful, and witty woman, an amazing person I wanted more than anything to call a friend.

"What are you looking at?" she asked suddenly. I continued to watch her with a small smile playing on my lips, although my eyes lost their dazed focus.

"Can we be friends?"

Her brows furrowed at my question.

"I thought we already were!" She said that as if I had asked if water was wet.

I giggled, leaning my head into her shoulder. "I'm happy that that's a fact."

She sighed with amused contentment. The silence hung between us for another few minutes, enveloping us comfortably, before Rosa spoke again. Her voice was low, this time, more relaxed. "You do know that last night was a date, right? I mean, not really, but Kai kinda thought of it as a date?"

I looked at her incredulously. "What?"

"Yeah, seriously! He would be ashamed to admit that he took you on a date with other people, but it was a date."

Kai and I were fucking dating now? How had I never become aware of that?

ANGEL

But Rosa didn't give me time to examine Kai's motives. She pulled me onto my feet, tossed me a pair of sweatpants, and forced a shirt over my head. Then, she led me down the hall and we both stomped down the stairs. The first thing I saw when we both entered the kitchen was my laptop and phone sitting on the counter. I gasped in surprise. "Yes! I can work now!"

Rosa nodded. "Mason picked it up from your house this morning. Found your keys on the counter, figured it was fine if he went in when no one answered the door the first few times he knocked." I dismissed the thought of my mother, since she would have already been at work when Mason arrived, and got to work myself, curling my legs under me on the couch and typing away at the device. I stopped occasionally to scribble notes and dates into the notebook. I would have to give Kai all my work at the end of the month, only a week away, and, in return, be granted a hearty paycheck.

Sometime between then and three-o'clock, Rosa looked up from her puzzle she had begun at the kitchen island and suggested that then would be a good time to cut my hair. After a moment of debate, I decided that I deserved a break and an excuse to put on music. "Do you listen to music?" I asked as Rosa pulled a container of hair pins from under the sink. "Yeah, but it's mostly classical. Not so much of the pop music that you probably listen to." I shrugged and tilted my head to the side, a devious glint in my eyes. "Guilty."

Rosa sat me down in a chair in the centre of the kitchen and wrapped a large plastic cape around my shoulders to keep my hair away from my clothing. I flinched slightly when she began to cut, but quickly stilled. I didn't want her to butcher it. I could feel her pinning up thick locks and pulling on other chunks. The amount of hair that fell to the kitchen floor was alarming, and she obviously wasn't just giving me a trim.

Eventually, Rosa did finish. She didn't cut it too short, either.

In fact, she only cut it slightly shorter in the back and on the sides. It was styled away from my eyes temporarily. Now that it wasn't so long, I could easily run my fingers through it and push it back without it falling back into my eyes so quickly.

"Ah! I love it!" I bounced happily as I stared at the mirror in my hand while a heavy beat urged me on from a speaker on the white countertop. Secretly, I was absolutely ecstatic for Kai to see my new hair. What would he think of it?

Whatever he thought about it, I would find out soon, because that was when the elevator signalled a new arrival.

"Damn, I like the hair, Luka," Mason said the moment his feet touched hardwood, instinctively bending to help Rosa sweep my hair into the waste bin. She thanked him for his help. "Thanks!" I replied, jumping slightly when a hand gripped my hip suddenly. I turned, looking up at Kaia with hopeful eyes. I was silent as his gaze swallowed my hair, his brows furrowed, giving little indication to what he was really thinking. Then his fingers reached up and flicked it away from my face lightly before I gathered the courage to speak up. "Do you like it?"

"I don't know what I was trying to picture when I thought about you getting a haircut...."

My face fell slightly. He obviously didn't like it as much as I hoped he would.

"But... I like it. It suits you."

My face immediately lit up; I smiled at him brightly.

I was about to move away from him to help Rosa and Mason clean up the mess I had helped make, but he suddenly pulled me back to his chest, thick arms wrapping around my waist like chains. His breath tickled my ear as he spoke, inducing goosebumps that decorated my upper arms.

"I also want to bring you somewhere tonight... if you'll let me...."

CHAPTER
TWENTY-FOUR

"BRING ME SOMEWHERE? Tonight?"

His voice was low, and I would be lying if I said it didn't scare me, but it was comforting just the same. "There's a club close to here that I want to bring you to. A BDSM club." I wasn't surprised that he would visit a place like that. There were probably lots of people that would cling to a hunk of meat like him there. The thought suddenly made me furious. "It's 'BYOT' night," he added. "So what does that mean?" I asked hesitantly. Kaia smirked. "Bring your own toy." But then his gaze turned soft and kind, hopeful. "I know that I really shouldn't be asking you this early. I mean, you did alright at the sex shop, but... I think you're ready for it. It's actually kind of fun once you get into it. We don't have to do a scene or anything if you aren't comfortable. I don't like doing scenes there, anyway."

I thought for a moment before shrugging. How bad could it be? "I've been to a club before."

Kai turned sheepish. "Yeah... I figured that, I guess."

"Ha. Gay," Mason chimed in, smiling lamely around a spoon of peanut butter. The two of us rolled our eyes.

The only thing that scared me, I realized, was how easily I would follow him.

I didn't know what to expect when Kai handed me a large paper bag that night.

In the bathroom, I gasped in surprise, though. It was sheer. Obviously, it was the finest clothing that could be bought; a pair of black jeans sewn with glittering gold threat and sleek black sneakers. The pants hugged me like a second skin. A dark mesh tank-top with a solid black piece of fabric only thick enough to cover my nipples completed the look. I felt like a stripper... a hooker. "Is it supposed to be this... revealing?" I called from his bathroom as I stared at myself in the mirror. That top was bothering me...

He entered a moment later; I blushed harshly as his gaze roamed over my body with a sudden hunger. "Yes. You look...," he trailed off, coming to turn me around and let his fingers ghost down my stomach. I shivered, completely forgetting the shirt. His finger tips could be felt through the mesh.

"Stunning."

My exhale burnt my nose even more than his touch. "I'm putting on a tank-top under this," I informed him evenly. The man chuckled. "Okay." It was easy to find one of his, since I didn't happen to have one with me. He was amused more than anything, especially since I had not yet realized what he was holding. It shone bright in the fluorescent bathroom lights. The metal glittered like a beacon, drawing my attention to it quickly. It was placed on my neck while both of us smiled with satisfaction. This time, my hair didn't get caught in the clasp.

Kai drove us to the club in a new car: a black *Maserati*. The seats in it were most comfortable, but I barely noticed that fact. I was too preoccupied with the man sitting beside me. "Are you nervous?" he asked. I shook my head while simultaneously pulling

ANGEL

on my knuckles in my lap. Sure, I had been to clubs, but none with a partner. He sighed. "Don't be." Would I be competing with others for Kai's affection? Would Kai want to sneak away with someone with more experience, someone more eager than myself? I was delighted to experience a club for the first time with Kai, but eagerness didn't make up for a lack of experience.

We pulled up beside a large building piled high with rentable living spaces. The ground floor was the club, designated by a large neon sign that read '*El Oculto Agujero*' in uppercase letters. It was one of the only lit places on the secluded street, save for the taco truck at the end to cater to the late-night bar scene.

"Are you sure you're okay with this?" he asked before we stepped out of the car. Kai had dressed himself in a pair of ripped blue jeans and a white t-shirt that hugged his muscles perfectly. I nodded and swallowed hard. I certainly wasn't scared, but insecurities and wariness did hold me back. "You're not okay with this," he said finally, after a moment of gauging my reaction. His eyes held guilt when he recognized what he obviously thought was a bad idea. "I'm sorry. I know I was walking a thin line here. I made a mistake."

He slipped his keys back into the ignition.

"N-No!" I said quickly, putting a hand on his arm. He looked back at me with furrowed brows. *Stop being a fucking pussy, Luka.* I took a deep, shaky breath and glanced at the club, working my knuckles furiously.

"No. It's okay. I've been here before. I just… I don't know, do you actually do scenes in these places?"

He gauged my features again before letting out a deep sigh. "No. I mean, yeah, I have with others, but I would never force you to do anything. Besides, we didn't even bring our own toy. Didn't think you'd want to." He allowed us to step out of the car, wrapped his arm around my shoulder once again, and watched me smile at the warmth. "Okay."

The interior of the club was much different than the exterior. Men and women bustled about, laughing and chatting together. I ogled at them. They weren't dressed in black leather or metal like in the movies. They wore normal clothing, as if they decided to come here with their partners after a long day at work. That's probably exactly what they were doing. For a moment, my senses were overwhelmed. So many colours surrounding me, blending with the heavy bass of a house mix. There were definitely more female submissives than men, judging by the amount that wore bulky, obvious collars, but I didn't feel so out of place when I saw a boy, roughly my age, flirting with a middle-aged man in the corner. He wore clothing similar to mine. Security guards stood beside each door, especially the large entrance to a hallway at the back of the bar to ensure that there were no underaged children trying to find their way inside. People walked to and fro, ignoring the guards dressed in black shirts and decorated with rippling muscles. They probably didn't see much belligerence in a place that demanded so much respect, but I had noticed at least a few people who were known on the corner as trouble. The building brought me straight back to my roots.

"Wow," I breathed, my eyes wide. Where to start? With Kai, the building held endless possibilities. The lights shone brighter. The music was more invigorating.

"Kai! You brought him!" A familiar voice interrupted my ogling.

Alice bounded around Kai and wrapped her arms around me. I leaned back slightly, surprised. Alice was dressed in a sheer black corset, embroidered with glinting jewels and dark-purple lace. Her black jeans gave no need for imagination. The look was tied together with a layer of glossy purple lipstick, low pigtails, and a pacifier strung around her neck with a strip of white leather.

"I-I didn't know you were part of this whole... BDSM thing," I

ANGEL

said nervously, smiling sheepishly as Kai wrapped an arm around my waist. Shouldn't I have expected it? I glanced up when a long pair of arms wrapped around Alice's shoulders, a cigarette hanging between the fingers of the woman behind her. "These your friends, baby?" The woman's half-masted eyes were done with sparkling reds and devious blacks, glinting gold in the lights of the club; her wild makeup matched her fiery-red hair. She brought her cigarette to her cherry lips and blew out a long puff of smoke. It curled into the air and up around her narrow nose. "Yeah. This is Luka," Alice replied, motioning to me with excitement. The utter energy that rolled off such a tiny girl was slightly terrifying. The woman, who I then assumed was her partner, obviously knew Kaia already. "Hey, Luka," she regarded me with disinterest. I smiled at her.

"Can we go get drinks now, Mommy?" Alice asked the woman, looking up at her innocently. The woman nodded. "Let's go, baby."

'Mommy' took Alice under her arm and turned her away towards the massive bar in the centre of the crowded club.

"I didn't think Alice had a Dominant," I said. Kai shrugged. "She always has been a sub, and I think she always will be. Some people outgrow it, but I think she'll stay as a little for a while," he replied as my gaze drifted over the club again. I would have to ask Kai what a 'little' was later.

In each corner of the club, a metal pole was erected from the floor and raised on a large table. They were all occupied by women at that moment. So it was a strip club, too? They have undergone renovations since my last visit. Kai noticed my staring and decided to correct my suspicions quickly. "They're open for anyone who wants to give a show. Some nights there's a big lineup for them."

"Oh...," I said, directing my gaze towards a sofa beside the door where a small group of young women eyed Kai, among other men around us, searching playfully for a friend for the night. They were beautiful. I resisted the urge to tell them off. One met my eyes and quickly found another person to set their sights on.

"Don't mind them. You're mine, Angel. Mine only."

He pulled me away from the couch and through the throngs of people towards the bar.

"Arche!? Is that you?"

The aging bartender suddenly perked up when he saw Kaia, obviously recognizing a familiar face. "John," Kaia greeted with a smile. "Damn, Kai it's been a while since I've seen you here. A year, maybe?" He slid a beer across the counter to a man waiting beside us before he could give us his full attention. "And who do we have here?" he looked between Kaia and I with a raised eyebrow. Kai smiled proudly and set his hands on my shoulders. "This is Luka. He's new."

"Ah...," John nodded. "Can I get you two anything? We have a special tonight. And it's on the house for new kids... if you're old enough. I assume he only got in because you got friends here, huh?" he said, motioning to me. Just because I was old enough to consent to sex didn't mean I was old enough to drink. I glanced at Kaia before he nodded, proud. "One special for him, then. Can you water it down a bit?" Neither of the men seemed to mind my adolescence as long as we all stayed responsible. John immediately got to work as we each took a seat at the bar. It was a massive wooden square, manned by a total of six bartenders. Once again, my gaze drifted to the poles in each corner of the room. Their occupants weren't really dancing; they were more giving lap dances from across the room. Their eyes roamed easily, not trained to one person, so they were obviously hoping to catch someone's attention.

"Here ya go, kid," John smiled and slid me the glass. "Thanks," I mumbled in reply, bringing the glass to my lips with a shaky hand. It was bitter at first, but then the flavour faded into a tangy fruit taste.

ANGEL

Kai had been watching the club, seeming to look for something. I knew he had found it when he looked back to me. "I'll be back in a minute. I'm getting a cigar," he said. I bit my lip and nodded as he stood and walked away quickly. I already wanted him back.

We seemed to be in a relationship different than just a play date. We were... more. Like Rosa said, he had apparently taken me on a date, more or less. Maybe she was right. Would Kai ever go for a boy like me? A boy who's only wish was to make a little cash? But I didn't want the cash as much as I wanted him anymore. The only thing that stopped me from becoming completely reliant on him was the constant pull of the thought of my mother at work. She would probably be home by that time. Dinner was waiting for her in the fridge.

"That's a plain collar," a voice interrupted my thoughts abruptly. Out of the corner of my eye, I could see John looking up too. The man couldn't have been a day older than Kaia. Chocolate-brown hair greased back and warm hazel eyes alienated him from the exotic faces in the club. His cheekbones were slightly low on his narrow face, which would have given him a more round face, if not for his slab of a jawline. His lips turned up in a kind smile. I could remember that smile from somewhere, although I was sure that my memory was playing tricks on me.

"Yeah... I guess it is a little bit," I mumbled, my finger immediately pulling at the dark leather lightly. He hummed as he stared at it. Yes, I was sure I had met this man before. His voice was hauntingly familiar.

"My name's Cade." He held a large hand out for me to shake.

I took it hesitantly. "Luka."

His grin widened, revealing a gold canine. It glinted with malice in the low light of the club. "So you came here with a friend, I'm guessing?" he asked. I nodded.

"Yeah, he just... moved away for a minute. He'll be back soon."

As I replied to him, John slid me water and continued to occupy himself with drinks, but I could tell he was listening to our conversation intently, probably watching out for his friend's sub. I prayed to god that he would intervene soon.

"I'm glad such a pretty thing has a dom... or sub."

"Yeah... right...."

"So, a collar, huh?" he asked.

It seemed like such an intimate question, and I wasn't sure if I wanted to answer. So I nodded, looking away. I flinched slightly but managed to keep my composure when his hand reached out to feel the soft leather of my collar. My eyes were wide with fear. Something about the man was odd. Working with people like him for years gave me good common sense, and I knew I had to listen to my gut feelings. But something about him was so... paralyzing. I *remembered* him from somewhere.

I could finally breathe when he pulled his hand back and stuffed it in his pocket. "It's... pretty."

There was a moment of uncomfortable silence between us, but he covered the awkwardness with another smirk.

"Well, Luka, if-," but Cade was cut off.

"How about you get lost, Cade? He's got a collar. Let him be." Finally, John has come to my aid.

I flashed him a stiff smile as Cade's eyes darkened and he straightened his jacket. Then he smiled back, although his looked much more convincing.

"Have a good night then, Luka. John."

Neither of us replied.

Then the man was gone as quickly as he appeared, and replaced by Kai almost as fast. I couldn't help but stare in the direction he left in, fading silently into the crowd.

ANGEL

Kai held a cigar firmly between his teeth. He puffed his chest out slightly. My hand wandered to the collar once again as John eyed Kai. "What?" he asked, noticing my hesitant starting. But my eyes suddenly widened when I realized that I knew exactly where I had seen Cade. He had been a customer of mine, one that had been rather kind. He had always paid a little extra and made sure we *both* finished with satisfaction. But we had never encroached on anything pertaining to this new lifestyle, so seeing him here confused me. The man must have recognized me.

"Nothing."

CHAPTER
TWENTY-FIVE

WE SPENT THE next few minutes chatting at the bar. But my eyes never strayed far from the hallway people entered and exited regularly. It seemed to be the busiest place in the club. "Are the scenes back there? Last time I was here, that space was closed." I said suddenly, setting down Kai's drink that I had been sipping at. I was probably a little bit tipsy by then, but what did it matter? Kai would bring me back home for my mother to take care of me if I got too drunk. Kai turned in his chair to follow my gaze before he looked back to me with hungry eyes. "You want to see?"

I nodded before he took my hand and quickly led me towards the hallway.

My mouth dropped to the floor.

There were three rooms, each of them holding different kinds of BDSM equipment. Whipping equipment, spanking benches, and suspensions filled the rooms, and even a cage sat in the corner of one of them. Vents decorated the walls to allow the circulation of new air. Men and women crowded around the equipment, leisurely indulging in the scenes that were taking place, occupying every one of the pieces that fit in the space.

"Do you ever come to watch them?" I asked as I witnessed a

girl count her last hit. Her flesh was fiery. Her Dominant, a man who looked old enough to be her father, leaned in towards her tear-streaked face to whisper comforts against her ear as he unbuckled her wrists and ankles. A few onlookers smiled joyfully at the pair. We couldn't recognize them, though, even if we knew them, because the man's face was covered in a black leather mask. The woman wore a small one over her eyes. It was never required, but I understood why people would want to hide their identity, even in a safe space.

"That's what this club is for. So people can feel comfortable enough to be themselves around each other outside their homes," he replied, setting a hand on my back. "Oh," I said quietly. "Do we have to do a scene? I... I don't think I can do that." The thought terrified me. How could anyone do something so intimate and private in front of so many people? I understood the poles in the front, but... My breath quickened at the thought. "No, of course not, Angel. Not if you don't want to," he replied gently.

I breathed a sigh of relief.

"Let's go back to the bar. I want another cigar," he added, leading me away with haste. He seemed to have sensed my urgency to escape those rooms. Once at the bar again, I downed another one of Kai's Moscow Mules and glanced repeatedly towards the poles that people danced on. Damn, I could go for some dancing right at that moment. The alcohol was obviously toying with my brain and nerves, firing them up for *something*.

"Do you mind?" I asked monotonously, motioning to the pole closest to us. He looked at me incredulously, obviously not believing my sudden nerve as he brought one of John's thick cigars to his lips. He just wasn't aware of my inability to hold my liquor. Kai shrugged and nodded after a small pause, watching my actions closely as I set my drink on the polished wood and stood on surprisingly solid legs. I was lucky to be able to slip up onto the pedestal quickly and silently, ignoring the glares I received from others who wanted a turn. The line I had chosen was short, so kicking someone off and finding a place above them wasn't too hard. A radio remix blasted from speakers in the floor, vibrating the walls around us and pumping energy through anyone within a one-mile radius.

I had never learnt how to pole dance. I hadn't even seen it done outside of magazines and the rare television show. But I had seen enough to know that if I made it at least relatively sexual, then I would do okay. I just wanted to dance, and I had the perfect audience.

I started with a slight sway of my hips, feeling the familiar beats worm their way into my muscles and veins, the metal pole acting like an energy conductor. The people faded away around me, churning into a single sound that was finally dissolved by the music. I sighed and held my arms against the cold metal cylinder as I flirted around the pole, curving my spine deliciously and catching eyes scandalously. The metal was cold, but the warm air around me kept my body hot and sweaty. The smoke in the air was intoxicating, but my mind was already hazy with the effects of the alcohol. I did workouts in my room during the day, simply to keep up appearances, but I could see how pole dancing was such an intense exercise.

Then my gaze met Kai's.

I gave a slight moan, my cheeks reddening before I realized the sound had been drowned by the music and crowd. A few men and women had gathered around my feet, grinning widely. An attractive brunet licked her lips as I executed a small twirl. But I didn't notice them in the least. There was only Kai, the energy, the music, and myself. I crouched in front of the pole slowly before standing again, feeling my thighs ache and my stomach roll. It all blended into the haze.

He had never looked so handsome. I was completely sure, even just for a second, that he felt the same way about me. His jaw was slightly slack, something I had never seen before, and his eyes were glazed with a sudden, uncontrollable lust. His usually perfectly slicked hair was slightly disheveled, and to top it all off, his boner was plainly noticeable. Even from there. The sight of him had me panting and aching for *him.*

But the moment ended quickly when I turned my head away, letting myself drop onto the floor lithely as hungry gazes followed me. The show had been brief; there were obviously other people who wanted a try. I had actually just done that. The realization hit me like a wall. I had pole danced, more or less, in front of dozens of people. In front of Alice. In front of John. In front of Kai.

And it hadn't been that bad, had it?

I bounced back to him, melting into the crowd as they returned to their own socializing and drinks. I gasped when his arm suddenly wrapped around my waist tightly and he began pulling a thick wad of cash from his pocket. He slammed it onto the slab of wood with his cigar and growled, "We're leaving." The man's eyes were black and territorial, glaring at anyone who glanced his way.

Even my mother, who had very few fears, would have been scared of Kai then. The group who had previously been eyeing the both of us flinched and looked away before Kai pushed me out of the club with his lips slightly pulled over his teeth in a snarl. "Look, I-I'm sorry, I d-didn't-," but he cut my confused apology off with a sudden, rough bite to my neck, digging his canines into my soft flesh, undoubtedly creating marks.

I gave a small whimper, the pain bringing tears to my eyes, before he licked the wound with a thick, wide lap of his soft tongue and a kiss. The sound ended in a small moan-like hum. Then Kai kissed me again, twice, on the collar bone, hurried and urgent. He hadn't told me he was into biting.

"We're leaving," he told me in a low, gruff voice. "O... kay?"

Kai took my hand in his, squeezing it until my fingers ached and they turned a dangerous shade of purple. His urgency scared me. He acted as if he didn't get me back to his home within the next thirty seconds, his control would finally come to an end. And I believed it. He all but threw me into his car, barely making sure my seatbelt was locked in place before he sped towards his apartment. My white-knuckle grip on the door was the only thing that kept me from crying out in shock and confusion.

We made it to his garage in two minutes flat, thanks to his disregard for yellow lights. My eyes strayed to the bulge in his lap. Once the engine was cut, he had pulled me onto his lap in under a second, pushing my thighs apart until I straddled him uncomfortably. it didn't feel much worse, though; my thighs were already aching from my show. His lips were on my skin just as fast as his driving; the man was licking, biting, and creating red marks that would last until at least tomorrow. Kai never sucked anything more than a sunburn-like bump into my skin. They faded within an hour, usually. The more he did that, the more I realized I loved being marked by Kai. It showed the world, preferably not my mother, though, that I was his, and his only.

I moaned, the alcohol numbing my senses until the only thing that existed on this planet was Kai and his mouth. His actions made my stomach clench and my teeth dig into my lower lip, drawing emotions and noises from deep within the recesses of my body. His lips were so soft, yet they had firm muscle to back them up when he needed. His tongue was rough and wet, a perfect combination for playing with my nipples until I was a drooling mess. "K-Kai!" I cried when he bit down rather hard on one of my sensitive buds as his hands mapped my body, gliding up and down along my spine. By then, both buds were slightly bruised and swollen, oversensitive, and aching for a break. He let his tongue loll around it, before pushing

ANGEL

it in and biting it suddenly. It was then rolled between his teeth like a candy. "Kai, pl-please, it... h-hurts!" It was agony to be in so much pain and experiencing so much pleasure in the same moment.

He gave a final lap at my chest before I felt a hand dip into the back of my shorts, the jean buttons being torn as he fought his way inside. I shouted when a finger was licked and buried to the knuckle without warning. "Kai! Hurts!" The pain came more from surprise than anything else.

Suddenly, he went still, pulling his hand away and gripping onto my hips tightly. I already missed his mouth and his hands. Why the fucking hell did he stop? That pain had been so good. His forehead rested against my chest, and I could feel his heavy breathing against my stomach. I wanted him to return to what he was doing to me immediately, and I knew he did, too, because his hands continued to squeeze and loosen repeatedly against my skin, as if he had to grab onto me in order to stop himself.

"Goddamnit," he cursed.

"Kai?"

"We can't do this. Damnit!"

"Wh-What? We can't...?" Did he suddenly not want me? Maybe he changed his mind about the whole 'sex' thing tonight. Maybe all the lust in his eyes was just a small faze induced by his downstairs brain instead of his upstairs one. The realization made my heart ache and my lip stick out in a hurt pout.

"Kai?" I asked again. "Why can't we?"

Finally he looked up, anger and amusement swirling together in his gaze. "Because you're drunk."

"I am not!" I gasped, appalled.

"You pole danced. You are very drunk."

"B-but... why?! What are you-," but I was cut off when he leaned back, throwing his head over the headrest behind him with a deep, frustrated groan.

"You're drunk, Luka. It'd be illegal if I had sex with you now. I'm sure you'd be totally into it if you were sober, but if I'm not mistaken, it would probably be rape now." I frowned, still distracted by his stiff erection that sat between my thighs, covered by overrated jeans. If I was sober, I would be able to realize that consenting to anything regarding BDSM would have been so incredibly dangerous; Kai was doing the right thing.

I was *totally* sober.

That was the same moment I suddenly felt the bile rise in my throat. My eyes widened. Panic set in. I had a split second to think, and instead of leaning over the side of the car like I should've done, my body tilted to the left.

I puked all over the shiny leather shotgun seat of his one-hundred-thousand-dollar *Maserati*.

CHAPTER
TWENTY-SIX

I WAS MORTIFIED, EVEN after Rosa's continuous insisting that all was fine. Mason told me with a smirk that Kai could replace his car, but I could never relive a party, before Rosa slapped him over the back of the head angrily. "Don't encourage him!"

Kai remained quiet, leading me upstairs with an arm around my waist. My hand was practically glued to my mouth, constantly covering it. Maybe I was blocking the putrid smell of alcohol and stomach acid. Maybe I was terrified that I would throw up again. I wasn't sure.

"Luka, it's fine that you threw up. Honestly, I would be worried if you were able to hold it in for the whole night," Kai told me. How the fuck was that supposed to make me feel any better?

He sat me on his bed, disappearing in his bathroom for a moment before he returned with a toothbrush, toothpaste, and a glass of water. "Drink it all." His words were an order. I sighed before throwing the water back. I grimaced slightly as it found its way down, but at least I no longer had the urge to vomit. "There. Now brush your teeth and we'll change you into some more comfortable clothing, hm?"

Once the water had settled slightly and my teeth were brushed, I was more aware of my slurred speech and hazy vision. Damnit, I *was* drunk. Had I ever even been tipsy before? Mom never kept alcohol around the house, so there were really no other opportunities. "Arms up," he ordered, pulling my revealing top over my head and replacing it with a massive t-shirt that fit larger than a dress would have. A band shirt. *Iron Maiden*. "Is this yours?" I asked. He nodded as he bent to slip my jeans off, leaving the boxers. "You like your pop music. I like my rock. My mother used to take me to concerts when I was younger with-," but he stopped himself mid-sentence. My brows furrowed as I waited for him to say a name. His friend? His uncle? His father? ... Her?

He shook his head and gave me a rare, kind smile to cover his agonized features. "I used to see bands live all the time. I save all my band shirts, but I don't keep most of them here."

"Oh...," I said quietly, playing with the hem of his *Iron Maiden* paraphernalia. He spoke to me like a child. I would be lying if I said I didn't like it, actually. It was so comforting, promising ecstasy and rough sex before a bubble bath and rainbows and unicorns later. Screw being drunk, I wanted sex *now*.

I straightened my back, wrapping my arms around his neck to pull him down towards me, before I adhered my lips to his. His eyes opened wide, and he gasped against my mouth. Maybe he didn't want the kiss with me. I had obviously caught him off-guard. Or maybe he was just getting the scent of alcohol and mint toothpaste. I thought maybe he would push away from me, but instead, he wrapped his own arms around my waist and pushed me backwards into the bed, setting a knee between my legs. I moaned when he pushed my arms above my head, trapping my wrists together with one hand and holding my cheek with the other.

God, I would never get used to this mouth. His lips were so soft and firm, brushing over mine like a feather, then applying the

ANGEL

perfect amount of pressure to deepen the kiss. I felt his tongue glide over my bottom lip, requesting entry. I gave it gladly, opening my jaw wider until he could slip his muscle between my teeth.

As he explored every nook and cranny of my hot cavern, saliva began to accumulate between us, mixing our spit together until we weren't sure who's was who's. Kai smelt like chocolate mixed with the finest Cuban cigars tonight, the scent embedding into my skin until my nose nearly burnt. It was so rich and abundant. Even the feel of the overnight stubble against my soft cheeks couldn't compare. His tongue licked a ring around my own before it burned a line down the inside of my cheek and he bit my bottom lip. I gasped in pain and the sudden jolt of blood that flowed to my groin.

Then he pulled away, our breath coming in ragged gasps. His eyes were blown wide and much darker than usual. A thin strand of saliva still connected us until gravity pulled it away from him and it dropped onto my swollen bottom lip.

"Damnit, Luka. Goddamnit," he cursed repeatedly, pushing his face against my neck. "What the hell."

My chest rose and fell heavily. "Being drunk is so underrated. I want you to fuck me," I blurted between gasps. His grip instantly tightened on my wrists and my hip. "If I hear you swear like that once more, I'll take you again, but I promise you won't like it," he growled in reply. It was an empty threat, but the memories that swirled in his eyes ordered me to leave the subject. I took a deep breath and nodded quickly, knowing that he certainly wasn't as angry as he seemed, just tired. "But please?" My erection was painful against my underwear. I could see his just as clearly. He sighed. "I'm not a rapist, Angel. You need to go to bed. Tonight was exhausting for you." There was that fatherly voice again, as if he was talking to a baby.

I pouted and he gave a smirk filled with amusement, leaning

back and allowing my hands to flop back to my sides.

"Sorry, baby. It's time to sleep."

....

My headache the next morning wasn't comparable with any one I had had before. "Jesus," I groaned, turning over and stuffing my face into a hot chest. The thin undertone of cigars and the bold scent told me that it was Kai. I could definitely get used to waking up like this. "If you're going to throw up, do it in the bucket on the floor, not in the bed," Kai told me suddenly. I groaned again. "No. You got any Advil?" I replied. "Advil isn't good for hangovers. You're having water instead. We'll get you an energy drink or something in a while." The man sat up with me to give me a glass of water that had been set on the nightstand. I was surprisingly thirsty.

"You're staying here today. I'm not letting you out with a hangover," he told me quietly. I nodded, my head still hazy. I was tired. And it *hurt*. I didn't have time to swallow back the bile before I suddenly leaned over the bed and let my few stomach contents drop into the plastic red bucket with a splash. So much for that water, then. I went into dry heaves before I felt Kai's large hand massaging up and down my spine, rubbing random shapes into my tense muscles. Still, he was silent. Kai was so different when he was alone with me, quieter. Less boisterous. I had a feeling that Mason fueled a lot of his emotions, good or bad, and without him, I was allowed to see the Kai hidden underneath. It was disturbing, but I realized that this was probably just the kind of guy he was. Privately a teddy bear. Sometimes a teddy bear with crystal meth being smuggled inside, but a teddy bear nonetheless.

When I leaned back, my eyes were drooping and I had to wipe the drool that had accumulated around my lips with the back of my hand. I didn't want to swallow and clean my mouth. When I

ANGEL

did, I winced. My throat was raw and sore, the taste of stomach acid burning and adding to the pain. But Kai wasn't fazed. My head tilted back against his chest and my eyes closed as he worked his thumbs into my shoulders. He was a masseur, too?

"God, that feels good," I moaned, my headache still pounding against my skull. At least I was comfortable. My eyes only cracked when the elevator opened to reveal Mason, smiling brightly with his chin held high. "Good morning, Lucika. Mr. Arche," he greeted, coming to stand in front of us. Kai stopped his massage therapy and I nearly whimpered, only slightly comforted by his arm that was wrapped around my shoulders and pulled me to his chest. "Good morning, Mason. Cancel my schedule for today. I'm staying home," he ordered with a kind, professional smile. "Sure. Even the call you planned to make to Roy? Your dad's been on you to do that forever. Do either of you want breakfast, too? Rosa is making omelettes downstairs."

I looked up at Kai, who immediately answered for me. I was sure I would vomit again at the sight of food. "Yeah, I'll call him tonight. Make some bacon with it, please," he told Mason, who left quickly. Kai's hands returned to my shoulders, working down and then up around my neck slowly. I leaned my head back against his chest again, my eyes closed.

"Do you remember anything from last night?"

His question forced my eyes open, my senses heightening momentarily. Truthfully, I didn't remember as much as I wanted to. I remembered the kiss. The bar. The pole dancing. I shivered at *that* thought. Maybe I had gotten under his skin more than I thought. Could he be feeling the same things I was? That seemed next to impossible.

"I guess. I remember some of it, I think."

He seemed satisfied with that answer, and we both turned silent until Mason returned with a tray of food and Kai had worked his hands down to my tailbone.

"The bacon's hot, so be careful," Mason warned as he set the tray on the bed beside us. There were two glasses filled with a beige liquid accompanying my breakfast omelet and bacon. I realized that they were probably Kai's calorie shakes. "Enjoy," Mason said as he turned on his heel and left us alone again. Kai returned to massaging my lower back muscles, but I quickly shook him off. "We should eat," I told him. Truthfully, the omelet stank and the bacon looked like a meal of grease. Good god, the hangover thing was *not* working for me. I wanted to throw up again just looking at it. But Kai ignored my hesitation, probably understanding my point of view, and instead grabbed one of the glasses. I watched as he tilted his head back and downed it in under ten seconds, the thick liquid gathering in a white moustache on his upper lip before he wiped it away.

"How many calories are in a calorie shake?" I asked. "There's about eight-hundred in one of these, I think," he replied as he reached for the other one. He suddenly seemed to think better of it and instead held it towards me. "Here, try some. Mason has never told me what it tastes like. Smells okay, though." I raised an eyebrow at the glass in his hand, taking it from him hesitantly. I smelled it first, bringing it to my nose and inhaling the musk of what I could only describe as the smell of flour or rice. Of course, there was no need for any added flavours. When I brought it to my lips, I almost puked again. It was cold and repulsively thick. The taste of barley and wheat was most bold, but the undertones of chemicals would leave a bitter flavour for hours after anyone drank it. I leaned back instantly, my face contorting with disgust while an amused smile played on his lips. "That is probably one of the most disgusting things I have ever tasted," I choked out, grabbing a piece of bacon in an attempt to chase the flavour away. "Yeah, I suppose it doesn't look very good. But sometimes Rosa puts crackers or something in it for texture, and I like that," he replied, taking a small sip. I sighed and cut away a piece of the omelet. I was hungry, but unwilling to eat an entire breakfast such as the one in front of me with such an irritated stomach.

"You didn't need to cancel your schedule or anything. I should go home and work, anyway," I told him. He shook his head.

"You don't think a day of relaxation would be nice? With me…?"

CHAPTER
TWENTY-SEVEN

I DIDN'T EAT MUCH of my breakfast after Kai finished his shakes, but he didn't seem too bothered. Mason retrieved the tray and dishes once we had finished and we were finally left alone. He must have had work to do, I was sure. "Is there anything specific that you want to do?" he asked, pulling my blanket off the floor and onto the bed. I smiled and pulled it to my chest. The texture hadn't changed very much over the years; my blanket was still just as soft as it had been when my mother first gifted it to me. "You want to just... relax? I don't know what you mean by 'alone time'," I replied. I was still tired and my throat still burnt. The headache pounding behind my eyes hadn't faded. He shrugged. "Do you want me to run you a bath?" I nodded eagerly, watching as he stood from the bed dressed only in his sweatpants and disappeared into his ensuite. Next, I heard the water running before he returned with a toothbrush and took my hands to pull me to my feet. "Leave the blanket," he said. I tossed it next to his pillow while I began brushing.

"Here we go," he smiled, lifting his band shirt over my head and letting it fall in a pool between our feet. "Are you coming in, too?" I dared to ask once I had spit the bubbled paste into the sink and rinsed my mouth quickly. Hunger suddenly flared in his eyes as his

ANGEL

fingers played with the hem of my boxers and he pulled me flush against his chest.

"Do you want me to?"

"Yes," I replied, biting my lip and looking up at him from under my dark lashes. A devious smirk spread across his face as he suddenly pulled my boxers down and ordered me to step out of the holes. I did so gladly, eager to get him in the tub with me. I didn't mind him undressing me, either. He squatted and balled my boxers into his fist. "Such a pretty boy," he whispered against my skin, pecking a light trail of soft kisses up my thigh. I blushed. He kissed me again.

"Let's get you in the bath then, Angel," he told me, finally standing and letting me step over the edge. The water was hot and filled with lavender-scented bubbles that rose almost too high to fit inside the tub. But I gasped when Kai suddenly dropped one of the bath bombs into the water, turning the bubbles orange. I could feel it dissolving around my feet. It tickled; I giggled. "That's the peach one," he told me as he let his sweat pants fall to the floor. He was right, the lavender scent was mixing with the smell of fresh-picked peaches. "I like your smell better," I blurted without a brain-to-mouth filter. I blushed immediately, but he only chuckled. "Me, too, Angel." I shrieked when he suddenly jumped over the side of the tub and splashed waves of water over the edge. They collected in a puddle around us, but I was certain that neither of us minded.

"I didn't think you'd stick around this long," he mumbled quietly as I turned around and sank back against his hard chest. I watched the bubbles pop with small fizzing sounds. "What do you mean?" I asked, tilting my head back until our gazes connected. I wasn't offended. "I thought it was going to be a one-night thing… I just didn't expect you to be… well, you."

He looked down, eyes searching mine with a hopeful and gentle expression. I wasn't sure how to reply, really, especially with his gaze burning into mine. I was caught, unable to react. The water paralyzed my body.

"I'm saying I want you to stay with me," he said finally.

The man's expression only changed when I rose and flipped myself to straddle his thighs. He was fretting a refusal to his offer. My brows furrowed. "Stay with you? Like... be a full-time submissive? Stay here for more than one or two nights a week?" He gave a smile. "Yes. That's exactly what I'm saying. I'll continue to pay you for your job and you'll continue to stay with me whether you want to keep the job or not. I want you to stay, Luka. I... like your company."

My mouth fell open slightly. Being a full-time sub for a sex god, Mr. Arche? A dream-come-true. Being able to spend so much time with a man who had grown to be a very good friend? A second dream-come-true.

"Yes," I said finally. It wasn't an eager reply, but it was just as sure.

"Yes, yes, yes," I repeated, reaching my arms up around his neck and curling my fingers into his soft hair. I tilted my head and began to kiss his jaw multiple times. "Yes, I'll be your sub. For as long as you'll want me." His arms wrapped around me, pulling me flush against him until I could feel his half-hard erection against my belly. I would be lying if I said I wasn't turned on too. I was in a bathtub with the man who occupied the dreams and fantasies that I never thought were possible.

Neither of us said anything more. He simply buried his head into my neck as we listened to the city around us, our own breaths the only movements rippling the calm waters surrounded by the scent of lavender, peaches, and an insane, unexplained love.

....

When our fingers and toes began to shrivel up, we both decided it was time to get out of the bath. He dried himself first, taking his time to slip a new pair of black sweat pants around his waist before he watched me stand and hop from inside the tub. The man then wrapped a fluffy white towel around me. I held it around my shoulders. My headache had receded. He handed me a pair of his boxers once I had given myself a running start and jumped onto the bed. There, my underwear was followed by a pair of jeans and a loose shirt. Kai folded my towel while we listened to the drain sucking water in the bathroom. His pants, fabric that certainly cost far too much, were only just being done up when Mason suddenly entered with a new tray of food in his hands. I realized it was already close to noon. We had spent almost an hour in that claw foot bathtub.

"Lunch. Rosa has to leave to grab some more groceries, so I'll be downstairs. The video games are callin' my name," he told us with a joyful smile before he left again. I could tell he was trying to stay out of our hair. Lunch was a platter of cheeses, fruits, and meats, releasing a scrumptious scent into the air. It was a smaller lunch, since breakfast hadn't been too long ago. "So, I have a question," I began, popping a cherry between my lips. I curled my legs under me. Kai joined me on the bed and crossed his legs, looking up expectantly as he took a bite of a piece of cheese. I could see why he might be drawn to the gooeyness of it. "I don't know if Mason wants you to talk about this, and I don't mind if it's private, but one of those first few nights he was driving me to and from home, I really triggered him about something, right?" It was hard to find the right words, but I was almost proud of what I had said. I didn't want to be quiet and wallow in the guilt. Kai nodded slowly. "He was upset, yeah. But he was fine."

I bit my lip. "I asked him about his mother. Did something happen between them? He was just... so angry."

Kai sighed, setting down his half-eaten slice of cheese. "Mason doesn't like to talk about it, but I think you should know. His mother was very young when she got pregnant with him, and she knew she wouldn't be able to afford to raise a kid. She was from Hawaii. She got caught up with the wrong people. He was three-years-old when he was forced into a human trafficking ring. Eventually, he ended up in a child soldiers camp across seas somewhere in the east. He was thirteen when he escaped." The pure ease in the man's reply was almost chilling.

My mouth dropped open. "Ch-child soldiers?! What the hell? So she just let them take her own kid?!" Kai nodded. "I chose my housemates for a reason. I help them as much as they help me. My family helped him back onto his feet once he returned to America, seeking shelter. My family took him in, more or less, for a little while."

"That's horrendous. Why didn't he say anything?! I would have never mentioned it if I thought-," but Kai shook his head. "He still struggles with it. No amount of apologies or therapists are ever going to change that. Just treat him as you normally would. He likes you, anyway."

"Really? After the memories I reminded him of?"

"Yeah. You're the first person that Rosa and Mason have really been able to connect with other than Abraham and I. You know they don't get out much."

"So... this means that Rosa has a story of her own? A story about how she met you?"

He chuckled and shook his head. "Rosa was one of Mason's first friends when he moved back to America. I met her through him."

"Oh," I said. That wasn't as badass as I thought it would be.

....

"Do you want to go out tonight?" Kai asked suddenly, looking up from his book. We had been lying on his bed, him reading while I

ANGEL

napped on and off. Kai had gone through two cigarettes during our time relaxing, and I hid myself in his blankets to mask the smell. After the second, he had promised that he had been trying to quit for almost a year. He was down to an average of three a day. On bad days, he admitted to an entire pack. Mason allowed him two packs a week and gave him a few of his expensive cigars if he still had a full pack left by the end of the week. I was proud of him. My mother hadn't tried to quit for years, but when she did, she had almost become a different person.

I reminded myself to ask Mason to drive me home that night, just to check on my mother and possibly make her dinner.

"Not really... can we stay at your house?"

"Sure. Do you like movies?"

I nodded against his side. "I used to watch movies all the time with Mom. But then we had to sell the computer, so no more pirated films for us." He chuckled. "I have a little bit of a selection downstairs. I promise we won't be watching any illegal movies." I peeked up at him from my new home in the sheets. "I'm thankful that my man isn't a criminal." A mischievous glint was evident in my eyes.

I didn't mention the fact that he stole my heart.

CHAPTER
TWENTY-EIGHT

HIS THEATRE ROOM on the main floor of his apartment, just beside his laundry room and pantry, was impressive. There were enough padded recliners for six people, a bar and kitchenette, and an eight-by-six-foot screen. It was by far the biggest in-home television I had ever seen. "A horror movie," I told Kai as he glanced through the movie selections on the tablet beside his recliner. I sat beside him, annoyed with the leather armrest between us. "I don't like horror flicks," he replied. I pouted slightly. "Why not? You've never seen *As Above So Below*? It was my mother's all-time favourite." He shrugged. "I've heard about it. I don't want to watch it."

"Why?"

"Because they're trapped somewhere they can't get out of. They're scared. I don't like watching people get scared."

I stared at him as he fired up his search engine, the lights dimming around us until the only remaining light came from the glow of the screen. He almost seemed as if he was speaking from experience, and the thought of Kai being trapped, alone, and scared alarmed me. But I decided to leave him alone; the man obviously didn't want to expand on the subject. "Can we watch a *Disney* movie instead? Mason likes those."

"You like *Disney* movies?"

Kai's guilty smile was all the answer I needed. I suppressed the laughter that nearly exploded from my chest at this new information and only stared at the man.

"We grew up watching them, okay?"

And at those words, I decided, if this is what being his sub meant, then I would be his sub. Forever. For as long as I could. I leaned against his shoulder, his arm slumped across my lap. His left hand gripped my left thigh, squeezing it when the movie he had chosen at random finally began. I didn't recognize it; Mason and Kaia must have had a plethora of children's films they liked. "Why am I finding it hard to believe that two grown men still watch childish films?" I mused. Kaia snorted and shrugged, glancing at me. "He doesn't like action movies. I don't enjoy horrors. So, it's this or romance," he replied.

"Romance isn't that bad," I chided.

"They can be pretty bad," he chuckled, flashing me a quizzical expression.

"Well, maybe if you stopped talking to Mason and I the entire time you watch a movie, you'd be able to get some good tips on romance. Then you could enjoy it more." My smirk, proof of my pride in my attitude, fell when Kai suddenly dropped the arm rest between us. It melded into the bottom of the couch he had just created before he gripped a lever on the side of his chair and flipped a foot rest out in front of us. He had just turned our two recliners into a bed. I could feel his arm trapping me in a second, clamping around my left hand and allowing him to smother my body with his. As my breath quickened and my brain clogged, I felt Kai's chest touching mine. His face was close too. I could feel his breath against my lips; it was hot and thick. It was another reason why I suddenly couldn't get enough oxygen into my body. "And what kinds of tips would I get?" he whispered. I swallowed hard, struggling to not choke on saliva. The man's teeth glinted in the low light like an animal's.

"Um... I—," but I was interrupted by his lips on mine. At first, my eyes were blown wide open, but I soon succumbed to his kiss. His tongue immediately found its way into my mouth, breaking through the wall of lips, before exploring my gums and ghosting over my teeth. It did a lap around my own muscle, flicking it playfully as his hands travelled down to my hips. I got the message, leaning forward and throwing a leg over his lap to straddle his thighs as people on the screen danced and sang. My hands went to his face, brushing over his chin and landing in his hair to grip the dark strands and pull his mouth closer to mine.

We both froze when a throat was cleared in the corner.

"What do you want, Mason?" Kai snarled, his furious gaze snapping toward his friend. Mason barely flinched, diverting his gaze to the floor, away from Kai's deadly glare. Even I was suddenly scared, my hands freezing on his chin. "James is here. He's waiting in your bedroom." Kai frowned, glancing at me momentarily. His gaze was uncertain; he had a big decision to make.

"Tell him I'm busy today." Hadn't he cleared his schedule?

Mason blanched. My brows pulled together. It wasn't like Mason to be surprised like that. "But Kai...," Mason trailed off, hesitating in front of me. "It's fine, Mason," Kai reassured his friend as he looked at me with an admiring smile. He reached to push a lock of hair behind my ear. "We can cancel our session today. Explain everything to him before he leaves."

Mason nodded, adamant on taking Kai with him to see James, but sluggishly pulled himself out of the theatre. Kai sighed as I relaxed against his chest, still straddling him, and the opening credits began to roll. "Who is James?"

ANGEL

"My therapist. He's also Mason's."

I gasped and looked at Kai incredulously. "What?! And you cancelled your session?! Kai, you can't do that, if you need to talk to a therapist, then-," but he put a hand over my mouth. I continued an attempt to talk through it, but he only tightened his hold, effectively silencing me. I licked his palm. He rolled his eyes.

"It's okay, Angel."

He let his hand slip away and drop onto my thigh once I was still.

"I don't need a therapist right now. I need you."

There was a moment between us when I really understood what he was saying, and I took a second to let it sink in. I wasn't realizing how big of a part I was playing in his life. But that still didn't give him any excuse to skip a session. He had a therapist for a reason. Then his mouth was on my neck, sucking and biting, while he removed his shirt. The moment was over. He would see James tomorrow. "Do you have any lube? Condom?" I asked. He nodded, "Behind you."

I leaned back to reach my hand into the leather pouch hanging on the back of the chair in front of us. He kept a rather large stock of condoms there, and I decided to be happy about it instead of worry over why he had so many condoms scattered around his apartment. "Can I put it on?" I asked timidly, my thighs tightening on either side of his. He nodded as he poured a generous amount of liquid onto his hand. Once he had tossed the lube to the side, he pulled my pants down to fit around my ass and drove his middle finger in to the base. My actions were paused. I bounced my hips slightly, although there was nothing to bounce on, really. One finger never compared to two. And two fingers never compared to dick. But at least he got bored after a few moments and added a second finger, scissoring and twisting them slowly.

I was planning to take my time and maybe blow him a little

while I applied the condom, but that idea had been flung out the window by then. Instead, I unbuttoned his pants to let his erection spring out before I pinched the tip of the condom and rolled it down the pulsing shaft with haste. He groaned at the touch. "Are you ready?" he asked in a husky growl. I nodded and buried my face in his neck, too eager to form a coherent 'yes'.

I yelped, suddenly seeing stars fly across my vision like fireworks, when he pulled my hips down to encase him fully, leaving no space for even an inch. Once I had taken a moment to settle, we began a quick, rhythmic pace that had my eyes rolling into the back of my head. Could my eyes roll further? Yes. Of course they could. My theory was proven when he wrapped his free digits around my length that touched his stomach. My nails dug into his shoulders as he pumped me heartily, gripping me with a kind of force that should have been painful. The pain in my behind was worse, though, blending with the pleasure like a vile potion. The edge was coming soon, I knew. It looked like Kai would get to finish with a blowjob today.

Kai could feel this as I spasmed around him. It only increased the hunger in his thrusts, hitting all the right places every time. I could feel him in my lungs, punching against my diaphragm and stealing my air. I held onto his shoulders to ground me as I met his thrusts; I was worried I would float away if I wasn't careful. "I'm g-gonna come," I breathed before licking two stripes across his neck and latching my lips to his. But he didn't give me the reply I was hoping for. "No, you're not," he breathed, sending new chills down my spine as I gasped against his mouth. His voice was rough and choked; he was just as flustered as myself. "You'll come when I say you can. Don't you dare do anything before then."

But he continued to pump me, his fingers almost begging me to shoot a full load across his stomach. And I wouldn't be able to stop it.

ANGEL

The realization and ceaseless thrusts against my prostate brought tears to accompany the fireworks as soft, broken gasps and cries escaped my throat. Didn't he know that my body, as much as I wished it would, didn't yet know how to obey his orders like my mind could?

I couldn't stop it.

With a loud moan, I came undone, letting hot liquid ooze over his fingers and onto his abdomen. The realization that I had failed to follow his directions, as hard as I had tried, made me want to sob. If I wasn't so busy still taking dick, I would have. It only took a few more thrusts for Kai to ejaculate, the condom swelling and heating up within me. After the breath holding and tensing muscles, he was quiet, pulling me close and panting against my chest. "I-I'm Sorry," I cried quietly, wiping my own tears away. I expected him to be angry. But, instead of introducing me to a new form of punishment, he leaned up and kissed away the watery bullets on my cheeks. They faded with the pain.

"It's okay, Angel," he reassured. Why was he so calm? Why wasn't he mad? Why wasn't he throwing me over his leg to paint handprints on me?

"It takes a while to teach yourself how to do that... I didn't expect you to really be able to... you're fine. You did amazing regardless," he assured in almost a whisper. My crying was only soft whimpering by the time he pulled me across his lap and kissed my forehead. Kai's gaze returned to the screen. He gave me a kind of reassurance that had been so outlandish and unfamiliar before I met him.

....

We left the movie theatre with flushed cheeks and tousled hair. The sex was sensuous, of course, but I could tell that there were some elements that he was starting to miss. We would definitely have to introduce more cuffs and blindfolds soon. This man was much more experienced than myself, and I got the sense that he was missing the sight of a destroyed submissive begging for mercy in that power exchange he dreamed of. I was thankful that he was willing to walk me through his practices instead of dragging me. Together, we took the stairs back up to his bedroom where we met Mason. But he was sitting with another man on one of the couches, and Kai immediately seemed confused. "James," Kai greeted hesitantly as the man stood with a smile.

He was older than Kai and Mason with greying charcoal hair and a wide smile that promised safety and kindness. He was taller than Kai, very lanky, but Kai made up for it with muscle. Those sunken, dark eyes and wrinkled, elongated face behind round glasses creeped me out.

I didn't miss how Kai slightly hid me behind his back. Was he ashamed of me? "Good afternoon, Kai. How was the movie?" Kai hesitated. I almost giggled. "It was fine," he replied finally. Mason stepped in quickly, "I said you would be a while, but he insisted on waiting for you." Kai nodded. James smiled before he caught sight of me. His eyes brightened. Mine flashed with panic. "And who's this?" He looked between Kai and I excitedly. Kai put an arm over my shoulder and pulled me to his side, suddenly seeming eager to introduce us. "This is Luka." Was he proud? Defensive? I wasn't sure. "Ah, Luka! I've heard a lot about you," James said excitedly, holding his hand out for me to shake. I took it and gave it a few satisfying pumps. "Hi." Had Kai been talking about me? All good things, I hoped.

"I thought you'd gone home already," Kai said suddenly. He was rather rude with the tone of voice he had chosen. I glared at him. James wasn't fazed. He simply shrugged and kept his smile.

"You can't skip sessions, Kai. I figured I'd wait until you had time later."

ANGEL

I hit him lightly in the arm. "I told you," I scolded. He couldn't just skip sessions. He needed them. Mason and Kai both did. I would never be as important as Kai's mental health. James chuckled as Kai smiled softly down at me. "Yes, you were right."

"I've already spoken a little bit with Mason. Would you like to catch up for a little while?" James asked, rubbing his palms together. Kai sighed and nodded before turning to me with that sheepish expression, his hand rubbing the back of my neck softly. "Go with Mason and get some dinner, hm?" I diverted my eyes and nodded, following Mason out into the hallway. James was speaking to Kai, but neither of us were paying attention. The last thing I saw before the heavy door closed was Kai's yearning gaze set on mine.

Rosa had finished her four-thousand-piece puzzle by the time Mason had led me to the kitchen: a stunning photo of a flower garden. "I'm gonna make mac-and-cheese with hotdogs for dinner. Are you alright with that?" Rosa asked. I nodded eagerly, overjoyed with the fact that it wasn't just me who ate those kinds of meals. Once given clearance, she set to work in the kitchen as I watched her, sitting on one of the dark wooden stools in front of the island. "It's Mason's favourite. He loves macaroni," Rosa smiled.

"Me?" he asked. The woman rolled her eyes. "No, the other Mason I eat dinner with. Dumbass." Rosa's smirk widened as she poured noodles into her pot. "Yep. He especially likes the shaped ones. You had the *SpiderMan* ones last time, right?" Her eyes narrowed with humorous mischief. Mason rolled his. I giggled, "Macaroni sounds great."

"I'm not saying I don't like them, but I don't think it was the *SpiderMan*-shaped noodles last time," Mason laughed as he took a seat beside me. He tilted his head to the ceiling as if he was trying to remember his previous macaroni meal. "Oh, yeah, you're right. *Disney Princesses*," Rosa said.

"Yes! That's it!" Mason exclaimed with ebullience.

We burst into laughter, only interjected when the phone in the corner of the room rang suddenly. I could tell it didn't get used much when Rosa and Mason looked to it in confusion. The woman picked it up hesitantly, twirling the cord in her fingers. "Hello?"

Rosa's brows furrowed and she looked at me after a small pause. Mason looked between Rosa and I. My gaze had frozen on Rosa's. "It's a Ms. Peach on the line for you. Do you want me to hang up?" My mouth fell open slightly in surprise. I had completely forgotten that I had given Ms. Peach Kaia's home number in case anything happened, like if something turned out bad and I didn't come home. It had taken a little while for me to fully trust Kai, but now his friends were obviously confused as to why someone would have their number and be asking for me.

"N-No, don't hang up," I said quickly, jumping around the countertop and taking it from her.

"Ms. Peach?"

"Boy!? Where have you been? Your mother is worried sick, kid. You've been away for two nights now and she doesn't know where on earth you went. Do you want me to tell her that you'll be gone until tomorrow or something?" Her rolled r's and heavily-pronounced words were familiar. The woman's speech reminded me of hot nights as I rolled around her yard and she playfully yelled at me to get lost. Her 'baby sitting' tactics were certainly questionable; I had seldom been allowed inside her house, and she told me to drink from her garden hose whenever I claimed to be thirsty. But she had been the only person my mother trusted well enough to leave me with.

"No, no, Ms. Peach, I'm coming home now. Is she okay?"

"You know your mother, boy. She's just worried. You've never done this to her before."

It was true. She was a strong and quiet person, but when it came

ANGEL

to me, she knew my normal behaviour, my habits, my schedule. And when I didn't stick to them, red flags immediately went up in her mind. She knew something was up, and she would have to be panicking badly for her to speak to Ms. Peach about her worries. "I'll be there in ten. Just tell her I'm okay, alright?" Ms. Peach made a hum of affirmation, so I hung up the phone as soon as she did. "Mason, can you give me a ride home? Like, now?" I asked, my eyes wide and urgent. Mason and Rosa exchanged a deeply worried glance. "Of course. What happened?" he replied. I shook my head and bounded past him towards the stairs. "Nothing, I just need to get home. Can we go?"

Mason sucked in a breath of air and nodded, pushing his keys into his pocket and following my hasty steps to the garage.

CHAPTER
TWENTY-NINE

"DO YOU NEED me to come in, too?" Mason asked. I shook my head. "No, my mother was just worried." He knew that something else was wrong. I knew I had a long night of explaining to do. Kaia would have to wait until tomorrow. I had forgotten all my work supplies at his house, too, so I would definitely have to get those. Payday was coming soon.

"Are you sure?"

I nodded as he turned onto our street. I was out of the car and closing the door before he had even come to a full stop in front of my house. "I'll talk to you tomorrow, Mason!" I called, waving quickly and turning to run up my driveway before I could get a reply. Inside my house, my nose immediately began to burn. "Mom?" I asked. Cigarette smoke made the air hazy, and it was hot. My eyes watered with the fumes.

"Luka," her grave voice sounded from the living room. I bounded inside and froze, my face falling. My mother was a mess. Her hair was disheveled and thrown up in the messiest of ponytails. Blue bags hung above her cheeks. Her oceanic orbs nearly disappeared in the blood-shot white. She grabbed one of the many cigarettes strewn around her and attempted to light it many times before she succeeded. Her hands were shaking too badly.

"Mom, I'm sorry," I breathed. Fuck, how had I messed up this bad? She looked at the coffee table, her eyes glazed.

"Mom?"

"Where did you go?" Her voice cracked. It was broken, as if she had been gurgling shards of glass. As if she had been crying. Her sudden reply made me flinch.

"What do you mean?"

There was a pause between us before she looked up. "Where the hell did you go? Where have you been? You're... you're lying to me about where you go at night."

Fuck. The headlights were turned on, and they were fucking bright. I was the deer and I could see the impact coming soon. This was the wrong time to tell her everything. Would she even understand? I had to come clean. She was my mother. She told me when I was born that she would love me forever and always. Did that still apply?

"Mom, I'm just... I found a good job, okay? I work for this guy, and he gave me everything I needed for it, so I don't want you to worry."

"What guy? You've been riding back and forth in fucking *Ferraris*!" she exclaimed, standing so fast I thought I had imagined it. I flinched again, scared. When was the last time I had heard her swear? My gaze fell to the floor. "Mom, I'm sorry..."

"Sorry?" she asked incredulously.

I looked back up at her. She was furious. Her eyes glowed with sudden energy, and it wasn't the good kind. "You're sorry you've been keeping your new phone a secret? Or the car rides? Or sneaking out late at night? Or the fucking toy I found under your bed?! You didn't hide it very well, you know. Did he give it to you?"

I nearly collapsed then. My legs had turned to jello. My lungs began to close. When had she been in my room? Why was she even looking at my hiding spot?

"Mom... Mom, I'm sorry. I'm so sorry."

What could I say? I felt as if I was arguing with a stranger. This wasn't my mother. This wasn't a side of her I had ever witnessed before. This was scary. With a deep sigh, she collapsed back into the couch. All the energy in the room seeped away, and she looked more exhausted than ever before. To say I was riddled with guilt was an understatement. She pushed her fingers against her temples, her eyes closed in agony. "Mom... if you want me to leave, I can. But I was just trying to help us. Help you." This was the best apology I could conjure, but I knew that it wouldn't save me if she wanted me out of the house.

"Luka... I'm not mad," she told me finally. Tears were gathering in my eyes by then. "You can stay. I'll never kick you out. You can leave when you want to leave." The breath that had accumulated in my lungs, causing them to scream for fresh air, was suddenly released and replaced with utter relief. "Thank you, Mom," I whispered. I didn't trust my voice to say anything louder.

I turned to leave the living room, not wanting to disturb her anymore. She needed a good night's rest that was uninterrupted by me. And I needed time

"Luka?"

I turned back to her slowly. "Yeah, Mom?" I really didn't want to hear anything more. She brought her cigarette to her trembling lips and took a deep inhale, only letting a long stream of smoke out into the air once it had sat in her lungs for a few seconds.

"Have you met someone?" the woman asked. I realized that *neither* of us could look at each other. "Yes," I replied. "I met him through work." *That* I could tell her. She was allowed to know that I was safe with him. "Are you happy?" she replied. The truthful answer was, "Yes." She sat in my reply for a minute or two. Was she pausing because she didn't believe me? Because I had just come out of the closet to her? I was beginning to panic, frozen in the doorway while I waited for the angry words to come flooding from her mouth.

"You may not see it yet, Lucika... but this guy is going to break your heart. And it will shatter. Just like mine did."

She didn't make any eye contact with me. I searched for her gaze, but I was never able to catch her eye. I gave up after a moment, her words sinking in. How could she know? Kai had promised to keep me as his slave for a while longer; I wouldn't know heartbreak if I stayed with him, I hoped. But her sincerity scared me; it was almost as if she had seen the future. And I didn't care for what she thought she saw.

"Goodnight, Mom," I said finally, rather rudely. I wanted to escape upstairs and hide myself in my sheets instead of facing her. Then I did, turning up the stairs to my room and shutting the door silently. She never looked me in the eyes when I left.

It was hard to fall asleep. Next to impossible, actually, after I realized I had left my beloved blanket at Kaia's house. My phone was also constantly giving me new message alerts. It even rang once, before I quickly turned it to vibrate. Who knew how many calls I got after that? I knew who they were from. I had left Kai when I told him I could stay overnight, and he had probably heard of the dramatic escape I made with Mason. I didn't want to speak with him or Mason or Rosa. I wanted to be alone for a while, knowing that my mother's life was crashing down around her while mine was just picking up. My mother didn't believe in me or my love.

My restless night was riddled with nightmares. Dark ones, lonely ones, scary ones. If Kai was there, he would be able to chase them away. We both would sleep soundly, despite his nightmares. After I woke with a gasp, Kai's name nearly leaving my lips, I abandoned sleep. My mother was upset, I was upset, Kaia was upset, and I was too scared to fix any of it. What if Kai really could break my heart? Would he really leave me for another sub? I was sure he would get bored one day, but I didn't see that day coming anytime soon. Instead of allowing anymore worries to flood my mind, I grabbed my phone off the nightstand and glanced through Kai's messages first.

"*Angel? Mason said you had to leave suddenly. Is everything alright?*"

"*I'm sorry I had to leave you so suddenly.*"

"*Answer me, Luka.*"

"*This isn't funny. Pick up the damn phone, Lucika.*"

"*If you don't reply soon, I'm coming over.*"

I then scrolled through the few messages left by Mason.

"*I stayed there for a few minutes after you went inside, but nothing seemed wrong. Is everything good?*"

"*You should tell Kai that you won't be staying with him tonight. He wants to know these things.*"

"*Luka, Answer Kai. He's walking on the ceiling.*"

"*Seriously, Kai will be over in ten minutes if you don't answer us. He thinks something happened to your mom.*"

After a moment of reading the messages again, the bright screen blurring in front of me, I messaged Mason.

"*I'm sorry. I was sleeping.*"

His reply was immediate.

"*Dude, Kaia is going insane.*"

I bit my lip. Would a man who was going insane over me ever break my heart?

"*How long does Kai normally keep his subs?*"

"*... Why?*"

"*Can you just answer? Please?*"

"*He never keeps them for more than a week or two. He likes changing it up. His partners do too.*"

"*So he's going to change me up soon?*" I had already been with him for close to a month.

"What the hell, Luka? Have you not heard anything I've told you about him? Why do you think he was so upset when you didn't answer any messages? He likes you. A lot."

"Well I'm sorry I didn't reply sooner. Goodnight, Mason."

"Wait, you should give Kai a call. Messages aren't enough. He just needs to know that you're okay."

But I shut off my phone, hopeful that I could get more sleep now than before. Mom had al

....

When I woke, I almost screamed. After a moment of panic, I started with wide, incredulous eyes up at Mason.

"God, you scared me!" I exclaimed. He looked at me apologetically as I quickly sat up. "How did you get in here? Did Mom let you in?" I asked as I rubbed the sleep out of my eyes. He shook his head. "I knocked, but no one answered. And you left your keys at our house last night. I let myself in. Sorry if I intruded." I shook my head, my brows furrowing. "She should have answered. She has the day off today, I think," I told him as I stood. I realized then that I was only in boxers, but Mason didn't seem to mind. After throwing on a shirt and jeans, I jumped down my stairs and opened my mother's bedroom door only a crack to peek inside.

The first thing I noticed was the package of *Nytol* sitting on the nightstand beside her. I sighed and closed the door. "She's sleeping. She probably will be for a while. You want some coffee or something?"

He nodded. "Sure."

"You take sugar? Milk?" I asked. Mason shook his head and took a seat at the dining room table. "This is your house?" he asked. I nodded and shrugged. My eyes stayed trained on my work. The water for coffee began boiling. "It's not much, but... it's home, I guess." His gaze roamed over my decrepit furniture and cracking ceiling. The house looked more like it was falling apart everyday. "And you... live here?" He obviously couldn't wrap his head around the appliances that were older than me and the tiled floors that looked as if they were ready to be torn up.

I sighed and poured his black coffee into a mug. "Yes, Mason, I live here. Some people aren't as fortunate as you."

He looked momentarily hurt, and I realized that he had probably a worse childhood than I did. I didn't even want to imagine the kind of horrors one would experience in a child soldiers camp.

I set his cup of coffee in front of him and took a seat, my head supported on my fist. "He was pretty upset last night, you know. He thought he did something wrong when you guys were in the theatre." He didn't give me a chance to apologize.

I glanced at Mason quickly, but then I diverted my gaze to the floor. "You don't know him as well as I do yet, but you can't just tell him you'll go eat dinner and then leave without telling anybody what was going on. I sat outside your house for half an hour after I dropped you off because he needed to know you were okay." I stared at him in shock, the floor forgotten. Then I sighed, deflating with guilt.

"Mason... I'm sorry I had to leave like that, okay? My mom works all day and then when she came home to an unusually empty house, she was upset. I... I explained to her about my job, kinda."

"Where does your mother work?"

"The diner down the street. You know the one on the corner between the thrift store and that drug store?" His brows furrowed. "But that's barely minimum wage."

I shrugged, scratching my arm nervously. "Yeah."

"How could you afford this place? Even with your job before, that wouldn't be enough to keep this place going, right? L.A. is expensive."

I shrugged. "It wasn't. Not until I got the job from Kai." His eyes softened. Now he knew, and Kai would know soon too. "I knew you didn't make a lot of money, but... this is really far under the poverty line, Luka."

I nodded slowly. "It was."

Mason sighed and nodded. "Well Kai wants me to take you back to his house, like, yesterday." I shook my head. "No. I have lots of clothes to wash, and I need to shop. I don't know when my mother ate last, so I gotta make sure she makes herself something."

"Kai's not going to like that. He'd rather hang with you instead of his work."

I tilted my chin up slightly. "I know." Kai would have to deal with being ghosted for a few more hours.

CHAPTER
THIRTY

MASON FINISHED HIS coffee, left, and my mother woke soon after that. My day was a maze of shopping, cleaning, eating, and sleeping. Mason picked me up at seven that night, much to my mother's dismay. She watched me speed away from the front room window, her face solemn and distant. I hoped she knew that I was doing this for *her*. "Did you have a productive day?" Mason asked. I shrugged, fiddling with my knuckles in my lap. He sighed and suddenly swerved onto a back road. "Where are we going?" I exclaimed, my hand immediately flying to grip the handle attached to the ceiling. Suddenly, I missed Rosa's driving.

"I'm taking you to Kai. But he's not at the apartment," Mason replied, stepping on the gas and swerving the car again. "Do you ever drive like this with Kai in the car?" I was struggling to keep my voice steady and free of any fear. Thank God Mason had been driving for most of his life, or I would have been more fearful. He shrugged. "Actually, he drives like this sometimes." I gritted my teeth and rolled my eyes, my knuckles turning white on the handle. When we came to a stop, it was sudden, both of us propelled forward towards the dashboard. I caught myself with trembling arms and stepped out of the car before I had the chance to puke. "Sorry, Luka. I'll

ANGEL

remember that you don't like my driving for next time." I mumbled a few curses at him as I caught my breath, staring up at the building in front of us. It was a restaurant, a fancy one. Not as modern as our previous date, but probably just as expensive. "Come on, follow me," Mason said, taking my hand and leading me quickly around to the side of the building. He motioned towards a small door. We were surrounded by mystery trash bags and concrete stains accented with blotches of discarded chewing gum. It stank like the bad side of L.A.

"Kai is through that door. Just take the stairs up to the top."

I blanched and glanced at the decrepit door nervously. "Um...." Was he planning to freaking kidnap me? Mason chuckled. "It's fine, Lucika. Kaia is waiting up there for you. He's been planning this for a while now. Just don't make him wait any longer," he told me earnestly. I pouted slightly, confused and hesitant, but I pulled myself away from him begrudgingly and opened the creaking metal door. I suppose every beautiful restaurant had a dark side, like the trash alley behind it.

The stairs were polished wood encased in a metal railing, leading the pathway up to the next level. I bit my lip as I began to climb them, my steps more curious than anything else, now. Once I had passed the fourth floor, I was getting out of breath. The jumbled voices from the crowded restaurant below had faded away on the third floor, and now the cool air was almost silent, save for the white traffic noise. At the top of the flights of stairs sat a large wooden door, different from the metal one below. This one was prettier, holding the same kind of charm as the restaurant. I opened it slowly, glancing around the top floor of the restaurant before I realized that I was standing on the roof.

My mouth fell open as I stared around the rooftop in awe. The scene that sat before me was stunning. It was a patio, probably used for special guests by the restaurant, filled with a dozen wooden tables surrounded by black, cushioned chairs. Candles illuminated each table, while the single wall on one side of the deck was festooned with hundreds of tiny glowing lights, as if the night sky had fallen onto this building, sending a soft yellow glow onto the ground and nearby seats.

But the place was empty, or so I thought, before I finally noticed a single figure sitting in the centre of the three rows of tables. Excitement suddenly bubbled inside me when I saw that undercut raven-black hair. "What is all this?" I breathed as I stopped beside his lonely table. His gaze darted up and drank me in as I bit my lip and anxiously waited for a reply. "This-," he said, "-is where you sit." His smirk was humorous; there was something funny occurring in his head. Or maybe I had already done something to make him smile.

I took a seat across from him, my eyes widening when I glanced up and realized we weren't alone. A waiter had materialized beside us with a crisp red dress shirt, black pants, and a black menu booklet in his hands that indicated his job. "Welcome to Rome's, Mr. Arche. Lucika. Have you decided what you would like to eat tonight? And would you like the wine menu?" His voice was kind, preppy, and strangely comforting, as if he would still be smiling and confident if the world collapsed around us suddenly.

Kai glanced to me. "Are you okay with the Rigatoni?"

"Um...." I glanced diffidently between the waiter and Kai. Was I supposed to know what Rigatoni was?

Kai chuckled under his breath before sighing. "We'll have the cabbage Rigatoni," he said, holding his hand out for the wine menu. The waiter nodded and waited patiently as Kai flipped through it slightly, glancing up as if he was mentally asking me what kind of wine he wanted. I continued to glance between him and the waiter

ANGEL

before the man caught my eye and gave me a kind smile. I blushed a deep rose and immediately looked away. "We'll start with a bottle of the Dorana twenty-ten," He said finally. The waiter nodded before he scurried away. Kai smiled at me from across the table then, but I was too anxious to meet his gaze. So, instead, I kicked my feet lightly and sat on my hands so I wouldn't pull at my knuckles. Kai sighed.

"This is a date, Luka. I've taken you on a date."

My eyes widened. "Wh-What? Why didn't you tell me?! I would have worn better clothes!" Kai chuckled again, straightening in his seat. "It's fine, Luka. Anyone who looks at you would be jealous." I blushed harder at his words as the waiter returned with a dark bottle of wine and set two glasses between us. "This one is actually compliments of the chef," he said with a smile as he poured us each a healthy helping of alcohol. I almost refused it, my previous drunk experience blooming in my mind.

"Thank you," Kai said as the man left the bottle on the table and scurried away again.

"I can't drink," I said. Kai shrugged. "As long as you aren't as drunk as you were last night. My replacement car hasn't come in yet, so don't ruin another one on the way home." I gave him a mortified expression. "B-but I- I didn't, I mean-." I stumbled over my words before he interrupted again with a laugh. "It's fine, Lucika. It's only a car. Even though Mason was upset about having to clean it out before we junked it. None of us will ever be able to get that stain out of that leather." I bit my lip and leaned back in my chair, taking my wine glass and holding his close to my lips. "Mason Crule, afraid of a little puke? I thought he was supposed to be a badass." Kai snorted at this and shrugged. "He's always been a bit of a germaphobe." We each chuckled and took a small sip of our drinks. I watched with a raised eyebrow as Kai smiled at me fondly, as if he was lost in thought. "What?" Bright pink dusted my cheeks. He continued to stare at me in the same fashion. "Just taking in the scenery." I looked away in an effort to hide my blush and found myself gawking at the darkening city below us. "Speaking of scenery...."

He followed my gaze and nodded. "It's pretty, isn't it? I have a view like this of the mountains in the Swiss Alps. Not of the city, of course, but you get the picture."

My mouth went slack a little. "You own a house there?" He nodded. Of course he did. "I'll take you there one day. My mother bought it for my birthday a year or two ago. Well, it was allowed to be in my name if i shared it with my siblings," he promised. I smiled, the dream seeming distant and unrealistic, although I had grown to know that nothing was unrealistic in Kai's eyes.

"So why do you think the chef sent his compliments?" I asked, creating conversation. Kai shrugged. "You remember James, right? He works nights here."

"Wow. So a chef by night and a therapist by day? That's an odd combination." He nodded. "He says he enjoys both professions, but honestly, I think he just hates sleep. He never gets any." I giggled and took a sip of water. This time, I was determined to balance out my food, alcohol, and water.

"So do you have any family other than your Mom around?" he asked. I shook my head. "My dad walked when he found out my mom was pregnant, and I'm pretty sure he had another kid from his previous relationship that he hadn't talked to before. But I've never met him, so I'm not sure if he really counts as family. Other than that it's only my mom and I." Kai nodded. "Do you get along with your mom?" I immediately thought back to last night. That was the first major fight we'd had in years. That was also the best we've ever held a conversation. "Yeah, all the time. We used to be best friends when I was younger, but I guess my rebellious teenager really came out after that."

ANGEL

The man across from me snorted. "I understand."

"What kind of family do you have?"

He hesitated slightly, and I hoped I hadn't ruined the dinner by making him think of 'Her', whoever she was. But I lightened up when he didn't let it faze him too much. "Actually, I have seven siblings. My mother and father had me before they decided that they were ready to open their home to others."

"Seriously? Seven adopted siblings? That's insane."

He laughed and nodded. "Yes, it got pretty hectic at times. Especially with the fact that my parents decided that every child they adopted was going to have some kind of disability or illness or *something*. They wanted to help kids who didn't have a family to love them, you know? It was supposed to be just fostering, but I guess they just couldn't stand to see a kid leave them."

"Wow. That's amazing. Huge kudos to your parents. It takes guts to do that."

He smiled. "I'll tell them you said that. They'll love to hear it. What's your mother like?" The question caught me off-guard, and I had to think for a moment before I answered. "She's really smart. Like a know-it-all university professor-smart. But she doesn't show it much. She also has a thing for cooking and children, but she doesn't cook much anymore. She hasn't spoken to a child since before I started growing up."

"Well, Rosa is always looking for a cooking mate. Bring your mother over one day and I'm sure they can go to town all afternoon." My eyes saddened. Would my mother ever support my relationship with Kai? His friends? She didn't understand it. But I understood her worries. I should be more worried too, but I wasn't. I felt as if nothing could go wrong around Kai. For the first time in my adult life, everything was perfect, but only when I was with him.

"What did you mean by disabilities? Like mental disabilities?"

Kai shook his head and waved his hand. "My family is kind of a mix of everything. My mother grew up with a pretty severe depression disorder, so she knows a few things about mental health and got some tips from old councillor friends. So she had a huge impact on my sister, Lily, when she moved in. She still struggles with her O.C.D. and anxiety today, but my mother helped her a lot. You should have seen her when she first came. She did *everything* because of her O.C.D. It was crippling."

"Wow... Kai, your family literally sounds really nice."

Kai burst into laughter.

"Do they? They'd laugh if they heard that. They're not always very fun. I got a brother who's missing his left leg, and my dad helped him all the time by decking his prosthetic out with wires and lights to make it look like a robot's leg. My brother loved it as a kid and still keeps his old legs."

I nodded, listening intently as the waiter dropped our meals off and disappeared.

CHAPTER
THIRTY-ONE

I POPPED A FORK full of noodles into my mouth and nearly moaned at the taste. It was fabulous. I would have to tell Kai to tell James that he was truly an amazing cook. "There are six men in the family including my father and I. The other four are my mom and sisters, Lily, Janet, and Saskia. I have two older brothers and two younger ones. I think one is actually younger than you."

"So you had the adult fazes, rebellious teenagers, and the responsibilities of taking care of a baby when you were a kid?" He nodded. "Yeah. Like I said, it's always been a little crazy in the Arche household."

"What do your mother and father do for work?" I asked, licking my gums to sweep away a piece of stray cabbage before I took a sip of water. "My mother is a neurosurgeon with a black belt in Karate and my father is a businessman like myself."

"Jeez, a neurosurgeon? That's incredible. Sounds like they set the bar pretty high. What do your siblings do for work?"

"Do you really want to know or are you prolonging the inevitable? I'm aching to hear about your extremely exciting life." I tilted my head to the side and gave him a look as if to say *'Seriously?'*.

He laughed before releasing a long sigh. "Actually, we all kinda chose different careers, despite my parents' urging towards business or the medical field. That just wasn't what we wanted to do, other than myself, who obviously followed in my father's footsteps."

"But being a businessman was what you wanted to do, right? You like it?"

He nodded and shrugged. "It gets stressful, but I've learned how to embrace it, I guess. The stress distracts me."

"So you have a really good relationship with your family?"

"Yeah. They've pretty much been just as close to me as Mason and Rosa my entire life."

I didn't know where else to go from that point in the conversation, and after a small pause, he took control.

"Do you have any good friends you talk to?"

I shook my head. "Not since junior high. But now I kinda consider Rosa and Mason to be friends." An excited smile crossed his features. "Me too." There was a pause between us as we enjoyed our meals and looked out across the city. I adored this view and the noises of horns and engines around us. A tiny bird chirped loudly and made a beeline for a shrub against the glowing wall. "What's your favourite colour?" I asked suddenly. He laughed, and I didn't expect him to answer, but he almost immediately replied, "Black."

"Black's not a colour."

"I like black."

"That's very... gothic Arche."

He broke into loud laughter momentarily, and I could only stare in awe. He ended his laugh session with a shake of his head and a sip of his wine. "Yes, I suppose it is. Do you have a favourite animal?" They were basic, cheesy date questions. But they fit; for once, it felt *natural*. We didn't know these facts about each other.

"Hm... I like... all animals. Especially soft ones, like my blanket," I replied after a moment of thought. "You?" He thought for a pause too. "I've always liked cats, I guess. My mother bought me a house

ANGEL

cat when I was younger, although I constantly begged her for a big cat." I giggled and shrugged. "Why don't you buy yourself one now? I'm sure you have the money...." How one would go about getting a big cat, I had no idea, but I was sure that if Kaia put his mind to it, he would get it eventually. He shrugged. "Rosa is allergic to cats, and I probably wouldn't have time to care for any kind of pet right now... especially if I got a big one. How would you feel about sharing a bed with a tiger?"

I scoffed, "I already do." Big cats weren't meant to be pets, anyway.

"So, what do you do for fun?" Kai asked, changing the subject. I tilted my head to the side slightly. "Like, what you spend your time doing on a weekend afternoon." I snorted. "I'm with you on weekend afternoons and a lot of time in between too." He snickered and nodded. "You're right, so what do you do when you're alone? To have fun. And I swear to god, if you say you like to play with dildos-," but I interrupted him suddenly. The first and only thing that came to mind. "Music."

He motioned for me to elaborate.

"I like music. All kinds. Pop, rock, classical. Any kind of tune I can sing or hum to, I'm happy. I... well, I love to sing, I guess. I like to dance too." They were understatements, but true. He raised an eyebrow. "You like music, hm?" I nodded enthusiastically. I loved it more than anything. Well, maybe not as much as Kai, but the music was an extremely close second.

We conversed far into the night, talking about anything and everything. Even after we finished the wine and our meals, we simply chatted until the moon had begun to rise above us. The sky was clear, revealing beautiful glowing stars. He paid by leaving a thick wad of cash on the table between us and took my hand before leading me back to the alley below. At the front of the restaurant sat his *Ferrari*, standing beautiful and sleek under the bright lights of the stores along this street. "Anywhere you want to go in particular?" he asked while we both buckled in. I thought for a moment before I shrugged. "Let's just... go to your place." I bit my lip and gave him a coy look. I didn't want to tell him straight that I had briefly popped into a tiny, cheap lingerie shop and bought something special for Kai earlier today as an apology. The surprise date had just made the night all the more special.

"Okay, Luka. Let's go to the apartment."

I could tell that he had read my features very clearly.

....

His lips were on mine before he even cut the engine in the empty garage.

"You taste... really... delicious," I muttered between kisses, licking at the flavour of expensive wine that still stuck to his lips. He chuckled, and I could feel his smile against my own before I was completely immersed in the feeling. "I'd say the same thing, but...," he growled, pulling me over his lap and attaching his mouth to my neck, ignoring my own statement. I realized that he wouldn't even be able to taste the salt on my skin like I could on his. He couldn't taste any cigar residue like I could. He couldn't taste the rich coffee scent and musk that rolled off his skin, lingering in my mouth until I broke away from him.

What he lost in taste, he made up for with other sensory details. I wondered if he could smell things too. I hoped I felt as good as he tasted. Kai's hands roamed up and down my sides, tracing my ribs before landing on my hips and squeezing slightly. "You want to go upstairs?" He asked, pecking a line of kisses along my jaw. I nodded eagerly before I was scooped up and thrown over his shoulder. I wasn't complaining; a face full of Kai's ass would make anyone's day, but I was slightly uncomfortable when I was slung over his shoulder.

I felt as if I was about to fall over his back, although I knew that he would never allow that to happen.

"K-Kai!" I exclaimed as I laughed, gripping onto the back of his silky coat. He only chuckled and bounced me lightly as we exited the elevator, climbed the stairs, and burnt a trail down the hall to his bedroom. I gasped when he threw me back over his shoulder and sent me falling onto the bed, the feather duvet engulfing me. Kai didn't waste any time before pouncing on me, grinding his thigh between my legs and against my growing erection. I released a low moan and attempted to grind back, desperate for any friction. "Look at you... I would have taken you out to dinner sooner if I had known that the night would end with this," Kai mumbled against my shirt, his fingers pulling at my nipples lightly through the clothing. My stomach twitched at his words and I arched my back with the stimulation against my chest.

"Kai... Kai...," I repeated his name desperately, my erection painful against my pants. We could both see a small wet spot forming at the front. "Excited, hm?" KaI grinned. I almost shouted, arching up again when a hand wrapped around my neck. It was tight; his fingers dipped into the holes between arteries and tendons. If he tightened his hold further, I knew that he would be capable of so much. He could send me to heaven. When he finally decided that he was through with my chest, I was a drooling, twitching mess. But I woke from my daze slightly when he slowly removed my jeans and took a deep inhale. I watched, waiting for his reaction. It was too soon to tell if he was turned off or on.

I watched his hungry eyes roam around my hips and waist as he grew enchanted by my new panties, garters, and stockings. They were purely lace across my front and back with simple strings on the sides, and we could both see my erection clearly through the dark mesh at my crotch. The only skin obstructed was the small patch under the two embroidered cherry blossom flowers on my left hip. He seemed to have a thing for those flowers, and I figured I would encroach on his subtle fetishes.

His eyes flashed with hunger, pain, and lust in a millisecond, before he scrambled to lift my shirt up and investigate further. Once he had the fabric pooled around my neck, he could see the black leather bulldog harness that encased my chest. Then I was suddenly flipped onto my back with a small yelp; he hadn't even given me time to explain my motives. "I like it," was all he growled, "I like it a lot." I smiled with joy, hiding my face in his satin sheets. He loved them sincerely. I could tell.

But the thought was forgotten when I felt him pushing the panties down my thighs and licking a wet stripe up my entrance. I gasped and pushed back against his face as he pulled me up towards his body. Before we went too far, I would take a shower and clean myself.

But that came *later*.

My moans were long and low, spilling from my lips as he pulled at the rim. His tongue was just as amazing as him when it lapped slowly and with a delicious pressure. I yelped, stars exploding in front of my eyes, when he added a finger, found my prostate, and wrapped his other hand around my erection. My hands began gripping the sheets as I trembled and squirmed, drool leaking from the corner of my lips and my eyes threatening to roll back in my head. The accumulating saliva was wiped frantically on a pillow; I wasn't sure which of us it belonged to. I was in a trance, lost in the ecstacy like I had fallen into a black hole.

But then his tongue and fingers were gone and I was flipped onto my back once again. I groaned, reality returning to me. "What... why did you... stop?" He knelt between my bare legs, undoing his own belt. My brows knitted together. "I'm not—I'm not *clean*," I warned nervously.

ANGEL

"Luka, I want to try something," he said abruptly. I could see his cock straining against the front of his trousers. I just wanted that. There was no time for games. "You don't want me cleaned out, or-," I was cut off by his reply, "I don't care about that now." I bit my lip and nodded, supporting myself on my elbows to listen to him. He almost seemed feral, driven by the hunger I had stirred inside him. "Have you ever heard of a urethral plug?" he asked, massaging my hips. I would need another massage afterwards, I was sure. My blood ran cold.

Yes, I fucking had heard of *that*.

"K-Kai, I-," but he cut me off. He could see the immediate fear in my wide eyes; I could tell that he didn't want to scare me off, despite the ferocity in his actions. "Luka, if you're against it, then we won't. But if you're even a tiny bit up for the challenge, then I'd like to try it with you." I stared at him like a deer caught in headlights, my breath quick and sharp. Connections had told me what the toy was. And what they told me was either absolutely horrifying or absolutely incredible. I didn't know who or what to believe. I only knew that the thought of it scared me to death.

"Luka," he whispered, placing his hand on my cheek.

My breath slowed, his suddenly soft and gentle touch grounding me instantly. I could do it, then. Kai would make it feel good, I realized, if I trusted him and allowed myself to submit. "O-Okay... I trust you," I stuttered, still fearful. That night, I was placing my complete and utter trust in the man. He seemed to understand this. His gaze promised that he wouldn't let me down.

He kissed my neck in an attempt at calming me before he began the real session, grabbing my wrists gently as our eyes closed and he slipped his tongue between my jaws. It flicked against my teeth before slipping away. "Is it okay if I chain you?" I was about to give a verbal reply, telling him that I was okay with that. But I hesitated, realizing that I really wasn't. To take a giant leap like that while being shackled to a bed and restrained was something I definitely wasn't ready for yet. I had a feeling that he knew that too.

I shook my head, no, jerkily, and he nodded. I hoped that I didn't hurt his feelings by telling him that I couldn't submit to him to such an extent, but he had to understand. He simply wouldn't be a good Dom if he didn't.

"Okay. That's okay. Just relax, Angel, this is about pleasure. I want to know when you feel good."

I moaned as his fingers entered me again, pushing and pulling at my supple walls. They were long and thin and perfect for grinding against that little ball of nerves. "It'll hurt a little bit, but soon it'll feel amazing, I promise," he said quietly, kissing my neck. I moaned and arched my back against his fingers just as they left me again. I groaned in frustration. "I… I like the hurt. Just do it."

He chuckled at my desperation and hushed me with a small, humorous smirk as he took my cock in his large hand and gave a few satisfying strokes. The stimulation sent white-hot bolts of lighting up my spine. That was when, during those seconds of shocking sensations, I felt a nudge of something cold and hard against my tip. I flinched away automatically, my breath quickening as I stared at Kai with a sudden fear. "This one isn't beaded, so it won't be as painful as the other ones, Lucika. Just remember the safe-words, baby," he told me as the object worked its way into my tiny slit. The man kept eye contact.

I threw my head back against the pillow, my hands flying to grab his wrists before the slightly warmed metal could intrude any further. My eyes were wide, even wider than before, and oxygen was suddenly trapped inside my lungs. There was no escape. A cry landed on my tongue.

"Y-Yellow!"

CHAPTER
THIRTY-TWO

KAI IMMEDIATELY FROZE, allowing me to catch my breath for a moment. "I-It hurts!" I exclaimed, biting my lip until I was sure I had broken the skin. "Breathe, Luka, you're doing fine," he insisted, stroking my cock gently. I whimpered and took a deep, wheezing breath. "I can do it quickly, Luka, just relax. It *will* feel amazing." I squeezed my eyes shut and nodded before he pushed it further in, eliciting a cry from me. It fucking hurt, merging with the ecstacy and incapacitating me. I was overdosing on stimulation, as if I was being fucked from the inside-out. I didn't like it at all. But, deep in my chest, that little bit of pleasure still had me hanging onto the string that held me above the water.

"You're doing so well, baby, it's all the way in," Kai cooed, rubbing soothing circles into my waist. My breathing was laboured and choppy, but he seemed to be happy that I was getting at least some air into my desperate lungs. I could feel it *inside me,* pulling the skin tight and rubbing it raw. My appendage jumped. I whimpered. But he knew this, the pain, and fondled my balls with the hopes of lightening my spirits. I jolted and yelped, the plug shifting inside me. Tears gathered in my eyes. My head thrashed on the pillow.

"Sh, Baby, Sh," Kai whispered, leaning forward and attaching his lips to mine. It momentarily distracted me from the sound of his zipper lowering and a condom opening. My shoulders nearly left the sheets when he slid his full length inside me with a single, slow thrust, my mouth falling open in a silent scream. Stars exploded into a glowing galaxy in front of my eyes, thrusting me into swirling pleasure until I was lost in euphoria. I could see his teeth grinding and his jaw flexing above me, sweat already beading on his skin. The room was hot, heated even further by our activity.

The pain was just as present, though, beyond the lewd images he offered. Somewhere in my brain, in a tiny corner, a piece of me laughed at myself. *You fucking masochist.*

Once he had bottomed out, he gave me a moment to grow accustomed to his size. Stretching around his cock was nothing like stretching around fingers. But I didn't want to pause. With each tiny movement, the plug moved and pushed against places I never knew existed, and I instantly abandoned the idea of 'waiting'. I pushed my body back against his cock roughly, satisfaction blooming inside me when I heard his deep intake of breath. But then I felt his appendage disappear; he hadn't even given a single solid thrust before he was gone, looming over me with a dominant gleam in his eyes. "Ride me," he growled, collapsing onto his back beside me. I was on him as soon as my mind registered his words, desperate for that first thrust. His muscles pulled taut as he fought the urge to thrust up into me. But he seemed satisfied once I began to bounce, curving my back and supporting my hands on his chest.

The room filled with moans and groans as I fell into a pace that made both our brains turn to mush.

Something felt unusual with Kaia that night. He was giving me the control. His world was dominated by deadlines, business, and controlling elements, and he funneled that into our scenes. But not tonight. Tonight, I was the one who would make him quiver with release. I was controlling the pace, the depth. He was putty in my hands for the next few minutes.

If only he would take out the fucking plug. I could feel the pressure building, and I was beginning to realize that I wouldn't be able to orgasm until he let me. So maybe I wasn't as in control as I thought...? I could feel him getting close, growing inside me slightly, if it was possible. With each stroke, my prostate felt as if it was on fire, burning and tingling and sending white-hot power around my body with every heartbeat.

"C-Can I come?" I cried, my nails digging into his chest. He gave a deep groan as he gripped my hips and pulled me against him with force, assisting with my bounces. "No... you can hold it, baby boy... you're doing great," he said, the words barely sliding through his grinding teeth. But there was nothing to hold. If he wasn't going to let me, then I couldn't. I was about to start begging, but my words were cut off when I felt his muscles tense, his hot seed filling the condom as he continued to thrust. The grip on my thighs tightened; I winced. His muscles pulled taut. I watched his chest freeze, quiver, and fall again before falling into a fast, deep rhythm.

"You can come now, baby," he breathed, pulling the plug out violently. I gave a yelp of ecstasy and finished with a few more thrusts before I allowed the release. My muscles tensed and I tilted my head back as I gave a loud cry, white, creamy liquid bursting across Kai's chest and up my stomach. He tossed the plug onto the nightstand.

It took a moment for the energy to leave my body. When it did, I was left as an empty shell, void of all motivation. Kai had softened inside me, but this barely registered with the fact that I was falling to the side. The world was simply tilting. It was slightly hypnotizing, actually, with the numbing sensations that encased my nerves. It wasn't as intense as what I felt before, but it was almost *better*, because I realized that it allowed me to focus on Kai alone. The bedroom melted away, even the sheets that turned to clouds. Kai instantly snapped out of his own trance when he saw me falling. My eyes were glossy and distant, and he at first expected me to catch myself. The man soon realized I wasn't, so he leaned up to catch me by supporting my upper arm with one hand. I gave a calm, hollow sigh as he sat up fully, scooting back so he could lean against the headboard without severing our connection. Kai began massaging my cheeks in an attempt to reel me back to reality. I could see him smiling at me with exhaustion hidden behind his eyes. The session had worn us both out. I blinked once, then twice, then quickly three times.

"There you are, Angel," he said, awe evident in his features. My brows furrowed, exhaustion still imprisoning my body. The room was coming back. I missed that feeling of floating. "Kai," I breathed, setting a shaky hand on his shoulder. His skin was hot. It helped to ground me as waves of chemicals rushed my brain, making it foggy. I pushed my sweaty forehead against his; I could feel his laboured breaths collide against my own.

"I almost lost you there, baby. That was amazing."

"Lost... me?"

He nodded and pulled out, the condom slipping off him easily. The smile on his face was so much wider than I ever expected it to be. "This wasn't even a very hard scene, and you... you did so well."

I collapsed against his chest without moving from straddling his waist. Our breaths were still catching up to us, so Kai leaned back against the mountain of pillows behind him and relaxed with his arms firmly wrapped around me. I pushed my head against his neck, breathing in musk. "Wow," I breathed, my head finally clearing. He hummed and chuckled. I was slightly uncomfortable with the stickiness between us and the perspiration that was yet to dry on our skin, but I wasn't necessarily ready to move yet.

"Thank you," Kai breathed rather suddenly, interrupting the silence.

ANGEL

"For what?" I replied against his collarbone. His fingers found my hair.

"For submitting to me. I know it might be hard."

I only snorted and rolled my face back into his neck. "I've had some practice."

Once our breathing had evened out, he stood and disappeared into his bathroom with the plug we had been using, only to return with a warm cloth and a clean torso. My head lulled back onto the pillows as I indulged in the soft, warm stimulation on my skin. "You want a bath?" he asked. I shook my head and rolled onto my side, holding my hand out to him. "Just come to bed, Kai," I smiled. The man sighed and nodded, discarding the cloth onto the bathroom counter and sliding under the covers where I had hidden my nude self. I managed to find my blanket hidden in mountains of sheets and pillows. We held it between us as exhaustion finally began to win the battle. I could tell he was tired too.

"Goodnight, Kai," I mumbled, stuffing my face into my fluffy blanket while Kai pushed himself against me snuggly. I had pleased him, and that made me happy. He was *satisfied*. We both were.

"Goodnight, Angel."

....

"My name's Cade," the man said. He gave me a devious smile, tilting his head to the side a little. I smiled kindly at him while I multitasked and searched the crowds of the club for Kai's raven hair.

"I'm Luka."

Cade's venomous grin widened, and I momentarily looked back to him out of politeness. "Well, Luka, why don't you join me and my sub?" I shook my head and gave him a bewildered expression. "I have a partner." He smirked and downed a shot that had been left on the bar countertop as I looked away from him. I needed to find Kai.

My stomach dropped.

No longer were there any random people in the crowd. Their noise was boisterous and the fact that most of them were drunk was obvious, but they were no longer the strangers anyone could feel comfortable with. As I searched those faces, I soon realized that I couldn't find Kai. Something within me told me that he wasn't just somewhere in the crowd. He was gone. *The utter abandonment that swept my heart up into a beating frenzy made me want to scream, yet nothing made it past the new lump in my throat.*

"Who's the lucky guy?"

I sat up in the sheets, my heartbeat deafening against my eardrums and my breath hitching in my throat. I was no longer in the club. There were no longer dozens of people in the room. It was a single Kai, my Kai, and his even, deep breaths against my now-empty pillow. "What the fuck," I mumbled under my breath, running my fingers through a sweaty head of hair. The dream wasn't scary; it was more confusing, unsettling. I hadn't dreamt since eleventh grade, the night I dropped out of high school. I had had a wet dream about the school's quarterback. And why was I suddenly remembering Cade, of all characters? The man may have encroached a little further than I deemed pleasant, but he seemed harmless enough. He had been nice to me the few times we met before.

I sighed and rolled out of Kai's feathery bed, making sure not to forget my blanket that had fallen to the floor during my sleep. I dropped it on my pillow, and Kai immediately reached out and pulled it towards his chest, burying his nose into the sudden comfort. I wanted to laugh a little, but decided not to risk waking Kai. He needed his sleep, and I needed to dress myself at least partially before I could go galloping around his home. I grabbed an old hoodie that had been discarded on the rocking chair in the corner probably months ago and slipped it over me. It was a rugby sweater from a high school team. Probably the team Kai had played on in his younger years. I made sure to add some boxers and sweatpants underneath too.

I took careful steps through the darkness, knowing that my screaming as I slipped down his staircase would most-likely wake the entire apartment. Eventually, I completed my journey into the kitchen without falling or slipping. What I was planning to do at the bottom, I wasn't sure. But I wasn't sure what to do after waking from my dream, either. There was too much adrenaline in my veins to return to sleep, so I took the next best thing. The clock on the wall read two-thirty. Mason would be awake soon. I would be able to spend my morning with him before Kai woke up. I leaned against the countertop, supporting myself on my elbows, and gazed around the living room with disinterest. Horns were already beginning to accumulate on the city floor, but the sun was far from rising.

It was surprisingly peaceful.

CHAPTER
THIRTY-THREE

WITHIN A FEW minutes I had decided to get to work on my computer, copying new numbers and notes down in the book along with it and working off the dim light proffered by the laptop. Then I found myself searching for music, accidentally clicking on a porn sight, and ultimately sitting in front of a blank search screen.

I bit my lip as I typed, "Kaia Arche" into the search engine.

Immediately, there were thousands of hits, mostly about his business and his family. I clicked on the images page. And, again, there were thousands of images of everybody but my man. They mostly included members of his family, especially his parents. A woman who had the same dark skin stood next to him in a photo. In another, the same woman was embracing a man who had many of the same features as Kai, the same jawline, the same black hair, although he was now riddled with greying streaks. As I continued to scroll, there were still very few photos that actually included Kai. The page was littered with photos of other people, too, who I suspected were his adoptive siblings. But I couldn't begin to guess who was who. They were important people in their communities, was all I knew for sure.

Then I landed on a picture of us. When we went to the mall, a photo had been snapped of us pausing in front of the lingerie shop. Of course. Seeing myself in a photo like this, featured on a sketchy reporting site, was boggling. His father had obviously made quite a name for himself.

I started when the refrigerator door opened, finally pulling my focus away from the computer. On instinct, I scrambled to shut the screen, and thought better of it after a moment. "Morning, Mason," I said. He was surprised that I was awake. "Hey, Luka. Couldn't sleep?" I nodded and shrugged. "I had a really weird dream."

"Yeah? A weird dream about... Kai?" he asked as he smirked and elbowed me playfully, a mischievous glint in his eyes. The milk jug in his hand sloshed. I glared at him half-heartedly. "No, Mason. I don't need wet dreams when I got the real thing... unlike you." He feigned being hurt. "Oh... oh, Luka, that was harsh." He put his hand on his heart and gave a heavy wheeze. We both laughed before the moment was over and Mason grabbed a cup from the cupboard. I took one, too, and filled it with water. The man beside me grimaced. Neither Kai nor Mason liked Los Angeles tap, and I couldn't blame them.

"Kai's always hated paparazzi. He doesn't get much, but when he does, oh boy. He's punched a guy before for getting in his face. That was when his dad's business was working out some settlement and they were getting extra attention in the media," he said, motioning to my open laptop. It glowed brightly in the darkness of the kitchen. A blush immediately formed on my cheeks when I realized I had been caught. "We've all been there, kid. You should sneak back into bed before Kai wakes up," he laughed. I pouted slightly before sighing and closing the device. "See you later, then," I waved as I stepped out of the kitchen. I watched his smile disappear below me.

When I reached the second floor, I was met with a Kai that was rolled in my blanket and snoring quietly. Thankfully, the noise I had created didn't bother him; he must have been used to it by now. I set the cup of water on the nightstand and collapsed onto the bed, waking him suddenly. He groaned and wrapped an arm around me. "Where did you go?"

I realized that there was more of a musk scent around us in the mornings. Maybe it rolled off his breath or he stirred it up while he tossed in the sheets. I decided now that I liked his coffee and chocolate combination better. "I went downstairs to just walk around a little, I guess. I had the weirdest dream last night." The man immediately raised an eyebrow as a smirk played on his lips and mischief sparked in his eyes. I laughed and slapped him away. "Oh my god, you and Mason are like evil twins!" He chuckled and pulled me back to him, enveloping me in musk and coffee. "Yeah, well, we grew up together. He kinda is my brother."

I snorted and looked out at the skyscrapers around us. "What are we gonna do today?"

He thought for a moment before he replied. "Actually, I have some things to tend to before noon. Then I was thinking your mother could come over. Rosa really wants to meet her." My mouth fell open. "R-Really?" He nodded. "I didn't know if she had the day off today, but I think she should come find out who you're really working for." I bit my lip and looked away. "Kai, I...." I didn't know how to finish my sentence. My mother would be uncomfortable and alienated in a house like Kai's. I didn't think she would even host the *idea* of meeting my boss. He frowned and leaned up on his elbow to look at me. "Does she not support your sexuality?" I shook my head quickly, scrambling to explain. "No, no, she supports me fine, I just... she doesn't understand. She doesn't think you're... good for me, I guess?"

He seemed hurt. "What do *you* think?"

"I think... I think you're happy. I seem to make you happy?"

ANGEL

"But do *you* think I'm good for you?"

A second of delay would reveal my uncertainty. Just because he made me happy didn't mean he was *good* for me. But my life felt *right* when I was working for him, whether it was in bed or at a desk. So how destroyed was I going to be when I had to say goodbye to him?

"I really like being with you. I think... that that's good."

He wasn't disagreeing; he stuffed his head in my neck and wound his arms tighter around me. "You and Mason can pick your mother up from her work later today. But until then, I have work to do." I finally released the breath I had been holding and let my head lull to the side to see outside the windows. we could catch a few more hours of sleep before the sun rose.

"Okay."

....

When I drove to my home with Mason later that evening, I wasn't sure what my game plan was. Would my mother want to come on one of her only breaks from work? She would support me, I knew, but would she like Kai? She believed that he would break my heart. Could she be right?

And as I opened my front door, I realized I had no idea what to say to her.

"Mom?" I called nervously from the entrance. Mason waited, idling beside the sidewalk outside. She appeared in the doorway to the kitchen, her looks slightly more gathered than yesterday. Mom looked at me expectantly, a cigarette hanging from her parched lips. "Um... I was just wondering if you wanted to come meet my... my boss." Her expression didn't change. I began to panic. "I-I know what you think about him, but I just want you to give him a chance. I have a friend who really wants to meet you, too, and I just thought... you know...."

She didn't reply for several moments.

"So you're taking me to see your boyfriend?"

I blushed harder than ever before and waved my arms frantically. "N-No! No, no, he's just... he's a good friend, and I-I...," I didn't know what to tell her. I sighed in an attempt to clear my mind. "I just want you to come with me. I'm... starting a life, Mom. Kind of. These are the first relationships I've had probably ever, and I want you to be part of it."

As I finished my reply, she blew out a long puff of smoke that dissolved into the air around us. "I can come... but I don't know how long I'll stay." A massive smile immediately lit up my features as I grabbed her hand and tugged her out the door, locking it quickly and smiling as I led her to the car. She stared in awe at the vehicle before I opened the door to let her in the back. "Ms. Roggy!" Mason smiled at her in the rear view. She jumped slightly at the mention of her name, but quickly pulled her composure back together and gave a forced flash of a smile. "That's me." Mason chuckled and turned in his seat to shake her hand. But then he paused, his eyes widening slightly as he held out his arm for her. My eyes narrowed at him when his mouth fell slightly slack and my mother met his gaze. Had I ever seen Mason caught off-guard?

He shook his head and smiled at her before I could decide if I was imagining the scene or not. "I'm Mason Crule. Call me Mason." She didn't shake the hand and instead smiled kindly to him. "My name is Teressa." Mason lit up like a child on Christmas morning. "A beautiful name for a beautiful woman." My mother looked to the ground, and I watched with a slight frown as her hand unconsciously moved to her packet of cigarettes inside her purse. She obviously had no idea what to do when she was complimented in such a way.

ANGEL

"Well, let's go, then. Traffic is gonna be hell," I said, interrupting them.

Had Mason just come on to my fucking mother?

The man nodded, unbothered, and flipped around in his seat as he sped away from my house.

I tried my best to forget what had just happened.

....

"G'morning, Abraham," I greeted with a smile. He gave me a bored expression. The man obviously had much better things to do than talk to his boss's boy toy. "Hey, kid." Mason nodded to him before Abraham looked back down to his paper, a thick cigar hanging from his plump lips. My mother followed last, her eyes wide, never settling on one place inside Kai's home. I watched her gaze eat away at the white sofas in the corner, sewn pieces she never dreamt of touching. She was quite obviously beside herself. "Come on, Mom. You haven't even seen the house yet," I said with a reassuring smile. I took her hand, rubbing my thumb against her knuckles comfortingly as I led her into the elevator. She was nervous, far from her comfort zone. I understood; I had been in the same boat the first night I visited Kai.

I refused to let go of her hand in the elevator, and she hung surprisingly close to me when the doors opened again. "Hey, Luka," Rosa smiled from behind the kitchen island. I smiled back as she caught sight of my mother. "And is this Ms. Roggy? I'm Rosa, Mr. Arche's friend... and cook." My mother was trying to be considerate, although I could feel her shaking slightly; she was more comfortable around this woman than Mason. "Hi...."

"Angel," Kai's deep voice rang around the room from where he sat at the couches.

My mother's head whipped around, her eyes narrowed slightly

before they widened. Kai stood and crossed the room and only a few long strides, stopping in front of us while I gripped my mother around her waist and motioned to Kai. I wouldn't allow her to run. "Mom, this is my boss, Kaia Arche."

"Call me Kai, Ms. Roggy," he smiled, shaking her hand. She gave a small smile and shook it back, probably out of fear or nervousness. Kai was so much different in front of new people. I knew that making a good first impression was everything to him, and he obviously wanted my mother to feel comfortable in his home. "Rosa is preparing dinner. I'd love for you to stay." My mother blanched and her mouth fell open. She actually had to *say* something, she realized. "I... Yes, sure. Of course. C-Call me Teressa," she stuttered finally. I could gradually feel the muscles in her spine loosen, and her hand slid further and further away from her cigarettes as she grew distracted.

Kai and I exchanged a victorious glance.

CHAPTER
THIRTY-FOUR

"Do you want anything to drink, Ms. Roggy?" Rosa asked. "No, thank you," she replied, her voice cracking as she stiffly took a seat at one of the black leather couches. "Hey, Rosa, do you think I could get a glass of juice while you're at it? Orange?" I asked. "Of course," Rosa replied immediately, and I could hear the fridge opening. "Thanks," I told her as she handed me the glass. I took a sip and set it on the coffee table. "So you've lived here your whole life, Teressa?" Kai asked, leaning back into the sofa with an arm slung over the back. I wanted to compliment him on the dark quarter shirt he wore; I wondered if he changed out of his formal clothing into something more comforting for my mother. She slowly shook her head. "I moved here from New York when I was seven."

Kai looked surprised. "New York? Los Angeles was a pretty big change, then, hm?" She shrugged and looked out at the city as I wrapped my arms around her and leaned my head against her shoulder. Kai watched with soft eyes when my mother barely flinched. I had always been comforted by her presence, and her by mine.

"I suppose it was. But I've gotten used to it now. They're both pretty big cities." Kaia nodded as Rosa briefly interrupted us from the kitchen. "You're all fine with Stroganoff, right?" We all looked to my mother for an answer. She was the guest, after all.

"Yeah. That sounds good."

We could hear Rosa returning to her work, pans and pots clinking and the fridge opening and closing. "Are you native to Los Angeles?" I didn't think my mother had the balls to ask the intimidating Kai Arche any questions about himself. Apparently I was wrong. Kai smiled and shook his head. "No. My family lived further up California, closer to Oregon."

"Whereabouts?"

"Around the Redwoods."

My mother's eyes lit up slightly; she was relaxing. She was adjusting to Kai, as much as she believed he was going to hurt me in some way. "I've never been, but I want to see the trees there. Is it pretty?"

"Yes, it's stunning. Maybe Luka will take you there one day." Her face fell, and I knew she doubted Kai with all her heart. He just didn't want to come on too strong and offer to take her to the Redwoods, though, as much as he shamelessly flaunted his parent's money. "You hungry, Mom?" I asked quietly, looking up at her as I gently swiped a lock of hair away from her eyes. She nodded, so I looked to Kai. We could hear Rosa finishing up her meal behind us; the noodles and ground beef had been pre-made earlier that day.

"Let's eat at the table." Kaia stood and led us to the other side of the room where he stored his mammoth dining table. Made from dark, solid wood, it wasn't necessarily part of a 'dining room', but it certainly wasn't any less grand. "It's very beautiful," my mother told her host. He nodded his thanks and pulled one of the twelve chairs out for her. "Teressa?"

My mother took a seat. "Thank you."

I sat beside the end of the table where Mom was placed across from Kaia, who folded his fingers together and supported his chin with them. "So do you have any plans for the next few weeks?" Kai asked, making conversation while we waited for dinner. My mother and I exchanged a glance before we both shook our heads. What was there to do when we lived from paycheck to paycheck? "I just have to work," I replied. "Me, too," she added. Kai seemed to be pondering our words, catching my eye. I decided to give him a coy smile. He raised an eyebrow like he was daring me to make a move on him in front of my mother. The woman looked down at her hands. "When exactly did you first start seeing my son?" the woman blurted, pulling us both from our silent conversation. I was shocked that my mother had asked such a forward question, but Kai simply smiled. "About a month ago."

My mother thought that we were in a romantic relationship. Could it be considered romantic? Had Kai ever entertained the thought of being my boyfriend? As much as I wished for it, that idea seemed far-fetched, even if he took me on dates. "Th-That's when I started working for him," I interjected, refusing to meet their eyes. Kai nodded as my mother glanced out at the city. She didn't seem upset by the news; she was expecting it. "What are your future plans with Luka? You're obviously having sex, and he works for you. How long does a boss-and-worker sexual relationship last?" I gasped, all colour washing from my face as I stared at my mother in shock. How ballsy was she going to get as the night progressed? It had to be a new record for her. "*Mom*," I breathed, flabbergasted. But Kai shook his head, both of them ignoring my outburst. "I consider Luka as my equal, Ms. Roggy. He will work for me as long as he wants, and I plan for him to stay." As long as Kai wanted me, I would stay forever, and those words made my heart melt. Again. But my mother didn't seem particularly satisfied with that answer. She was about to say something more, but Rosa suddenly interrupted with plates of food decorating her arms.

"Thank you, Rosa," Kai said warmly. She gave a low reply. Kai and I both began eating, but my mother only stared at her stroganoff longingly. Something in her gaze, which was set on the steaming mushrooms and noodles, was sad and diffident. "Are you not hungry, Mom?" I asked quietly, knowing that I was far from the truth. She shook her head. "N-No... I just... Is this free?" Her question obviously surprised Kai. His brows pulled together and he dropped his fork onto his plate, allowing her his full attention. "Of course. You're my guest tonight. I would never make any guest pay for food."

She nodded slowly and picked up her fork. I smiled at the image of her attempting not to moan at the taste. Rosa really did make some of the best stroganoff, and none of us could deny it... well, Kaia could. I could see him grimacing at the meal from the corner of my eye. "I remember when I was younger I used to make stroganoff with hotdogs because I couldn't afford beef. Actually, it's pretty good too. Rosa should try it sometime." I laughed quietly at my mother's words. "Mm... hotdogs with *anything* is good." The struggle food always brought me back to my roots. She snorted. "It was that or fish, so...."

Kai watched us with amusement from across the dark table. "Sounds good... maybe I can get Rosa to make something like that for Luka. He enjoys eating hotdogs." A devious smirk began to grow on his face as he glanced at me.

I almost choked, amusement forgotten.

But my mother didn't catch on, or at least she was hiding it well, and I thanked all the gods I could within the next few seconds for that fact.

....

"Thank you for coming, Mom. I know you don't like this, and I can't explain it very well, but-." She cut me off by setting a hand

ANGEL

on my shoulder. Dinner was fabulous, although Kai merely played with his food, drawing figure-eights in the noodles and pushing the sauce to one side of the plate. After our meal, my mother was anxious to leave. She wanted to get home and sleep before her busy shift tomorrow.

"It's okay, Lucika. You're happy... that's good."

There was sadness in her voice. She wasn't jealous of me. She was lonely. My bottom lip immediately stuck out. "I can come home tonight. I have to do dishes and stuff anyway," I told her. She shook her head and looked up at Mason who stood beside his *Ferrari*. "I'll just go home and rest. I'm tired. Just... don't go getting any STDs, okay? And, also, tell Rosa that next time she makes stroganoff she should add some jalapeño peppers to it. I used to do that for your father and he loved it. Kai might like it a little spicy since he didn't seem to enjoy it very much tonight."

I blanched at her advice.

"O-Okay... and you don't go overworking yourself, okay? I promise I'll be home tomorrow to make you dinner." She nodded as Mason held the car door open for her. He caught my eye as he closed it behind her, so I sent him a warning glare. He replied with a sheepish smile as the door was slammed.

Then her window was being rolled down.

"Oh, Luka?"

"Yeah?" I leaned into the window. Her amusement-filled gaze scared me.

"Since apparently you enjoy 'eating hotdogs' so much, make sure Rosa makes some for you. Wouldn't want you to be deprived."

My mouth dropped to the cold cement floor.

"I-... no! W-What?" The woman knew exactly what she was talking about, and her raised eyebrows certainly exposed me to her actual thoughts.

"Have a good night, Luka. I'll see you at home."

"What?"

But the window was already rolling up, forcing my fingers away and creating a wall between us. Together, they pulled out of the garage. I wondered how my mother would enjoy his driving as I wrapped my arms around myself. It was cold in that concrete box, even more so knowing that Kai had just revealed something so personal to my mother. I would never live it down. I had a good reason to be scared.

Don't you dare crash, Mason.

Upstairs, I met Rosa in the kitchen where she finished wiping her counters. "My mom said that jalapeño peppers in stroganoff are really good." She paused and thought for a moment. "I've never thought of that. But Kai likes spicy things, so maybe he'll eat it if I add something like that."

"But he can't taste it, can't he?"

"No. But he can feel the heat."

"Oh."

I took the rag from Rosa's hand and began rinsing it in the sink, watching the murky water spiral down the drain before I felt arms around my waist and a head resting between my shoulder blades. Rosa had disappeared, leaving the two of us alone. Dishes were mostly done.

"Your mother is nice," Kai said against my spine.

"Seriously? You know, she totally caught onto your stupid hotdog thing. But…that was the most conversation I've seen her have with anyone in years." He kissed three of the vertebrae in my neck softly, humming with content against my t-shirt. He didn't seem to care for my predicament. Kai only seemed focused on the peaceful moment.

"Kai?"

ANGEL

"Hm?"

I wasn't sure exactly what I was *planning* to say. Maybe my mother woke me from whatever sad trance I had been in. Maybe she had helped me realize my priorities. All I knew was that the words that came out of my mouth weren't the ones I cycled through my brain.

"I think I love you. Like really love you."

I had only known the man for a month, and I couldn't let him go. He had wrapped his hands around my heart, and I wouldn't be able to leave without having it torn away. His breathing hitched. I shivered. There was silence until I turned around, wrapping my arms around his neck. He stared down at me, his expression blank and waiting, processing.

"Why?"

I was dumbfounded for a moment. Why did I love him? Why wouldn't I? He was caring and kind, and he seemed to know more about me than I knew about myself. He had scars and fears that ran incredibly deep, and that's what made him one of the strongest people I knew. That night I met him was like a light suddenly turning on in the middle of the dark, dangerous path I was being led down. What hadn't he done to make me love him? I didn't care about our past or our future. He was there, right then, and he was one of the few things I valued. Like an anchor, holding me hostage so I wouldn't float away. Not only had he saved me, but he had also created a bond with me that was so unfamiliar for so long, I wasn't sure exactly what it was at first.

So how was I supposed to reply?

CHAPTER
THIRTY-FIVE

HE KISSED MY neck gently; I leaned my head in the opposite direction to reveal more skin. He was obviously overjoyed and encouraged, because his lips immediately clamped onto the pale flesh and began leaving darker marks.

"Well?" he asked between kisses.

"Do I need a reason that I can explain to you?"

I shook my head and allowed a breathy whimper to spring from my lips. My eyes fluttered shut. He didn't reply. Instead, he moved on to my collarbone, leaving a line of hickeys to my shoulder. "Can we... take this to the bedroom?" I asked. I sounded exhausted, although the blood pumping through my veins promised a very long night. Kai stopped his raid on my skin, only to sweep me into his arms bridal-style. "Of course, Angel." I kissed the daily-shaved flesh beneath his chin with a smile, riveted by the prickle of his barely-there stubble as he clutched me close to his chest. The sun was setting over Santa Monica, but the sheets were still warmed by its rays when he dropped me on his bed. I could tell he was anxious to get the show on the road, judging by how he pounced onto the sheets with me the first chance he got.

"Kai?" I pulled away from his lips far enough to look him in the eyes. His brows furrowed like he thought he had done something wrong. I comforted him by pulling lightly at his dark locks, carding my fingers through the strands before twirling them and digging my digits back into his scalp. With my pleading gaze, I silently asked him to do a scene with me, to destroy me. No anal that night, I decided, but that didn't mean we couldn't have fun. "Can I get a wand out?" The man hovering above me had gauged my expression perfectly, and I expected him to begin with rough, demanding movements. But he instead gently turned my head back up to meet his soft eyes, his fingers grazing over my cheek bone while I nodded jerkily.

"I asked a lot from you last time. Are you sure?"

I smirked and pushed his lips back to mine. They connected perfectly, like they were meant to be together. His tongue lolled across my upper gums before diving between my cheeks and gently toying with my own muscle. Meanwhile, his arms wrapped around my waist, pulling me up against his rocky chest. I moaned at the friction against my clothed erection, despite the many layers of heavy fabric between us. We both wanted our outfits gone. Kai gave me just enough space to sit up and pull my shirt over my head, letting it fall to the ground with a soft, comforting noise before he closed the space between us again, making it his duty to turn my lips as puffy and purple as possible. He was about to remove his own shirt, but I instead began unbuttoning it, letting each hole pop away with a heart-stopping, sluggish pace. Kaia didn't seem to mind, though. He was too preoccupied with my body, his hands roaming my sides, daring to tickle my ribs on the way back to my hips. Finally, I pushed the shirt away from his shoulders and watched as he reared up to take it all the way off, his muscles rippling under his skin. I could only stare in awe before he bent to attach his lips to my chest. I gasped. Kai's tongue licked rings around my nipples, teasing and pushing the little nubs in until I was arching off the bed, soft moans falling from my wet lips like invisible waterfalls.

"Kai... s-stop," I managed to choke, grabbing his hair roughly. He immediately recoiled to give me his full attention, obviously expecting something serious to leave my mouth. I instead leaned forward, undoing his belt buckle and lowering his zipper in only a few swift movements. Kai gasped when I engulfed his pulsing cock, taking it as far down my throat as I could. It smelled bitter and salty, how it should. I would need to work on my skill, I knew, but Kai hadn't given me any tips. Neither had people on the streets; I had learnt purely from their breathy moans and gasps. I flicked my tongue around the head before plunging my tongue beneath the foreskin and creating another ring around it. Superb tastes danced on my tongue. "God... Luka," Kaia groaned, throwing his head back and supporting himself on his muscular thighs as his hands dug into my hair. Maybe I didn't need as much schooling as I thought.

Without warning, I pushed his appendage up against his stomach and sucked both balls into my mouth, fondling them against my teeth and tongue. He jolted and groaned again, creating music for no one else's ears but our own.

"Keep going, Angel...."

This only encouraged me, and I soon had his cock shoved against the back of my throat, the heavy scent of musk and sweat burning my nose. The man groaned again, pulling my hair weakly. I gave one final suck from base to tip before finally pulling off with a popping sound, wiping my mouth with the back of my hand. He hadn't finished, but he didn't seem angry, either. "You're getting good at that," he breathed as he pushed me onto my back. I giggled. "I learn from the best, I guess." He slipped off my shorts and discarded them to the side. Then his pants followed. His boxers, my boxers.

The man bent and bit my nipple suddenly while I arched and moaned. My spine stretched and pulled at muscles that were too

ANGEL

tight to be moved, stimulating nerves that were stale and forgotten . "M-More, Kai," I whined. He chuckled and kissed my navel. "We're taking this slow. Be patient, Angel."

Why? Hadn't he understood that I wanted it fast? That I wanted it hard? That I wouldn't be satisfied until I was sobbing in his bathtub while he cleaned me with the softest cloth he owned?

I nodded feverishly before Kai wrapped his hand around my engorged limb. Through my nose, I breathed heavily, willing myself not to orgasm after such pitiful stimulation. A fingernail was dragged from the base to the tip. He scratched at the sensitive head, uniting pain with pleasure. When I keened, he returned all five fingers to the shaft and pumped me firmly. After a few moments of quiet moans and whimpers, he finally pulled his hand away and rested both on the backs of my thighs. "Let me get a wand," he ordered, standing. The vibrator was stashed in the bottom drawer of his nightstand for easy access. I realized that it must have been a powerful one, since it needed a three-prong outlet to plug the beast into.

For a moment, I thought he would begin to assault me with it, pushing me to my limit in seconds and ultimately depleting my ability to form coherent words on the highest setting. But he instead pulled the cord and turned it to the first, lowest setting. The buzzing was quiet and calming, then refreshing and exciting when it was pressed lightly against the underside of my erection. "Yes...," I moaned, gyrating against it. He moved opposite me, adding to the pleasure.

"Faster," I ordered, somehow feeling sure that I would get what I wanted.

But that was never how it worked with Kaia.

"Here. You hold it. Press the button on the side to make it go faster," the man ordered, sitting back on his haunches beside me. He stared with a mischievous glint in his eye, *daring* me to follow his orders. I did. The button was easy to find. My breath caught in my throat when the vibrations grew more intense; I brought the end up to my sensitive head. At that rate, I would be coming in no time. "Ah—*yes,*" I breathed, gripping the sheets with my free hand. I had almost forgotten the man sitting beside me, his eyes swallowing every movement I made. The hand holding the toy shook slightly with the bliss coursing strong through my nerves. My knees trembled.

"Now put it back to the first setting," Kai ordered suddenly.

What?

It was hard to do as I was told; my body didn't seem to want to oblige. But my mind was, and that was the hardest part. My thumb, twitching and struggling to find the switch, eventually did put the toy on the first setting. It was surprising how fast my body relaxed, like I had broken chains that bound me to my release. Suddenly, it wasn't so hard to follow his orders; my mind was clearer. My pounding chest was slowing, and my breathing wasn't so ragged.

"Put it on the third setting."

"What?" I said aloud. He gave me a deadpan expression, allowing me no opportunity to object. "Put it on the third setting." Was this his game? A scene meant to edge me until he ran out of settings? Until he was satisfied?

"Or put it on the fourth. Try the fifth?"

"I'll come if I do that!" I exclaimed, knowing that he was setting me up for failure. He shook his head, brows knitted together. "Only if you let yourself. You have…," the man checked his watch, "… eighteen minutes left. Then you can come." I stared at him in horror, frozen to the sheets. I prayed to find some hint of a lie or insincerity in his gaze. After a second or two, I had found nothing.

"Put it onto the fifth setting. Now." His impatience in his voice was finally divulged. With a deep breath, I pushed the button

ANGEL

and brought the vibrations up to an intense, loud hum. It wasn't calming anymore. Instead, it made my stomach knot with fear. On a vibration that high, there was no hope in holding out for eighteen minutes. But what would the ramifications be if I failed? Would he force more orgasms on me? Edge me? Slap me until I was screaming for mercy? What kind of punishments could he formulate?

When I brought the vibrator down against my shaft again, my mind forgot the eighteen minutes. The punishment was tossed out the window. In under a second, it was only the toy and I, pulling me closer and closer to the release I ached for. My muscles pulled taut again. My eyes closed. I sucked my bottom lip between my teeth. The high setting burned. My legs shook. Kaia's view must have been rather nice, seeing my knuckles turn white and tremble on the wand's handle as I helped myself to pleasure that he knew he would soon take away. But I couldn't think about that then. As much as my mind objected, my body couldn't, too overpowered by the pleasure coursing through my nerves and igniting my groin in white-hot fire. "I'm gonna come, Kai," I whined, bucking up against the toy. He frowned. "No. Turn it off. Lift it away. You can do that." As I whimpered, Kai glared, knowing that I was dangerously close to the edge. The tension was almost too much, consuming my mind and eating at my sanity. With the last of my strength, I pulled back against my straining limbs. In the same second, when the vibrations left me, the grimace of heavenly agony fell from my face. My chest rose and fell slower, more even.

"Good boy. Fifteen minutes left."

I gave a cry of objection, wanting to curse him for forcing me to create my own discipline. I hated him for it, but I also found myself wanting him. I wanted his hands on me instead of the vibrator. My thoughts ceased when Kai himself decided that I had had a long enough rest. The man took his index finger and pushed the vibrating tip that hovered just above my skin against my shaft. Already, I was close to the edge, drowning in spiraling pleasure. I wondered how long it had been since we began. It seemed like hours.

"Careful, baby… careful!"

Again, I raised it, my body momentarily arching up to follow the vibrations. This time, my face was contorted by silent sobs. I shook my head. "I was so close!" I told him.

"Ten more minutes," was his only reply.

There was *no way* I would be able to endure ten more minutes. His gaze promised me that I would have to… or face the consequences.

CHAPTER
THIRTY-SIX

EVER SINCE THE dream I'd had a few nights ago, I was slightly on edge. It was a strange dream, and it shouldn't have bothered me as much as it did, but now that I had spent a few nights in my own bed, the unsettling feeling in my stomach was only growing in strength. Why did the memory of Cade bother me so much? Why was he haunting me? He had been a nice guy, maybe a little creepy, but nice.

My house was silent and lonely. The noises of the city faded slightly in the outskirts of Los Angeles, but my love for Kai definitely did not.

Maybe he didn't love me like I loved him, but I felt as if he did. It was better than nothing. Nonetheless, I felt as if a pair of eyes were on me at all times. In the shower, I nearly screamed when I heard my mother's footsteps passing by the door. I had forgotten that she was home. I was almost *scared*. If I was allowed to, I wouldn't even be able to jack myself off. I felt too exposed, like everywhere I went, there would be someone who was watching me from around the corner. I had forgotten how uncomfortable my bed was too. I had decided to leave my blanket at Kai's house, secretly because I wanted something there to remind him of me. I had a fear of being forgotten or thrown to the side now, and anything I could do to help that was a blessing.

"*Are you awake?*" I texted Kai at midnight. He probably wouldn't be sleeping, but I also didn't want to intrude on his sleep schedule if he was. I waited for several minutes, my brows furrowing. He would either have answered immediately or he was sleeping. Or, he was sleeping with someone else. I shivered at the thought.

I only received a notification when I was reaching to set my phone on my nightstand. Immediately I read it, my eyes widening.

"*Kai had a nightmare. A bad one. Rosa wants to take him to the hospital, but James is coming over to see him first. This is Mason. I apologize for not replying sooner.*"

"*What?! What happened? Why the hospital? Tell me how he is when James gets there,*" I replied, my thin fingers typing faster than I thought possible. I began to panic, breaking into a cold sweat.

"*I have to go, Luka. Can you come over? I know it's late, but Kai's asking for you. Rosa will be there to pick you up soon if you can meet her.*"

"*Of course. I'll be waiting.*"

I shut off my phone and threw my covers to the side, frantically pulling on a pair of sweatpants and a long-sleeved shirt before I grabbed my keys and bounded outside. My mother wouldn't have heard, as she was probably going through her second bottle of sleeping pills. It would take at least twenty minutes for Rosa to get there, and an additional twenty minutes to get back to Kai's house. An extra fifteen if we were to meet them at the hospital. I waited for ten before I began to pace on my dead lawn. I just hoped that Kai would be okay. He was strong, unlike myself, but these nightmares had the power to warp him into a broken, terrified mess.

As suspected, I had to wait another ten minutes before the *Bentley's* engine reached my ears from the end of my street. When Rosa parked beside me, I didn't waste time with a greeting as I slid inside and buckled myself to the seat. "Is he going to the hospital?"

ANGEL

My voice was shaking. She shook her head, her dark eyes focused on the road. She looked concerned for her boss. Maybe this was bad, worse than I thought, but I couldn't tell when she refused to look at me.

"He'll be staying at the tower, but Mason told me to hurry you over there."

I nodded, my fingers pulling at my knuckles for the first time in a long time.

....

Rosa barely even had time to stop the car before I was out and jogging towards the elevator. Only when I got closer to the doors and looked behind me did I see that her eyes were bloodshot, as if she had been crying, and she had a darkening bruise under her left eye. "What happened?" I asked in horror, freezing with my hand just over the elevator buttons. She looked away, diverting her eyes as if she was ashamed. "Kai hit me," she whispered.

My breathing stopped. "He... hit you?" Kai would have never hit Rosa. He would never hit anyone unless they deserved it. Rosa would never deserve it. I didn't know what to do. Kai had hurt a good friend of mine; there was a twinge of hate in my heart for the man who hurt her. She shook her head, immediately defending Kaia himself. "He had another episode. He used to get them when he was younger, but they've cleared up for the last few years."

"An episode?" I asked as we walked quickly to the elevator together. "Sometimes he can wake up and still think he's in his nightmare or he can lose control of his actions. You know, like... a night terror. It's not really him when he gets like that."

"And... And he hit you? But... Kai wouldn't hit you, would he?" She shook her head. "No. He was trying to protect himself, thinking I was... a bad person. Mason had to restrain him before you got here. He's calmed down since and James has been sitting with him." I ran a hand through my dishevelled hair, knowing I needed to be strong when I saw him. He would be a mess.

I was right.

When we rode the elevator and made it to the top floor of his apartment space, Kai sat on one of his couches wrapped in my blanket, his hair matted and sweaty and his eyes wild and frantic. I could see him, especially his hands, trembling from across the large room. James sat in front of him on the edge of the coffee table, pushing sweaty stray locks away from his face and mumbling to him comfortingly. Again, there was that fatherly aura around James. At the sound of the elevator, James turned his head, eagerly searching for me, before he stood and left Kai sitting by the reflective windows.

"Luka," he greeted when he had crossed the room to me.

"How is he?"

"Not good. He's shaken up pretty bad, but he'll be okay in a little while. We're working to get his medication figured out; he's not usually this bad."

I watched as Kai brought his hands to his face, supporting his elbows on his knees, and kept them there. He looked agonizingly sad. "We'll leave you two alone. He's been asking for you," James added as he stepped past me and joined Rosa and Mason in the elevator. I could only give a nervous nod before the doors closed and we were left alone. But how was I supposed to comfort him? I had never done that for anyone before, but even my own mother.

I realized that it was what I wanted. Since I saw Mason sitting with Kai with his head in Mason's hands, I wanted to be that person. I just never realized how difficult that job was, how scary. "Hey, Kai," I began quietly, coming to stand beside him slowly, unsure of what he would do. His watery gaze snapped up to me. My breath hitched slightly. He *was* a mess. The man was dangerously pale, and his shaking didn't seem to be improving. He was terrified, broken, and all it took was one night terror to unman him. His coffee scent was over-sweet, causing my nose to scrunch up against the burn.

"Luka," he breathed, throwing out his arm in a flash and whimpering when he couldn't reach me. To soothe him, I quickly took a seat beside him, hip to hip, before his arms wrapped around me. I gasped slightly, his grip like iron chains. His fingers dug painfully into my back, as if he was afraid I would vanish at any second. "Are you okay?" I choked, wincing when his fingers dug in further and pushed against bone. He released a shaky, hot breath against my chest, but stayed silent until I pushed him back to look at him. Tears rocketed down his face. His breathing was uneven and forced.

I couldn't look at him anymore. There was too much pain and grief on the surface. If I stared too long, it would act as quicksand. Instead, I wrapped my arms around his neck and shoulders and pulled him to my chest, beginning a slow rocking motion. It seemed to calm him a little. The man simply gripped my shirt and whimpered against me as I hushed him.

Eventually, he cried himself to sleep with his head on my lap, facing my stomach. I had moved to the end of the couch so Kai had room to lie down. My fingers worked through his dark hair in an effort to comfort him. James had come to check on us once, excitement evident on his face.

"He's the luckiest man alive to have you, Luka," James told me, pushing his hands into his pockets. I looked up at him in confusion. "He is?" He nodded and slowly took a seat across from me. "You know he talks about you all the time, right? He... admires you, in a way."

"Isn't telling me this kinda against your privacy policy?" I didn't believe him.

"He told me that I could tell you if he couldn't."

I pursued my lips. "Oh. So am I... helping him?"

James nodded. "Absolutely."

I nodded absently and looked out across the city, my mind wandering aimlessly. The windows reflected my bleak face. James leaned back against the couch and followed my gaze. There was a moment of silence as we sat together in the dim lighting, Kai's soft, even breaths the only sound that broke the quiet. He mumbled something unintelligible to himself. Once I hushed him by rubbing at his scalp, he fell silent again.

"He wants you to move in with him. Has he told you that?" I looked at him in shock. "Don't you think that's kinda early? I mean... our relationship is still really young."

"Yeah. He said that too. But I do want to tell you that you're really good for him. He's made a massive improvement over the last month."

"I just don't understand how I could have done that. I'm just the hooker who wanted some extra cash." James laughed quietly instead of giving me a reply. I sighed.

"I guess he's grown on me too. I just don't know how to help him. I feel like my abilities are coming to an end." James shook his head. "No, no. You're doing amazing. Just keep doing what you're doing."

I sighed and shrugged. "I guess he seems happy with me, at least. I'm happy, too, I think."

"He's overjoyed when he sees you, trust me. I wouldn't know what to do if he came to me saying you had left." I bit my lip and nodded. "In all honesty, I've had the best month in my life with him."

"Promise me you won't leave him. He's like a son to me."

With that, I glanced down at Kai, my hand toying with his hair lightly. Tears no longer fell from his eyes. Instead, he stared at my stomach with a doleful expression, as if he had been awake for days instead of what I hoped were seconds. But when his gaze snapped up to meet mine, I knew he had heard it all. He just couldn't say it himself. I took a deep breath before answering James.

"I promise... I don't want to leave. And I'll do everything in my power to stay with him."

CHAPTER
THIRTY-SEVEN

I WOKE UP THE next morning with a headache and an instant memory of the night before. But I never remembered being put in Kai's bed, which was where I realized I was. Kai lay next to me, his hair falling into his face and covering his eyes. I moved it away from his features, pushing it behind his ear as his eyes twitched. I froze, fearful I had woken him. Instead of being angry, he rolled further towards me while he cleared his throat groggily, pushing his forehead against mine. I smiled and closed my eyes again, dwelling on his scent. We were both quite obviously awake.

"I'm sorry about last night."

My eyes flew open, directly in front of Kai's black gaze that watched me.

"Why? What's there to be sorry about?"

"I didn't know what to do. I'm sorry."

I shook my head, wanting to hit him for apologizing. "Don't be sorry. I came. Of course I got here as fast as I could. You don't need to apologize." He took comfort from my words and nodded as he pulled my leg over his waist, massaging my thigh lightly. There was nothing sexual in the act, only repose. "How much do you remember from last night?" I asked, unable to resist asking. "I remember the nightmare. I always remember those... but not much after that.

ANGEL

I remember falling asleep on the couch with you. And then waking up before James left." I bit my lip at the memory slightly as he continued. "And then I carried you to the bed. I knew my Angel hadn't gotten his full eight hours yet." I shrugged, a smirk rising on my features. "Well, I do need my beauty sleep. And so do you." He smiled and nudged his nose against mine. "So... what did you think about what James said last night?" I knew he was talking about moving in, but I also knew I couldn't, not until I really knew that we could stay together. We treated each other like boyfriends, yet our relationship felt so *temporary*. It hurt, but it was true.

"I... can't. Not now," I mumbled. His soft expression didn't change like I thought it would. "We've only known each other for a month, Kai."

He nodded. "But this month-and-a-bit has been one of the best... for me."

I frowned. "And for me too. But I can't move in now. I have to take care of my mother. We... can reconsider it months from now. Does that sound good?" Kai sighed and nodded as he played absentmindedly with the hem of my boxers. The man didn't seem disappointed, at least. "You know, you really should have installed some kind of balcony for your room," I told him suddenly. My gaze had drifted over his shoulder to stare out at the morning sun. He raised an amused eyebrow at me.

"What? You have a nice view that's kinda going to waste is all I'm saying...," I added.

He chuckled and sat up, shaking his head. "I do have a balcony."

I gave him a stare as if to say "... *the fuck are you talking about?*" with my upper lip slightly pulled over my teeth in confusion, as if I smelled something rotten. He laughed at my expressions. "You think I bought myself an apartment without anywhere to stand outside in private and enjoy the Santa Monica sunsets?" I shrugged, realizing that he would have never settled without an outdoor relaxation area.

"Put this on," he ordered, handing me his rugby sweater. I did so with excitement, breathing in coffee beans and the fading scent of sweaty teenage musk. "You should show me your rugby abilities sometime," I said as he took my hands and pulled me to my feet. "Now that you mention it, yeah, actually, that might be fun. Maybe I'll get some buddies together and we could have a game," he told me while he led me across the room, our hands connected. Excitement bubbled inside me when I realized that we were entering that second elevator, only accessible from his bedroom. "Would I play?" I asked. I wasn't sure exactly what rugby entailed. I knew it was a lot of running, like most sports, and it resembled football in many ways. So maybe I *wasn't* prepared for a game. Kai immediately shook his head. "No. I guarantee that the people I play with weigh at least fifty pounds more than you do. I'm not ever letting my Angel be crushed."

I giggled as he placed a kiss on my cheek, although his words held extra undertones of a warning.

"Who do you play with? High school buddies? Business friends?" For an unexplained reason, I just couldn't imagine Kai with a group of fun, boisterous men. He was just too cold when he spoke to other people, especially people he did business with. After hearing him curse over the phone to business partners a few times, I realized that he had probably created a reputation for himself. "Mostly guys I visit the gym with. It gets lonely working out at home alone. That's why I visit the gym down close to your place."

That was why he was out that first night we met. Mason visited the same gym too.

The elevator doors were closed, and we lurched slightly when we were pulled to what I could only guess was the roof. When the doors opened and I had grown accustomed to the bright light that blinded us, I realized I was right.

ANGEL

"Wow," I breathed.

We had entered into a small glass and wood building with a modern and uniquely geometrical design. There was a small square bar and seating area on the side, complete with a gas fireplace sitting in the centre. On the other side of the bar was a pool table, a ping pong table, and a foosball table. The place wasn't just for Kaia, I was sure. It was meant for the tenants in the entire building. Outside sat a hot tub beside a ring of padded outdoor seats set in a circle around a wood-burning fire pit. To see it all lit up at night would have been stunning, especially with the slight, ocean-tinted breeze that ruffled our hair. There was something refreshing about the wind up there, especially in the summer heat.

"No one else in the apartments below me really uses this place, but... you like it?" Kai asked, wrapping an arm around my waist.

I nodded eagerly. "This is awesome!"

He chuckled and led me outside where the sun stained the dark hardwood floors a bright gold. They were hot on my bare feet too. I wondered why I had never taken advantage of the top floor.

"I don't come up here often. Sometimes Rosa will come up here, though. And Mason loves the hot tub."

I laughed at the thought of his bodyguard relaxing in a pool, shades perched on his head and one of Rosa's cocktails in his hand. Kai leaned over the glass railing, supported on his elbows as he stared off over the other buildings around us. He had a sliver of a view of the ocean too. "This is so cool. You should move your bed into the building and move the bar if no one even uses it. You could wake up and step outside into the fresh air every morning," I told him. He sighed. "I've thought about that. But I like my bedroom, and then I remember the other people I share the space with. They're nice people, but... there isn't even a bathroom up here."

I nodded with a small, dismissive shrug. He was making sense.

"So, what do you plan to do today?" I asked. It felt wrong to talk about work in a setting like the one around us. The hot tub seemed to call to me. Kaia shrugged. "I have to get some work done today. That means I'll probably be in my office until I decide to sleep."

"I have to work too. I'll keep you company," I told him. The smile he replied with was calming. He took my hand to lead me back inside.

....

As much as I wanted to spend the night with him, I realized I also wanted to see my mother for once too. I missed her, and what little bit of a relationship we had before was crumbling. So, I managed to convince Kai to let me leave after a few hours of quietly working and shaking the apartment with a brief drum solo before showering him with goodbye kisses. He only chuckled, but I knew that he was afraid to spend the night alone. Again. Neither of us wanted a repeat of last night, but if he had another night terror, I promised him that I would be by his side as soon as Mason or Rosa picked me up.

During our week away from each other, we still conversed daily over texting. He even called me Thursday night, and I panicked, thinking he could have had another nightmare.

"Kai? Are you okay?" I immediately answered my phone, turning off my music. My work for the day was sitting between my legs, halfway done. He only chuckled. "I'm fine, Angel. Don't worry about me too much. I just wanted to hear your voice." My heart melted instantly, and a wide smile broke out across my face as I relaxed into my pillows and blankets.

"Has work been okay?" I asked.

"Eh... it's as good as work can get, I suppose. I'm trying to close a deal in Korea for my father, but those guys just aren't taking my price." I could hear the annoyance and exhaustion in his voice. He probably hadn't slept much at all within the last few days. I wasn't sure if it was my place to put him to bed.

"Well, that's *Kim Jong-un*'s loss."

He laughed. "It was South Korea, but it was the dealer's loss, yes."

There was a moment of silence between us as my foot toyed with the blinds above my bed. They were riveting in a peculiar, uninteresting way. "I'm really missing you right now, you know," I stated finally. Then I sighed.

"Me too."

We hung up soon after he claimed to be late for a conference call with a few of his father's associates. He seemed stressed and tired, but I knew that he had no intention of calling it a night. He needed his sleep, since Kai had told me that he would be taking me out tomorrow, but refused to relay any other information. I was too excited to sleep, staying up to blast music and create myself a comfortable nest of blankets and sheets.

"So, what are you doing tonight? Preparing for the big surprise tomorrow?" I texted him again at ten-thirty.

"Nope. I don't need to prepare much for it. What are you up to?"

I bit my lip as I typed. I had done something akin to sexting before, so should have expected it again sooner or later.

"I'm being horny at the moment... and I really, really need you to fix it."

My cock was already straining against my boxers, so I sent him a quick picture of it. He didn't reply back for a moment, and I hoped that he was getting in his car to get his ass over to my house.

"Well now I'm horny. What am I gonna do with you?"

"Make me scream your name?"

"Mm... that's a good idea. But how would I prep you? I would probably start at your chest...."

My hand immediately brushed over one nipple before pinching

it lightly. No, he hadn't given me permission yet, (Really, I didn't need it. We weren't together or in the middle of a scene) but I could tell what this was going to turn into. Never had I expected him to play along so eagerly. I bit my lip and closed my eyes, my little buds instantly standing at attention. I rolled them periodically in one hand, tugging and massaging them. The stimulations sent bolts of lightning to my groin.

"*Let me see that pretty little cock of yours, baby boy,*" he texted after a minute. I debated whether I should just take another photo without the underwear, but my mind instead led me to more lewd thoughts. For once, I didn't mind the dirty images flashing behind my eyes. So, instead of sending him another average dick pic, I opted for a different idea, reaching under my bed to grab the bright dildo and little bottle of lube. I also grabbed a large black sharpie from the drawer in my nightstand. After a few moments, I stretched myself enough to fit it in comfortably, and I resisted the urge to thrust against the toy. Across the handle of the dildo, the word "KAI" was written in bold, black ink. If I caught the right angle, one would clearly be able to read it before the dildo disappeared inside my straining entrance.

I sat in front of the tall mirror that hung on the back of my door, my legs spread to show Kai's prize. With my boxers having been taken off minutes ago, my cock stood straight up against my stomach, a tiny dribble of milky liquid melting down the side. I sent the photo to him, hoping he would be as aroused as I was.

"*I really want you, Daddy,*" I texted.

"*Jesus, Angel. Maybe I'll just cancel the plans tomorrow and we can stay in bed all day.*"

"*No. I need you. Now.*"

I was aching for him. I could almost *taste* him.

"*Fuck yourself with the toy.*"

ANGEL

Fuck. Kai obviously wasn't going to come over, but I was going to take what I could get. So I took a deep breath and leaned forward, nearly dropping the phone when I pulled the toy out slowly. Then I pushed it back in with a little more force, lighting firecrackers inside me. "God," I breathed, my eyes closing again and my breathing becoming quicker and more laboured. "Fuck," I moaned as I began to fuck myself with more passion than before, allowing myself to fall until my cheek was pressed into my stained carpet. I only opened my eyes wide enough to see what Kai had texted me, nearly dropping my phone in the process. Double-tasking was hard, but not impossible.

"Does it feel good, baby?"

I whimpered and decided to call him instead, my free hand finally coming to wrap around my shaft. The speaker button trembled with my gaze, so my finger had trouble finding it.

"It's not as big as you... Kai, I need to come. I can't hold it."

A tiny puddle of seed leaked onto the carpet, adding a new stain that would haunt me more than any other one. The pressure against my prostate was building with each new thrust, and I found myself trembling and whining as my eyes rolled back in my head. Faintly, I could hear him panting too. "I know you can't, Angel. Let it out."

With that, I released a loose, breathy cry, my body stiffening and arching violently as I watched stars explode and seed spill across my carpet, turning the dark material an even darker brown.

CHAPTER
THIRTY-EIGHT

MASON WAS AT my house around five PM The next day. Kai had told me to wear something casual. I was determined to give him a boner when he saw me, although he never told me what he specifically liked his subs to wear besides high heels and sex toys, of course. I just hoped that I wouldn't be going to a place with too many people. So, I met Mason dressed in a pair of dark short-shorts. Above that, I had put on an old playboy t-shirt and tucked it into the shorts. Once inside the vehicle, Mason gave me a small look, but didn't instigate the subject any further.

"Are we going to the tower?" I asked. Mason shook his head. "I'm dropping you off at your surprise. Alice will be there, too, so you won't be lonely."

"Won't be lonely for what?"

But Mason didn't answer. His thumbs moved on the wheel to an unfamiliar rap song, and he honked twice at a woman who couldn't seem to stay off the phone and notice the green light ahead. Even when I asked if he would give me a hint, he ignored me.

I was confused when we first pulled into a high school parking lot, but only until Mason motioned around the back. "The field is behind the school. I think most of his buddies are already there." I realized he must be playing a game of Rugby. Excitement suddenly bubbled inside me, and a smile sprung loose across my face. I nodded and thanked him before closing the *Ferrari's* door and walking quickly down the side of the school, my hands in my pockets.

"Luka!" A shrill, deafening shout filled my ears before two short arms wrapped and my neck and her stubby legs around my waist. "You look so fucking cute today! You cut your hair!" Alice exclaimed. I was too busy trying not to fall over with the new weight. "Uh, Sorry," she said, dropping to the ground. Even with my height, she only stood at my shoulder. "So are you excited to watch our lovers beat each other up?" I shook my head, no, quickly as she led me to a large set of metal bleachers beside the turf. I didn't expect her Domme friend to be there, and I suddenly worried for Kai. The sun was just beginning to lower, casting yellow light across the back of the school and field. From where we sat, we could see a group of people gathered in the centre. Out of the two teams that stood together, I struggled to pick out Kai.

"Kai is jersey number twenty-seven. Genova's number is ten," she told me, pointing as the teams did a cheer and moved into formation. The jerseys were different colours, all from different high school teams or professional rugby players.

"Wasn't she 'Mommy' last time I saw you?"

She nodded, unfazed. "I'm her little. And when I'm not in my headspace, which I usually am, she's my friend… or, well, a motherly figure."

"Kai was saying something about that. What's a 'little space'?"

She glanced at me then back to the field, sticking her hands under hips and swinging her feet lightly. "Well, my headspace age is about four-to-six-years-old. It's a long subject to explain. It's… a coping mechanism to me. Kinda like therapy, I guess. It helps me. That's really the only way I know how to explain it."

"Oh... so she takes care of you like a mother when you're in your headspace?"

She shrugged. "Yeah, kinda. Well, I guess she's more like a lover mother." She giggled.

"So you're a motherfucker?"

We both exploded into laughter; I was glad she didn't take my joke the wrong way.

As the game began, I realized that despite what I expected, rugby was even tougher of a sport than football. There was no padding, not even long pants, and the unforgiving ground when players were tackled—it was rough. My back straightened when Kai's shirt was grabbed and he was pulled to the ground by a man who was roughly the same size. I watched him hit the pitch harder than I hoped, his body creating a noise that I prayed wasn't his spine. A moment later, I realized that the noise had only been his pained grunt. I could see him wince even from where I sat. Kai would be sore tomorrow.

"Ah... I love her so much. You're a fucking beast, Mama!" Alice screamed from beside me. I cringed away from the noise as she waved her arms in the air and smiled from ear to ear.

I watched as Alice's girlfriend shoved the ball under her arm and rammed straight through Kaia, nearly pushing his feet off the ground when her shoulder met his chest. Alice was right, she was a beast. And Kaia was taking a lot of hits; it amused me to realize that he really wasn't all that good at the sport. But I could see that he was happy playing it again.

Genova was beautiful with her wavy, fiery-orange hair and cold, forest-green eyes. She was also the tallest of all the men in the group, standing at least six-foot-five. Alice's partner was probably closer to seven feet tall, actually, with a massive rack and beautiful curves that any straight man would drool over. I didn't realize until then that she had swirls of tattoos spreading up her thighs, symbols I only

ANGEL

recognized from customers with gang affiliation. I could tell that she had a hard shell and a venomous attitude, and that Alice had crumbled it in her tiny hands.

"How did you snag her?"

Alice laughed and leaned into my shoulder. "That's a long story too."

I smiled as we watched the ferocity of the game unfold.

When it was over, we watched the men and woman shake hands before dispersing. Genova's team had won fourteen-to-ten. Alice and I dashed across the field to jump into our lovers' arms. "I'm all sweaty, Luka," Kai laughed. I only giggled and kissed him hard on the lips as he held me. "You took a pretty good hit there. I never realized how violent this game was," I told him after I had tickled his tonsils successfully. He shrugged. "I'll be okay. I'm just getting old, I guess," he smirked. I laughed and looked to Alice, who sat in her friend's arms and leaned her head against the woman's. "Good game, Genova," Kai said respectfully. Genova nodded, a permanent frown set on her face like concrete. She seemed so cold, yet Alice smiled all the while. "You ready to go, Socket?" Genova asked Alice. Alice nodded tiredly against Genova's shoulder before they turned away, leaving us in the middle of the field as the sun set, sending a long shadowy outline on the field behind us. "I could see you from across the field. You're like a beacon with those legs," he purred, letting me stand and wrap my arms around his neck. Sweaty, post-workout Kai was definitely something I could get used to. Kai pulled me further to him, his obvious erection pressing against my hip. I smirked. "That was the point."

....

The constant feeling that someone was watching me had disappeared for a good while, but the next morning, as I woke with sore muscles and an aching back, (the night had been a lesson on impact play)

I resisted the urge to search the room for anyone trying to sneak a peek at us. "Kai," I mumbled, pushing his shoulder. He didn't stir, so I gave another shove. He groaned and swatted me away. "Kai," I repeated, pushing him again. "Do we have security cameras in this place?" He moaned and looked up at me with the messiest mop of hair and groggy, glazed eyes. "What? No," he told me before flopping back onto his stomach and shoving his face into his pillow. He was adamant on getting more sleep before he would have to get up and work. "That's why we have roommates and a doorman," he added, barely audible. He was obviously equally exhausted and sore as I was after last night's game and sexual encounters that followed.

I frowned and threw my legs over the edge of the bed. "I'll be back," I promised. He was already snoring by the time the door closed behind me. I met Mason in the kitchen where he and Rosa played *Mario Kart* before anyone was up for breakfast. They were careful to keep quiet, as soundproof as the building was. "G'morning, Luka," Mason said, his eyes trained on the large screen. Rosa mimicked his greeting, paying little attention to me. "Hey, guys, do you have security cameras in this place?" I asked, ignoring their greetings. Both looked at each other before glancing at me, their faces filled with confusion. I assented, it was a peculiar question to ask on a Monday morning, but Kai's answer couldn't be trusted in his state.

"Um... no. Kai didn't like the idea of someone constantly being able to see the inside of his house," Rosa told me, "So there are only cameras in the elevator and down at the building's entrances." I nodded slowly and wrapped my arms around myself, frustration mingling with the anxiety. I felt so exposed, as if all the eyes of an invisible crowd were on me. Maybe I was going crazy. "Are you okay, Luka?" Mason asked, pausing their game. I nodded absently, my mind distant, and took a seat at the island. Their attention was on me, causing my heart rate to quicken even more.

ANGEL

"Yeah... I'm just bothered, I guess. Maybe it's hormones."

Mason snorted. "Join the club. I haven't gotten any pussy in months."

Rosa hit him over the back of his head with her game controller.

CHAPTER
THIRTY-NINE

KAI WAS STILL snoring by the time I made it back to his bedroom. So, I decided to take a shower, hoping it would calm me. Undressing myself was strenuous, but once I had enclosed myself in the spacious tile box and let the scalding water relieve my tense muscles, a soft smile invaded my face.

"You're taking a shower without me?" Kai's voice made me jump, safety from the exposed feeling melting away in an instant. "Woah," he soothed, setting a hand on my hip. He was nude, lightly pushing his morning erection against my tailbone. "It's just me. Why are you like this all of the sudden?" I nearly moaned when his hands found my shoulders and he began massaging away the tension as my heart rate calmed. "I don't know. I guess that dream really weirded me out," I mumbled, leaning my head back against his shoulder as his steamers turned on around us.

"You mean the wet dream?"

I hit him in the arm playfully, pausing his massage. "It wasn't a wet dream!"

He laughed and fell silent for me to continue. "It was just really odd. And it had nothing to do with stalkers or anything, but ever since, I've been really on edge."

"Yeah, I can feel that," he replied, finding a new knot between

ANGEL

my shoulder blades. He worked it out slowly. I pouted. "How the heck did you even learn how to give people five-star massages?" He chuckled and shrugged, the spray of the shower pulling his hair down onto his face far enough for him to pause his work and swipe it away. "My sister, Lily, used to do a lot of sports medicine before she dropped that career. Now she's a teacher."

"Oh," I said finally.

"So... about the dream. What was I doing in it?" I wasn't sure if his voice was still playful. Did he want me to explain a fantasy or was he truly concerned about the images I saw?

I sighed and turned around, his hands finally falling to rest on my hips. Water dripped down Kai's face before cascading down his chiselled chest and over his erection. "Just forget it. I'm probably just going insane, anyway. No big deal," I concluded, patting his chest lightly. His brows furrowed, and the first chunk of a word escaped his lips before I hushed him. "Forget it," I repeated, already lowering myself to my knees without breaking eye contact. He got the message and his eyes darkened considerably when I took his length into my mouth, sucking the tip just to shut him the hell up. "I used to have to take care of this by myself in the morning if a sub hadn't stayed over from the night before," he told me as his fingers burrowed into my hair, pulling lightly. I hummed in reply and rolled my tongue around the head before thrusting it against his sensitive slit. He gave a low moan, his grip tightening on my hair. The thought of Kai jacking himself off was undeniably a turn-on.

The musky scent burnt my nose, but I powered through until milky liquid began bubbling down my throat. I took as much of him as I could and let it slide against the sensitive flesh of the back of my tongue. I did my best to suppress the urge to gag. My tongue quivered around him with the effort. "God, that's good. You're great at this," he mumbled, throwing his head back and closing his eyes. I fondled his balls before taking both of them into my mouth, sucking harshly. He jolted slightly before his cock dripped more liquid down into my face. Luckily, the bathroom tiles weren't too uncomfortable under my bare knees, and the water was only slightly blinding, falling over both of us like a hot blanket. It comforted me, allowed my throat to relax. I continued to fondle him as I took his cock back to my throat and sucked as hard as possible, my muscles screaming in protest.

"Angel," he breathed as his other hand joined the first one and he gripped my head above each ear. The man's thumbs swiped at my matted, wet hair. The waterfall smoothed it immediately. His voice wasn't exactly a statement, but it wasn't a question, either. Nonetheless, I got the message. My own erection stood straight, as if it was pointing to Kai, wanting him. A light hand gripped it and jerked it slowly, careful not to bring me to orgasm but enough to relieve the burn. He began mercilessly thrusting into my mouth, and I was careful not to let him feel any teeth. It was rough. I was forced to squeeze my eyes tight to block them from the oncoming spray of the shower, but I also felt burning tears accumulate behind my lids. My vision spun. There wasn't even any time to gag before the next thrust came, filling my mouth with more water and meat. Although it sounded much like a version of hell, I *loved* the choking hazard. I loved the increase of grunts when he grew close. I loved to know that *I* was the reason he didn't have to jerk himself off in the morning.

His orgasm was sudden and unpredicted, seed shooting down my throat and dribbling out of my cheeks when it had filled the small space. He pulled out, and I was left to choke and cough against the floor, milky liquid falling to the tile in front of my knees. There was no effort made to swallow it. Kai squatted beside me slowly, his brows pulled together, as I rubbed water away from my

ANGEL

eyes and struggled not to puke. It was a satisfying struggle, though, the feeling of being well-used. The raw flesh of my throat was a reminder that I had pleased him greatly.

"S-Sorry," I choked, coughing again. He knelt to take my face between his hands, the choking already subsiding. "Good boy," he praised. I smiled lazily, finally meeting his gaze with my own drowsy eyes. "I did good?" I asked eagerly. He chuckled and helped me to my feet, nodding, so we could finish washing. He spent the last thirty minutes of our shower cleaning me thoroughly and reassuring himself that my body had been scrubbed from head-to-toe. I did the same to him.

I released a yelp when he hoisted me up against his shoulder, supporting me on his arm once the shower turned off. He didn't even bother to grab a towel as he entered his bedroom and let me fall backwards onto the bed. I frowned slightly. "My hair is gonna soak your sheets."

He smirked and shrugged. "That's why Rosa knows how to change them." Kai supported his weight on one knee that he pushed between my legs, sucking a line of red spots across my chest and narrowly missing my nipples. I moaned with frustration at the lack of stimulation. The sound turned into a small, whimpering cry when he gripped my erection in his large hand. My back arched off the bed; stars burst across my vision. "Kai," I sighed, almost instantly feeling the edge of my orgasm. His hand was moving fast. "I'm close. Can I come?" I asked, struggling to move my grinding jaw. His strokes were firm and satisfying, turning my legs to jelly. I was so close, all I needed was a pump or two more—

"No," he replied, his grip suddenly stilling on my cock and squeezing hard at the base. My hips bucked off the bed as waves of both pain and pleasure coursed through me.

"You have to promise me something first."

I panted and gripped the wet satin sheets. "Wh-What?!" Could I not get through one single orgasm without him interrupting me?

"Promise me that you'll use it for me if I bought a dancing pole."

My eyes widened incredulously and I leaned up onto my elbows to look at him in shock. "Seriously?! You're holding that against me right now?! You manipulative dick..."

"Yes," he deadpanned. Kai ignored my name-calling.

I brought both hands to cover my face and flopped back onto the bed. "One damn club, Kai, and you're ready for me to be your stripper? All I wanted was one morning orgasm!"

He shrugged. "Just say yes and you can have it." Kai unexpectedly brushed the palm of his other hand over my sensitive head, eliciting a loud keen from my throat. The single movement was enough to make me crumble. "F-Fine! Okay! I promise I'll do it!" He seemed satisfied with my answer, since he softened his grip, jerked me slightly, and allowed release, my hips bucking as I whined and gripped the sheets. My eyes rolled back in my head before I closed them, allowing ecstasy to dominate my body. Once I was panting and slightly trembling with the aftershocks, Kai used his feather comforter cover to wipe away the milky liquid that decorated my stomach.

"Hey, Kai, I got a question," I breathed as he flopped onto the bed beside me, wetting the sheets even further. "Shoot," he replied. He didn't seem smug after his victory. The towel around his waist was loose and fell halfway down his ass.

"Why did Genova call Alice 'Socket' yesterday? I've heard a lot of nicknames, but 'Socket' doesn't sound very romantic." Kai shrugged. "It's not supposed to be. I'm sure she'll explain it to you one day, but she was known as 'Socket' in her old job. I don't know the details, but I know it has something to do with eye sockets." My brows furrowed with worry and confusion. "Eye sockets? That's...

ANGEL

okay...." Kai chuckled and sat up, noting my confusion. I was sure that it confused him too. "Yeah, it's a little odd. But I'm sure it would make sense if she explained it." I nodded and shrugged as we both dressed ourselves.

"So, I actually have a question for you,"

"Another question?"

"How would you feel about meeting my parents?"

My mouth fell open slightly, and my brain momentarily froze with terror. He had already met my mother, and we had been together for almost two months, more or less. But there was something about meeting his parents, Mr. and Mrs. Arche, that held much higher expectations. They were powerful, and what would I do if they didn't like me? Had Kai brought anyone home before? Would they allow a former sex worker into their home? Kai sighed, realizing my fear. "You can think about it. I just didn't want to come to you the day before and tell you that we're going to see them tomorrow. I'll be leaving in two weeks for a family reunion, and I wanted you to come. It's the parents and siblings, nothing big."

So it wasn't just his parents, it was his entire fucking family. Now I had to impress his siblings, too? The thought haunted me, sent my mind reeling with panic, as I stood and pulled a shirt and yesterday's shorts over my body. Kai did the same, although his outfit showed much less skin. He kissed me lightly on the cheek and took my hand as the hallway he pulled me into led us down to the kitchen. "Like I said, you can think about it. But just know that they'll love you no matter what."

"You don't know that," I mumbled as I took a seat at one of the islands. Rosa and Mason had disappeared. He frowned and grabbed a frying pan from under the counter, cursing Rosa quietly for leaving him without breakfast. "Trust me, I know my family better than anyone else. They're a little quirky, but they know a real gem when they see one." I blushed and looked away, a small smirk working onto his lips as he flipped on the stove. His words somehow calmed me.

But, within a few moments, his smirk disappeared and he began glancing between the pot, the stove, and the fridge. "So... do you want, like, eggs?" The poor man seemed utterly confused. I giggled. "Scrambled eggs, sure," I told him, watching as he nodded absentmindedly and glanced around the kitchen for answers. He was obviously trying to keep his confusion inconspicuous. "Do you not know how to make eggs?" I asked, attempting to control the laughter threatening to bubble off my lips. I pursed my lips and looked at him with my eyebrows raised.

"I don't know how to cook anything, so just... gimme a few minutes to figure this out."

I watched as he rooted through the fridge in search of butter or eggs. I sighed and walked around the counter to set a light hand on his back, grabbing the eggs from the top shelf above his head and the butter from the drawer in the door. The milk was snatched from the bottom shelf too.

"Here. I'll show you."

He smiled and wrapped his thick arms around my waist as I set a bowl on the counter and began to crack them, softly explaining the steps I was taking. I could feel him breathing against my shoulder. He kissed the flesh my shirt had left exposed lightly. He wasn't paying attention.

CHAPTER
FORTY

"IT'LL GET EASIER as you do it more often, but try not to get too many shells in it or you'll be getting some extra crunchy nutrition in your eggs," I told him, cracking the cold, white balls against the edge of the pan before emptying the contents of the shells into the bowl. He watched with his chin set on my shoulder, his hands following mine lazily with his own egg. I had already fished two shell chunks from the pan.

"Has Rosa seriously never taught you how to cook anything?"

"No. I don't really watch her cook anything, either," he replied.

"What about your mother? Didn't she cook for you guys?"

"Sometimes, but she didn't have a lot of time when she was on-call, so she usually had the maid do it for us. She's built-up her seniority since then so she can get a lot of time off, but that certainly isn't spent cooking."

"What does she do in her free time?"

"She does wine. Lots and lots of wine."

I frowned. "So you've never had a big home-cooked meal made by your mother or father?"

"I guess not. Sometimes they would help around the kitchen, though. The housekeeper and parents were never allowed to do the dishes, though, that was our job."

I sighed and poured the beaten eggs into the skillet. They crackled; I turned down the heat. "Now you just have to stir it."
With that, I shrugged away from him and pushed the spatula into his palm. "Try not to make a mess." He raised an eyebrow at me before sighing and flipping the eggs as best he could. His actions were futile; I would be cleaning it all morning.

Twenty minutes later, Kaia had managed to get at least *some* of the eggs into a bowl and make the kitchen somewhat presentable. Rosa would be having a cow, we knew, when she saw our mess, but we had time before then. "These are pretty good," I told him as he watched me shovel the food into my mouth from across the counter. I sat on the edge of the granite slab, holding the bowl of eggs and ketchup close to my chin. "I could've just asked Rosa to make it," he mumbled. I rolled my eyes with a smirk. "And give up the chance to see Kaia Arche slave over a stove? Never." He scoffed and came to stand between my legs, taking my bowl of eggs and setting it on the counter. I smiled at him with bright eyes as he gave me a coy look from under his dark lashes. "Y'know, I was thinking you could do something special today," he told me, light fingers finding my stomach under his *Skillet* t-shirt as I played with the buttons on his grey dress shirt.

"Special?" I asked as he brushed the pads of his fingers over the fat that had begun to bloom on my belly. It wasn't too noticeable, but it bothered me nonetheless. To avoid the reminder, I took his hand and rubbed my thumb over his knuckles. "I've asked Rosa to take you for a drive around L.A. today. She has a few stops to make on the way, but the rest is for you to enjoy and for Rosa to be your chauffeur." I pouted slightly. He pursed his lips. "I have a few things to take care of here. Believe it or not, I have to work," Kai told me apologetically. "It's fine. I'm sure Rosa will have enough energy for the two of us, anyway," I sighed. He scoffed and gripped the front of my shirt. "You'll have fun. I promise," he told me, before pulling my lips to his in a searing kiss.

....

"Take this," Rosa ordered, holding a credit card against my stomach inconspicuously. She glanced around the busy street. I was most definitely *not* supposed to be in possession of Kaia's credit card. My brows furrowed as I did as I was told. "Is there a reason as to why you're giving me this? Don't you dare tell me the code. I don't want to be a thief." My voice bordered on venomous. It was a lousy question, though, since we stood in the centre of the fashion district. People passed us quickly with overflowing bags and boxes stacked in their arms. I would definitely be using it for the duration of the day.

"Because I'm taking you shopping and that card doesn't have a very small limit on how much money you can spend. Kai got paid today. Have at it," she replied. It sounded like a question, as if her answer was obvious.

"Shopping for what?"

She held open the glass door of the closest shop for me and snorted. "For you, obviously,"

I sighed, knowing that there was no fighting her.

....

"You like it?" I asked, giving Rosa a twirl as I stepped out of the dressing room. Apparel shopping was amazing, especially when I had a friend and money to do it with. She nodded eagerly. "Kai would drop dead if he saw you in those," she promised me, and I laughed, looking down at the denim shorts around my waist. The word 'Devil' was sewn across the back in thick, maroon thread. "I like them," I declared before disappearing back into the dressing room. We had visited too many shops to count, and we were forced to make regular trips back to the car to drop off our bags. Rosa and I had briefly stopped at a women's fashion store, too, since I felt that she had been a little left out. As she glanced through racks of blouses, my eyes caught a flash of red in the corner. With a second glance, I realized they were glittering red five-and-three-quarter-inch platform stilettos.

And they were fucking gorgeous.

"Have you heard of his fetish?" Rosa whispered suddenly, following my gaze. Slightly horrified that she knew such information, I nodded quickly, blushing and diverting my eyes.

But Rosa set a hand on my shoulder and smirked, drawing my attention back up.

"What's your size?"

....

After shopping, we stopped at a taco stand to grab some grub and fill our rumbling stomachs. Rosa promised that it was on her long list of favourite places to eat, and I didn't blame her.

"Where to now?" I asked through a mouthful of food. Rosa shrugged. "You wanna go somewhere fun? We have a museum of death here, y'know." I shrugged the idea away. She immediately moved on to new ideas. "Or we could go buy half the albums at that big record shop. I like that place." My eyes lit up. "Record shop? Yeah, let's go there!"

She laughed before we both shoved the last bits of our food into our mouths and hopped off the concrete ledge we had eaten on.

"Then hurry the hell up!"

....

The sex was great. I was being paid. The man I woke up with that morning could beat any model that ever existed. I was well-fed and in a relationship with a BDSM-crazed man whose parents were worth half a million dollars.

But this.... this was heaven.

Hundreds upon thousands of records and albums were lined up in order as if they were asking to be blasted through the best-quality speakers. "Kai told me that you liked music, so I wanted to take you here sometime," Rosa told me. I was too excited to reply, my mouth hanging open as I quivered and gawked at the scenery around me. My legs shook with the urge to glance over every album in the store.

I ran off before even thinking of thanking her.

Through isles upon isles, I could see customers picking through their favourite artists. There was a smell in the hot store, almost of sweat and bodies accented with excitement. It was intoxicating. The pop section was a popular one, and the same with metal. As I passed the classical display, I picked out a record for Kai. The man who stood behind the register at the back of the store couldn't hide his surprise when we eventually dropped our total of thirty-two compact discs in front of him. "You guys like music, huh?" he asked, rounding them up tentatively. "He does," Rosa replied, leaning against the counter and pointing to me as she watched the man over her *Gucci* sunglasses.

I blushed and shrugged. I had bought a few of them for Kai, artists I thought he might like.

As the man pushed our CD's into a plastic bag, I turned to Rosa with a sudden, crazy idea coming to my mind. I couldn't even stop it before it escaped my lips.

"Hey, Rosa, do you have anything other than your ears pierced?"

....

"You're fucking insane," Rosa told me, locking the car doors as we sat in a random parking garage. "I don't know... I've always kinda wanted a cool piercing like that," I replied. The distraught woman scoffed and threw her hands into the air. "Oh yeah, let's just go get your cock pierced then!" She was angry; I could feel the heat rolling off her. "I didn't say that I definitely wanted a Prince Albert! I just said it could be an option. That or my nipples," I mumbled. Her eyes flashed with rage. "Luka, even if I did let you, Kai would have my ass hanging on the wall. Subs that don't ask their doms if they can be pierced? He's gonna flip his shit faster than Mason runs from cougars at the bar."

"But what if he likes it? You don't even have to come in with me. We can just say that I ran away from you and got my body pierced without running it by anyone first." Rosa rolled her eyes. "Yeah, my ass is still gonna be over the fireplace. I'm supposed to be keeping track of you today. He doesn't even know that I'm letting you use his card because mine maxed a week ago. You know that I'm already in trouble, right?"

"Come on, please? We can leave the dick for another day, I just want my chest pierced."

"I got you heels. He'll love those just fine. Why do you need metal sticking through your nipple?"

"Because many reasons. Kai may-or-may-not like them. I like them. They look hot. If he doesn't like them then I take them out, easy! I really do want them, though." She glared at me, but I knew that she was considering it. My eyes brightened with hope, knowing she couldn't resist my pleas. After a moment, she released an exasperated sigh. "You know what, fine! I don't care! But if Kai knocks on my bedroom door looking for blood, I'm coming after you first."

I could only give her a massive, victorious smile.

The drive to the parlor that Rosa chose was short. She knew it well, apparently, since she had gotten more than a few tattoos and body modifications done there, and once knew the owner personally.

ANGEL

After a few moments of sweet talking, she managed to snag an artist and convince them that she did not need an appointment. The woman, whom Rosa hadn't met before, eventually decided that Rosa was correct, judging by the fact that they had no other bookings for the next hour. A lonely man tattooed a young woman in the corner. The buzz from his machine was the only noise created in the room.

She led us to a back room, had me sit on a table, and handed me a form to sign. The pen that was then lent to me made my stomach drop. Rosa's killer expression forced me to sign it without reading the title. I never knew that I would be capable of making such bad decisions. Rosa would never let me pull out, though.

The artist urged me to relax, breathe, and explained the procedure to me. She included a friend, another woman covered in dark tattoos and multiple piercings.

"And... little pinch," the woman told me gently when the setup and disinfecting was finally completed. I looked at the wall.

Annica was tall, middle-aged, wore a white beanie, and her hair had been bleached far too many times to be deemed healthy. But she was nice, asking me how many piercings I had gotten before or if I was nervous. When I nodded, she only smiled and shrugged. "Everyone's nervous. But it looks good as hell when it's all over." Her accomplice agreed.

Rosa's hard glare aimed at me from the corner was much worse than the suspense of getting a hole punched through me, though. Her limbs were crossed and her posture was stiff. As was her mouth, stuck in a straight line and barely twitching when the woman brought the needle towards my chest. The pinch and burn came quick, drawing sharp tears to my eyes. My face twitched as the metal, which had been hovering harmlessly above me a moment ago, sat as a horizontal barbell piercing on my left nub of nerves. I hadn't noticed the pain of the other one yet. The other was a ring.

"Dumbass," Rosa mumbled. How could anyone do the same to their penis?

After I had been given strict instructions on how to keep my new jewellery clean and avoid infection, I was set free with a kind of giddy nervousness trembling in my bones. It ached each time my nipples rubbed against my shirt. They were both overly-sensitive, my lips twitching each time my chest was brushed.

"Not feeling too good now, huh?" Rosa smirked as we climbed into her car. I had never seen her so smug, angry.

I pouted slightly. "Whatever. I like it. It'll feel better soon."

She scoffed. "You're gonna be in pain for weeks."

"Shut up."

....

Rosa and I made a snack of pita bread and hummus once we had returned home, but my spirits ultimately brightened when Kai stepped through the elevator doors into the kitchen.

"Hey," I breathed, feeling his arms wrap around my waist lightly as Rosa left us to finish her chores. "Did you have a fun time?" he asked. I nodded eagerly. "Yeah! I got a whole bunch of records to listen to. I even picked up a few for you." Kai gave a small, exhausted smile. "I'm excited, then." I sighed and turned around to put a hand on his cheek as he trapped me between him and the counter. "Long day, hm?" He shrugged. "My ears are kinda ringing from how much bullshit they've had to tune out, but other than that, I'm just ready for a nap, really."

I nodded, refusing to laugh at his sad, tired attempt at a joke. It genuinely bothered me to see him in such a state. "Then let's go take a nap…" I wondered if he really wanted a rest or if he wanted to release some pent-up frustration. I knew that we were both tired; I just hoped he wouldn't wake the dragon when I showed him my new piercings.

CHAPTER
FORTY-ONE

"SO, HAVE YOU thought about it?" Kai asked, hovering above me on the bed. "About what?" I replied, wrapping my arms around his neck as his fingers swept over my stomach lightly. Any higher and he would feel the metal. "About meeting my family. They really want to learn more about you." I bit my lip and averted my gaze. "I mean, I guess I'll go, but... are you sure I won't get eaten alive in a house full of Arches?" Kaia laughed and shook his head. "No guarantees, but even if you are missing a few chunks, then my mother can always stitch you back up." This didn't help. I deflated into the bed. "I'm gonna die!"

Kai sighed at my outburst. "Luka, I haven't brought very many people home before. I think they'll be too stunned that you actually exist to think about eating you."

My brows furrowed and I tilted my head to the side slightly. "You've never been in a relationship that serious?"

He shook his head. "Once or twice, but... not for a few years now."

"Wow," I breathed. How could someone so attractive have so few serious relationships? He had to have brought *somebody* home at least more than a few times. "I don't believe that," I told him flatly. He scoffed and said, "It's true. I promise. Can we have sex now?"

I bit my lip and nodded, coyly watching him from under my lashes. His gaze darkened as he began leaving sluggish kisses on my neck, his hands ghosting up my stomach. I straightened my back and prepared myself for the anger or the delight, whichever came first. His fingers traced my ribs lightly, pushing against each one before he hit my nipples. When the pads of his fingers came in contact with the cold metal, he froze, his lips stopping mid-hickey on my neck. I would have missed the heat his mouth created if I wasn't so nervous.

"Lucika Roggy," he breathed against my jugular, testing to see if he was going insane by pressing lightly on my left nipple. I flinched harshly, wanting to punch him for the act that brought pain and crippling sensitivity, before he reared up to look at me with confusion that almost seemed hurt.

"What are those on your chest?"

I pulled on my knuckles and met his gaze bravely. "Take my shirt off and you'll find out." The man gave me a slight side eye, probably wondering how I had conjured the balls to do what he thought I had done. What I *had* done. His hands found my chest again and pulled experimentally at one of my hard buds. I almost screamed and arched off the bed. This time, I did punch him lightly in the chest. He seemed to understand why I did it, though, and wasn't angry. Immediately, he retracted his fingers and soothed me by placing a hand on my cheek.

"Lucika Roggy, did you get your nipples pierced?" despite his comforting and calming touch, his words produced terror. I flinched when he pulled my shirt over my head and tossed it to the floor with a soft flutter of cloth. I couldn't read his expression. Was he mad? If he was, he'd be furious. Was he turned on by this? If he was, I wasn't going to be able to walk tomorrow, even if he *was* exhausted.

"Why did my boy get his chest pierced?"

ANGEL

I pouted slightly at the question, finally falling into a headspace that would allow me to *be his boy*. His words worried me. Did he not like them? Did I not please him? His hand was placed on my cheek again. This time, it burnt. It twitched.

"It doesn't matter why I got them. I just want to know if you like them."

His jaw fell slack. I noticed the bulge in his pants.

Then his hand was raised, the palm flashing bright in the corner of my vision. I had seen a hand like that before. Not his, though. I was confused as to who's hand it was. Would my master hit me?

I didn't have time to flinch away before he slapped me. It wasn't very hard, but more startling, shocking. My flesh stung. I hung onto the pain for as long as I could. When it faded and I opened my eyes, the gaze I was met with wasn't nearly as hard. He wasn't as angry, if that's what he had been. I silently asked for more. I *welcomed* it.

"Thank you," was all I could whimper.

"For one, I'm pissed that Rosa would Let you do this. And, second, this is one of the hottest things I have ever seen you do." Kai whispered the last part against my earlobe before his tongue shot out and he licked it. I shivered. I wanted more pain. I deserved it. I *craved* it.

"*One* of the hottest things?" I moaned, my eyes closing when he reattached his lips to my neck. My hand subconsciously travelled up to massage my cheek. I resisted the urge to slap myself again, just to imitate that feeling of being dominated. He mumbled an affirmation as he pinched them and rolled one between his thumb and forefinger. I jolted and cried out, my nails digging into his clothed shoulder. Suddenly, my eyes were open wide. "K-Kai! They're still... really sensitive. They hurt." I blushed crimson as I complained, but he only smiled victoriously. "Isn't that a good thing, baby?"

My mouth fell open, my eyes wide, but I couldn't utter a word before he thrust his tongue into my mouth and began pulling on my chest, abusing my sensitive piercings until I was pushing my chest against his and whimpering for more. The pain sprouting from my raw skin was fiery. His fingers had found my throbbing erection. The man squeezed the tip harshly before wrapping his hot hand around it. I was rocking against his hand as I moaned and whimpered, spiralling into a black hole of pleasure. But, when my eyes opened to meet soft beige sheets, I realized I had been flipped and cuffed to the bed, both hands immobilized, and the intoxicated feeling was suddenly gone. It was replaced with uncertainty. I wasn't *scared* of him; how could I be? He was giving me what I wanted. His fingers disappeared, leaving me to whimper as a blindfold was tied over my eyes.

"But just because they're hot doesn't mean you don't deserve a punishment. I can't believe you really thought you could do this without permission… while being mine," he told me quietly, his lips tickling the soft flesh below my ear. The man's voice was dangerous.

My breathing became erratic with excitement. "P-Punishment?"

"You'll get six paddles," he told me.

"Please." I couldn't stop the words from rolling off my tongue. The word wasn't meant to make him stop; I was welcoming anything he was willing to give me. His hand was massaging me first, giving my milky flesh the occasional, firm slap. It was nothing to be screaming over; it surely wasn't the paddle.

Then there was no hand on my behind. My fists clenched. I readied myself. "Do you want me to count them out loud? Or just get it over with?" His voice was softer this time, comforting. I felt him move to grab the leather-wrapped wooden board from under his bed.

I nodded jerkily, my mouth dry and my head spinning wildly. "Use your words, Angel," he warned, his hand gliding up my spine slowly before he reached my neck and squeezed it. The action grounded me. "No… just do it, please."

The bed dipped as he repositioned himself next to me.

"Relax, baby. It'll be over soon," he promised, rubbing my back soothingly. Three slaps were placed on my bottom first with his hand. I could only attempt to brace myself for the onslaught. Until the flesh was a soft pink, he wouldn't dare touch me with a paddle. "Keep that ass up or you'll be looking at double the hits." I whimpered at his soft phrase, and he took his chance to lay the first smack against my ass, the slap of wood on skin resonating throughout the bedroom.

I yelped loudly as waves of pain shot up my spine, the cuffs clinking against the wood headboard. Despite what I hoped, the sharp sting lingered even after the paddle was pulled away. It was different, so much more overwhelming than the slap to the face I had earned. Kai had a knee over both of my legs, holding them captive when I tried to squirm away from him.

"That's one," Kai told me, pausing to let me catch my breath. The paddle was bigger than his hand; he brought it down with so much more strength than he had with any other tool.

With the second impact, the pain was more intense, and tears gathered in my eyes as my back arched deeply. I managed to keep silent. The shock had left me. The third-which came quickly and didn't allow me the extra few seconds to breathe after he had counted the second one aloud-elicited a long, agonized keen from the back of my throat.

"Do you want me to stop?" he asked in that low, innocent whisper.

The restraints were clicking loudly. He held me fast, almost painfully. "Please," I cried, "It hurts, Kai."

"Aw. Poor baby."

Instantly, my deflated cock stood achingly erect. I licked up the drool threatening to escape the corner of my mouth.

He brought that paddle down so hard, that silent sob I had trapped in my chest was released as a wail. He made it clear that I wouldn't be escaping him unless I used any safe-words, although we knew that I could stand the pain. I could always stand the pain.

By the time he had counted to six, tears were leaking through the blindfold, my wrists were bruised, and my ass was decorated in purple lines and fiery-red hues. I heard the paddle fall to the floor as he rushed to unhook the leather cuffs. I sobbed when they fell to the bed, the lack of blood circulation turning them numb and cold. Kai removed the blindfold before his arms wrapped around me. I struggled to relax with the nearly unbearable pain on my backside, arching away from his lap with a soft whimper when I was placed on it.

"I'm sorry," I cried. "I'm sorry."

"I didn't punish you because you didn't ask permission. I punished you because you got it done without *telling me.*"

I sobbed and nodded quickly, clinging to him as he pulled me, gently this time, into his lap and attached his lips to my cheek. His kisses were soft and didn't leave stinging marks like his previous actions; I didn't welcome them at first. I only cried and tilted my head away, whining when he leaned back, allowing me space, and brushed the hair from my leaking eyes. I could also tell that he was trying to be careful not to let my bottom brush the sheets. He failed a few times, and I cried out before he could hush me. I was sure that Kaia would tend to my skin later, after he was sure the pain had subsided.

But I jolted from my serene daze when he brushed the tip of my cock, the back of his hand sliding down the length slowly. It was hard, painful.

"Just come, baby boy. You did good," Kai soothed, wrapping his hand around me and jerking it a few times. I was so close already, only a few touches and I was tensing. The room was shadowed, but it seemed to swirl with colour as hot spurts of liquid shot over his hand, landing on his fingers and my milky skin. It turned patches of his dark flesh white.

"You want a bath?" he asked once the aftershocks had reduced to slight trembles.

I shook my head and clenched my throat against another whine. It came out in a choked growl that made him attempt to kiss away the pain. "N-No."

"Just some lotion before you sleep, then."

I only nodded before he landed a kiss on my forehead and pulled away to grab his supplies and clean the seed from our flesh.

....

Another week went by, and I spent as much of it as I could with my mother. With the new paycheck, we could get all our bills paid on-time and not a penny short. The leftovers were spent on a shopping spree for my mother, where I let her indulge in things she had never experienced before. Maybe it was the freedom from constantly feeling as if she could never make enough money, or maybe it was the fact that she had the first proper meal since spending dinner at Kai's house. Whatever it was, she was beautiful when she wasn't passed out on the couch or her bed with an empty pack of cigarettes next to her. Her smoking habits were fading. She went through a pack in a few days instead of one. She even began to ignore the sleeping pills on her dresser.

The one thing that bothered me most was Mason. He would spend his days asking me about her, how she was doing, if she needed anything, what I had done with her the day before. He was like a lost puppy who had finally found its owner. But, when I asked her if she had any attraction to Mason, she replied with, "Who's that?" as she gave me a confused side eye. I only laughed and waved my hand.

"Nobody. Just an admirer."

Her confusion deepened. "Admirer? Of you?"

I shook my head. "No, Mom. Of you."

She seemed stunned for a moment, but shook her head and looked at her hands, hiding her blush from everyone but me in the small restaurant I knew she would enjoy eating in. "Yeah... right."

I frowned. "Mason is Kai's friend, remember? The one who picked you up and dropped you off the night you came over to his house for dinner?"

"Oh... him. He made a move on me while he was driving me home, I think. It's been a while, but I'm pretty sure that's what it was."

I blanched.

"He *what*?!"

CHAPTER
FORTY-TWO

"How far away is your parents' house?" I asked as Kaia packed his bag. Mine was all ready to go. "We aren't going to my parents' permanent house. They own a property up close to Mount Baker, so we'll be driving there." I pouted and thought for a moment. "I don't know where that is." He sighed and pecked my lips lightly, taking one of his pairs of boxers from my hands and tossing it into his suitcase. "Do you want to take anything extra with you?" he asked me, his lips lingering close to mine. I raised an eyebrow. "Extra?" I didn't think we would be having any sex on the trip. It was a family gathering. He snorted. "Luka, you can't expect me to go an entire four-to-six days without sex. I'd die." I laughed and wrapped my arms around his neck, pulling on his tie to bring him closer. "And having your parents hear you having sex is any better?"

He nodded eagerly; I hit him playfully. "Go pack. You're just horny."

"Of course I am!"

Kaia went to work collecting his toiletries. Down the hall, I could hear Rosa and Mason arguing over bath towels. Somewhere in the conversation, she had switched to Mandarin, although Mason was still replying to her in English. Their voices faded downstairs.

Once our bags had been packed, there were still twenty minutes to wait before Mason concluded his argument with Rosa.

"We all ready to go?" Mason asked, loading his own bag into the *Bentley*. Kai nodded and motioned me into the car. "Is Rosa coming?" I asked. "No. She's staying here with Abraham," Mason replied, climbing into the driver's seat beside Kai. "Is Rosa still pissed that you took her towel?" Kai asked, looking to his friend with amusement. "It's not her towel," he grumbled. Kai shrugged with amusement. "Well, it really doesn't matter. She's been drying her coochie with it either way. You guys are basically having sex."

Mason was too horrified to reply.

I buckled my seatbelt and looked into the front seats where the two men sat, Kai glancing around the garage mindlessly and Mason starting the engine. "It's a twenty-hour drive, give or take, so I hope you brought something to entertain yourself with," Mason told me as we pulled out onto the busy street.

"Twenty hours? Can you drive for that long?" I asked him incredulously.

"Hell no. Kai'll take over in a while."

Kai scoffed and gripped the handle above the window. "But only if I can survive the suicide seat with your driving first." Mason looked at Kai, appalled. "My driving is better than yours!" Kaia rolled his eyes. "Yeah, it's better until you're sitting in a ditch beside one of my most expensive cars." I watched with wide eyes from the back as they bickered, glancing from one to the other. "Oh, come on. I paid you back. I can drive pretty good the rest of the time."

"And you'd drive like that with Luka in the car? What are you gonna do with Teressa when you get her son killed?" I straightened in the back seat, glaring at Mason in the rear view. "I'll... move to China, maybe? I'll go live with Rosa's pals. I don't want that beast on my trail, thank you." I only frowned at him. "Beast? You were the one who apparently made a move on her." He scoffed, his fingers nervously carding through his hair. "She told you that, huh?"

"Yep."

"Am I in trouble?"

"Yes, Mason. Yes you are."

The car fell into silence after that. As promised, Kai took over as the sun began to set. But I didn't mind the pause on the side of the road. I had never left Los Angeles, let alone travel all the way up to Washington. The weather changed too. Thick clouds covered mountain tops in the distance instead of the usual scalding-hot flat land that stretched on for miles close to L.A. I simply admired the view, leaning my head against the window and focusing on forgetting about the anxiety of meeting his parents. My mother would have loved to come. I knew, deep down, that she wanted to follow me when I told her that I would be taking a weekend off with Kai. She only nodded absently when I added the fact that there was extra cash in the closet and some fixings for sandwiches and pasta in the fridge. She understood that the trip was for me, and me only.

To my surprise, as the sky turned a darkening shade of blue, Mason fell asleep, and I lost the stimulation of their quiet chat. I had never realized how much of a talker Kai was. They could talk about anything and everything together, and I was envious of that relationship. How could they be so different and get along so well?

"Can we put some music on?" I asked, handing Kai my phone. He nodded and plugged it into the dash with one hand on the steering wheel, careful to keep his eyes on the road. He seemed like he had more trouble driving the average car than his motorbike. Kai lowered the music volume to a soft hum when I asked him a new question, though. "Why do you drive up to Washington? Why don't you just take a little plane instead? It would be way faster." Kai shrugged. "It's kinda a ritual for us to drive there. Mason likes it, so why not?" I nodded. "So... do you have any aunts or uncles that are gonna be there?"

He shook his head. "My parents are single kids, so no. But I am an uncle to Lily's kids. She's got two that'll be there."

"How old?"

"Jeremy and Kara are five. They're twins."

"... You think they'll like me?" I asked nervously, pulling on my knuckles.

Kai sighed and caught my eye in the rear view mirror. "Luka, they'll love you. Honestly, you'll probably be the most normal person in the house."

"Seriously?"

He snorted. "Yeah, don't tell them I said that, though. Then they might *actually* eat you."

....

It was nearing five AM when we pulled up to the Arche Mansion after driving for twenty miles through dense, quiet forest. It stood high on a ridge, overlooking valleys and hills below. Mount Baker faded into the clouds on the horizon, and Mount Saint Helens was just barely visible above the trees on the other side of the home.

And the house was stunning. High, curved arches and beautifully stained dark wood decorated the home, helping it blend into the surrounding forest. The windows made up a lot of the wall space, so the views from every side of the home must have been gorgeous. A select few displayed a soft glow from inside. "You like it?" Kai asked, resting a hand on my hip as Mason stumbled out of the car groggily. His foot caught on the edge of the doorframe and he nearly landed face-first on the cement. Kai and I ignored him. "It's so pretty," I breathed in reply, watching bats fly in circles above us, illuminated by the soft glow from the home.

"Let's go inside, shall we?" Kai added, tossing his keys over his shoulder to Mason, who caught them jerkily. I heard him curse Kaia under his breath before turning back to the car. The driveway was made up of light concrete and bricks, paving a path specifically for expensive dress shoes and high heels. "Most of them are probably asleep," Kai mumbled as he opened the door silently. We were immediately met by a colourful grand staircase and ridiculously high ceilings, complete with intricate gold crown mouldings and a massive, silver chandelier hanging above us. Even the carpet under our feet was a spotless, velvety red. "Wow," I said simply, finding new things to look at with every passing second. "You should see my parents' permanent residence."

I breathed a laugh. "I can't imagine."

"You must be exhausted. Let's go up to our room, hm?" he suggested. I could already feel the gentle urge of his arm on my back to lead me away. But I put a hand on his shoulder and looked up at him with my best puppy dog eyes. "Can we explore instead? I want to see the rest. I swear I'm not tired." Only some of it was the truth, but I was determined to investigate more of Kai's life. I had known him for almost three months and I hadn't even met his family yet. He sighed and nodded.

"Sure... just stay quiet. The twins are probably awake, and they smell fear." I laughed while he wrapped his arm in mine, smirking as he proceeded to lead me through the house. We were met by more reds and golds, a dominant colour in the house, which was accented with whites and browns. "It's got eight bedrooms, two dens, four-and-a-half bathrooms, a few family rooms, a gym, a pool, an entertainment room, a wine cellar, a four-car garage, and a rooftop and backyard terrace," Kai told me as he led me through a kitchen complete with three ovens and two sinks. This was obviously meant for large groups of people, specifically for the Arche family, I decided. They must rent it out to large parties when they aren't using the home.

"Is there any kind of room that this place doesn't have?" Kai shook his head. "Not really. Zach wanted to install a bunker underneath it, but Mom said 'hell no'."

I giggled. "Why no dungeon?"

He snorted, but didn't reply as we entered the living room. There was no television in front of the mammoth, white couches, but the view of the Olympic National Forest could top any television premier.

"Uncle Kai!" Two voices suddenly rang through the home from behind us, and I barely had time to turn before I had two tiny, blonde, baby-faced children running through my legs and attaching themselves to Kai. "Hey!" Kai smiled, immediately lifting a tiny girl into his arms. His sudden excitement shocked me, and I could only stare at his wide smile. She giggled loudly, her joyous laughter echoing through the room as she wrapped her arms around her uncle's neck. "Damn, you're getting heavy," Kai told her, kissing her cheek and hugging her brother close at his side. "Your husband is pretty, Uncle Kai," the boy, who I assumed was Jeremy, told Kara, looking up at me with wide, bottomless eyes. My chin fell to the floor when Kai simply chuckled. "This is my boyfriend. We aren't married, kiddo." My mouth still didn't close with the fact that he just declared me as his boyfriend. The boy put his thumb in his mouth and began to suck gently, staring up at me with curiosity. "Hey," I said, waving shyly with a kind smile. Jeremy's expression didn't change, and I glanced at Kai nervously. Was I supposed to do something else for him?

"How about you two go find Uncle Mason? Help him carry the bags upstairs," Kai said finally, setting Kara on the floor beside her brother. They took off in a run, bounding through the house as if

ANGEL

they were overdosing on candy. "How can they have so much energy this early in the morning?" I asked as we watched them disappear.

"I haven't the foggiest."

I sighed and turned back around to yawn at the window. "Okay. Now I'm tired. You think we can take a nap before we have to meet the family?" He snorted and nodded, taking my hand and leading my back to the grand staircase where we climbed it slowly.

"Of course."

Really, I wasn't sure if I ever wanted to wake up. That would mean I would have to face his family… which could very well end me.

CHAPTER
FORTY-THREE

I WOKE WITH A start, realizing quickly that I was not in Kai's nor my own bed before remembering that I was spending most of my week with Kai's family. "What time is it?" I mumbled groggily, rolling over to where Kai leaned against the headboard reading. He flipped his wrist to briefly check his watch. "Almost ten. Some of them should be up by now."

"Okay," I yawned, "let me get dressed." I stumbled to my feet and put on a pair of jeans and a plain t-shirt that had grown too small for Kai many years ago. He watched as I struggled to fit the jeans over my hips, but was able to button them relatively easily. They were tight, though, and I knew I needed new ones soon.

I realized before I had lay down for a nap that Kai and I would be sharing a room, almost like what we were doing in L.A. I was sure he had other beds for me to sleep on, but I had a feeling that he wanted me to sleep in his. The bedroom wasn't nearly the same size as his at home, but it was spacious enough for a small seating area and large dresser. I was yet to step out onto the balcony it also had, and I knew that I would have to indulge in that view sooner or later.

"Do you smell that?" I asked, pulling my shirt down. He nodded. "That would be Janet's breakfast bagels. Go down and try one."

My brows pulled together, and I began to pull on my knuckles as my teeth gently tugged at my lip. Meeting his sister and family for the first time alone? No-fucking-thank you. Kai sighed and stood to button his white dress shirt. "Okay, okay. Let's go, Angel," he sighed, curling his fingers over mine and leading me out the door. I broke into a cold sweat by the time I crossed the top step of the grand staircase. I almost fell down the steps when a head poked out of the doorway to the left. The man looked to be at least as old as Kai, with the longest raven-black braided hair I had ever seen. It was almost the same colour as Kai's, along with his skin tone. "Damn... he's a lot younger than I imagined," the man commented, his thick right eyebrow raising as he stared me down and licked his lips devilishly. There was barely any feature resemblance between Kaia and who I assumed was his adopted brother, as this guy obviously had some kind of Asian blood in him. "Well, I told you he was nineteen. What did you expect?" Kai retorted. "I expected an old, old man, Kai. A fossil. Oh, wait, that's just you," he replied before disappearing behind the wall. "We're the same age!" Kaia yelled in frustration.

I put a hand over my mouth to muffle my laughter while Kai pouted and we entered the kitchen together. "Hey! The pure-bred is here!" a stunningly beautiful woman threw her arms around Kai to embrace him in a warm hug. "Hey, Janet," he smiled, hugging her back and kissing her cheek lightly. She pulled away to smile widely at me, glancing between the two of us. "And could this be Luka?" I blushed and gave her a sheepish smile. Kai put his arm around my waist and smirked victoriously, as if he was showing me off as a prize. "I'm Janet, Kai's sister," she introduced herself, shaking my hand with practiced politeness. Janet was short and thin with dark-brown curls, translucent skin, and large, hazel eyes hidden behind her square glasses. I adored the single dimple she had on her right cheek. She seemed like the motherly type, but I could also tell that she had a mischievous streak in her.

"Hey," I mumbled in reply.

"I've got a few bagels ready. You better get them before the twins snag them all," she told us, motioning to the counter across the room. I smiled at her as we turned away, Kai still clutching me close. "What's with 'Pure-bred'?" I asked under my breath. Kai glanced back to his adopted sister before leaning his face towards mine to whisper, "It's kinda a joke that they made. I'm the pure-bred because I'm the only child in the family who's blood-related to Mom and Dad."

"Y'know, I thought your family would be more... ya know, dark. Like the *Addams family* or something." He laughed loudly. Janet shot us, specifically me, a brief look. "Well, you never know. You haven't met the rest of them."

Lily Arche, a woman with a constant smile and glass-half-full personality, joined us soon after I had finished my first bagel. "I'm Lily," she introduced herself before Kai had the chance, embracing me in a kind hug instead of shaking my outstretched hand.

"Mama! Look how pretty Uncle Kai's husband is!" Jeremy told his mother, putting a hand on her leg and tugging on her loose jeans. "Baby, he's not Uncle Kai's husband. Luka is his boyfriend," Lily corrected, handing her child a bagel. "Take this and go play, guys. Share with your sister, too, Jer," she told her son before he took the food and began to chase after his sister. "Your bagels are really pretty, Aunt Janet!" Jeremy added before he and his sister disappeared. "What's with everything being pretty?" Kai asked, holding me close as I ripped chunks off my bagel and popped them between my lips. I chewed slowly. It was delicious. Definitely homemade. "It's another phase. Everything is pretty to them. They're still convinced that you have a husband, too," she sighed. Kai snorted and shrugged. "That's okay. Let them be. How have you been?"

"Tired. The kids are exhausting, but other than that, not too bad, I guess."

ANGEL

"You excited for this week?" I asked, attempting to make further conversation. She laughed. "Trust me, Luka. It's gonna be fun."

"Yeah, lots of fun. Laurent says you won't last the next few days," Kai's brother declared, appearing behind us. I could tell that Zach was getting on Kai's nerves already; he seemed to have that effect on people. "And you guys bet on that, hm?" Kai retorted, coming to my defence. "Yep. Four-hundred says he'll be gone by Monday, but I think he'll at least last until Thursday," he replied. I frowned slightly. Kaia sighed. "You're still a dick, huh, Zach?"

Zach gave a lopsided smile and nodded happily. "Yep!"

....

I still couldn't see anything different with his family. No quirks, no disabilities. Lily joined her kids in one of the living rooms while Janet and Zach cleaned the few dishes that were left in the kitchen. Breakfast had come and gone. "My parents aren't here yet, I guess. But they have to drive from Belfair, so you'll get to meet them soon," Kai promised. He had taken me out into the hallway to stand beside the grand staircase. "Y'know, your family isn't that different. They seem pretty normal," I commented. Kai shrugged, pursing his lips. "Well, they all have their own things that make them them. I told them to be nice to you."

"You told them to be nice to me?"

"Trust me, they were being really nice. Especially Zach."

I sighed and wrapped my arms around myself. So far, I was feeling fairly welcomed, save for Zach's comments. I had a feeling that he really couldn't control himself, much like Mason. "I've just never done this before. My mom isn't a big family person, y'know." Kai put a comforting hand on my arm. "I know, Luka. Once my mother gets here, I promise that they'll be a lot better behaved." I nodded sheepishly, but my eyes widened and my arms dropped to my sides when his hand found my ass, squeezing harshly. "We'll all be better behaved," Kai promised against my ear, and I shivered before he leaned away as if those words hadn't just left his mouth.

"I'll be back in a second. Let me get something from our room, then I might show you the view we get at the back of the house," Kai promised before he darted up the stairs two at a time, leaving me to stand alone at the bottom of the steps.

"Hey, Luka," Janet entered the hallway smiling. She was one of the few people in the house that weren't too hard on my nerves. "Hey," I mumbled, expecting her to pass me. But she stopped, so I decided to meet her gaze. I wasn't planning to make eye contact. "So...," she crossed her arms over her chest, "What's your secret?" I could only stare at her for a moment, frozen by confusion. "My secret?" I asked finally. "He looked different when I saw him at first, and I thought maybe he was just happy to see us and have a vacation for once, but...." She trailed off and licked her lips profusely, as if she was trying to gather her words with her tongue.

"But?"

"But then he laughed," she told me, "I thought maybe he was possessed or something. But you're the only thing that's changed."

"Does he not laugh around his family?"

"Not like that. That was different. I've never seen him that... free. I mean, he used to, but... not since..."

My brows furrowed. "Oh... well, I guess he seems pretty happy when he's around me, but he's usually like that around people he knows, right?" Janet shook her head. "No. I mean, he's told you about her, right?"

Her? Did I suddenly have competition? Kai hadn't exposed many hints to the fact that there was a girl behind the scenes, so I had disregarded them to respect his privacy, but hearing it from his family brought new life to 'Her'. The hair on my arms stood straight. Should I have been worried about Janet's news? It seemed as though her words suddenly summoned my deepest fears. "N-No... what girl? Kai's...Kai's gay, isn't he?" Janet jumped, shaking her head and waving her arms. "No, no, I mean, he doesn't care about body parts, but, um, she's dead. I was just wondering if he's ever shared anything with you." The woman's bottom lip protruded slightly, like she had just ruined one of Kai's biggest secrets. I had a feeling that that was the case.

"I hope you're not being mean to him," Kai warned suddenly as he limped down the stairs. Both of us visibly flinched and froze. "What's wrong?" I asked, putting my trembling hands on the railing and watching his steps with concern. Janet folded her hands behind her back and fell silent. "Nothing. I hurt my knee playing rugby. It just started acting up," Kai replied, finally reaching me and putting an arm around my waist.

"Getting old, huh, Kai?" Janet taunted. But her voice was distracted, hesitant. "Not as old as you, you old hag," Kai retorted, flipping his middle finger up at her and turning us away from his sister. Janet didn't say anything more, but that sad gleam in her eyes still hadn't left when I gave a brief glance back at her. I could tell that her mouth would be closed on the subject for some time.

CHAPTER
FORTY-FOUR

"I COULD SIT OUT here all day," I declared, staring off at the scene before me. Most of the mansion was elevated on one side by wooden pilings, which gave us a stunning view of Mount Baker and a small lake that sat far below us. "I know. I don't think our cityscape will ever beat this view," he replied, leaning heavily on the intricate metal railing lined by small potted shrubs and nests of chirping little birds that called the deck home. I had to squint my eyes against the bright sun before I put a hand over my forehead to block it. "You mean your cityscape," I corrected, leaning into him. "Mhm," he hummed absently.

"Do you guys use the lake down there? Can you even get to it?" I asked, motioning below us. Kaia nodded. "Yep. It's a bit of a hike, but it's absolutely worth it. We'd spend hours down there when we were all younger. And that was even before we found a way onto the trestle."

"The trestle?"

"You see the old train tracks down there? It isn't used anymore, but there's a trestle that runs over the lake. We always used to climb it and use a rope swing to jump off it. Or we'd see who could make up the most insane diving routines." My smile was huge. "That sounds so awesome." I imagined a fifteen-year-old Kaia laughing

ANGEL

and jumping off the ledge with the most carefree of minds. Did he know 'her' back then?

Kai chuckled and nodded. "It definitely is."

....

Kai and his siblings were the first to greet his parents when they arrived.

"Ah, my babies! You all look so beautiful!" she exclaimed, throwing her arms around Zach as Mr. Arche greeted his adopted daughters warmly. Kai's other siblings, Alex and Laurent, were yet to arrive. His third sister and younger brother, Saskia and Kennith, drove with Mrs. Arche and her husband. Kennith was already in the house somewhere refusing to show himself, as I understood. I waited uncomfortably in the living room, standing against the wall while pulling on my knuckles until they were sore and red. I felt as if I was intruding, being part of their get-together when I wasn't family in the slightest. I was hesitant to finally meet the top dogs. "Hey, Mom," I heard Kai greet his mother happily after giving his father a brief hug. "Kaia! You look good," his mother replied. "Never been better," he told her, sending his mother a flash of a smile as they pulled away from each other.

"I heard that you've been busy with a little boy from the City of the Angels," she said. His family went silent. The only thing I could hear was the pounding of my own heart against my rib cage. "Luka? Quit hiding, babe," Kai ordered, and I began to panic. Did they know about my past, who I was? He had set me up to be the star of the show, the main course. I was about to be eaten!

So, I took a deep breath and straightened my shirt before carding a hand through my hair in an attempt to calm any rogue strands. Then I turned out of the doorway to the living room. His mother's eyes lit up immediately. I stared in fear as she crossed the foyer to me. Mrs. Arche was a short woman with a bulky build, and her skin was much darker in person. Her hair was curly and greying, thrown up into a loose bun wrapped by a little piece of fabric with Nigerian flags printed across it. She was an elegant woman. As she crossed the floor, her small, narrow, black eyes scrutinized me mercilessly. Her face had a masculine shape to it; the observation made me uncomfortable. "It's Luka, correct?" she asked with a sudden smile. It wasn't malicious, but it wasn't kind, either, almost like she just wasn't sure what to think of me yet, or her mind hadn't decided if I was friend or foe. "Y-Yeah. That's me," I replied, shaking her hand jerkily. I was sure she would pull away quickly once she felt the sweat on my palm. But, instead, she put an arm around my own and pulled me close to her side, a stiff smile plastered onto her face. "Call me Aja, dear," she told me kindly as she turned us towards Kai. "Kaia Jenkins Arche, how old is this boy?"

I finally knew what her smile meant. She was furious.

Kai's own smile fell like a plane with engine failure. He obviously hoped that his mother wouldn't do this. He licked his lips and looked to his brother for help, his expression just as fearful as my own. Zach shrugged and looked back at him with sympathy. "Nineteen," he said finally.

Aja gasped. "Kaia!"

"H-He'll be twenty soon!" Kai exclaimed in a desperate attempt to save himself. But his mother's nostrils only flared while her eyes blazed. "I'll be twenty in December," I said quietly, hoping to calm her. She glanced at me and shooed Kai away. "You, hush," she told me, "And Kaia, help your father with our bags." Kai frowned, his chin rising to challenge his mother. Did he ever think he could really conquer her? "But I-," he began, but his mother snarled, "Is Mason here?"

"Yeah, but-."

ANGEL

"So he can help too. Run along, boys," she waved, turning us away. The two of us already had whiplash from her sudden changes in mood; I wondered how Mr. Arche kept his head attached to his shoulders. Zach gave a low laugh and patted his brother on the back as he passed him, earning a glare from my boyfriend.

"Zach, you're in charge of unpacking our things. Get busy."

"What? What did I do?!"

But his mother ignored him as we passed the grand staircase, Aja taking my hand and pulling me away. When I looked back to find Kaia's gaze, I realized that he was being dragged too. My mouth opened to object, but my breath had been stolen by surprise.

Then we disappeared from each other's sight.

I was reeling from Aja's surprise attacks, and it took me a moment to take a breath and smile nervously at the few women that herded me towards the other side of the house. They were quiet, stealing glances but not quite making eye contact with me. At first, I thought that maybe Saskia was mute. She had been silent since she entered the house, even refusing to say hello to her siblings. She hung behind her father, searching the room with evaluating eyes that promised knowledge and a wise soul behind them. "Hey, I'm Luka," I said quietly to Saskia as we followed Aja through the home. Her skin was much darker than Kai's or Aja's, and her hair was a massive mane of pitch-black curls. Her cheeks were littered with acne scars, but the beauty of her features and shining, brown eyes drew one's gaze away from her subtle flaws. I wasn't sure what to do when she simply stared at the photos on the walls, her head turned away. What had I done wrong for her to already want to ignore me?

But Lily, who followed behind us, tapped her on the shoulder, making Saskia jump slightly. She whipped her head around to her sister, who began to sign to her with a soft smile.

Saskia wasn't mute. She was deaf.

"This is Luka," Lily said aloud as she signed, spelling out the letters of my name with her fingers. Saskia looked at me wearily, and I grinned at her brightly. "She can read your lips, so it's okay to talk to her as long as she can see your face," Lily told me.

"I'm Saskia," she mumbled shyly, turning her head away slightly. Her voice was slurred, and the syllables weren't pronounced the best, but anyone could still know what she was saying.

"I'm afraid I don't know any sign language," I said.

She shrugged and signed a quick few words to Lily. "Most people don't," Saskia told me before she turned away again and ended the conversation. "Don't mind her. She just doesn't know you yet. She said you and Kai look good together," Lily told me. "Thanks," I said sheepishly, blushing and turning away. "Aren't the guys kinda just… relaxing now? I don't want to intrude on girl time or anything," I said nervously. I felt exposed, especially with the fact that I wanted to be with Kai. Why had they separated us? Aja laughed, a fleeting image of the devil flashing in her eyes. "No, Luka. We're just going to learn a little more about you." Her words only scared me worse, although nothing could have prepared me for the interrogation that was to come once they had trapped me in a side room of couches.

"Has Kai taken you to Paris yet?"

"Exactly how long have you been together?"

"You wrapped it before you tapped it, right?"

"Don't be stupid, Lily. He's a guy. He can't get pregnant."

"Yeah, but who knows how many venereal diseases Kai has!"

"Did he seriously ask you to move in with him?"

I stared at the women who sat around me, their legs curled under them on the bright leather sofas. Even after they had asked so many questions, they still came back for more. I had been waiting for half an hour for them to run out of inquiries. "One question at a time, ladies," Aja soothed. Her voice was always kind, but she also

ANGEL

knew how to twist it until she demanded submission. We had all definitely submitted to her. I couldn't imagine growing up with such large shoes to fill, especially with her over-sized personality and ego that stretched the fabric of the legacy.

Saskia signed furiously to me, and Lily translated just as quickly as she shot her own questions. As I struggled to answer the onslaught, I sent a quick SOS text to Kai.

"Send help. I don't know how to answer these questions."

"They're just excited. They haven't tasted fresh meat like yours in years. Not since Jeremy and Kara were born. But we all know you do taste pretty good... ;)."

"YOUR. TASTE BUDS. ARE. USELESS! HELP ME."

Either Kai was on his way or he had decided to ignore me because I no longer got any new notifications from him.

"N-No, Kai hasn't taken me to Paris. We've only been together for about three months now, and I don't think that's long enough for us to move in together," I stuttered, struggling to find words that wouldn't conjure new questions. But, of course, the women found a way. "How exactly did you meet my son?" Aja asked, sending me the best of her cold, scrutinizing gaze. I couldn't tell her that, either. How would she react if I told her that I had been a hooker for a majority of my life and made a chance encounter with Kai because he was in need of entertainment for a night? I stumbled over my words, my mouth opening and closing silently, as if I was a fish gasping for water.

"Mrs. Arche?" A soft voice suddenly sounded from the corner, accompanied by a small knock. It was a housekeeper, but, disappointingly, it wasn't Rosa. "Yes, Charlie?" Aja asked, raising her chin at the woman. The woman shrunk against her offences and bowed her head. "Mrs. Arche, Mr. Kai is asking for Mr. Luka. He says it's urgent."

Aja raised an eyebrow. "Does he now?" I looked to Kai's mother with dimming hopes and rising fear.

But, thankfully, she nodded and waved me away. "Have fun, then, darling." Her bright, joyful personality was back, but I didn't waste any time hanging around to enjoy it. Charlie, after I had nearly flown into her arms with gratitude, led me through the maze of halls slowly, her heels tapping against the floor deafeningly. "Do you always wear those? They must be uncomfortable to wear all day," I said. She turned to give me a kind smile, her cherry-blond hair falling over her shoulder in beautiful waves. "I've gotten used to them. I've never seen you here before, though. Are you a new kid they've adopted?" she replied. I shook my head. "No. I'm Kai's boyfriend, actually. How long have you worked for the Arches?" Charlie shrugged. "Too long to remember. I mostly do work for Mr. and Mrs. Arche, though. I've never worked with their children much."

"Oh," I replied simply as she led me through a small door at the bottom of a tall, narrow staircase. Despite its small size, it was lit brightly and coloured with a deep red. She opened the door without another word and motioned me through it.

"Right through here, Luka," she said.

I followed her directions and entered the room.

CHAPTER
FORTY-FIVE

THE MEN SAT on a series of cherry-red leather sofas in the centre of a massive balcony overlooking an equally spacious garage filled with new cars and classics. Although it was indoor, they relaxed under glowing party lights as they nursed beers. "Goddamn, you survived?" Zach suddenly exclaimed, ending the laughter and conversation. Mason had joined them, along with another potential brother, who sat quietly in a wheelchair beside Zach. "Kai saved him," Mason smiled, throwing his arm over the back of the couch. "Of course," Kai replied as I crossed the room to him, despite having to dodge multiple chairs and game tables.

"They're merciless. But you'll learn to love them," Mr. Arche promised, holding out his hand for me to shake. "Call me Micheal, Luka." I smiled and shook it firmly, his skin soft and his muscles tight. Micheal Arche had a gentle complexion, and he was obviously considerably more generous than his wife. An aging face with the occasional line or wrinkle was shaped so similar to Kai's, the guy would only have to change his skin colour to be an older version of his son. Greying-blue eyes and black hair added to his soft, patient aura. "And this is Laurent. He's our eldest," Micheal added, motioning to the man beside Zach. He looked healthy despite the black wheelchair he sat in, his hands folded in his lap. "Hey, Luka," he greeted, smiling at me with eyes that were just as black as Kai's. His skin was just as dark, too, although his hair had been buzzed short, almost to the scalp. It was, again, obvious that he wasn't related to Kai by blood.

"I was just telling them how you like to sing," Kai said behind me. I turned to gawk at him. "You were?"

"Do you play any instruments?" Micheal asked, refusing to let Kai reply. He hoisted an ankle onto his knee, flattening the fabric of his dress pants and pinching a little chunk of dust away from them. I shook my head. "Shame. You can't be part of the family until you at least know how to play a girl," Zach smirked at me. His father sent him a soft warning glare. "You all play instruments?" I asked, sitting beside Kai and letting him wrap his arm around my shoulder. I took a sip from his beer. He raised a quick eyebrow at me, as if to say, *'don't be getting drunk in front of my family this early.'* I rolled my eyes and smiled at the men as they answered my question. After a moment, I had learnt that both Michael and his wife played the piano, Janet the cello, Lily the violin, Alex the guitar, and, of course, Kaia the drums. I was impressed with their talents. Money really did mean success, even in hobbies.

"Speaking of Kennith, is he here? I still haven't seen him."

"Yeah, and he hasn't seen any of us, either," Zach smirked. Laurent punched him lightly on the shoulder and glared at his sibling, but I had yet to understand what I thought was Zacharia's attempt at making a joke. His amount of levity was jarring. "That's alright. He's probably reading. Leave him be," Michael said, kicking his feet up onto the glass coffee table between us. "So, how did you and Kaia meet?" Laurent asked us. The man was timid, quiet. "It's Kai," Kai mumbled. Even with the fancy crown moulding and cars, the Arche family was just as fitful as any other. Meanwhile, I choked on my own saliva and coughed harshly before looking up at Kai with wide eyes. "Luka was in the specialty business," Mason came to

ANGEL

my rescue unexpectedly. I stuffed my face into the palm of my hand. At least he hadn't identified me as a *hooker* like I expected him to.

I didn't miss the small smirk that sat on Kai's perfect lips.

....

The day was spent chatting, and none of us realized how late it had gotten until most of us were suffering from hunger pains. The women had moved to the (comparably) small balcony off the kitchen and spoke in a nonchalant circle of iced tea and pool-side recliners. A man had joined them, either Kennith or Alex, I concluded. "Hey, Pure-blood," the man greeted, departing from the women when he noticed us standing in the doorway. "Hey, Alex," Kai replied, throwing his arms around his equally-muscled brother and patting his back. "This is Luka, I assume?" Alex asked, smiling at me. He resembled Mason quite a bit, despite the five inches of height Alex had on Kai's friend. The guy was mammoth. "Hey," I mumbled sheepishly. Alex gave a jaw-dropping, pearl-white smile. The man was attractive. A pair of dog tags dangled and shone bright on his white t-shirt. "Hey, Luka. Have you seen Kennith around? I thought he would be with you guys."

"No. He's probably upstairs," Kai replied, and Alex shrugged. "Well, someone's gotta go get him, then. It sounds like Charlie's getting ready to make dinner." We all listened for a moment as their parents fought idly in the kitchen about sandwiches before the maid came to break them up. "You guys go get him. By the time you convince him to leave his room, dinner will probably be ready." Kai scoffed. "Yeah. Let's go, Angel." He took my hand and led me out of the kitchen, tracing our steps back up to the second floor. "Is Kennith a vampire or something?" I asked as he led me down the long hallway. He seemed to live like a hermit. A large door sat at the end; we stopped a few feet away from it. "He's not a vampire.

He's blind," he told me in a hushed voice. I wasn't very surprised, but I didn't blame the guy for not wanting to leave his room. "Is he older than you?" I asked. Kaia shook his head and knocked on the door quietly. "Leave, Kaia," a venomous voice sounded from the other side of the door. The voice was ready, prepared to tell us off. I realized that Kennith could be worse than his adoptive mother. "Don't be like that, Ken. You want dinner?" Kaia asked. There was a pause before the voice answered quietly. "No. Please... go away." Kai only frowned at the white wooden board dividing the man's bedroom from the hallway for a moment before he sighed and lowered himself onto one knee. "What are you doing?" I asked in a whisper as he picked an object from his pocket and stuck it into the door. That metal pick was soon joined by a second one, and he rattled them together inside the lock piece.

Kaia was picking his brother's lock. I understood that Kennith locking himself in his room was something that happened more than often; Kai had come prepared.

I jumped when the door was thrown open to reveal a teenage boy, probably even younger than me. He wasn't wearing the dark glasses I expected, but instead let his glazed, blue eyes stare at nothing for all to see. "Seriously, Kai. You're such a f-," but he froze mid-sentence. "Who's with you?" he asked, his brows pulling together under the small, dark fringe of hair that hung over his eyes, held in place by his grey beanie. He had an eyebrow piercing over his right eye and arrow or two of hoops in his ears. A septum piercing hung above his thin lips, thick and intimidating. I wondered if he could see well enough to notice the piercings in the mirror or if anyone had told him that they accented his angelic, angular face.

"This is Luka. Boyfriend," Kaia replied, putting a hand on my waist. Kennith grimaced with disdain. "Whatever. Keep him the hell away from me. Go eat your damn dinner, fag. I'm not hungry," he told us before the door was slammed shut loudly. My introduction hadn't fazed him.

I cowered against Kai as he sighed. "Don't mind him. He's always been like that."

....

Dinner was exciting. I had many questions asked about my family and where I came from, but that subject was a rather boring one. As I learnt more about his family, I felt more like a part of it. There was no homophobia, save for Kennith's hurtful remark. Kai didn't seem too fazed as he smiled at me from across the massive dining table that seemed more as if it was meant for kings and queens than everyday people.

So, instead of ignoring my raging hard-on, boredom, and following the conversation, I gave Kai a coy look. He merely glanced at me before looking back to his mother and continuing his conversation. I wasn't humiliated to sit around his family while so aroused. They couldn't see my lower half under the table, anyway. I bit my lip and gently slid off my shoe, deserting it on the hardwood floor to slide my foot up his calf. It was a rather long stretch for me, but I managed to find his body without having to sink under the narrow table. Only I noticed how he flinched and briefly glared at me. He was not happy with my actions, but he would enjoy it soon enough. Surprisingly, he didn't move his leg away. It only stopped bouncing as I traced the hem of his dress pants, creeping along his thigh and slowly towards his crotch. Kai was beginning to squirm, shooting me daggers with his eyes. '*Not around them,*' he seemed to warn. I could only smirk and finally find his bulge with my foot, poking at it experimentally with my toes.

Kaia rolled his hands into large fists on the table, anger and pleasure hidden behind his tight, polite smile. His Adam's apple bobbed as his jaw flexed, his meal forgotten.

"Kai, are you planning any trips for Luka and yourself?" Lily asked. Her brother looked up from me, his cheeks flushed and his eyes dark. "Yeah, I thought you said that you haven't gone anywhere for a few months. You're always going to new places for work," Michael contributed. I was surprised he didn't release a groan when I finally added more pressure to his cock, rubbing it lightly with the ball of my foot. "Um... yeah, I actually wasn't sure how much Luka likes to travel. I wanted to take him to a music festival somewhere. Or maybe to somewhere tropical?" Kai stammered. "That sounds fun," I said, smiling devilishly. It was fucking adorable to see him so flustered. The more pressure I added, the deeper his blush became. He bit his lip and momentarily closed his eyes when I switched from a counter-clockwise to clockwise massage. "Take him to Canada. You can come visit me and see the moose there," Lily giggled, and I laughed too. When I caught Kai's gaze again, I paused and rested my foot against the inside of his thigh, muscles rippling as he breathed heavily. The glare he was giving me was deadly, and I debated whether I really wanted trouble added to the oncoming punishment.

So I let it fall to the ground, slipping my shoe back on as easily as it was removed.

Kai still didn't relax, his shoulders remaining tense and brooding through the meal. I remained quiet, never looking back to Kai in fear of the anger I would see. I was satisfied, though, the giddy feeling in my belly hanging around even after the family had finished and decided that conversation could continue over dishes.

"That-," Kai began, inconspicuously squeezing my ass in the corner of the kitchen as the family helped clean it up, "-was a dirty move." Lily shot us an amused glance.

"You gonna punish me?" I asked under my breath. He visibly shivered. I smirked up at him. "Yes. Yes, I'm going to-," but his

ANGEL

mother shoved a plate of sandwiches and chips towards me, interrupting our conversation quite rudely. "You've been volunteered as tribute to bring the devil his food," she told me with a smile.

"Bring what to who?"

Kai immediately frowned at his mother, fist clenching against my tailbone. "Let Alex or someone do it." She gave a warning glare to Kai before shrugging him away. "Kennith. Upstairs, room at the end of the hall to your right. Luka can go while you dry dishes, Kaia." Kaia deflated. "Mom, Kennith called me a-a... a name earlier today. He's in a mood. Luka doesn't need to be around that. If he doesn't want dinner, then he's not gonna come."

"You hush. I'm not just gonna let him *not* have dinner," she replied, frowning, "And you, Luka, just relax. It's just like meeting a new friend!" Aja smiled joyfully at me before she walked away and began to assist Lily at one of the two sinks. I looked to Kai with wide eyes. He sighed. "Just... make sure he eats it, okay? Maybe you'll break the unbreakable code and finally get through to his tiny brain that not everyone hates him."

"But he hates *me*!" I whisper-yelled. A tiny hand pulled on my back pocket, so I looked down at Kara angrily. "Kennith likes pretty things. Smile at him," she told me with a large grin. The girl didn't soothe my racing heart, but she did brighten my spirits slightly. My frown turned up into a worried expression. Kaia, seeming to forget his predicament, smiled at her. For a moment, I wasn't so worried about meeting new family members with an uneasy belly full of food and butterflies.

"Kaia, come dry the dishes or you'll be doing them all by yourself!" his mother threatened loudly. The man smiled at me apologetically. "Sorry, Babe. Gotta run." With that, he threw his drying towel over his shoulder and bounded away to take his place among his family.

He left me to face the devil.

CHAPTER
FORTY-SIX

I CLIMBED THE STEPS slowly, dreading the meeting between Kennith and myself. When I reached his room, I knocked very gently on the door and took a large step back. The plate was shaking in my hands, and I prayed I wouldn't drop it. "Seriously, get the hell out of here," Kennith greeted me, his door open only a crack. "Um... I have dinner for you, though." He scoffed and closed the door. "Give it to someone who wants it!"

I sighed and wracked my brain for new ideas. "Kennith... you should, um, eat it. Seriously. I don't want to be standing in front of your door just as much as you don't want me standing in front of your door." *Good job, Luka. That made sense.*

"...can't you just leave?"

"I'll just put it on your desk or bed or something, then I'll leave."

After a moment or two of more silence, I worried that he had decided to ignore me. I wouldn't blame him; I would have done the same thing. I nearly jumped with joy when he opened the door, his oceanic eyes trained on the floor. "Just... put it on the dresser. What is it?" He let me step past him, and I took a deep breath before answering. "Bean sprouts, tuna, and some kind of sauce that I think everyone in this house but me can pronounce. Oh, and also some hot sauce. Kai said you liked it hot."

ANGEL

"I guess," he replied, folding his arms around himself and biting his lip as I set it on the dresser beside his bed. The room was decorated with boring, faded colours and very little clutter. He kept only what he needed and put it back in the same spot every time he used something.

"So... how long have you been with Kai, exactly?"

And just like that, the Arche household devil had begun a conversation with me. He really wasn't as bad as I thought he would be. Much easier to talk to, despite his unapproachable bravado. My reply was quick and joyful. "Three months now. How old were you when you came into the family?"

"Three. I was born blind. Kai actually... uh, he helped me a lot. He helped all of us."

I then noticed the massive shelf of books behind me. One of the rows of books were impossibly thick, and they all looked exactly the same. 'The Holy Bible' was written in beautiful, thick cursive across the spines. "Are you religious?" I asked. I didn't mean to change the subject, but Kennith has piqued my curiosity.

He paused, stuffing his hands in his pockets and sitting on the edge of his bed. He obviously knew his way around his bedroom easily, despite the fact that he didn't even live there permanently. "Not really. It's just kinda a hobby. Kai bought me those big books a few weeks ago, and now I'm re-reading them while I'm here."

"They're in braille, right?"

"Obviously." I ignored the slight venom in his voice.

"Have you ever thought about pursuing something in religion? I bet you could get a pretty cool job at a museum or something," I said, putting my hands on my hips as I studied the books. Underneath the cursive sat rows of tiny raised dots, probably a translation of the title. He scoffed. "Yeah. Whatever."

"Seriously. If you like it, you should just go for it."

"What are you pursuing? You sound young, so you still have time."

"I'm nineteen. Not that young."

He scoffed quietly. "You're like a baby to Kai!"

"Oh, come on! I'm legal. That's all that matters." I was tired of the age card. Kennith sighed, considering our relationship. "I guess you guys really love each other, huh?"

I opened my mouth to answer, but then I paused. I told him I loved him a few times before. The gleam in his eyes told me that he loved me too. But had he ever actually said it to me? Did that gleam really prove anything? "I... yeah. I guess we really like each other. I mean, I'm meeting his parents, right?" I said finally. Kennith's eyebrows pulled together disbelievingly. "Right...."

"So, you just like reading about religion?" I asked, opening one of the books and silently flipping through the thick pages. They were all blank, save for the tiny dots that poked up. The pads of my fingers ghosted over them momentarily. "Yeah. I mean, it's for the philosophy of it. It's kinda either reading braille or listening to music. I can't do a lot of other stuff." I perked up and set the book back on the white, wooden shelf. "What kind of music do you listen to?" He shrugged. "You can look. They're in the drawer closest to the corner there." He motioned in the general vicinity of the wall, but his aim was off from the corner. I ignored that fact and opened the drawer to see dozens of discs. Tiny braille stickers were taped to the covers, obviously so he could know which CDs were which. "Wow," I said as I filed through them. "You don't really seem like the classical type." He scoffed and scratched the back of his neck. "Mom played them a lot. I don't really like music with any actual words in it. It's just too much extra noise, you know?"

"Yeah. I get that."

Neither of us were sure what to say next. The silence dragged

ANGEL

on for a few moments, but I eventually grew bored and closed the drawer. My actions didn't seem to stop the quiet between us. I didn't want to leave him. Maybe he wanted some company while he ate? Under his rude bravado sat a kid who was simply cursed with the loss of his vision and dreams that only he thought would never be pursued.

"... are you still here?"

"Oh, yeah, sorry. Are you gonna come downstairs to eat? I heard that they were planning on playing some games outside. Maybe we can get them to put on some *Beethoven*." He sighed and crisscrossed his legs on the bed. "No thanks. But... tell Kai that I'm sorry I called him a fag. I didn't mean it. I think he knows that. We try to keep discrimination at a minimum in this house." I nodded, knowing that he couldn't see me. "Don't worry about it. I'll tell him. Enjoy your dinner, I guess?" It felt strange to connect to someone so young. Most boys had tossed me to the side after I attempted to make them my friends. But the kid seemed okay with it. "Have fun with the fam," he replied, feeling for his sandwich discreetly. I left him once he had successfully found the plate, closing the door rather loudly so he knew that I had left.

"I was worried you were eaten alive up there," Kai told me when I entered the kitchen again. "Yeah. He said he was sorry for calling you names," I replied. His family had disappeared, leaving only Zach, Kai, and Mason to finish the few dishes that were left on the counter. Even the maid had abandoned them. I decided to help, grabbing a towel and snatching a plate from Kaia's hands. "So, Luka, about your mother," Mason began suddenly, dropping a glass on the drying rack after he had cleaned it in the bubbles that went up to his elbows. "About my mother," I replied with a raised eyebrow. "Do you think she would say yes if I asked her out?" I paused, anger boiling inside me until I was sure it would explode all over Mason.

The dish in my hands was set gently on the counter so I could give him my full attention.

"And what if *I* say no?"

"Oh shit," Zach laughed from the other side of Mason. I glared at him, too, which silenced him quickly.

"I'll be nice to her, I promise! I'm really not that bad of a guy."

Kaia watched, intrigued and amused.

"Where would you take her?"

Mason thought for a minute. "Maybe to a nice restaurant. Buy her a nice meal and take her out for a car ride around the city...?"

I scoffed. "Good. Stay the hell away from her."

"What?! What's wrong with dinner and a drive?"

I glared at him, my hand on my hip. "First of all, she'll hate any nice dinner. Buy her a burrito and you guys can eat in your car outside my house. Then she will leave your car after a small conversation over Mexican food. Second, you will not drive *anywhere* with her in the vehicle."

"I mean, it's not a horrible date," Zach mumbled. "So, if she doesn't do elegant, I'll buy her a burrito," Mason added. He was losing hope.

Kai sighed and put a hand on my shoulder to draw me away from the conversation. He could feel my anger rolling off me in waves. "Why don't you let me take care of the date? Let me set it up?" I gaped up at him. "You?"

"You enjoyed our dates, didn't you? I promise, your mother will have fun. And Mason will not be overstepping boundaries, will you, Mason?" It was a slight warning. I looked at him with a warning glare.

"Right. No overstepped boundaries. Got it."

I would know if he did anything wrong. And he wouldn't survive the night if he were to encroach on my mother's boundaries.

ANGEL

....

Around ten-o'clock, the family was seated outside under the stars. The Washington wilderness was beautiful, especially around that time of year. Halloween was coming fast. A gasoline fire pit sat in the center of our ring of patio furniture. Lily relaxed on a loveseat with her children curled up and asleep at her sides. I wondered who the father was. Maybe he wasn't part of the picture. Couples were cuddled against their significant others while the unfortunate singles were left to fend for themselves in the chilly air of the patio. I was grateful for Kai then. I always had been, but in that moment, I was simply *happy*. His family had welcomed me as one of their own by then. I was surprised by how easily that had happened. Kai's arm tightened around my shoulder when I adjusted my head against his shoulder.

"You tired?" he asked quietly. "No," I whispered a reply as I gently pried his fingers from his bottle and took a small swing of his beer. Thankfully, Kai was very wary about his drinking habits. He didn't like to be drunk or tipsy at all. At the moment, everyone had been talking about animal encounters in their neighborhoods. I was shocked to find that the Arche family lived all over the world, from Dubai, to Australia, to Vancouver.

"Did any of you hear about the cougar we had by my house?" Lily asked her family. "No, we didn't. Did it get any pets or animals?" her father replied, his interest piqued. "Was it you?" Zach asked in all seriousness. We all got a good laugh, but my own laughter was cut short when I noticed a movement in the glowing kitchen window.

"I'll be back. Getting us all more beer," I said hurriedly as I unhooked myself from Kai. He seemed hurt, but I smiled and took one last sip of his beer before leaving the group to settle his nerves. They continued on with their conversation without me, grateful for the promise of more alcohol.

"Hey, Kennith," I said, closing the sliding glass door behind me. He stood at the sink washing his hands. Or trying to, at least. The soap had fallen into the large, metal basin and he was feeling around for the slippery, hand-made chunk lethargically. "Hey," he said. I silently grabbed the soap and put it in the palm of his hand.

"...thanks, Luka."

I shrugged. "It's no problem. Did you like your sandwich?"

"Yeah. Nice and hot. Just how I like it."

"Good. Do you want to come sit outside? There's lots of room next to Kai and I. I promise we don't bite... that much." I hoped he could hear the smile in my voice. But, despite my best efforts, he hesitated. "Um... no, thanks. I'm good. I got audio books upstairs that I haven't listened to yet."

"Oh. Okay, then. Have a good night, I guess," I said, my spirits dimming.

"Night, Luka."

We both turned away from each other, but I stopped suddenly when he called for me again. I was hopeful. "Hey, Luka?"

"Yeah?" I asked, my gaze moving to him slowly.

"How long have you been his sub?"

A fear-like chill jolted through me. "Wh-What?" I whispered in shock. How did the conversation suddenly tilt to *that?*

"He said he didn't like keeping his subs for a long time. And now you're here. How long has he really been with you?"

"... how do you know so much about BDSM? The rest of his family doesn't know, right?"

"Just answer the question."

"I've been with him three months, like I told you. Are you, like, a sub? Or a dom? How does that all work with... you know...." I didn't know what to say. It would be like wearing a blindfold every time he had sex. My senses were destroyed even *without* a blindfold. He wasn't of legal age, either.

"I'm not in the lifestyle."

"Oh… but when did you find out about Kai's… hobby?"

He shrugged. "Fourteen. I kinda got wrapped up in Kai's things. The dumbass left his shit out on his bed… I know he doesn't make it a lifestyle, though, per-se. That's why the family doesn't know much about it."

I panicked. "But he didn't… does he even know that you knew about his life at the time?"

"Not at the time. But I told him later on," he assured. I sighed with relief and licked the panic off my lips. "Yeah. O-Okay."

"Whatever. Go have fun. I got shit to do."

"Have a nice night, Kenneth," I replied in a shaky voice. But he was already finding his way up the stairs, obviously ignoring my goodbye. I almost walked back out onto the patio without the beer.

CHAPTER
FORTY-SEVEN

"WOW. TONIGHT WENT pretty nice, huh?" I said as Kai changed into his sleepwear and took a seat on the edge of the king bed. He smiled and motioned me towards him. I came to stand between his legs. "Did you have fun?" he asked.

"Yeah. Kennith is actually pretty nice. I had a good gab sesh with him," I replied playfully. He snorted. "A gab sesh, hm?" I nodded and played with the collar of his shirt, straightening and pressing it with careful fingers. I didn't meet his eyes, although I could feel his content gaze trained on my face. "Today, when I was talking with Kennith, he said that you helped him a lot. Ya know, with his lack of sight and... yeah, his sight. I just wanted to say that that's pretty cool. You don't seem like the family type, and now I'm seeing a whole new you."

"Do you like it?"

"Y-Yeah. It's... inspiring, I guess."

Kaia wrapped his arms around my waist and pushed his face against my stomach. I smiled when he kissed it gently. My stomach quivered with the sting of his stubble against my sensitive flesh. Lazy fingers carded through his hair. "Did you bring any condoms?" he asked against my belly. I sputtered a laugh. "I thought we were having a moment! No, I did not bring any condoms!" He pouted as he pulled me back onto the bed until I was straddling his waist. "That's okay. Just a little more clean up when we're done." But I shook my head. "No. We cannot have sex here. Not in a house full of people."

"But Mason and Rosa live with me and we still have sex with them in the house."

"Yeah, but they don't sleep right beside us. Most of the time, they're passed out on the couches downstairs." I stopped to listen to Kai's parents speaking in the master bedroom next door. "We'll just keep quiet, then. You have a punishment waiting too." I had forgotten about that, but I couldn't contain my laughter as he pulled me down to his face. "Kai! Your parents are going to murder us and throw our bodies in the lake!"

"Oh, let them," he replied with a smirk as he kissed me passionately. I sighed and melted against him as I felt his hands work themselves under my shirt and pull at the tiny piercings on my chest. Thankfully, they were healing nicely, but that didn't make them any less sensitive than before. "Ah... Kai," I groaned, leaning to suck on his neck. His libidinous tongue found my chest. The man licked a searing stripe up one of my buds, catching the ring slightly. I jolted and moaned, covering my mouth desperately. "No, Angel. Let them hear," Kai breathed, taking my hand and twisting my fingers into his on the bed as he rolled my nipple between his teeth, tiny bolts of hot pleasure shooting straight to my groin. "Ya know, I brought some things with me... we could have our own little scene here," Kai suggested, pinching my nipple lightly. It felt like a hell of a lot more than a pinch, though. I hissed and dug my nails into his shoulders. "K-Kai... I don't want them to hear us." He chuckled darkly. The man drove a hand under his belt and pulled a dark object from his boxers.

"Don't worry."

I wasn't sure what he meant until he pushed the object into my mouth, wrapped it around my head, and hooked it together in the back. The scent of him engulfed my face; it was strong and jarring. The item in my mouth was quickly identified as a shiny red ball gag that he must have been carrying in his boxers since before we retired to our rooms. I blushed harshly and diverted my eyes as he took in my new accessory. As he smiled devilishly, I bit down experimentally on the ball. Hard plastic.

"Beautiful," he said, grasping my ass and squeezing. My eyebrows pulled together as I unhooked the gag behind my head and pulled it away. I could tell he was about to begin his chiding, but I interrupted him. "Before you yell... I have a surprise for you." The man raised an eyebrow but let me up, watching as I crossed the room and entered the bathroom.

The red high heels had been hidden under the sink out of fear of him finding them in my bag.

"Should I be worried?" Kaia asked from the bedroom. I smirked and undressed, leaving only my cherry blossom panties and heels. I wrapped the gag around my neck temporarily before gathering the courage to stand and leave the bathroom. I took a deep breath and stepped out into the dim lighting offered by Kai's bedside lamp. At first, he only noticed my panties, and he smiled, but his smile fell when he noticed the shoes. Originally, I thought that he didn't like them. His blank stare told me many things, but I wasn't sure which was true. I gave an experimental twirl and smiled a little at him. "So... you like?"

He stayed silent and stared, his Adam's apple bobbing when he swallowed hard and finally nodded very slowly.

"....does that mean I won't be able to walk tomorrow?"

It was a moment before he could choke out an answer through

ANGEL

gritted teeth: "It means you won't be able to walk for a week."

In an attempt to ignore the shivers against my spine, I crossed the room and straddled Kai's lap again. He seemed to break from his trance, since he finally made eye contact with me. His eyes were terrifying, hiding none of his lust, as if that thoughtless beast had been released.

"Get on the floor," he ordered. I frowned. "Why?"

"Just do it." His voice was an absolute order, telling me clearly that questioning him would only make my situation worse. I had put him in the perfect headspace for an opportunity I wouldn't get again for a while. So, I did as I was told slowly, making him wait. He didn't like that, though. Instead, a large hand suddenly gripped my hair while he moved from the bed, dragging me with him. I almost cried out when I thought he was about to rip my hair from its roots. But it didn't last long. Kai dragged me to the dresser in the corner and quietly ordered me to stay still and silent before he disappeared into the bathroom. I could hear him moving things, rustling chains and buckles. The sounds were softened by leather. When he reappeared, he held my collar, a leather leash, and a pair of cuffs.

"Wh-What are we doing tonight?" I asked. There was fear in my voice and excitement in my chest. He knelt and kissed me on my cheek as a reply, leaving me to stare as he carefully wrapped the collar and cuffs around me. Then, the ball gag was added. He attached the leash to me and tied it to the dresser's leg. A soft tug promised him that it was secure. I whimpered. "Why...?" I tried to ask. The gag reduced my words to muffled groans. Kai shushed me by grabbing my neck in one hand, thrusting it back against the floor, and putting his lips on mine, kissing me deeply. It was full of lust and heat, a deep, raging hunger. The back of my head burned where it had collided with hardwood. Tears rushed to my eyes at his ferocity.

Then he left me, half-hard, and watching as I frowned in those adorable heels and panties that he loved. I sat up slowly, disoriented, and watched him fall back to sit and lean against the end of the bed before he unzipped his pants, drawing his underwear down slowly. My stomach clenched when his half-hard length popped up, finally free from its confines. He stroked himself to an erection, those black eyes never straying from my own. In only a few moments, I was just as hard as he was.

Why was he all the way over there? Why wouldn't he come over and fuck me?

My eyes widened and my breathing picked up when he groaned lowly, his firm hand jacking himself off as I wasn't even there. He refused to speak; his eyes said everything. They were taunting me... and I hated it.

I whined when bliss began to creep over Kai's face. He was nowhere close to finishing, but the way he pursed his lips and gritted his teeth elicited a sudden, insuppressible groan from me. In an unconscious attempt to ease the burn of my own erection, I leaned forward and looked up at him with my cheek pressed against the carpet. I was sure my face was fiery red by then, and I wanted to beg for him to let me touch him.

The ache in my gut wasn't just my arousal. It was almost abandonment, or at least something like it. Why couldn't I touch him? Why wasn't he allowing me to take him to the back of my throat like I wanted to so, so badly? I wanted to cry knowing that he would come without my hands on him. He was going to come without his hands on *me*.

"Mm... Luka," Kai moaned under his breath as he stroked himself. His arm was jacking faster. He could see the end. I gave a whimper, wanting to yell and cry for him. I instead began pulling on the cuffs and leash in an attempt to reach him. All I gained were marks on my neck from where the collar was digging in, and I only pulled back when I began cutting off my airway. When I looked up again, my eyes widened and I nearly ejaculated to the image that sat in front of me. Kai had come, semen ruining his chest that hammered up and down. His head was lolled back against the bed.

It almost brought me to tears. Almost.

"Please...," I whined. It broke Kai from his post-orgasm trance. In a second, he had packaged himself back into his pants and crawled back to me. I didn't look up at him until he forced me to, after he had untied the leash and removed the collar. When he noticed the marks under my jaw, he rubbed those away too. Meanwhile, I scrambled to lick the milky liquid from his belly, savoring rippling muscles over thin layers of fat he hadn't bench-pressed away.

"It hurts," I told him quietly when there was nothing more to taste but saliva. I was worried I would have alerted his family. At least Jeremy and Kara weren't knocking at our door.

Kai stayed silent as he pulled me across his lap, my wrists still aching with the urge to release the pressure at my crotch.

"Th-That's- that was cruel," I groaned against his ear. I gave another moan when he pulled my underwear down and began stroking me slowly. The pace was okay; it calmed my racing heart. I had received the night's punishment, and there was lots more to come.

....

"Come on, Lucika. Can't you find him?" Cade whispered, setting both hands on my shoulders. My eyes were wide with fear, my breath coming in small gasps.

Where was he? Had he left? Was I alone? Those people in the club were more menacing than ever before, knowing that they were the wall between Kai and I.

"Find him quick, Angel... or else I might be the only one who can

take you home tonight."

I turned to him in shock and horror, only to meet the devious, gold-laden smirk and glinting eyes of Caden himself.

I woke in a cold sweat, my heart pounding like a wild animal against my rib cage. My entire body ached, but the adrenaline helped me ignore the pain. There were no more clubs or horrible people who only wanted to separate Kai and I, just the white ceiling that I stared up at. I took a deep breath in an attempt to calm my shaking body. The adrenalin was racing, and it probably would be for some time.

"Christ," I cursed as I sat up with a grimace, running a hand over my face. But when I looked up and around the room, I didn't see the doorway to the bathroom like I should have. Instead, I got a view of the shadowy figure standing in front of it at the foot of the bed. It was a man dressed in black, silently watching as my heart stopped and I froze in terror.

The shadows concealed his face, and I couldn't manage to do anything more than remain frozen like a deer caught in headlights. Even my scream was locked in my throat, fighting its way out and gaining no ground in the battle. Kai stayed asleep, his soft breathing the only sound that reverberated off the walls. I couldn't even hear my own heartbeat against my ears. Neither of us moved. He was surely just a shadow, right? He had to be. He was too still. This place was too large for him to have broken into, climbed the staircase, made it past all the bedrooms, and Kennith, who would still be awake and could hear everything. It just wasn't realistic.

In what felt like a split second, I gathered the courage to reach over to my left and turn on the light, but I fumbled with the switch, and it took what felt like an entire minute to flip it.

Within a few seconds, the soft glow illuminated the room.

But it was empty.

ANGEL

The doorway to the bathroom wasn't blocked. There was no man watching Kai and I as we slept. I could finally breathe. I released it in a quivering sigh and sucked fresh air back in with a gasp, one hand clutching my hair and digging into my scalp as my eyes scanned the room one final time. It was silent.

Very cold, but silent.

I decided to turn off the light and climb out of bed, careful not to disrupt Kai too much. He mumbled something unintelligible and pushed his face deeper into his pillow. I never understood how he could be a stomach-sleeper, although I had bigger problems. Sighing, I stiffly crossed the room until I stood in the center of it, immediately noticing the *whoosh* of air in front of the balcony door. The curtains blew ominously, reminding me almost of a jellyfish or a stingray swimming in water. It let me briefly forget about the ache that still lingered from the hours before.

I picked up Kai's shirt to throw around my shoulders and stepped outside, enchanted by the view before me. The darkness only added to the beauty. Thick clouds accented the bright stars that poked through the gaps, and the diluted moonlight glittered off the lake below like thousands of tiny diamonds. Without any light pollution, it was easy to get lost in the beauty. And just like that, the tension in my shoulders was gone. The image of the shadow man had escaped my mind, because it was just my imagination, after all, wasn't it?

CHAPTER
FORTY-EIGHT

I DIDN'T WANT ANY more nightmares. They were bizarre and creepy, and they gave me an intensifying sense of dread. I stood on the balcony for only a few moments. It was cold out there, but I was almost too scared to move. If I turned around, would that man be there again? Something in my stomach held all my muscles in place so I was unable to even twitch.

That changed when a hot chest came in contact with my back and arms wrapped around my waist like a cage. The image of the shadow flooded back to my mind, so I jolted away. "S-Stop!" I exclaimed without thought, pushing the arms and chest firmly, my arms and legs flailing. I only froze when my foot had returned to the floor after landing a kick in the man's crotch in my struggle to get away from him as fast as possible, a loud grunt of agony echoing through the silent forest below us. Whoever I had kicked was just kicked *hard*.

I stared wide-eyed at Kai, who's eyes were just as round, glazed with pain. His hand cupped his groin with white knuckles, and I realized that he was nude. The man's jaw was tight and his free hand just barely supported him on one knee against the ground. He was the first one to say anything, as I was unable to utter any words through my hand that covered my mouth in horror. "Why did... ugh, why did you just... do that?" Both of us were silent for a moment as he struggled through the first few waves of agony. Then Kai rolled to his side, clenching his thighs together and running his free hand down his face.

My hand fell to my chest, my own mouth opening and closing. But no words came out. "I-I'm sorry!" I choked finally.

"I know... why did you kick me? Why?"

He was confused and probably angry, but there was something else in his eyes that I couldn't identify. Something sad. Something horrified. I had just given him homemade, surprise CBT, and he obviously wasn't all that impressed.

"I thought I saw a guy here. You scared me."

"What?" He was still pained, but worried. The man sat up.

"I... I think it was a dream. But I saw a guy in our bedroom. When I turned on the light, he was gone. The balcony door was wide open." Kaia stiffly hoisted himself back onto his feet, grimacing. One arm supported him on the doorframe. "I locked that before I went to sleep. How long ago was this?"

"Five minutes, maybe? I'm not sure."

He licked his lips and glanced back into the bedroom as he took a few steps towards me. He was evaluating the situation, wondering, hoping, that I was playing a painful prank on him. Something in his eyes clicked, and I could see the muscles in his jaw working and grinding. "Put some clothes on. I'm calling the police," he told me as he pulled us back inside and locked the balcony door.

"B-But I'm sure it was just part of my nightmare. Maybe the doors were blown open by the wind." I was desperate to know that I was only imagining everything. He ignored me and began dressing himself.

....

There were three police cars sitting outside the home within the next hour. Lily clutched her children close in the kitchen while Aja and Michael spoke with a pair of officers in the foyer. I had already gone over my experience with another officer, so I decided to move away from the commotion and rest my face in my hands as I sat on one of the sofas in the living room closest to the kitchen. I could hear Kai's deep voice echoing from another room as he spoke to a man and a woman in uniform. They fell silent after a moment.

"Hey," Kai said. I jumped at his entry. He took a seat beside me and leaned his shoulder against my own. Neither of us gained any comfort from it. "I'm so sorry I kicked you," I told him sincerely, as if I was begging for forgiveness. He shook his head and sat beside me. "Don't be. I shouldn't have snuck up on you, anyway." I scoffed. "Like that has anything to do with it. Are they going to search the woods around here? Have they searched the house?" I asked, immediately thinking of Jeremy and Kara. Had an uninvited stranger actually been in the house? What if the balcony doors really had been left open?

"They've searched the house, but there's nothing telling us where he could have gone. Not even a rope or anything for him to climb up onto the balcony with."

"He had to have gotten here somehow, though. He either took a car or ran miles through the woods."

"Yeah. And he's got a half-hour head start. But they're gonna bring dogs in and search for a while." I sighed. "He was in the house, Kai. I'm sure I saw him. Right there. What if he had done something to Kara or Jeremy? Or anyone?" Kai shook his head and scooted closer; our hips touched. "Try not to think like that. It's scary, but he didn't do anything. Everyone's safe and accounted for. I don't think anything was even stolen."

I nodded. "Thankfully, but isn't that weird? Why was someone

ANGEL

even here if they didn't come to steal?"

"Are you alright, dear?" Aja said suddenly, appearing beside us with her husband's arm around her shoulders. "Y-Yeah... just a little shaken up," I replied. She put her hand over mine and squeezed it. "You're family now, Luka. You-," but she was cut off by her grandchildren bounding through the living room and yelling for their uncle.

"Uncle Kai! Are you and Uncle Luka okay?"

He nodded and scooped up his nephew. "We're fine, kiddo," Kai promised. *Missing a testicle, but fine.*

"Is Kennith still upstairs? Alex went up to talk to him a little while ago." Aja said to Michael quietly. I perked up and looked at them hopefully. "I can go check on him."

"Thank you, dear."

I gave Kai a quick peck on the cheek before I stood and bounded up the stairs, careful to dodge the police woman who took notes on a pad in front of our bedroom door. I knocked on Kennith's door before I entered, but he was already standing in front of the entrance. "What was all the commotion out there?" he asked. The boy didn't sound particularly interested.

"The police are here. You should come downstairs."

"Yeah. A guy came and searched my room, talking about a guy in your bedroom. I figured I would be fine up here."

"Police have searched the house. I think they're gonna bring in a dog or two to search around the woods, but he's probably long gone by now."

"Good. But I'm staying up here. I've been reading for six hours straight now, and my fingers hurt. I'm gonna sleep." He began to close his door, but I put a hand on his arm, making him freeze. His reaction startled me; I tried not to make him anymore uncomfortable by pulling away slowly. "You should come downstairs. I think your parents want everyone in one place where they know where you are." Kennith hesitated, obviously resenting the idea of doing so. "I'll come with you. And you can bring a book or something, too," I suggested. Thankfully, he finally caved. "Fine. Can you grab the one on my bed?" I hurried to snatch the heavy chapter from the Holy Bible off his soft, grey sheets before following him out of the door.

I had never seen a walking stick in Kennith's hands. Instead, he guided himself with his hand on the wall, his thin fingers tracing door frames and feeling for the end of the hallway. He was damn slow too. "Normally I've memorized roughly how many steps it is from my bedroom to the stairs, but I don't come here much," he mumbled. I shrugged despite the fact that he couldn't see the action. "That's okay. I got time." Kennith's brows furrowed slightly in concentration, his footsteps shuffling and unsure. After a few moments of watching the end of the hallway approach agonizingly slow and finally making it to the edge of the stairs, he paused. I was about to ask him what the hold up was, but he began to feel for my arm. I gave him my hand immediately. The colour left his face. "I've never been good at walking down stairs," he explained in a suddenly diffident, hesitant voice.

I instantly held his arm with both hands, prepared to ensure that neither of us fell. "I don't mind."

....

"I really hope this didn't ruin our vacation," I mumbled to Kai. We stood in the kitchen alone. Most of the family was trying to get another hour or two of sleep before the sun rose. Mason was staying awake despite Aja's begging for him to lie down for even just a little while. I didn't know everything about Mason's past, but I knew that the police had kicked him into survival mode, and he was beginning

ANGEL

to walk slow laps around the inside of the home. Kai promised that there was nothing we could do when he shut himself down like that. Lily had finally gotten her children back to sleep, but decided to stay outside on the kitchen's balcony with Alex and Zach. Laurent sat in the living room, headphones perched on his head and napping on and off while the rest of the family went to bed. Everyone knew that none of us would get much sleep, if any, tonight, no matter how hard we faked it.

He shook his head. "Nonsense. I actually think I heard Janet talking about going to the lake tomorrow, and the kids definitely won't be leaving until they've taken a dive." I released a half-hearted breath of a laugh. "Sounds good... maybe Mason will take a dunk with us?" Kaia scoffed. "Maybe. But I hope you're ready to pull a lot of strings."

I smirked. "Born ready."

"Are you sure you don't just want him to drown?"

My mouth fell open in mock shock. "Kai!"

"No, I mean with your mom and all," he said hastily. I sighed at the unwanted memory. "Yeah. That. I just... don't like him hanging out with her. Even if you set up the date, I'm scared for her sake, ya know?" He snorted and leaned back against the counter, his arms folded over his chest. "If she's what you're worried about, I think you can forget about it. Mason is an intractable teddy bear, for the most part. She might need to be afraid of being humoured to death."

"No, Kai, that's not what I'm saying," I said with an exasperated sigh. He frowned and let me elaborate. "It crushed her when my dad left. She's terrified to give her heart to anyone else, and I know that Mason isn't a bad guy, but neither of us want her to get hurt."

"Have you not explained this to Mason?" He asked. I fell silent and shook my head. Kai shrugged. "If I were you, that would be my next move. Or at least make sure that your mother knows what's happening. I don't see the issue with a date, though."

I sighed and pinched the bridge of my nose between my forefinger and thumb. A headache had bloomed soon after the police dogs had begun to bark when they first pulled up to the house.

"You wanna go back to bed? You look exhausted," Kai told me. I shook my head, the image of the man flashing behind my lids once again. Kaia caught on quickly and put his hands on my arms to gain my full attention. "Luka, that guy isn't coming back. We've got police notified, and Mason is watching for anything within a one-mile radius. You need to sleep."

"Maybe. But you do, too," I replied, resting my hand on his cheek as my thumb swept over one of the dark bags that hung under his eyes. He was constantly tired, and I could tell that he didn't sleep as much as I initially thought. Having a stranger in his bedroom during the night certainly didn't help.

CHAPTER
FORTY-NINE

"HEY, MASON," I said hesitantly as I entered the small seating area on the far side of the house. He sat slouched in a chair, his narrowed eyes watching the trees sway gently outside. I hoped they were calming to him. "You shouldn't pull on your knuckles like that," he told me, his gaze trained on the darkness.

I paused when I saw the black handgun resting on the small table beside him.

"Are you going to bed sometime soon? You should sleep," I choked. Initially, I thought he was going to ignore me, but then he adjusted himself slightly and cleared his throat. "I'll be awake for a while. Go sleep, Luka."

"But I can't sleep knowing that you're awake down here. I don't think the guy is coming back."

"You don't know that. Go. To. Sleep."

I sighed and let my hands fall to my sides, determined. "Okay. Just... at least try to sleep? You're tired. We all are."

He fell silent. I began to pout. He, out of the corner of his eye, glanced at me, and sighed, surrendering.

"I'll go to bed soon, okay?"

I immediately lightened up and nodded. "Okay. Sleep

well, Mason."

"G'night, Lucika."

I met Kaia in our bedroom. I paused in the doorway, as if the room was somehow poisonous. What if the man did come back? What if the police dogs that were outside weren't able to pick up a scent to follow? What if the police officers had missed something and he was still lingering somewhere inside the house? "Luka. Are you listening?" Kai's voice shook me from my thoughts, and my gaze flashed to his. "Come sleep. The bags under your eyes are twitching."

I frowned and crossed the room to sit on the edge of the bed. "Mason isn't gonna sleep any time soon, is he?"

Kai shook his head. "Angel, Mason was raised in war, for war. Those instincts will never leave him." I deflated. "He's been torn away from most of his family, people he trusted and loved. Especially his daughter. Her mother doesn't like her staying with Mason. But he gets lonely. That's why he needs your mother, Luka, that's what you need to understand. That's why he's not sleeping tonight," he told me.

"That he needs someone close to keep him company?" I asked, looking up at Kai.

"It's not just that. It's more… you'd understand better if you were with him when he was young."

With a tired sniffle, I looked at the floor. Mason had always looked happy. I understood later how lonely he could be, even in a room full of people. I also understood that Kai had been torn, and was finally realizing that Mason no longer had the mental capacity to be held on a leash. He was changing. So Kai had to too. "Look, Angel, don't worry yourself now. Your mother is going to kill us all if I bring you back with sleep deprivation." I silently allowed him to pull me under the sheets and against his hot chest, his breaths evening out as I traced his lean muscles with a cold finger.

ANGEL

"Hey, Kai?" I asked.

"Hm?"

"Can I get a raise?"

"You want a pay raise?"

I nodded against his side, my eyes closing slightly against the rich chocolate scent that I had stirred up. "I want my mom to quit her job and find something she actually might enjoy. But I can't do that on my current paycheck." He hummed groggily and closed his eyes. "I'll give you a pay raise. Name your price...." But I was too tired to reply. Instead, we allowed the silence to consume us.

....

I would be lying if I said I didn't stay awake half the night out of fear. But Kai held me close even in his sleep, and my heart was calmed by the hot arm that hung around my shoulders. When I woke from my fitful sleep, Kai was missing. I glanced at the bathroom and visibly relaxed when I saw him finish shaving at the sink. This time, it wasn't dark, and there was no shadow. "G'morning," I mumbled, stretching as he rinsed and tapped his face dry with a white, fluffy towel.

"Good morning," he hummed, crossing the room and leaning down to land a kiss on my cheek. Before he could leave, I wrapped my arms around his neck, pulling him back so I could shove my face against the patch of skin where his shoulder and neck connected. "You smell really good. I like your shaving cream." He chuckled and kissed me again, this time letting his tongue swipe lightly over my upper lip. "I'll keep that in mind," he told me sincerely. "Y'know, maybe you could grow out your beard. I'm kinda curious about how it would look."

He scoffed. "Trust me. It doesn't suit me."

After breakfast, Kai's family and I took a hike to the lake. Under our clothes, we wore swim trunks and bikinis, adding to the excitement that we concealed with sunscreen and the effort of carrying bags of towels and inflatable plastic tubes until we actually reached the water. The trail was thin and winding, but the beautiful greenery and singing birds compensated for the many tripping hazards. Despite the fact that it was mid-October, the sun was shining bright and hot, filtering through the trees and lighting our way with bright yellows and fluorescent greens. Only a few dead leaves littered the ground, the only sign that winter was coming.

"Are we there yet?" Kara groaned as she grabbed her mother's hand. "Nope," she replied, popping the 'p'. I smiled at them, Kai and I bringing up the rear. "How well do you swim?" he asked. I shrugged. "Not the best. But I know how to not drown." He chuckled and pursed his lips, shrugging. "Good enough." Another ten minutes of walking, and we came to a break in the trees. Beyond that sat a small lake, roughly a quarter-mile wide. As promised, wood pillars held up the metal train tracks that offered a web of shade on the water. The twins raced each other to the water and splashed their way through it, stirring up tiny droplets that shone in the light.

"This place is beautiful," I said, watching a bird cross the lake and stop to land on the trestle. I could see the tiny outline of it against the sky. Kai nodded with a small smile. "That it is."

"So, first one to the trestle gets to choose who does dishes tonight?" Zach challenged the men. I wished that Laurent could have taken the trek with us, but he promised he would enjoy watching his football game at the house in his wheelchair. Charlie could keep him company.

Kai patted Zach on the chest before suddenly taking off toward the hill on the other side of the lake, Mason and Alex hot on their trail. Zacharia had worn a leg built for sporting; he could keep up with his brothers while they climbed the hill, but would have to remove it before jumping into the lake. I watched them as the women, less excited by the siblings' competition, eased into the water slowly, Michael standing nearby with his hands in his pockets and obviously enjoying the scenery that he built with his wife. Aja floated on an inflatable chair. The woman's skin glittered like gold in the sun. So did Kai's. The only one who didn't seem to be engaged was Saskia, who sat on the rocky shore and wrapped her arms around her legs. She had brought her sketchbook with her to keep her occupied.

"Come in, Uncle Luka! The water's freezing!" Kara called. I pulled my shirt over my head, leaving only my black swim trunks. I waded out with a small smile that twitched slightly when I shifted a new body part into the water. It was *cold*, especially on my piercings. Swimming wasn't recommended for piercings that were still healing, so I would be sure to clean them once we returned home. "The lake is fed by glacier water, so it's cold all year," Lily said, lifting her son up by his armpits and tossing him back into the water. Jeremy shrieked and laughed as the soft waves engulfed him. "I've never been to a lake like this," I replied, letting my knees give out under me so my head would fall under the surface. After a few moments, my limbs would be numb, anyway, so the temperature only bothered me in the first few minutes. I glanced up at the trestle when I surfaced again and swung my dripping hair from my face, my hand shielding my eyes from the glaring sun. Alex had made it to the top first. The four men tip-toed their way across the tracks. Without any guard rails for him to hold on to, I could tell that Mason was struggling with the height. His dark form was hunched and trembling under the sun.

The boys stopped at the centre, speaking with each other briefly. After a moment, they had decided that Kai would go first, and he picked up the rope that sat on the tracks. We watched him take a deep breath before running over the opposite side of the bridge so he could swing down towards us.

And when he swung, he *swung*.

Before he released his grip on the worn, knotted rope, he was nearly level with the bridge, his body spinning back and flipping a few times before he landed, creating an explosion of a splash. He surfaced a few feet away, already kicking and paddling toward the shore. I immediately began to swim out to him; the water was invigorating against my thrashing limbs. I was much slower, but when he reached me, he wrapped his arms around me and began to tread water. Kai's skin was like fire against the icy water. I could feel every ripple of muscle beneath the calm waves.

Above us, Alex took the simple cannon-ball method.

I laughed and wrapped my arms around Kai's neck, reveling in the perfection of the moment.

CHAPTER FIFTY

WE ARRIVED BACK home in L.A. a week later, just before a rare storm began to rage over the city. Rosa was excited to have us back home; she complained that Abraham had never been all that good at video games. Mason couldn't wait to return to the alcohol stash he hadn't previously been able to access.

We were unfazed by the weather, sitting together in the darkness of his bathroom as rain pelted against the windows. There was no lighting other than the soft glow from the city and the occasional crack of lightning to illuminate our faces. "I used to hate thunderstorms. They scared the shit out of me, but now all they do is calm me down," Kai said quietly, his rising chest adjusting me slightly as I relaxed against him. Both his arms hung over the sides of his soaking tub, but I was more content to let mine float idly on the top of the water, creating ripples that were only broken by my legs that were curled towards my chest comfortably.

"I've never minded them. They're kinda exciting, actually," I replied. We both fell silent once again, ignoring his phone that vibrated momentarily on the counter across the room.

"I have a session with James tomorrow. I think he also wants to speak to you," he told me. "Why?" I asked, leaning my head back so

I could look at his upside-down face. A small smile found his lips. "I think he just wants to get to know you, honestly."

"Get to know me?"

He nodded and let his arms fall beneath the water to wrap loosely around my stomach. He wasn't about to elaborate on the subject. "Y'know, Janet stopped me in the hallway once when we were at the vacation house," I began. He stayed silent, staring out at the city as he listened. "And she was asking me what my secret was. Why you were so happy there."

"Why was I so happy? She asked that?" I nodded. "She told me that something was different. Like you had a new spark in your eyes. Like she just… saw you differently that day." I didn't know what I was expecting as an answer, but all I procured was silence for a few moments.

"Luka, my life has been black-and-white for years. I thought I had colour and excitement, I thought I had friends and the people I met at the bars. Then... yeah, that spark of colour was probably you. You did that. I just never realized how deprived I was." His words were quiet and hesitant, but I knew they were sincere. I turned around slowly, straddling his hips and creating soft splashes as my arms wrapped around his neck. My fingers carded through his hair, pausing to toy with the soft fuzz of his undercut. He only stared at my body, admiring the way his stomach touched mine and tracing my jaw and collarbone. His hand swiped a stray lock of dark hair behind my ear. "So I guess we kinda saved each other, huh?" I realized.

He smiled. "Looks like it."

....

"Hey, Mom," I said, closing the front door behind me. She looked up from her bowl of cereal with tired eyes. I was surprised, though,

ANGEL

because it looked as if she had gotten a lot more sleep than I thought she would have while I was gone. "Hi. Did you have fun?" I nodded and took a seat beside her after dropping my bag in the living room. "Yeah. It was awesome. I bet you'd really like his sisters if you met them." She nodded absently, confused by the fact that I had sat beside her instead of darting straight to my bedroom. She knew something was coming.

"Can I tell you something without you thinking that I'm pulling your chain?" I asked her.

She raised an eyebrow. "What is it?"

I bit my lip and smiled. "I was thinking... you could quit your job."

She only started.

"I'm serious. I'm making money now. And with the raise, we can pay the rent on this place and buy necessities, plus your paycheck." I could tell that she didn't believe me, even though she wanted to with all her heart. "You can quit your job and find somewhere you like. You could do some low-wage or volunteer kinda stuff. Things you want, Mom. I'm... I'm sick of seeing you like this at that stupid job. You don't deserve it. You never did." At first, I thought that she still didn't believe my words. I was ready to tell her as many times as necessary, but then her eyes began to water.

"You're not kidding?"

I shook my head with visible excitement before she slowly pushed her arms around me, hugging me close and holding my head under her chin. She hadn't done that since I was very young. "You're a good kid, Luka." As always, her words held more meaning than anyone but myself could understand.

With my mother happy and my eyes drooping, I decided that I didn't want to bother her anymore than I already had. She needed her sleep too. Without dinner, I climbed the stairs to my bedroom and collapsed, releasing a huff of air as the sheets swallowed me. I decided to call Kai before throwing in the towel.

"Have the police found anything more on our visitor at your parents' house?" I was always connected to Kai via phone, especially when I spent the night at my own house. My bed would never amount to his, but the comforting smell of my pillows and blankets conjured familiar and safe memories. "Not a lot. The trail fell pretty cold after a mile or two. Spend the night with me if you're still wary of him." His voice was clear and well-rested, contrary to mine. I sighed. "I'm staying with Mom tonight. I have my own house, remember?"

"Seriously. I want you here. We still don't know who that guy was and why he was there."

I snorted. "And you think he followed us all the way back to L.A.?"

As if.

....

I woke to the sound of birds, car horns, and my mother clanging pots downstairs. When was the last time my mother ever actually used that many pots? When had she ever even gone in that drawer? I tossed my covers onto the floor and threw on a pair of shorts and a thin tank-top before jumping down the stairs. My steps were like skips, fast and carefree. What met me was the last thing that I expected. Mason sat at our dining room table, a steaming mug of coffee held between his hands. My mother glanced up briefly when I entered. I would have yelled at Mason if I hadn't suddenly remembered Kai's words. He at least deserved a chance, and I would begrudgingly give him a small one.

"What are you looking for?" I asked. "Frying pan. I want some eggs," she replied. "In the cabinet behind you," I told her.

ANGEL

"Morning, Mr. Luka," Mason dared to speak up. I flashed him a stiff smile. "Hey, Mason. You came for coffee?" He shrugged. "Mr. Arche wanted you to have this back. You need it if you really want to work for that raise." He fabricated a laptop from beneath the table, handing it out to me along with my notebooks. "Thanks."

"Do you want me to make it, Ms. Roggy? I'm not too bad with a frying pan," Mason suggested suddenly. My mother paused as she set her eggs on the counter. He didn't waste any time rising and coming to stand beside her. "You go drink some coffee, hm? And I'll work my magic." They had obviously conversed a little, enough to get to know each other, at least, because when she sat down, she didn't have her own mug.

Instead, she began to sip from Mason's.

As appalled as I was, I was still able to tug my phone from my pocket angrily and speed-dial that familiar number, preparing to go ape-shit. Why was he with my mother? Didn't he have work to do for Kai? "Please don't tell me that this is their date," I told Kai, barely acknowledging his jovial greeting.

"What?"

"Mason is in my house making breakfast for my mother. You need to start guarding your bodyguard."

"He was supposed to be picking you up. We have to go out and look for a suit for you."

"A suit? Why?"

"There's a charity ball my family and some of their friends are doing tomorrow night, and I was hoping you would come with me." I smirked. "You're inviting me as your date?"

"Yes. It's going to be a big party with a lot of very important people. I figured you fit into that list of people." I blushed and bit my lip. "What's the charity for?"

"It's actually for a few different charities in the family. That and some of the money will be going to the children's hospital. I mean, we gotta stay rich somehow, right? You wouldn't believe the tax exemptions we get."

"Wow," I breathed. He chuckled. It was only an excuse to dress up for his family. "Guests can wear either red or black, and that's why I need to buy you a red dress." I rolled my eyes. "Very funny, Kai." Kai only chuckled before he sighed. "Just let Mason finish his coffee. He says that your mom is good company."

I blanched, suddenly horrified. "So you *knew* that he was over here to chat up my mom?"

He hung up on me, and I could only stare at the phone in shock and anger.

"Your stupid brother just hung up on me," I seethed, returning to the kitchen. Mason popped a sugar cube between his lips. Eggs crackled in his pan. He leaned against our counter while he waited to flip them. "Why?"

"Because neither of you can freaking own up to anything." I wasn't completely sincere, but the fact that Kai was being so relaxed about having his best friend in my house without telling me angered me.

"Wow. That's so unlike me," Mason feigned his hurt with an uncontrollable smirk. My mother slurped at her coffee and shook her head.

"They're boys, Luka. They don't understand that owning up to things can get them laid. You have to sweet talk your partner, not hang up on them."

Mason's smirk crumbled. It made morbid joy bloom in my chest.

"I'm a boy, mom."

"Exactly. Learn from their stupid mistakes so you can stop making them yourself."

"Wow. Thanks for the support," I snorted.

ANGEL

....

"You could wear a red suit. That would be hot. It would make a statement, too," Kai suggested, pausing beside a helmet shop and admiring the motorbike gear that glinted at him from the opposite side of the window. I pulled lightly on his arm, urging him towards the high-end clothing store across the mall. We didn't have time to window shop. "Who said I was wearing red? What if I want to wear black?" He scoffed. "I'm wearing black. No question about it. And... I kinda made a deal with Alex that if I got you to wear red to the gala, I would be able to have his old Harley." My eyes narrowed at him. "Can't you just buy your own damn bikes?" The man chuckled, amused at my anger. It only made me boil. "What's the fun in that? He'll be down by one favorite automobile by Sunday night." I pouted as we entered the shop, immediately greeted by a worker who stank of perfume and cats. She seemed kind and bright, though, upon meeting her. "Can I help you two with anything today?"

Kai nodded, handing her a folded slip of paper. "Our measurements. A red suit for him and a black for me." I frowned at him, but he ignored me. The woman, who's name tag read 'Cathleen', nodded and looked up at me. "What kind of red? I can show you our colour swatches." I glanced up at Kai nervously. He nodded and nudged me in her direction. I could only shoot him a few anxious glances before I was led away by Cathleen, the back doors opening into a back storage room neatly organized with fabric and a single, small sewing machine. It was built for small repairs and extra adjustments, not making the actual suites the company made. On the wall hung a small ring of fabrics.

"I like that one," I told her, a bright cherry-red catching my eye as she flipped through them. She nodded and scribbled it onto a piece of paper. "We have a few styles that you can choose from," she pulled me towards the back of the room. "I have some styles in the book back here that aren't on the floor yet. Are you looking for something more modern or classy? What's the occasion?"

I shrugged. "I honestly don't know. It's for a party. A fundraiser. Whichever one you like best, I guess?" Her immediate reaction was to smile and nod. "I have just the style. You like this one?" Cathleen motioned to a sharp and well-fitted suit jacket, double breasted with a structured silhouette. It was just as stunning as every other item of clothing in the shop. Kai had advised me to refrain from inspecting the prices, but I couldn't help but reach out and glimpse the tag taped to the edge of the laminated page.

I gasped and immediately dropped it. "Is there a problem?" Cathleen asked.

My throat and smile were tight when I answered. "No. Everything's fine. I like this one."

CHAPTER
FIFTY-ONE

"**A**NGEL." A SOFT hand was shaking me awake to end my nap that afternoon. My lack of sleep during the night was becoming a problem. I groaned and swatted it away. "Angel, get up, you need to eat dinner," the voice told me. "I don't want to," I mumbled to Kai. He sighed and let his hand fall onto the bed. "Thanks, Mason," he said, before the door shut and we were left alone. One eye opened to see the handle turn and stop. Suddenly, the bed dipped and I was slowly hoisted into his lap, my head on his shoulder. I hit his arm weakly, refusing to wake "Why are you so tired all of the sudden?" he asked. "Haven't been sleeping well," I replied through a yawn. His brows pulled together slightly. The sun was setting slowly behind the skyscrapers of L.A. That was okay, though. I could just blast music until the sun returned tomorrow.

I hadn't convinced Kai.

I ran a hand through my hair, prolonging the inevitable. "I told you... I'm just paranoid," I mumbled finally, pushing myself out of his lap. Between us sat a tray of gourmet cheeses and meats, accompanied by bright fruits and a pitcher of juice. "You looked like you weren't up for eating something heavy, so I told Rosa to make you something that wasn't too hard on the stomach," he explained. I shrugged and licked my lips slowly. He was obviously waiting for me to elaborate, but I hesitated. "I can't help if you don't tell me. Or I could call James and have him here in the next half-hour." Eventually, I gave in, and he listened silently as I explained my predicaments. "I was having nightmares first. And then I felt like I didn't have any privacy. Like somebody was always watching me. And it's just been getting worse." I paused and watched him nod slowly. But he stayed silent, so I decided to bravely continue. "And then the guy came to your parents' house. I had a nightmare that night, and when I woke up, he was just... standing there. I haven't really been sleeping well since, and the paranoia isn't going away, either."

His jaw worked as he thought for a moment, setting one elbow on his knee and his hand on the other. "Do you mind if I ask what the nightmares are about?" I shrugged and diverted my eyes. "They're always about the night we went to the club. You're ... like... I can't find you." You left me."

"Odd... I'm going to call James. He'll talk to you for a while," he told me, beginning to stand and pull out his phone in a hurry, as if he was angry. But I could see in his eyes that he was simply worried. My hand shot out to grip his arm. Kai's attention was immediately on me. "You don't need to. I'll be okay. Can we just eat?" After a moment of obvious inner conflict, he sighed and discarded his phone into his pocket once again, calming enough to take a seat beside me as I pulled my legs to my chest and popped a grape between my lips. "We can get you medicine for it. I used to take a lot of medication for anxiety. They help."

I didn't reply to Kai.

"Eat some," I ordered as I held a slice of gouda towards him. With a sigh, he snatched it straight from my fingers with his teeth, smiling when I did.

ANGEL

....

"I don't know how to act at these things," I told Kai the next day, buttoning my suit. I looked fairly good in my cherry-red suit jacket and pants, accented with a black tie and dress shirt. I knew that I would be much more prominent than Kai in the crowd, who wore his black... well, his black everything.

"That's okay. As long as you're kind, people will be kind to you," he promised, planting a kiss behind my ear. On instinct, I tilted my head to give him better access before he pulled away. "I'll be there with you the entire time anyway," Kai added. I smiled and nodded. "Well, are we leaving the-," but I was cut off when he pushed me onto the bed, peppering kisses on my neck.

"K-Kai! I don't have the time or fabric to cover hickeys tonight!" He chuckled and flipped me onto my stomach, my spread knees supporting my waist above the bed so my ass was efficiently shoved up against his crotch. "What are you d-doing?!" I exclaimed, already clutching the sheets. I could hear his smirk as he replied, "Having some fun. This is the best way to break in a new suit, you know?" My retort was instantly caught in my throat when he pulled down my slacks and his saliva-dripping fingers were at my hole, sucking and tugging on the rosy pucker. Again, I wasn't clean, nor exactly in the mood to waste time. But that didn't mean I wasn't in the mood for fun. "Ah... Kai," I moaned, pushing against his hand. One dug into my hip as he thrust his index finger as deep as possible, reaching places that had me curling my toes and arching my back. "Ah... don't stop," I moaned, throwing my head back. I could only hope that my cock hadn't already stained the new pants that I gyrated against my palm.

"Sorry, Baby. We're stopping for now," he told me, and his touch was suddenly gone; it had felt like only a few seconds since he began his assault. "Wait! N-No! What are you-." I pouted and sighed, abandoning my complaints before wrapping my arms around his neck. I deflated with a sigh. "Well, now I'm horny." He only laughed and pulled me to my feet. "Don't worry. There'll be lots of people for you to come in front of."

"Oh, shut up. I doubt many people there will be interested in my sex life." Kai smirked and pulled me flush against him. "Actually, there will be about five-hundred people there. And some of them are Zach's friends..."

Yep. I was fucked.

"How much money do they expect to raise?"

"Tickets for the night are five-hundred dollars each. Plus there will be auctions and opportunities for extra donations." My eyebrows rose to my hairline. "Five-hundred dollars? You spent a thousand bucks to get us into a charity event?"

He shrugged. "It all goes to good causes. I've spent a lot more on a lot less."

"And you were talking about a surprise? What kind of surprise? If it's pole dancers, I'm leaving." Kai laughed. "Don't worry, you'll get your turn. The pole I ordered should be here within the next few days."

CHAPTER
FIFTY-TWO

WHEN MASON PULLED up to the mansion, I could only gawk at the clothing and cars, shining reds and glinting blacks, accompanied by glittering paint jobs and sleek automobile models. "I guess everyone here is pretty rich, huh?" I asked, gaping up at the building towering above us. Decorous people passed us. "Well... I guess they're not swimming in it. They're more... *bathing* in money," Kai replied, buttoning the top button of his suit. He briefly paused in the doorway to hand the receiver our tickets as I absorbed the scenery around me carefully. The foyer immediately opened up into a glowing, golden ballroom, crystal chandeliers and a warm smell that wafted through the air on a soft stream of breeze that floated in through open doors. It invaded my senses and set the scene in the ballroom. That and the noise, which was a melting pot of laughter, chatter, and soft music being played from the corner by a string quartet.

"This place is really pretty," I told him. He wrapped an arm around my waist as Mason and Rosa disappeared into the crowd. "Champagne, sir?" a man asked suddenly on our right, and Kai grabbed a tall sparkling glass. "Thank you." I frowned up at him as he pulled us away.

"Why don't I get any?"

He pushed his head back and swallowed the glass's contents with one mouthful. I could tell that Kai made the most of his parent's events. "Because-," he replied, setting the empty glass on a passing tray held by another woman dressed in the same clean apron and neat bow around her neck, "-you aren't getting drunk tonight. Especially not since I have plans for us later." The dark glint in his eyes told me that whatever he had planned should scare and excite me more than anything.

Women wore fluorescent red gowns, which were followed closely by men in black tuxedos and sharp haircuts. I was yet to see a man wearing a red suit. My eyes narrowed, almost angry at him. I should have caught on when he said that he had made a deal with his brother.

"I see what you did. I hope you enjoy that damned bike." My voice, although I really couldn't help it, held much more humour than venom. Kai ignored me, although he couldn't keep that devilish smile off his face. "Come on. I want to find Genova," he told me. I couldn't help but follow him as quickly as possible into the dense crowd, eager to meet someone that wasn't as rich and more familiar. We found her standing alone in a corner, her eyes dark and half-masted in an oppressive glare. She was dressed in a sleek, black suit, her mile-long legs defined wonderfully under the dark fabric. Finally, I wasn't alone. "Genova," he greeted with a smile. She glared up at him briefly and unfolded her arms from under her breasts. "Your knee still bothering you?" she hissed, almost as if she actually cared. Kai shook his head and smiled kindly despite her venom. "Not anymore. Where has Alice run off to?" She shrugged. "Went to get me some alcohol. Socket better not be drinking any, or she'll be fucked for the rest of the night."

Kai flinched slightly at the unexpected mention of his least-favorite word, but recovered quickly, straightening his jacket and

ANGEL

dropping his empty champagne glass on a passing tray. "I'm sure she's just getting lost in the crowd. She'll find you soon enough. She's pretty late past her bedtime, huh? And the night hasn't even started yet." Genova glanced at her wristwatch and rolled her eyes. "Yeah. She's gonna be a bitch to get to sleep tonight unless I get her asleep in the car. Been in a really young headspace all night too."

"Wow. Must be a new record for her. She's-," but Kai was cut short by a panting Alice racing to her caregiver. "I got it, I got it! The guy at the bar said I was really pretty. Then he gave me his number, but I swallowed the paper." The girl's voice was odd, pronunciation contorted almost like a child's. I stared in confusion at Alice as she explained to Genova. She took both shots, throwing her head back and letting them disappear down her throat without a wince. "Thank you, Baby. You ate his number?" Alice nodded eagerly, her low pigtails bouncing. Genova smirked and pulled her lover to her side. "Good girl."

"Don't ever change, Alice," Kai told the girl with a laugh. Kai was wasting no time making his rounds to more familiar faces. The man grabbed my hand and began leading me away. I waved to Alice before she disappeared behind us. We met his brother once Kai had found his bearings in the sea of bodies. "Hey! Pure-blood!" Zach's voice drew us in another direction. "Hey, Zach," Kai smiled, embracing his brother in a hug. Zacharia then patted me on the back.

"Have you ever been to one of these before?"

I shook my head.

"That's fine. I'm sure Kaia can show you the ropes."

Kai only glared. "It's Kai." His brother ignored him. Instead, he only waved for more drinks.

The bidding began about halfway through the night as it neared ten-thirty. Donated items like paintings and cars were auctioned off at stunning prices. Kai placed bids on many items, but failed to reach his goal, and instead only took home a wallet full of money. That new car he had been eyeing as a Christmas present for Mason had been lost. A few people had begun shows, magic demonstrations and singing short tunes for entertainment as the night wore on. A Tombola wall was set up under the grand staircase across the room where people bought packages of mystery goods for thousands of dollars. I was happy to see that people would donate so much money for something worth next to nothing.

Finally, the music was turned down low, and Zach climbed the steps of the small, cramped stage with his mother and father. My grip was tighter than necessary on Kaia's arm, but he didn't seem to mind. "Good evening, everyone," Zach began, the crowd quieting to soft whispers littered throughout. "The bids are in. I'm going up to stand beside Zach. The family always does. We helped organize the charities," Kai informed me. I nodded. "Okay. Have fun," I replied, before he kissed my cheek and turned away from me. Without him, I felt like an outcast, shining bright in my red suite. I wasn't his partner anymore, I was the lost puppy he had left in the crowd. No longer did I have an owner to guide me.

As the Arche family made their way onto the stage and assembled around the podium, Zach continued talking, introducing his parents and brother. The rest of Kai's siblings hadn't been associated with the event. His mother and father said a few words to the crowd. I clapped when everybody else did, unsure of what most of their words meant. Their speeches were so much more complicated than 'Thank you for helping us raise money'. Kai shot me a wink, brightening my spirits considerably. I played with my hands almost giddily.

Once they had thanked their guests for attending the gala, a massive wave of applause erupted around me. Their clapping was obviously fueled by the alcohol that had been provided to them. I hoped they all had rides for the night.

But the only reason why I hadn't immediately begun applauding my man was a face that caught my eye from within the dense crowd when I glanced to my left. His dark eyes stared back at me from under black lashes, staring into my soul and even further, the eyes of the man who had dominated my nightmares. A devious smirk crossed Cade's face, causing my own to falter. I blinked a few times, wishing him away. He stood there for a few moments, never breaking eye contact, before a man leaned back in front of him and he suddenly disappeared, melting into a sea of bright reds and blacks. Even when he wasn't there, I could almost see his smile lingering behind my eyelids.

My gaze immediately searched for Kai's again, seeking the comfort I would gain from just a glance. Pure fear set itself inside my chest, the memory of the man in our bedroom, of him sitting on the barstool at the club, him taunting me as I searched for Kai in an ocean of people. My veins turned to little tubes of ice as the applause turned malicious.

Watching Kai from what seemed like a mile away made me sick. I wanted him beside me; I didn't want to be alone anymore. "Feel free to linger for drinks," Zachary declared, earning himself a final round of applause, before the crowd dispersed and returned to their conversations. Kai met me at the bottom of the stairs to the podium, bouncing down them as if his family's words had raised his spirits. He seemed to glow with joy for a moment before his fingers entwined with mine at his waist. I squeezed his hand hard. A few people were filing out of the building, but most had decided to stay for a few more performances and drinks. "Excuse us, guys," he told Rosa and Mason. The pair exchanged a glance before they stepped to the side and allowed us to pass. They were probably hoping that we wouldn't abandon them there in our rush to get home and get freaky. We made a beeline for the doors. I hadn't realized how deprived of air I was until I was outside, taking in the fresh night breeze that rolled off the nearby beaches.

"We raised a lot of money tonight. My family is impressed with all the guests," Kai said, stuffing his hands in his pockets and slowing our steps into a soft stroll down the side of the rented mansion, following the long line of cars that had been parked there. The air was silent despite the dimming party taking place inside. "Yeah... you guys did really well," I said absently. Why was Cade there? Why was he haunting me?

"You looked petrified from the stage for a moment there. What's wrong?" I jumped slightly at his question, but he only caught my eye and searched my gaze for answers. "What did you see?" I swallowed hard and looked away, my nails digging into my palm. Was I being paranoid? Was I trying to avoid something that could be more than I thought?

"Can we talk about this at home?" I choked. Something in his expression changed, lightened. Mine never did. "My home?"

My mouth fell open slightly. "Y-Yeah. Your house. Later."

I had had enough. Once we left, I was finally beginning to feel comfortable with Kai's arms wrapped around me in the back seat. Mason drove while Rosa, drowsy with the copious amounts of alcohol she consumed, fell asleep in shotgun. The soft hum of the engine and faint horns were enough to calm anyone's nerves, adding to the warmth of Kai as he cuddled up against my chest.

....

"Are you fucking with me?"

I woke to the sound of Kai swearing into his phone across the room, his back to me. I silently adjusted my head against my pillow as my brows furrowed, watching his hand move to his forehead anxiously. My gaze was still clearing; I blinked sleepy residue from my eyes. I was sore from the night before, an ache settling deep in my core as a reminder of Kai's power and ferocity. His hand fell to rest on his hip. He had thrown on a simple pair of jeans and a t-shirt, abnormal attire for him. His body language scared me.

"Why do you think the case can be reopened?" He paused for a moment as the person on the other side of the line spoke to him. "Jesus-fucking-Christ. And you think he took her there?" There was another pause as he gave an exasperated sigh. "Okay. Okay. Just... keep me posted... p-please." He turned his phone off and stuffed it into his pocket before he spun and froze, realizing that I was finally awake. He seemed scared that I had caught him in the act of *something*. I sat up groggily, taking a deep breath of his morning musk. "What happened?"

"Nothing," he replied a little too hastily, but he continued talking before I could ask any more questions. "I have to go out for a while. Mason'll drop you back at your place after Rosa has made you breakfast."

"Where are you going?" He stood and made his way across the room to his closet, selecting the suit he would wear for the day. He was rushing. "Out," Kai said. I pouted. What place was so secret? "Are you going to tell me what happened last night now or later? I have to go," he told me curtly, and I was shocked for a moment at his impudent behaviour. The man didn't react when I shot him a glare. "I... I'll tell you later. Go do what you need to do," I told him quietly, my fingers pulling on my knuckles in my bare lap. Kai, who was in such a rush a moment ago, sighed and let his arms fall to his sides. The suit brushed the floor. He looked to me, knowing that I was hurt, and shook his head.

"My wife died a few years ago. Did you know that?"

At first, his words didn't even register in my mind. Someone died? *Oh. Wife.*

My gaze snapped up to his, swimming with horrified shock. Kai had been married? To a girl? *Married?!* Who was she? Why hadn't he talked about her? How could I only be learning of her existence then? Why did he just decide to drop a bombshell like that?

But he didn't seem to notice my appalled state; I could see the anguish in his eyes that blinded him. "*What?*" I breathed.

"They... caught the man who did it."

"They caught... *what?*" My inability to wrap my head around this new information frustrated me. Kai needed me now, but all I could do was stare at his broken expression.

I had spent too much time. Kaia only left without another word, the bedroom door closing with a terrorizing slam before the silence and heartbeat in my ears was my only company.

....

"Hey, Mom," I greeted, leaning my head against her shoulder as I dropped my small bag in the doorway. "I found a new job," she said suddenly, not bothering to reply. I immediately perked up from the depression Kai had set me in that morning. The fact that he swore so violently scared me more than the fact that he refused to tell me where he was going. He always kept me notified of what his day consisted of, even if it was a boring schedule.

"Yeah? What did you find?"

It was energizing to be free from the light cloud of smoke that usually hung around the house. A single butt sat in the green ashtray that had been placed out of the way in the corner of the kitchen. "You know that cheap little restaurant down the street? I heard that they needed a new cook who knew their way around food well enough to help make a decent meal. I figured I wouldn't lose anything if I tried. Even when they said that minimum wage would be a reality for the pay. It's a little less than I was making before,

ANGEL

but...." A bright, ear-to-ear smile covered my face as I threw my arms around her. Almost, *almost,* I forgot about Kai's wife. "You're gonna be a chef, Mom! That's so cool!" She sighed and shook me off playfully. "Go run off with your boyfriend," she told me, a spark of playfulness evident in her sharp gaze, a glow of humor I hadn't seen in years.

If only I could run off with him. That morning, he had run away from me.

My expression fell. She frowned at it, realizing that while her world had just brightened, mine had crash-landed. "What happened?" Her voice didn't sound like it used to; she sounded like she *cared.* "I don't really want to talk about it," I replied, forcing my gaze away from hers. She didn't try to follow it; I would talk to her when I was ready to. Until then, she trusted me to be okay. I was always okay.

"I'm just gonna go upstairs. Tell me if you want me to make lunch or something." Truthfully, all I wanted to do was sleep. She seemed to understand, nodding and turning away from me.

My room hadn't changed. It was still cold in the winter months, the bed was still messy and stale, and my CDs were untouched. The blankets were familiar and almost warm when I returned to them. For once, I didn't feel as if I needed Kai to heat them.

"*Hey Mason,*" I texted as I sat bundled in my comforter. Heavy rock pounded against my eardrums through the headphones Kai had bought me only a few days before. I had downloaded a few albums onto my phone recently.

"*Hey, Luka,*" he texted back. "*You good?*"

"*Kai had a wife?*"

"*He told you that?*"

"*He said that she died. Something about reopening a case.*"

"*Yeah. I honestly thought you kinda knew about her.*"

I seethed at my device. How would I have been able to know that I wasn't the love of his life like he showed me so many times?

"*You thought I knew?*"

"*Yeah… Kai should be telling you this.*"

"*Why didn't he?*"

"*Well, if you got a call saying that the same person who killed your wife might be on the prowl, wouldn't you be shaken, too?*"

"*They never got the person who killed her? What happened?*"

There were a few moments of a pause before a new message was delivered from him.

"*Like I said. I'm not the one who should be telling you this. He's doing his best. Try not to worry too much.*"

CHAPTER
FIFTY-THREE

TO SAY THAT it felt odd to stay at home was an understatement. There was no chest to curl up to at night, so I was freezing. There was no company during the day, so I was lonely. I found myself unmotivated to do anything. Music hadn't even been played in days. All I did was work and sleep. Eating became a problem too. I was gaining weight fast—I had been since I started seeing Kai—and I didn't know how to stop. Was Kai purposely ignoring me? Why had he refused to pick up the two calls I had made to him the night before? Did he not need me as his sub anymore? Was this the heartbreak my mother had promised me? I still didn't want to believe that he would leave me after all our time together. Wouldn't he at least *talk* to me if it was all over? Wouldn't he at least talk to me if he needed a shoulder to cry on? He was raised better, I knew, but I was beginning to run out of conclusions.

"*Just tell me that you're okay*," I texted him, not bothering to read the dozen other texts I had sent him over the last week-and-a-half. There had been no replies, not even a peep from Mason. He discontinued contact with me only a few days before, much to my dismay. Tears gathered in my eyes, and I angrily wiped them away. The action only summoned more, and soon I was sobbing into my pillow. I missed him. Was it all a lie? Was he loving me to replace his wife, someone to fill the hole she left? Didn't I save him? Wouldn't that mean *something?*

My mother, thankfully, was working a later shift at her new job, which she was enjoying. I had never seen her so happy. Once I was alone, I was able to scream and cry and throw my own tantrum. *'Fuck you, Kai,'* I thought to myself, scalding tears staining my pillow. *'Fuck you, fuck you, fuck you'.*

Soon, even my mother had begun to worry about me. She brought fresh sandwiches up to my room when she had the chance, switching the new plates with the stale, dirty platters that she had left in the days before. I began to feel light-headed from crying so often. How could some asshole make me feel so horrible? "Luka...," she began, "I don't want to say I told you so, but this was inevitable." She paused before sighing, glancing around my bedroom instead of looking me in the eyes. "You should go out somewhere. Go get some dinner." I only rolled over to glare at the wall as I listened to the door close with a click. I *wanted* to go out somewhere. I could show Kai that I didn't need him. Did I want him to be jealous? Could I betray him like that? No, he had betrayed me; he *lied* to me. He had dropped me, a temporary replacement, like a new hit album, and he damn well better feel regretful. I almost wanted him to miss me, even if my stomach churned at the thought of Kai being in so much distress.

I slowly sat up, stretching forgotten muscles and pulling on ligaments that had nearly turned to stone. "Fuck," I mumbled to myself as I stood on trembling legs. I took the stairs to the main floor one step at a time until I had completed my journey to the bathroom. Instead of undressing immediately, I collapsed on the toilet and rested my elbows on my knees, out of breath. I was already exhausted, void of the emotions that usually kept me going through the day, although I knew that a scalding shower would wake me up efficiently. It burnt my skin, turning it a fiery-red and making it itch. The pain only lasted a moment, though, until I could force my towel around my shoulders and rub away the burn. As I dressed myself after my shower, my muscles felt rejuvenated, like I was slowly waking from a deep sleep.

"I'm going out. See ya, mom," I hollered on my way out the door. The entrance was closed before she could reply. My journey would be a long walk when I didn't have a chauffeur to drive me anywhere, I soon realized sadly. A constant ache had nestled itself inside my chest with that sadness. Whether it was fed by the loneliness or my complete lack of exercise over the last few days, I had no idea. All I knew was that it would take a while to reach *El Oculto Agujero* and that I had left my collar at home.

I passed many places filled with memories—not all of them bad. Sex work wasn't always a negative job. Sometimes Ellie, a kindhearted former customer of mine, would always have an ice cream sandwich saved for just before I left her. As I passed her apartment building, I glanced up into her window. It was dark. The sun was just beginning to fade, casting the building in shadow. She wouldn't be home from work yet; I didn't want to say hello, anyway. Down the street, my mother's favorite restaurant sat, its doors locked and a '*for lease*' sign taped to the window. Beyond it, the nearly-empty street that would carry me to the club. I couldn't decide if it would take me to a place I *wanted* to go or a place that would take away my sadness.

What was the difference?

Outside the club was quieter than the last time I visited. A couple chatted just beside the entrance, but other than that, there was no one in sight. What if there was no one there who would do anything with me? Was I there to have sex?

"Hey, it's John, right?" I asked nervously once I made my way across the floor of Kai's favorite club. I was right, the place wasn't very lively, although the rooms in the back were fairly full. The bartender looked up at me as he poured a shot and passed it to the man who brooded beside me. "Yeah... wait, you were with Kai, right? I didn't see him come in."

"He's, um, not here right now. At least, I think he isn't."

He raised an eyebrow and took my appearance in more closely. He would notice the bags under my bloodshot eyes and denim shorts with the word *'Devil'* sewn across the ass. They were supposed to be for only Kai's eyes. His gaze lingered on my bare neck. "You got bored with each other or something?" I shrugged his question off. "Can I get a shot? Something dry and strong?"

His pause revealed his idea of kicking me out of this club. He seemed to know that I would be eaten alive, but that's exactly what I wanted. The man put both hands on the counter and leaned forward. "You got any ID with ya, kid?" I licked my lips and glanced around me. "Come on. Just one? It's been a rough week." John's nostrils flared as he thought, glowering as me. Finally, he sighed and grabbed a shot glass. "Just one. Watered down. Stay safe, kid." I smiled at him and threw the drink back, finally deciding that I didn't like alcohol.

The club was still slightly crowded. Every few moments, I would catch the eye of a man or woman staring me down before they diverted their gaze, and I soon felt the loneliness ebb away; there was only the thirst for a distraction. I didn't want to think about him anymore, so I began to wander the club, daring to poke my head into the rooms at the back where lewd scenes were taking place. A young man spanked his wife in the corner while a woman electrocuted her sub across the room. I watched him writhe in pleasure and pain for a moment, remembering how I used to do the same thing under Kai's control.

ANGEL

"You aren't wearing a collar," a deep voice said from behind me. I turned quickly, my eyes level to the man's wide chest. "No, sir," I muttered, looking up at him with wide eyes. He stared down with a hungry expression as if he was the wolf and I was a sheep. "Wow. You're trained pretty well. Looking for anyone to be with tonight?" His words gave me déjà vu, reminding me of a long-forgotten time of slaving over others and convincing people that a little bit of cash would mean a blowjob, or at least a good handjob. I shrugged and diverted my eyes. *Make them think you're not interested. Draw them in. Make them work for it.* He was built large and tough, and I could tell that he had been in the lifestyle for many years. "Hey, May!" the man called suddenly, waving a tall woman towards us. I flinched as she approached, a sinister smile widening on her face. "Oh, I've never seen you here before. Fresh meat just waiting to do a scene, hm?" May hooked her arm around mine and began to forcefully drag me towards another room. Panic filled me, suddenly suffocating me. I didn't like May. She had been drinking; I could smell it, and I wasn't exactly looking forward to doing a scene with a girl. I wanted a *man*, or at least a sober female. My consciousness called me sexist from the back of my mind.

I needed to get out. This time wasn't like the night Kai brought me to the club. It wasn't a safe place anymore, not with a woman like May. "S-Stop it!" I cried, pushing her away. She gasped and glared at me when she was shoved into another body behind her. I didn't wait to get any more of a reaction before I attempted to slide through the crowd. The deafening music drowned out all sounds as I shoved past people, earning myself mumbled *'fuck you's* and *'watch it's*. Some people even pushed back, tears flowing in my eyes. I only got a single "*Sorry*" from a girl who was quite obviously spending her first time in a BDSM bar searching frantically for her friends. I felt bad for her.

I wanted out. I wanted to go home where it was safe. Safe with Kai. Why did he leave me there?

My sense of direction was lost until a hand suddenly wrapped around my upper arm and pulled me to the left, knocking the air from my lungs. I would have begun screaming if the room I was pulled into wasn't silent. The only sounds inside were the muffled voices and low bass of the music from the other side of the slammed door. "Are you alright?" the man asked, his voice immediately sending chills up my spine. My hand that supported me on the wall curled into a fist. I recognized the voice; it was the one that had been haunting me for months. I slowly looked up with wide eyes, meeting Cade's narrowed gaze.

Fuck.

My body instantly began preparing to run screaming, but before I could execute my escape, he asked a question that shocked me: "Do you want any water?"

He was a bad man. He was sinister in my dreams. And now he was asking if I was thirsty? If I was okay? "Wh... What?" I asked. He sighed. "Take a seat," he told me gently, crossing the room to the small table where I would find bottles of water, tea, and coffee for guests. "A guy like you gets eaten alive out there. Why were you alone?" he asked.

I swallowed hard and glanced around the room, a bedroom, I realized. A king bed sat in the center with racks of equipment arranged around it. It was beautiful in my eyes, although Kai was the only thing missing. "The room is only used for reservations. It's normally pretty private or for a small group of select audience. They film porn in here, too, sometimes," he explained, suddenly holding a bottle of water towards me. I took it with numb fingers, removed the cap, and glanced inside at the clear liquid. I remembered my mother's voice, "*It's hard to drug water. Normally you can taste it or it'll turn the water murky."*

"Water," he clarified. "I barely loosened the cap for you." He could obviously see my hands shaking. I willed them to stop.

I licked my lips and threw it back, the cool water immediately comforting my churning stomach. How could just a sip taste so *good?*

"Didn't you have a sub? Where is she?" I asked, already gaining confidence as my strength returned. Maybe this man wasn't as bad as I initially thought. He was treating me as if I was a friend, not a sub or some slave he needed to win over. "He didn't want to stay. I'm not the kind of guy who likes to stay with one person for too long, either, ya know?" His smirk was kind, obviously an attempt to lighten my spirits. I tried to smile, but it failed miserably halfway through. "Yeah... I get that."

"Seriously. Sit down. You look pale," he told me. I slowly relaxed onto the black leather sofa in front of the double doors, swallowing hard when I earned a small head rush. Obviously, I was dehydrated and tired. I took a new gulp of water. "Thanks for helping me and all, but aren't you here to look for subs? I mean, I'm one, but I'm just kinda... not into it-," but he shook his head and took a seat beside me. "You're a guy who was in trouble. Figured that if there is a special person looking for you, I better not get in the way."

I could only breathe a sigh of relief, toying absently with the bottle in my lap. "Thanks, but... there's no dom."

"Please. A boy like you gets snapped up with a contract in an hour," Cade chuckled. I shrugged, a headache beginning to burn behind my eyelids

"No. There's no partner. Not anymore."

He nodded slowly, my headache intensifying. With a wince, I realized that it wasn't as much of a headache anymore. I was beginning to feel tired, and it wasn't because of my lack of sleep. It was an exhaustion that tugged on my brain harder than anything before, like I could sleep for days. Sounds faded around me; the heavy beat outside distorted and grew muffled. My vision wavered; I closed my eyes in an attempt to clear it. When I opened them again, I brought both hands to my temples, not realizing the bottle and cap that fell to the floor and splattered the remnants of my water across the hardwood. "Wh-What...?" I groaned, my fingers pulling at my hair in pain. My stomach was beginning to hurt.

"You dropped your water, Lucika," Cade said with mock sadness. His words made my chest burst with panic. With a soft moan, I doubled over and wrapped my arms around my stomach. "Wha-What did you... y-you drugged me?" I grumbled in horror, twisting to look up at him with swirling vision and squinted eyes. How did he drug *water*? I wanted to be scared. I wanted to cry and run. I wanted Kai, but my body wasn't responding. I was *stuck*.

I watched Cade stand slowly, moving in front of me and blocking the suddenly harsh light.

"It's only a special little roofie. Now I'll inject you with a potent aphrodisiac. Don't worry, Lucika. I'll take good care of you."

CHAPTER
FIFTY-FOUR

"CADE... PLEASE," I sobbed, my erection obvious and uncontrollable. My body was hot, too hot. It made my head fuzzy with pressure; I dropped it, squeezing my eyes shut. The light burned along with my organs. I was tired, disoriented, aroused. The injection site on my thigh burnt. "Sh...," he whispered with a soft smile, lifting my chin with the end of a small whip and forcing me to look up at him. The cushion of the couch induced vertigo. "You'll behave for me, won't you?" With that, he swept me into his arms, all one-hundred-and-sixty pounds, and threw me onto the bed, eliciting a loud yelp of pain from my parched lips. The water seemed to dry my mouth even further. "Please stop. Just let me go," I sobbed, gripping the sheets. My body refused to listen to my commands when I told it to scramble away. It was almost like my body *wanted* someone to touch it, wanted *him*. A firm hand held me down as he cut my clothes off my body, pushing them onto the floor before I felt cold cuffs wrap around my wrists. "Help!" I attempted to scream. Instead, my voice came as a hoarse, broken cry. I tried kicking him; my movements were lackadaisical. He sat on my thigh, twisting it over the other painfully.

Cade's figure towered over me once he was comfortably straddling me, engulfing me in darkness and forcing the light away. Just his image was enough to pull the air from my lungs and suffocate me.

"Damnit, Cade! Get the fuck off him!"

Two hands were thrown over Cade's shoulders before he was torn away from me, tossed to the side like a rag doll. Through my tears and the sudden bright light, I could see John, Standing over Cade with something akin to disbelief on his face. Again, a sob shook me. I pulled against the chains. "You fucking *bastard,*" John snarled at the man who had just barely gotten his footing back. Despite his tone, he comforted me; at least he wasn't Cade. For a moment, Cade stared at John, mulling over his options in his mind. Run? Fight? Could he take on John, a man who could probably even beat Kai in a fist match? He was big, and the horsepower behind his muscular system was something that no one wanted to deal with. So, Cade decided to flee. He rose from his fighting stance to make a dash to the back of the room; the emergency exit. John didn't follow him, though, thankfully. He turned to me when he knew that Cade had escaped, his face solemn and worried. The man worked hastily to undo the clasps on my wrists, and when they were free, I wrapped my arms around myself, crying softly. I wasn't safe yet; Kai wasn't there. "Did he hurt you?" John asked, sliding a quick hand over my cheek that had been bruised recently. I shook my head. "I just—scary," I replied through sobs. He nodded, sighed, and helped me scoot to the edge of the bed. "The police have been called. I, uh, called Kai too. Are you okay, though? Nothing hurts?"

"M-Muh-My head," I told him. It was throbbing, really. The roofie still had me exhausted too. My skin still burnt.

"Kai will be here soon," John tried to comfort. I could tell that he wasn't sure how to help me. We didn't know each other well, and I wasn't acting very open when I had my head buried in my knees. "My head really h-hurts," I whined, pulling harshly at my hair. It was a pulsing ache, an agony that wrapped my skull in layers of fire.

ANGEL

My headache only made me cry harder. "You'll make it worse... just take a breath," he said. I shook my head. Again, a new spark of fire grew into a flame behind my eyelids; I squeezed them shut and whimpered loudly. It happened *so fast*, and my spinning world wasn't slowing down. Was Cade gone? Would he come back? Where was Kai?

"I want Kai," I wailed.

My lungs gave one last pull of air before the room stopped spinning abruptly, but it only stopped spinning because everything turned black.

....

At least when I woke, I was comfortable. I didn't wake on my hard, age-old bed or in the club. I was being rocked in strong arms, which improved my headache considerably. Kai was singing under his breath, the soft, blue light of the morning illuminating his bedroom. I tried to mentally make a checklist for my body. A wire protruded from my hand where an IV line was attached. My wrists were bound with gauze, dark bruises decorating my arms. My hips were sore from Cade's crushing weight.

Kai continued singing a tune I didn't recognize, slightly off-key and very slow, as I was sure it was a heavier song with many guitar solos. I inhaled a raspy breath and experimentally placed my hand on his chest. My fingers curled out of my fist slowly, smoothing the wrinkles in his shirt. Kai froze, stopping his rocking motion and singing to look down at me with too many emotions to count. Anger, regret, sadness, anguish. Whose fault was that? Mine? His?

"Kai," I croaked. "Sh... you're safe now. Caden will never do this to you again. No one will," he told me sincerely, scrambling to comfort me. I shook my head and tried to smile up at him, too weak to conjure anything more than a hopeful expression. Why was he here? Where was he when I needed him? Could I trust him at all?

He visibly relaxed as tears gathered in his eyes. But Kai looked away before I could comfort him, rocking me in his lap once again as he stared blankly out at the cloudy morning. I was nearly asleep again by the time I began to wonder how long we had been sitting in silence. My pain was beginning to intensify as the drugs wore off and new muscles awakened. "It hurts? A lot?" The question he gave me caught me off-guard, but I should have been expecting it, shouldn't I? If he didn't care about me anymore then I wouldn't be sitting in his arms. So why did he leave me? Why did I suddenly learn of his wife?

"It hurts a little," I played it down. Immediately, he leaned forward to push a syringe against the tube attached to me. "N-No, they'll make me tired!" I jumped to stop him, pain searing through my body and leaving me paralyzed for a moment as tears gathered in my eyes. My left thigh was particularly bruised. "Sh, Luka, breathe. I won't give you any if you don't want it," he whispered, soothing me with soft touches.

"You've been asleep for almost a whole twenty-four hours. Do you remember anything?" he asked. I thought for a moment, remembering only Cade's hands and his sinister smirk. But after a moment of rocking, I remembered the needles, then the chains. "He drugged me. Then he chained me up and he-... he tried to—," I broke off into a whimper. "Sh. You don't have to tell me. I was just hoping that you didn't remember anything," he replied as his lips burrowed into my hair. "I'm really sorry. I was alone. You weren't answering my messages, I thought you didn't want this anymore. I thought-," but he cut me off when I began to cry. "Angel, I should be the one apologizing. I left you alone. How could I have done that to you? I just...," but he trailed off in horror, his eyes wishing him to say what he wanted. Fear prevented him from opening his mouth. "You just what? What happened?" I sniffed. I could see his walls come back up in a second when he shook his head. "Nothing happened, I-," but I put my hand on his cheek, forcing him to meet my yearning gaze. "Tell me, Kai. It's about your wife, right?" The man was obviously terrified. Years of blood, sweat, and tears had built the person he was in that moment, but whatever was troubling him was about to tear down his entire empire, so I could see why he would be a little hesitant.

"You can tell me. You can trust me." At the moment, I didn't care that he had left me for so long. I needed to know that he was okay, no matter how much he hurt me by hiding himself. He obviously had reasons for it; he loved me, I knew. Kai gave a shaky breath, on the verge of crying.

"Her name was Cherry," he began in a broken voice, his vocal cords pulled taut with the amount of strength needed to keep himself from breaking into fits of sobs. My expression didn't change. I could only listen, or I knew he would run again, like he had done a week ago. And he couldn't run anymore. Not from this.

CHAPTER
FIFTY-FIVE

"SHE WAS MY wife. We got married on the fourth of August about seven years ago." He swallowed hard, his gaze never leaving mine as he searched for strength. He seemed to have found it since he continued with the same small voice and tight jaw. "One night, a few years back, the both of us were kidnapped by a man I now know as Markus Valur. He had friends who joined in, but he was always the most memorable." I couldn't hold my gasp. Even if I was to speak, it wouldn't have stopped Kai. Once he started on this, no one could stop him. The words were like a tsunami; that wall he had been fortifying for years had finally fallen, and it had been pathetically easy to knock it down. "He raped us both every day for almost three months in an underground hideaway in the woods. He was the one who first introduced her to the BDSM world. Before, it was merely fantasies I played with when I was young. We lived there, surrounded by things like chains and whips. He brought us food, water, and sometimes a deck of cards. But one of the things I hated most was his swearing. Every other word from his mouth was either 'fuck' or 'bitch'."

I traced my finger lightly across his cheekbone as bullets of salty liquid fell from our eyes. "She had been anorexic for the last few years of her life. But, despite that, Cherry was always really feisty.

She tried to escape...," his voice faltered and he closed his eyes in agony, a soft sob leaving his chest. It was filled with anguish, bits of his memories falling down his cheeks as boiling tears. On instinct, I pulled him into a hug and let him lean down into my sore shoulder as his body shook. "But when he caught her, h-he... he killed her. He hung her in f-front of me. He made me watch. I... can still remember her face when she died. When I knew she was... When I knew she was g-gone." His voice broke off into a soft wail muffled by my skin.

"Sh," I tried to soothe him, knowing it would never work. I rubbed his back lightly and leaned my cheek against his head, trying to rock us both while I was still seated between his legs. His fingers curled into my shirt. "It's okay. Breathe, Kai."

"She loved cherry blossoms. We had a huge cherry blossom tree in our backyard when we were younger, and when the buds bloomed, we would try to see who could climb to the top fastest," he croaked after a moment of crying. "That's why you like cherry blossoms so much. Because they remind you of her," I realized. So... was he fucking me because he loved me or because I reminded him of his love? "I know what it sounds like," he licked his trembling lips, "I get it if you can't forgive me for this. For... For not telling you. You just... filled the gap like no one else could. You look nothing like her, but... she's in your eyes. They hold something extra, but they also hold her spirit. And I couldn't let that go, that feeling of not being alone. When she left me, I was just... alone." I had heard that kind of sentence from my mother. 'Alone' meant so much more than *Alone*.

I wiped away my own tears before reaching up and wiping away his. He kissed my hand and held it close. "They never found the guy. She never even knew the name of the man who took her life. Then, that morning, I got a call from the lead detective on our old case. He said that another couple had been taken, and it fit the same description as our kidnapping."

"It was the same man?" I asked in horror. Suddenly, he leaned back, wiping his eyes furiously with the sleeves of his black shirt. Kai sniffed loudly, his nose full of snot. "They, uh, they found him. He got sloppy. A fucking sixty-year-old guy trying to rape two newlyweds." I understood why he couldn't look me in the eye.

"Jesus," I breathed.

I knew I needed to know his story. He needed to tell me. But did I want to know? How many nightmares would I have after *that*?

"And then, when I got that call from John after he found you in the club, I just... I forgot why I left you alone. All I saw was her." I was trying to feel his agony, his anguish. A sub's pain is a Dominant's pain... and vice-versa. "I couldn't stand to make contact with anyone. I even refused to see James. I gave Mason a dislocated shoulder the other night during a night terror, and for you to see that... I don't want to think about what I could have done if you were with me that night. You don't need to see me like that." My brows furrowed with sadness as I forced him to look at me with those dinner-plate eyes. The man was terrified, whether of memories or how much he had let past the floodgates, I didn't know. "It's okay," I whispered. My thumb swiped under his eyes again to move the fresh drops away from his cheeks. The skin was becoming inflamed. "It's okay."

He deflated, his head dropping and his arms wrapping around my waist tighter, as if yearning for any kind of body heat after leaning away from me for so long. "I don't know what I did to deserve you. I told you that you saved me, and that you were the colour in my black-and-white vision," he shook his head, "But you're so much more. You're my world, Luka. I... I love you. So, so much. I love you as much as I loved her. But she's gone, and you're here… you're *here.*"

I leaned my forehead against his and smoothed down the sides of his wild hair. "*I'm here.*"

"I love you, Luka," he repeated, finally meeting my bloodshot eyes with his own. The message he sent with them said more words than anyone could express.

"I love you."

He didn't need to say anything more. I could hear the utter sincerity in his voice. I could tell that he had been needing to tell me those words for a while. My heart glowed at them. I was prepared to reply with 'I love you, too' or 'I'm happy I wasn't the only one', but only for a moment. Suddenly, my small smile fell, remembering *him.*

"You called him Caden," I said, leaning away with a wince, grimace, and horrified realization on my features.

He sighed, knowing exactly what I meant with only a sentence.

"Caden is well-known in the community."

"What?" My body and mind ached to talk about him. The only memories I had of him were no longer innocent ones from the night we first met at the bar or when he had been a customer of mine. But I needed to know. Kai obviously knew something about him, something that could send my foundations quaking.

"He was my Dominant."

My eyebrows rose to my hairline. Kai, the sexy, badass god that destroyed me during every session, had been a submissive? "You were once a sub. Right," I said in disbelief. His story just wasn't adding up to me. The man chuckled sadly. "It's true. I was in a constant state of depression after my wife died. And I found out through him that a good scene can help me forget about it all. It was like a drug." But then his tone turned dark, horrifying memories filling his eyes. "But he was never a nice person. It took me an entire two years to realize that. Not only was he a horrible person, but also a horrible Dominant. He didn't believe in aftercare or safe-words. He always told his subs when they tried to use a safe-word that 'if they can't make it through a single goddamn scene, then they shouldn't be a sub'. It was just... how I thought it was. How it was supposed to be. I couldn't recognize him as the abusive egomaniac he was."

My lip began to tremble all over again at his words. "That's... I'm sorry, Kai."

He averted his eyes and pulled me back into his comfortable lap. By then my body was really hurting, and I could no longer ignore it after the jostling. "Painkillers," I whined desperately, a hand subconsciously cradling my head. His hand was instantly at the syringe, pushing it into the long tube. "They'll make you tired. But you need to sleep anyway." His words only made me panic, my heartbeat increasing and my eyes widening. "Y-You won't leave me, will you?" My hands gripped his shirt feebly. "Just stay here like this."

"Luka, sh, I'm not leaving you. I won't. I promise," he soothed, prying my aching fingers from the cloth and pushing them against my side. "I'll be here. Just sleep." Could I trust him? I was already getting drowsy. Of course, he would be there. He had to be. He knew that I would be there for him, and in return, he needed to be there for me. He couldn't run after telling me what he had.

....

The sun was shining when I woke. Thankfully, the drizzle of rain disappeared as I slept, and the light shone through the bag of saline fluid that hung above me. I rolled over and stretched tight muscles, searching for Kai. "Are you hungry?" his voice rang out, comforting me from where he sat on the edge of the bed beside my stomach. I shook my head, aggravating it. "Lay with me." Kai could only nod and smile, his body turned towards me. "Are you sure you don't

ANGEL

want a shower? You can take one if you're careful."

"No," I whined, making grabby-hands for him, and he chuckled. "Fine. But then you're taking one tonight." I nodded and grabbed his arm as he climbed under the sheets with me, careful of my IV. "Mason'll come up soon and take that out as long as you drink lots of water," Kai promised, wrapping an arm around my waist and pulling me toward his chest. His other arm wrapped around my shoulders like a vice. Kai sighed as he got comfortable, pushing his lips into the back of my neck and taking a deep whiff of my scent. I briefly wondered what I smelt like to him before an idea popped into my mind, a distant ache that had finally risen to the surface. "Have they caught Cade yet?" I asked. Kai stiffened, staying silent. I tried to focus on anything else in those few seconds.

"You can tell me, Kai," I said softly when he didn't say anything. "He can't get me here when I'm with you. I know that."

"He's still at large. I didn't want to tell you until you were healthy," he told me slowly, as if any sudden movements would upset me, but I didn't feel any panic. Not in his arms.

"He seems to have skipped town. Police raided his apartment to find everything but him and a suitcase of clothes. I told them that he's probably in a safe house around Phoenix. He's taken me there a few times when I was with him." At that, I rolled to face him with furrowed brows. "Why didn't you just run?" Kai was obviously hesitant to answer me, and I understood why. How traumatic would the time with Caden have been? To go through a relationship like that for years, let alone one night? "Because I was a depressed man who had just lost his wife. My mind was screwed up. Badly. I would have killed for anything to help me forget about her. Like I said, he... BDSM was like a drug to me. But I know how to make it safe for me now. I taught myself how to turn the pain into pleasure, not punishment. I know how to keep partners safe too." He seemed to be reassuring himself that he was better than Caden or his past self, even after all these years. I vowed to remind him as often as necessary that he was not who he used to be, and he would never have to be that person ever again.

I could only watch him with a sad gaze, my lip threatening to wobble. Finally, he sighed, focusing on brushing his thumb over the soft flesh of my navel. "My entire family was destroyed after Cherry died. My siblings were close to her, and my parents began to shut me out, blinded by their grief. I was alone, and I eventually decided that it was my fault. Because *I* was the one who got away." I gasped, opening my mouth to object, but he raised his hand to silence me. "I know now that I was wrong. James taught me that. But at the time, it gave me an escape and a punishment, one that I believed I deserved."

"What made you leave?"

"He dropped me, actually. I was getting too old for him, I guess. He likes them young and new. That's probably why he went after you. That and the fact that he knew I was your partner." I pursed my lips and nodded, absorbing the new information. "Probably why he's been following me," I mumbled. He raised his head quickly, eyes suddenly wild. Memory lane was forgotten.

"What?"

The only thing I could do was sigh, knowing he would go off anyway. "I honestly think he's been following me. Since the club. He was at the gala too. That's what I was hoping to tell you that night."

"Since... the club? Since the freaking club?" Kai was growing increasingly agitated. He jumped from the bed and jostled me in the process, nearly enough to start a new headache. "Sorry, sorry," he apologized immediately. "Just... since the freaking bar. Why didn't you tell me? Why didn't you tell *someone*?! I hadn't even noticed anything. I'm so sorry, Luka."

ANGEL

I shrugged, my eyes sad. "I'm sorry... It's not your fault. Neither of us knew."

"Can I come in? You have a visitor," Rosa's voice interrupted us as she opened the bedroom door just enough to pop her face into the room. At the sound of her voice, I tried to sit up, wincing through my excitement. "Rosa!" She gave me a wide smile as she held the door for a figure behind her: my mother. "Mom," I sighed in relief. She crossed the room to my outstretched arms and jumped onto the bed to wrap me in a hug. "Don't ever do that again," she said sternly, forcing my gaze to lock with hers. "Worrying the hell out of your mother. Who the hell does that? Do you know how many times Mason has tried to ask me out?"

My smile fell. "What?"

Rosa and Kai muffled their laughter as I began to seethe. "That son of a... gonna beat his ass...." I began to mumble curses as I struggled out of the bed, despite Kai instantly urging me to stay. "He can't just torment my mother like that, he-," but then I froze when I noticed my mother's expression. Guilt. Humour. Obvious withheld information. My eyes widened with disbelief. "You had sex with him, didn't you?" I asked in complete horror. My mother knew she was caught by then. Her mouth opened and closed like a fish as she fought to find something to say. "I mean, I went and visited you in the hospital last night. A-And then he was at our house, okay? He said I shouldn't be alone with you transported to Kai's home and one thing led to another, and, well...."

"Mason is not going to become my stepfather. No god-damned way!" I shouted, pulling the needle out of the back of my hand and running around the bed, past the pole that had been erected in the center of the room, and out into the hallway. Luckily, I wasn't completely nude. Instead, I only wore a pair of Kai's boxers and one of his shirts. "Mason!" I yelled for him. Kai and Rosa were hot on my trail. "Luka, you're going to fall down the damn stairs!" he exclaimed. But Rosa only laughed and said, "He's in the garage." If it wasn't for my fiery rage and the pain that fueled it, I would have collapsed already. At the bottom of the flight of stairs in the middle of his apartment, I slammed the button beside the elevator, which opened promptly. It seemed to sense my anger and lack of patience.

Mason jumped and dropped a wrench that clattered to the cement floor when I threw the heavy door to the garage open. Across the garage, a couple stood beside their own car and turned to look at the commotion. They were obviously people who rented apartments below Kai. I paid them no mind. "Hey, Luka. What's the rush?" Mason greeted.

"*What's the rush?*" I mocked, crossing the room in a fit of rage. "What's the fucking rush?"

Mason stood with furrowed brows, obviously confused, but only before I conjured the entirety of my strength and kicked him square in the balls.

CHAPTER
FIFTY-SIX

"I'M NOT APOLOGIZING," I seethed to Kai, ignoring Mason's groans of pain as he rolled on the floor beside one of Kai's vehicles where he had been clutching his crotch and curling into a fetal position for the past two minutes. Kaia had managed to get me to sit on a stool where I finally felt the worst of my injuries. "What the hell, Luka." I winced and glared at Mason, hoping it would worsen his pain. "Worth it." He chuckled. "You incapacitated my bodyguard. Not gonna lie, it was a good kick."

"What the hell, Kai... you're freaking encouraging him?" Mason groaned, burying his face into his elbow. "You're the one who slept with Teressa. Not to mention you did the dirty while Luka was knocked out," Kai retorted, obviously growing increasingly worked up when he mentioned me.

"Are you okay yet, Mason?" my mother asked, kneeling in front of the man. "No," I told them firmly, shaking my head. "You are not comforting him. Step away, mom." With that, Mason released a breath of a laugh. "At least the sex was good, right, Teressa?"

"Mason-!" I yelled, jumping to my feet and lunging towards him. That was it. He had found the end of my fuse, and it had been lit a long time ago. At that moment, I was seeing red. "Luka!" Kai bellowed, sweeping me off my feet to cut me off and dragging me out of the room before I could reach Mason. "Get a damn hold of yourself." I was thrown over his shoulder as I reached for Mason fruitlessly, hollering curses to him until the door to the foyer slammed shut. "He can't just do that to my mother!" I exclaimed. Kai set me in the chair beside Abraham. He sat at his front desk and barely paid us a glance. From the corner of my eye, I could see him send us a sideways glance. Kai put both his hands on my shoulders. "I understand, Angel, but they're consenting adults. Your mother is a smart woman. She knows how to handle Mason." I clamped my mouth shut and glared at both him and the door behind him. Truthfully, that wasn't the entirety of what I was worried about. Yes, I worried that my mother would get hurt again, but I was beginning to realize that she was only with Mason because she truly believed that he was a good man. And he was, for the most part, if you could see past his inappropriate jokes and crude personality. If she could trust him in that way, then I could eventually understand their relationship.

But if they were together, then would that make me his stepson? I shivered at the thought.

....

Three weeks later, it was safe to say that I had basically moved in with Kai, despite my intentions to stay at home. I had been sleeping most of the time too, allowing myself to succumb to the depression I had welcomed. I wasn't sure what to do; I wasn't *sad*, per-say. All I knew was that my energy was gone, my stomach was in constant turmoil, and I wasn't sure if I wanted to hide it from Kai. He was trying to keep me busy and distracted, but, despite his best efforts, I woke many times during the night. He could do nothing but attempt to calm me. Some nights it worked. Some nights I was left with bloodshot eyes and a body racked with tremors. Kai, thankfully, only experienced one nightmare during this time, and he fell

ANGEL

asleep soon afterwards. Cade sat in the back of my mind constantly, continuing to fuel my nightmares. He stayed at large, increasing my anxiety by the day. The painful memories and fears didn't leave, and neither did Kai's constant worry over me. Mom helped me often, staying at Kai's house whenever she had a few hours away from work or home.

"You're kinda on your own now, Mom," I told her nervously as she sat next to me on the sofa on a scalding November afternoon. She sighed and nodded, playing with her hands in her lap and diverting her gaze. I wondered if I looked the same when I was caught in a compromising situation. "I'm not that alone, I guess. Mason has been helping a little bit around there. You know that old window that was broken beside the door? The one that was letting all the bugs in the house?" I nodded slowly; I had slightly come to terms with the two of them, as long as Mason and I weren't in the same room for too long. Honestly, my outburst was rather embarrassing to think about. "Well, he fixed that. I don't have to worry about spiders in my bed anymore," she told me. I perked up. "He fixed that leaking pipe under the sink too. He's been just... keeping me company, you know?" My smile fell slightly. "Are you sure about him, Mom?"

She was obviously confused. "Sure about him?"

"Mason is a good guy. He really is. But how do you trust him so easily? So quickly?"

My mother didn't miss a beat before she answered with a hopeful smile, leaning towards me. "How did you trust Kai so easily and quickly when you met him?"

Touché.

....

"How do you feel about going for a vacation?" Kai asked the morning my mood seemed to be at its worst. Waking up with Kai wrapped around me was definitely something I could get used to, though. "A vacation where?" I replied, closing my eyes and reveling in his light stubble that grazed across my shoulder. He hummed lightly, tracing an invisible line up my arm and down to my hip. The touch made me shiver. "How about...," he trailed off in thought as he lightly gripped my ass, causing me to squirm. "How about we take a week or two on my parents' yacht and spend some time in Mexico?" I sighed and rolled towards him. I replied with a small smile before pulling him into a soft kiss. But Kai had other intentions, and immediately deepened it. It was almost instinct to turn up the heat. "I like waking up with you. I missed that when you weren't here," he told me. I leaned back to meet his awe-filled gaze. My only reaction was to laugh. "As long as you can put up with my morning breath." Soon, he was laughing, too, and I rolled to straddle his stomach with a wide smile. I could feel his large erection against my tailbone, poking between my cheeks. "We should go somewhere cold. I want to see snow," I told him as I pulled our thick comforter around my shoulders and threw a shadow over Kai. "You've never seen it in person, hm?" I nodded. "When I was really young, Los Angeles got a super light dusting that blew in from the San Gabriel mountains. It was barely enough to turn anything white, but it was pretty."

"So you want to see a real snowfall this winter?"

I nodded as I drew a heart around his left nipple with my finger. I should have titty-twisted him, just for the fun of it. "Do you want to celebrate Christmas with me?"

"Of course. My family always spends Christmas together. We should invite them and your mom somewhere for the holidays."

"You guys go somewhere different every year?" He nodded. "We fight about where to go, but mom's decision always wins."

"I'm not really surprised. We should also invite Alice and

Genova." With that, Kai burst into laughter, but I only stared in confusion. "Do we not want Alice and Genova there...?" The man shook his head and quieted his laughter. "Genova just... probably isn't the person who you would want at a family reunion."

"Why?"

"Doesn't matter. I'm just saying that you should get chills when you think of her. She isn't always the best person." I decided to stay quiet on the subject. I really didn't know Genova, did I?

"We should get up," he declared. My mood was brighter, I realized, especially when Kai suggested a shower together. After an hour under the water, we had played for long enough, and got out to dress ourselves in relaxed weekend attire. Rosa greeted us with coffee and vegan bacon downstairs. Kai indulged in one of his shakes. Over our breakfast, the three of us chatted and decided on our day's activities. Mason had left earlier in the day to do errands and visit his daughter, I was told.

Once dishes were washed, that stupid cowlick in my hair had finally gone down, and Rosa had selected her daily bottle of rum to add to a litre of coke, Kai and I went down to the garage. We had work to do, and Rosa's alcoholic weekends weren't going to ground us.

"I'll be here," Kai said as I unbuckled my seatbelt. From the garage, we had taken one of the cars and drove through a fast food restaurant to get a breakfast for myself that tasted more decent than Rosa's cruelty-free breakfast. "I don't think my mom is even gonna go for this. She hasn't been on a vacation in... ever," I sighed. I was only finishing my breakfast wrap in the short time we had been sitting in front of my house. Kai nodded. "That's why you need to get her to come." I gathered my garbage, stuffed it in the bag, and stepped out of the car. I was about to close the door before Kai leaned over the seat, squinting against the harsh sun. "Hey, Luka, you should, um..."

My brows pulled together. "I should what?"

"Nevermind."

All that earned him was a roll of my eyes before I slammed the car door. As if I hadn't heard *that* one before. In the same fucking car. I crossed our lawn and opened my door, expecting my mother to be relaxing on the couch with a book or making herself an easy lunch, since the door was already unlocked. But I was met with the sound of small banging on the other side of the house. "Mom?" I called hesitantly. I was sure that our shower had broken again. The water made that noise in the pipes often if the water ran for too long. Something else Mason could fix, I realized.

When there was no reply, I hastily approached my mother's closed bedroom and opened it wide, wide enough to take in too much of the horrific scene in front of me, then and forever etched into my retinas. I wasn't sure why I thought she would be hitting anything in her *bedroom.*

Mason mercilessly pounded into my mother, eliciting soft moans from both of them as he buried his head into her shoulder and whispered soft, unknown words to her—not that I wanted to know what they were at the moment. The banging I had heard was the bedpost against the wall. Could they not bother to hang a simple sheet over the both of them? Could they not have locked the fucking door? Both of them froze, their heads turning quickly to me as if they were deer in headlights. We stared at each other for a moment before I realized that the heavy pit in my stomach was the urge to leave as fast as fucking possible.

"I'm going on a vacation. I'll be back never," I choked before frantically reaching for the door handle and closing it with a slam.

CHAPTER FIFTY-SEVEN

"I'M SURE THERE were lots of other things you could have seen that would have been way worse," Kai tried to soothe as we cruised through the streets of L.A. I stared at him incredulously. "What could be worse than that?!" Kai chuckled with a shrug, taking a rather sharp turn toward Alice's adult shop. "You can tell her later. I'm sure they'll be busy for a while."

"I'm mad that you knew. You were about to stop me! Do you know how bad I need holy water eyedrops now?" Kai burst into laughter. "I'm sure Alice can find you something to forget it all." His slightly devious voice darkened with lust for a moment. He pulled into one of the many empty spots in front of the store before we both stepped out of his shiny, orange *Bugatti*. Once inside, I was expecting Alice's excited greeting to ring across the store as she jumped on us with hugs and kisses. But we were instead greeted by silence. "Probably in the back with Genova. Go look around, Luka," Kai ordered, leaving me. I bit my lip and followed his directions, getting an eyeful of the vibrators that hung on the wall next to me.

"Is it in yet?" I heard Kai ask quietly from across the silent store. I wasn't meaning to eavesdrop; Kai's voice was rather loud. In the corner of my eye, I could see a woman examining dildos a few aisles down, but other than that, the place was empty and quiet enough for sound to travel far. The excitement was already coursing sharp through my veins. "Yep," I listened to Alice's reply.

When Kai returned, I diverted my eyes, guilty. He carried a small box under his arm inconspicuously as I absently grabbed a blindfold off the rack in front of me. It was made with a beautiful, shiny black leather and had the word *'slave'* imprinted across it. "Did you get what you needed?" I asked. "Yeah. You like this?" he replied, taking the hand that held the blindfold and examining it in my grasp. "It would look a hell of a lot better on you than it does on the shelf." I only blushed and shrugged, although I didn't return it to the rack and instead handed it to him. He smirked victoriously.

"Kai," a voice sounded from beside the front door. We both looked to Genova and met her cold glare. I shivered at the sight; those eyes were *venomous*. The woman had just been leaving. "He's not in Phoenix, but a friend of mine found him on a security camera in Houston. My guess is he's heading towards Havana. He's got friends there," she told us. "Cade?" I asked. Was Genova part of the police department? She didn't seem like a cop kind of girl. She seemed more like the one to run from them. "Good guess, genius," she hissed, and I flinched. "Thank you, Genova," Kai interjected, his voice twisting into a warning. But Genova obviously didn't like to be snapped at. "Fuck you." The woman paid us both another glare before turning with a flip of her hair and exiting the shop. "Buh-bye, Mumma!" Alice called as the door closed, bells jingling. What was Genova's fucking problem?

"She's looking for Cade? She isn't a cop, though, is she?" I asked, looking up at Kai with a worried expression. I was hurt, too, by her words. He sighed. "She's not a cop. She just has friends. And sorry about that. She decided that she didn't want to take her happy pills this week."

"She has friends who look at security videos in Houston?" I asked.

"Yeah."

I nodded, still lacking information. Kai was probably right. I probably didn't want to know that much about Genova Donatella.

"So, are you going somewhere cold for Christmas?" Alice said, wrapping her arm around mine and leaning her head against my shoulder. "Possibly," Kai replied. "What about you and Genova?" I asked. She pulled away and shrugged. "She wants to go to New York and find some old friends of hers. She wasn't happy when they ripped her off on their last deal. Then maybe we'll go get high together for a weekend somewhere in Europe."

"Then why does she want to go there if she isn't happy with them?" I was confused, but Kai certainly wasn't. He glanced around the shop, obviously wanting to leave. There was money in his hand already; he was ready to pay for the blindfold and get the hell out. He didn't want me talking about Genova with her girlfriend, I knew, because it wasn't a secret that Kai disliked Genova.

"I don't really know what she wants to do there. She said it in Italian, but I think it was something along the lines of 'Turn them into a puree with a machete and mail the remains to their parents.'." My eyes widened slightly before I shot Kai, who gave a stiff smile, a concerned glance. "Well, I hope it works out for your girlfriend.... have a nice night," I told Alice as I stepped away slowly. She only smiled and excitedly waved goodbye, refusing Kai's money for the blindfold. "Have fun with your new toys, Luka!" I hoped the "toy" that Kai had bought would be exciting, although I never had to worry about a dull moment while sharing a bed with *him*. "Thanks," I mumbled.

....

Kai took me to James's restaurant where he had reserved a table for the night. The stars weren't visible, but the city lights compensated.

"Kai!" James greeted excitedly. I didn't expect him to meet us up there, but Kai was obviously happy with the fact that he carried a bottle of rum and another of Coke. We were both settled into a small nook in the corner of the deck, overlooking the street below us as the sun began to set over the city. It reflected off the glass buildings around us in golds and oranges.

"James," Kai smiled. "I'm glad you came. Gives me a chance to thank you," he told Kaia as he set the bottles between us. "Don't thank me. Thank Luka," Kai replied. I gave them both a confused side eye. "What are we thanking me for?" James laughed. "For your mother! She works harder than any other cook in my kitchen, and I'm told she never even attended an official culinary school." Mom had taken many culinary classes in high school and spent a year or two working in a kitchen before she started dating my father. My mouth dropped open. "Th-There's a m-mistake, I...," but then I made eye contact with Kai, who was smiling giddily. Had he arranged this? Could he be the angel that my mother had been waiting for?

"You did this?" I asked, the lid to my excitement nearly popping off. My voice shook with the effort used to compose myself. Kai nodded, biting his lip and grinning. With that, I jumped from my seat and around the table to wrap my arms around Kai's neck. "I love you so much!" I exclaimed to Kai before jumping into Jame's chest. "Thank you so much for letting her work with you! She'll never be able to tell you how grateful she is." James chuckled and rubbed my shoulder. "She's telling me with the meals she's helping to put out. She's a pretty good cook, if I do say so myself. She would be a very talented chef if she went to school."

I sat back down, pushing my hands under my thighs and swinging my legs. "Drink your treats. It's my favourite pairing. And Luka-," he said, looking to me, "-not too much rum. I don't need

ANGEL

the police on me now." I laughed and nodded as James clapped his hands together and rubbed them joyfully. "So, what can I get you two." I was surprised when Kai looked at me expectantly. "You want me to...?" I motioned to my own chest as I stared at him incredulously. He nodded.

"Okay. Do you have anything with fish? Like a seafood platter?"

"Of course. A large to share?"

"Yeah. That sounds great, James. Can you add a side of gravy to it?" Kai asked.

He snorted. "I forgot about that. Coming right up."

Once James had left us, I folded my hands on the table and leaned toward him. "Gravy with seafood?"

Kai shrugged. "They make a good spicy gravy here. Then I found that it pairs well with seafood. It helps me forget about the texture."

We chatted throughout the meal, careful to stray away from any conversation on Cherry or Cade. It was my first time trying oysters, and I decided that I loved them. By the time Kai had swallowed his last bit of gravy, he had finished a quarter of the rum himself and we had shared the entire bottle of Coke. James came to take our meals as if he were a waiter dressed in a black chef's coat. "I'll be back in a minute. Just heading to the washroom," Kai said suddenly, standing and leaving James and I once James had reached our table. We watched him go, and I expected James to take our plates and leave me alone with my drink, but I was apparently mistaken.

"May I sit, Luka?"

I nodded and motioned to Kai's seat. "Yeah. Of course."

Was it about Cherry? Was Kai still struggling even after telling me about his wife? Stupid, stupid, of course he was. He always would. She was fucking murdered in front of him.

"How have you been feeling since the incident with Cade?" The question caught me off-guard, and my brain took a moment before

I could reply. "Okay, I guess. Better with Kai around," I told him nervously. My fingers worked on my knuckles under the table. I pushed a stray lock of hair behind my ear. It had been growing back since the summer. James nodded, his brows furrowed slightly. "He's been doing really well too. You're probably feeling unsafe with Cade not being locked up yet." I shrugged and traced my finger around the rim of my glass mindlessly. "Cade is running. A-And last I heard he was in Houston. Far away from me." I knew what I should have been feeling. I was safe in L.A. Caden wasn't even in the *city*. So why did I feel his eyes on me from around every corner? Why was I so scared that he would come after me again? Why did I only feel safe when I was asleep or curled in Kai's sheets? "Luka, it's okay to be shaken up after what you went through. It was traumatic. I'm just telling you that if you need to talk to anyone, I can help. It's my job."

He watched me hopefully from across the table before he stood, taking my reluctant silence as his cue to leave. "Have a good night, Lucika," he smiled, passing an approaching Kai and heading for the kitchen.

CHAPTER
FIFTY-EIGHT

THE NEXT DAY, Kai grew busy with his work. He was in his office since early in the morning; I hadn't even woken up with him in bed with me. So, instead of letting me sit around the apartment and do my own work like I planned, Rosa treated my mother and I to dinner and took us to a small Mexican restaurant in Hollywood. Afterwards, as the hot sun set and began to cast familiar shadows across the city, we walked the Hollywood Boulevard and admired the famous names that passed under our feet. I began to wonder about the famous songwriters and singers featured there, and what I wouldn't give to see my name on one of the gold stars. What if I wrote my own song? Would I be able to reach the top with just one hit? Probably not. But I would have written and sung my own music. How many people could say that? "Hey, Luka!" Rosa gained my attention as she waved me down the sidewalk. "What kind of ice cream do you want?" My mother stood beside her nervously as I shrugged absently and stuffed my hands in my jean pockets. "Vanilla, I guess?" Rosa rolled her eyes and turned to the man behind his flavours. "How about a liquorice cone, a strawberry cone, and a bowl of maple," she told him. He nodded while I sighed. My mother wound her arm around mine and took her cup of maple ice cream before I was given my cone of strawberry.

"So, Luka...," my mother began as we strolled past businesses and tourists, licking at our treat. Her voice was quiet and curious, unusual. "Are you planning on marrying Kaia?" I nearly choked on my cone, a chunk of it falling and catching on the end of my shirt before I could regain my composure. "I-I don't think so... we've only been dating for, like, half a year," I told her. She nodded slowly. Kai wouldn't marry me. I was a good boyfriend and companion, but I didn't think that marriage had crossed either of our minds. I didn't exactly see a point in marriage, anyway, because we didn't have a specific culture that called for it. We didn't quite need the legality of marriage yet, either. I didn't need a thousand-dollar ceremony to tell Kaia that I would love him forever. He knew.

"Oh," she said. She didn't seem disheartened by my reply, but she also didn't seem to mind either way. Mason must have really been getting to her, poisoning her with his lazy nature. "And are you and Mason getting serious?" She rolled her eyes playfully. "Please. I haven't even met his daughter." My face and bright mood fell. "Oh yeah. A step-sister too."

"Oh, hush," she scolded, swatting me lightly on the shoulder. I only laughed half-heartedly as Rosa followed us toward Santa Monica.

....

"Come for me, Luka. Such a good boy," Cade smirked as he landed another swat on my ass with his flogger. I screamed, nowhere close to an orgasm. The chain around my neck pinched my skin tightly as I pulled on my restraints and tore at my flesh. "Please stop," I sobbed. This time, I didn't have a gag on. He ignored me until I caught the eye of the figure relaxing on the sofa across the room, his black gaze scanning me smugly from behind that thick hair. He held a black, glinting Wartenberg pinwheel between his long fingers, lighting fireworks of terror between

my lungs. My stomach dropped when I identified him as Kai himself, watching me as if we were an erotic scene unfolding instead of a horrifying experience. "Ah-ah, look at me, Lucika. Don't pay attention to him. He's just a guest," Cade smirked as the paddle came down across my spine, eliciting a crack from the aching bones—

I woke with a yelp, sitting up and immediately scanning the room for Cade. I half expected Kai to be watching me, but I was alone. Maybe that was even worse. I almost instantly began to sob, panic forcing strong gasps to enter my throat and never make it to my lungs. Tears burnt my eyes and disrupted my vision as my hands dug into my scalp. So suddenly, it had come over me, *engulfed* me, like a tidal wave.

I screamed.

Within a minute, Kai was bursting through the door, followed closely by Rosa. I didn't give any thought to Mason's absence. "K-Kuh-Kai I can-t... I n-need—," I told him desperately, barely comprehensible as he jumped onto the bed beside me. "What happened?" His words weren't as comforting as he wanted them to be. True panic flashed in his eyes.

"M-Make it stuh-stop!" *There is fire in my lungs.*

"Luka, calm down," he said in a shaking voice. "Tell me what happened."

"I-I-It hurts!" I wailed as my vision began to waver and the room began to spin. My neck and face burnt faintly from where I had scratched the skin raw in just the few moments my head had been spinning. Rosa jumped onto the bed beside me and helped pull my hands away from my head to see the damage. I missed the horror-stricken expression on her face before she shook her head. "I think it's a panic attack," she said to Kai. "This isn't like the ones you used to have."

"Just breathe, Luka. Close your eyes and try to get air," Kai consoled. It was difficult for his voice to break through the haze and panic that enveloped my senses, but I managed to clamp my eyes shut tight and push my face against Rosa's chest. She smelt like flowers and something more musky and bitter. It helped soothe my cold sweat tickling my spine and ringing in my ears, but my throat still ached for fresh air. Rosa and Kai restrained my arms when I began to scratch at my neck once again. Tiny blood droplets were already forming there; they couldn't do much to help me but talk me through it, just as I saw Mason do for Kai in the past. "I've messaged James. He's on his way over here," Kai's voice broke through that haze. "Just breathe, baby. You'll have help in a few minutes. Just take deep breaths. I know it hurts a lot." As I was told this, Rosa bundled me in my blanket that Kai grabbed off the end of the bed. His scent surrounded me and began to calm me slowly, although it wasn't nearly as strong as the real man. It hurt to panic, to be so scared and realizing that I had next to no control over my own body. Why had my lungs been so against me?

"Do you want to go downstairs? I'll make you a drink in the kitchen," Rosa asked as she rubbed my back in soft, even strokes. I gave a pathetic nod before she helped me to my feet, keeping her actions slow and soothing while my hammering chest calmed. My knees threatened to give out under me as they trembled. We limped together down the stairs and into the kitchen where she let me collapse on one of the dark sofas. By the time I was left in a ball, I was panting. Still, I was thankful to have most of my airway under my own control. Mason was there when I glanced up, shooting me a smile. I was exhausted, so Rosa left me to slip into a dazed, vacant mindset as she spoke quietly with Kaia in the kitchen. Soon, the voices faded. Mason's smile turned sad.

I stayed in this headspace until I wasn't sure how long I had been sitting there. When I looked up from the coffee table, the room and sky were still dark.

"Hey, Luka," James greeted quietly on my left. His words had startled me from my daze, and I began to scramble into a sitting position on the couch. "No, no, it's okay. You're good where you are," he told me, and I hesitantly relaxed, wrapping myself deeper in the blanket. "Here, Luka. It's pretty hot," Rosa told me as she set a steaming mug of hot chocolate on the table next to my head. "Thanks." My voice cracked. I flinched. "Can you get us your first aid kit? He's got some nasty cuts here," James asked Rosa. She and Kai must have been waiting for the doctor to arrive; I felt like a psych patient, although James would be a much better fit to take care of me, both physically and mentally. Rosa nodded and made a beeline towards the stairway to retrieve the medical kit while Kai appeared behind me. "I'm going to leave you with James. Talk with him alone. Is that okay?" I nodded, unable to really hear what he was telling me. All I could register was his lips in my hair, kissing away the itch I had had before. Mason flirted past James to follow Kai when he left the room.

"Is that hot chocolate?" James asked gently. I sat up to inspect it, too, and grimaced slightly when the blanket fell across my neck and chest. "That's what Rosa said."

"Looks good. You should try a bit. Maybe I can get her to make me a batch." He was making idle conversation, probably an attempt to calm me further, distract me. I bit my lip and shook my head after watching the steam roll off the top and disperse into the air. Too hot. James's brows furrowed as he stood suddenly and crossed the room to the refrigerator. "Maybe Kai still has some of his go-juice cubes. Rosa puts them in her iced coffee sometimes," he told me as he pulled a small baggie out of the freezer. I watched him pop a small, brown cube into his mouth before he returned to me and dropped one in my own mug. "Iced coffee. It's pretty bitter without something to go with it, but it should cool your drink down," I nodded as he winked at me and returned to his seat on the coffee table, resting his elbows on his knees and sighing hesitantly. Coffee never kept me awake all that long, but the caffeine could rearrange my intestines better than Kai ever could. One little coffee cube wouldn't hurt me, I decided. "So... Luka," he began. He caught my eye. I found his gaze strangely calming. "Why do you think you had a panic attack?"

I licked my lips before answering. My fear of Cade was starting to make me feel stupid and embarrassed. He couldn't get me there. But why did it feel like he could?

"B-Because of the nightmare."

"Can you tell me what it was about?"

I nodded, but my lips refused to work. Something in my mind screamed at me to keep quiet, to stay silent so Cade wouldn't be able to find me.

"I... I was at the club. Cade was... it was when he tried to rape me. But...." I didn't know how to finish, and I thankfully didn't have to, since Rosa finally returned with a large box under her arm. James's eyes never left mine. "Here ya go. Tell me what you use so I can replace it all," she told James before sending me a small smile and leaving us. "I was told that John had gotten there just in time," James fretted. He was horrified, his bushy, grey brows seeming to fluff up like a cat's tail. My throat was momentarily closed tight, constricting my airway and vocal cords until I was sure I was turning a different colour. "Yeah, yeah, he didn't actually... he didn't-," but the tears were coming back. I stopped, and in that time, James did his best to soothe me. "Okay... tell me when you're ready." James waited patiently and only glanced at the box briefly to slowly remove each item one-by-one. "Kai was there," I said finally. James's expression didn't change. "You mean in your nightmare...

ANGEL

Was he just watching or touching you? Was he trying to save you?"

"W-Watching," I choked. I felt as if another panic attack was coming, consuming what little light was left in my mind. "He was... h-holding—... He was... part of it. With Cade." A tear burnt my cheek and settled under my chin as James began dabbing at my neck with alcohol-soaked gauze. He apologized when I jolted and winced. I wondered if he had even heard me; it looked more like he was focused on my wounds instead. "I-I'm not scared of him, I don't know why I had the dream. I know Kai wouldn't do that," I explained quickly. He shook his head. "No one's blaming you. The mind can make you see some scary things sometimes. You're a sexual assault survivor now, Luka. It's a long road that most people never completely recover from. It's part of you, but that doesn't ever make any of it—the aftermath or the experience—your fault," he soothed as cooling ointment was rubbed into my skin. Gauze was then wrapped around me with the lightest touch before he taped it together.

"Thanks."

James shrugged. "No problem."

James chatted with me about everything after bandaging my self-inflicted wounds. I told him more about my experience. I told him about my life before I met Kai. We even found ourselves talking about how I could ground myself after nightmares and some tips on battling PTSD. I found that the more I spoke with him, the more I relaxed. He was someone who could calm an entire room of angry people, I could tell. "Do you want me to stay with you for a while longer? Do you think you can get back to sleep?" he asked. I shook my head. "I'll be okay. Thanks, James." He nodded and stood, pulling out his phone. "I won't tell Kai anything from the meeting if you don't want me to. But I'm sure he'll be very interested in how you're doing. I have to get back to work."

"No. D-Don't tell him anything. Thank you, really."

"Goodnight, Luka," he told me quietly. The man turned and left, leaving me alone with what was left of my steaming drink.

CHAPTER
FIFTY-NINE

THE DAY WOULD be one for work and relaxation, hopefully. Wrapped in mounds of blankets, especially my own that carried Kai's comforting musk, with the windows on the fogged setting and mellow music playing softly from across the room, I began on weeks of bank reports and records. I had taken a quick shower before Rosa delivered a grilled ham and cheese sandwich around noon, and I didn't expect her back until she was sure I was finished with my plate, at least forty-five minutes. Kai stayed in his office for most of the day. When he finally did return to his bedroom, I wrapped my arms around his neck to pull him onto the bed with me. He breathed a surprised laugh and put a hand on my ass and the other on my lower back. "You missed me," he said into my neck. "Truthfully, I would have enjoyed seeing *anybody*. My work was boring, for sure," I replied with a sharp, searing kiss to his lips. His chest was warm under mine, and he smiled up at me. "I thought you would never take a break," I said, pulling myself up until I was straddling his stomach. "I didn't want to stay. I wanted to be with you." There was no hesitancy in his tone when he told me that, swiping my hair behind my ear. "I'm glad I wasn't the only one." My smile was huge until his slow hand found my crotch. I shuffled back slightly until my ass, wrapped in a layer of boxers and another of his sweatpants, gyrated against his clothed cock. He closed his eyes and let his head fall back against the pillow. "Mm... yes, Angel." His praise only made me wiggle and squirm more, working his belt open and the fly down on his pants. My lips were around his length the second I had popped it free from its confinements. His hips bucked up involuntarily, and I could only smile. I did that.

But the thought disappeared when I drove a hand under my boxers and began rubbing myself. "Ah... Kai," I moaned, my eyes closing and my head tilting back. His cock was then forgotten, standing tall above his hips and aching for my touch once again. I would get back to it eventually. I could *feel* the heat radiating off it. He twitched when he realized he was no longer getting any special treatment. "Ah-ah," he chided, taking my chin firmly in one hand and shaking it harder than necessary. I liked the sting of his fingers against my jaw bone, he knew. I expected him to slap me like I wanted him to; I wanted to feel that *hurt.* But, instead, he flipped me onto the bed and closed my thighs, drawing my garments off my legs and onto the floor. Then he grabbed a bottle of lube off my bedside table. I expected him to prepare me, even just a little, until I felt the liquid being poured over my cock. A breathy moan escaped me, long and sensual, as he spread it across my testicles and over my erection and stomach. My back arched as sweet, innocent pleasure rushed through my body like a lightning bolt. "Just remember, Angel... you're not allowed to come," he whispered as he lubed up his stiff member and stared me down with hungry, half-lidded eyes.

The moment was ruined.

"Wh-Why?" I whimpered in a broken voice as he closed my thighs around his cock. It shaped beautifully to the contour of my balls and up the underside of my limb, as if it was destined to be there. My calves sat on his left shoulder, and if I wasn't occupied, I would have been tempted to run my toes through his hair. "Because

ANGEL

what's the fun in that?" he replied in his dark, silky voice. I whimpered as he began to move, shifting between my honey-like thighs. "I love this," he breathed, my pleasure building with each thrust. His words barely made it past my drums as I threw my head back and gave him a low groan. The orgasm would be hard to ignore. Impossible, even. The friction was awesome, sending me into a whirlpool of colours and hot, heavy breathing. I could feel his hands on my thighs. They were tight and firm, squeezing the fat until we both knew there would be bruises forming by tomorrow. It hurt—but I loved it. He owned me, and he was making sure of it like an animal marking its territory.

After a few moments, I could feel my climax approaching. The knot was forming, and it was going to explode soon. I needed to come like a fish needed water, and I was fucking thirsty. "Hold it, Luka. Maybe, if you're good, I'll let you come before tomorrow," he whispered to me, his eyes blazing with his own oncoming ejaculation. My spirits began to fall, and so did my restraints. If I held it any longer, I swore I would explode. The searing, blissful pain was unbearable. My eyes closed as I grimaced and whined, squirming and aching for the sweet release.

"Breathe, Luka. You can do this, just relax. You're getting too worked up," Kai soothed softly. His fingers were on my chest, massaging the tight muscles slowly as I felt him fall into a more sedated pace. He was allowing me the smallest of breaks. I hadn't realized that I was holding my breath until I released it, my lungs finally relaxing. My nails dug into the bed sheets until they nearly ripped, but, thankfully, his blankets were used to being manhandled. All of them were, except maybe my own blanket, which had begun to sport small holes on the edges. As much as I wanted a new one, I didn't know if I was quite ready to let the old one go.

Through my haze, I failed to notice Kai dangerously near his release. He began thrusting again. I only focused on my breathing, as commanded, as I grimaced and pursed my lips tightly, my eyes squeezed shut against the onslaught. Then he stiffened and bucked his hips more frantically than before. He gasped and huffed while his milky seed spilled across my stomach and chest. Some even made it as far as my chin, just out of my tongue's reach. Finally, he stilled, both of us gasping for air. "Please," I whimpered. "P-Please let me..." I was on the verge of tears, although I was rather proud of myself for being able to hold out for so long. "Sh," he soothed as he slid away and let my legs fall straight against the bed. I was a quivering, disgusting mess compared to him, who reimmersed himself in his dress pants and straightened his wrinkle-less shirt. "Just a moment, Angel, you're doing beautifully," he hushed before disappearing into the bathroom, only to return with a hot cloth. I immediately gripped onto his bicep and breathed in his comforting scent.

"You were such a good boy, Luka. You can come now," he told me once he had wiped me down. Then his hand was around my cock. I gasped and tensed under it. There was no more restraint necessary by then, just unadulterated, simple rapture. No more than five firm pumps were all that were needed before I was spilling onto his hand and arching over the bed. Stars swirled into my vision as he coaxed me through the overwhelming, amazing turmoil in my body.

"I love you Kai," I breathed, my eyes fluttering closed with exhaustion once I was finally spent and pliant in his care. There was no exhaustion like that experienced after an orgasm. He only chuckled. "I love you, too, Angel." I could hear him then washing his hands and dropping the cloth in the hamper before the bed dipped and I was pulled against his chest. No blankets or sheets, just us and nothing in between. "Are you asleep, Angel?" he asked suddenly, his silky voice only a calm whisper, as if he had just disconnected a phone call with his mother instead of having had sex. If he continued

ANGEL

rubbing my shoulder and cheek with his thumb like he was, then yes, I would be asleep very soon. "No," I breathed, nothing more than a huff of air that carried the occasional sound wave.

I was asleep before he could reply.

....

I woke forty-five minutes later with lighter shoulders and a cleared mind.

"Did you sleep well?" he asked from his seat on the edge of the bed with one knee on the sheets under him and the other hanging off the side. Kai sipped at one of his calorie shakes slowly, seeming to be quietly enjoying the evening. "Mhm," I replied as I darted across the bed to find his lap. He moved his drink out of my way and welcomed me, letting my smaller frame curl against his chest. "I thought you only drank those in the morning and ate a little bit throughout the day," I hummed as he gulped down half of the thick shake. "I guess I wasn't hungry this morning," he replied. I snorted and I pursed my lips. "Because you were too tired from my keeping you awake?" I assumed my question would make the air around us pregnant with unspoken words, but that was exactly what I wanted. He was hesitating. I waited patiently. "Luka...," he began. He set his drink on my bedside table and pulled me out of his lap so we could have an official conversation. His eyes met mine and seemed to search for any pain, but he hadn't even said anything yet.

"I get that the nightmares aren't stopping, and I think you need to see James more often. Look how often I go visit him... even *I'm* still healing. And I was kidnapped, what, five years ago? Six?"

My gaze fell onto the sheets. "But your meetings and business stuff... I don't want to talk to him alone anymore. And you're busy a lot of the time," I said. He shook his head. I was beginning to feel as if I was being ridiculous. "Meetings and business can be postponed.

You can't." I wanted to make more excuses. I was scared of talking, scared that if I told anyone the details of my experience, the mention of his name would summon Cade.

"Thank you," I mumbled. I wasn't sure how long I could hold out; Kai could certainly tell that I was reaching the end.

CHAPTER SIXTY

"**PLEASE...**," I SOBBED.

My nightmares and terrors were becoming increasingly worse, and the fact that Caden was still MIA was not helping. "G-Get off me!" I cried, fighting against Kai's restraints. Kai might have been able to calm me down if he released me. *Air* was what I wanted, not comfort. But he continued trying his best to make me accept that warm place in his arms. I couldn't tell him, so what was he supposed to do? I was delirious and broken, only half-awake from a terrible night terror and aching for something that was near impossible. "I know, Luka, sh, I'm sorry," Kai attempted to soothe. He had abandoned telling me to stop what felt like hours ago. His hands held my wrists tight so I wouldn't slip them away and add new, angry lines to his body, but he couldn't end my pain-filled cries and exclamations. His hands were Cade's. His face was Cade's. I could feel the bed sheets and my lungs closed knowing that they felt so much similar to the ones in the club.

"Get it the fuck off me! Puh-Please!"

A shiver trapped his spine and he pushed his head against my collar bone. '*It's not her,*' he reminded himself silently. His wife had cried like that the first time Markus had strapped a vibratory to her and expected her to be pleasured.

'She's gone. Luka is here. It's just Luka.'

I suddenly released an ear-splitting scream in agony. Kai jumped and gasped. "Sh... it's okay, Angel, I got you." I seemed to quiet down after that, having released some pent-up steam. I mumbled incoherent pleas and curses under my breath as Kai grasped both my wrists in his lap and rubbed random shapes into my back with the other. "I got you, Luka. You're safe."

It was a long night for the both of us, especially since Kai woke early and couldn't fall back asleep. He walked a few laps around the kitchen, took a shower, spent some time in the gym downstairs, and finally returned to his bedroom to read. I had woken momentarily when he jostled the bed. Quickly, I was back asleep. There were seven days until Christmas Day. Six until my birthday.

I woke for the second time exhausted and ready for a nap. "Luka?" Kai asked, startling me from my sleepy haze. I realized that I was being held against a familiar chest with comforting arms. Kai was sitting against the headboard with my head against his knee. His book had been discarded to the side. "Good morning," I smiled groggily up at him. The bags under his eyes were dark and disturbing, as if he had gotten no sleep at all that night. He was pale and his eyes were blood-shot. My smile immediately fell. "What's wrong?"

"You don't remember," he whispered. I stared at him with confusion in my gaze as he took one of my hands gently in his. His expression was agonized. "God, I'm so sorry. I didn't mean to hold them so tight." He planted a feathery kiss on my wrist, which was, by that morning, a pale lavender colour. "What happened?" I asked. "Night terror. Like the ones I get, but... scarier." My brows pulled together as panic surged through my veins like icy water. "What happened? Did I do something bad?" I wasn't surprised that I had a night terror. They were getting increasingly worse during most nights. But could it have been that bad to have impacted Kai so

ANGEL

horribly? Kaia's head shook with fervor. "No, no, Luka. You did nothing bad. Nothing." I nodded slowly, wishing to drop the conversation. It was obviously hurting him. With a sad sigh, I pushed my head under his arm, forcing my way up against his chest. "I don't remember anything," I whimpered, repeating what he had told me. I could remember colour. I could *feel* it. It had built in my brain, created a painful pressure and a disorienting flash of swirls and violent lines. I remembered that it looked like a knotted ball of yarn, tangled and confusing. But it wasn't exactly a nightmare. That had come before the haze.

"Are we going anywhere special for the holidays? Have you made a decision?" I asked. The subject was dodged, saved for a sad, rainy day, and an idea for a brighter future replaced it. He thought for a moment, hesitant to move away from the former conversation but eager to know that I was happier when I ignored the night's adventures. "Definitely the Alps. But... I almost want to go there with you alone. Away from my family for the first time in my life. Is that selfish?" I shook my head, smirking as I ran my finger down his Adam's apple. It bobbed when he swallowed. "Not if I can be in the middle of nowhere with you... for multiple nights... with no one to hear me scream your name."

"That's what I was thinking."

Our smiles were genuine for a good few minutes. When I was satisfied with the glowing teeth I saw, I put my chin on my fist and looked up at him with wide eyes. The man stared back, gaze briefly wandering to his novel. "Can I ask you a question?" I asked. He had probably thought that I was about to fall back asleep. "Shoot," he replied. There was no hesitancy in his voice. "It's about you and your wife... specifically you," I told him hesitantly as I rubbed the back of my neck and looked up at him from under my lashes. Kai didn't stiffen or lean away as I thought he would. Instead, he rested his head against the top of mine and intertwined his hand with mine on the bed between us. He tickled my scalp with his lips. "What's your question?" he asked bravely. I took a deep breath. "How did you escape?"

His breath hitched. I didn't expect him to reply. "Cherry was murdered after about two months. During the third month, I was... I wasn't myself. A part of me knew I needed to get out, so... so I gained his trust." I didn't look up at him. Our hands worked, danced together in his lap. I had the urge to interrupt him worriedly, but I clamped my mouth shut and curled further into his side, forcing him to reposition his head on mine. "I told him I loved him, and he, in turn, started to trust me. He was obviously disturbed, and I eventually managed to convince him to let me play some games on his phone, you know, just to keep me occupied. It took a long time, though."

I gripped his hand tighter. The only movement was my thumb brushing over his.

"But instead of games, I texted my mother. I couldn't tell her where I was, but she knew that I was alive. I could only tell her that I was underground in a forest, but that was enough."

"But... they didn't get a location. How could they have found you if they had no idea what forest you were even in?"

"Cherry's body was found three days before I sent the text in a ditch between a road and a patch of land close to Forks. That's up in Washington, about two hours from the home we were living in at the time."

"And you were in that patch of land?"

He nodded. "And I was in that patch of land. They combed the woods and stirred up leaves until they found me, but...," he trailed off.

"But what?" I encouraged.

ANGEL

"But they said I wasn't myself. My parents tell me that my entire personality changed when I was rescued. They say that I still don't resemble the person I was before. That and I started struggling with things like my anger and flashbacks. Some days, I was *catatonic, empty, errant.*"

"Is that linked to your PTSD?"

"Yes. And it got bad again when... we were apart for that time. I was just... angry. All the time. Scared and furious. I've lost count of how many times I lashed out at Rosa and Mason when you were gone. Flashbacks too. I would be sitting quietly and then I would be hit with a vivid memory. Like I could smell him. I could hear her. Like I was still there."

"When did it stop? When you were younger, I mean."

"Truthfully? It never really stopped. Even before I met you, I would be lucky to get past with two or three big flashbacks a month. James helped with them a lot, too, so if I felt like anything was off, I would just call him, despite the fact that I didn't always enjoy our sessions."

"Good," I said. "I would be hitting you right now if you hadn't gotten help."

He raised an eyebrow and leaned away. "You'd be hitting me?"

"Well...," I pursed my lips, "Kai, we both know you can be... hardheaded." His eyelids drooped and he smirked as he rolled over me and pushed down the sheets. "Am I? '*Hardheaded*'?

"Oh my god!" I laughed. "You're like a wild animal!"

He chuckled. Had he forgotten our previous discussion? It was almost as if I had made him forget it all or that it had simply slipped from his mind on its own. Maybe we would share the pain now.

CHAPTER
SIXTY-ONE

"**I** REALLY WANT TO go to your home in the Alps," I told him. The mall was crowded, but Kai was eager to find a new motorbike helmet for me today. "We could go somewhere warm, y'know. Everyone in the family owns houses pretty much everywhere. Dad gave me an apartment for my twenty-fifth birthday in Australia. I rent it out most of the time." I rolled my eyes. "You know what I got for my twenty-fifth birthday?" He chuckled. "Nothing, yet. You're still nineteen."

"Exactly. Nothing." Kai only laughed and plucked a large helmet off a shelf. "Try this one." It was matte black and sleek with a single silver racing stripe up the centre of the round oval-style helmet. Simple and pretty. "How does it feel? Is it too loose?" he asked. I shook my head and gave a goofy smile through my lop-sided window of view. "Feels good." Kai removed it from my head, ruffling my hair with a wide grin. "Let's go then, Angel."

With the wind ripping through our clothes and our hair becoming matted and dead under our helmets, Kaia drove me home. I left him with a short kiss and my new helmet. He seemed sad that I had to leave him. Inside the house that my mother had warmed with the oven, I took note that she had vacuumed, and I promised myself that I would do the dishes and dust before I went to bed. "Hey, mom, I was wondering something," I said quietly, leaning against the doorframe to our kitchen. It was amazing how accustomed I had become to a chef's kitchen and laundry that was already done. But, as much as Kai wanted me to stay at his home, I decided it was time to spend at least a dinner with my own mother. She looked up from the small pot she was stirring with her eyebrows raised expectantly.

"What do you want for Christmas?"

I could tell that she was shocked for a moment. In past years, we had never exactly celebrated Christmas. There just wasn't a lot of money to spare for many gifts or even a turkey dinner from the grocery store. She simply brought home whatever food was leftover from the diner. Maybe half a pie, too, if there was any left by the end of her shift. "Nothing," she told me. I expected the answer, but my brows still furrowed. "Nothing? Are you sure? You don't want anything?"

"I already have you and Mason, and I lasted nineteen years with even less than that." I blanched and finally nodded slowly, my arms uncrossing and falling to my sides. "Dinner's ready," she told me as she placed the pot on the dining table and passed me a fork to accompany my bowl. "What is it?" I asked, picking excitedly at it after pouring a portion into my dish. "Chili. Rosa gave me a recipe she got from an old boyfriend. She said that he didn't work out, but the food sure did." I laughed and nodded, taking a seat at the small, circular table. "That sounds like her."

Mom only hummed and shovelled a spoonful of food into her mouth.

....

"I have it all planned out."

"Do you?"

We had both been on the fence about where to go. Both of us

wanted to spend time with our family, but we also wanted to relax together alone in the middle of nowhere. Kai nodded. "We're going to the mountains for a few days together for your birthday and our own Christmas, and then we're taking a jet to Canada for a holiday with everyone on the twenty-sixth. Teressa will be taking a flight with Mason and Rosa up to Yellowknife. Lily lives there."

"Wow. You got it all figured out."

"Like I said."

I paused and bit at my lip as I ate the final bits of my pancake and Kai slowly finished his shake. "So... what do you want for Christmas?" What could anyone buy for a man who had it all? A mischievous glint crossed his eyes before he pulled me into his lap over the comforter he was wrapped in. His lips were almost as sweet as my pancake syrup. "How does that song go? All I want for Christmas is... you? Wrapped in leather, silk, rope and chained to a bed, preferably, but I'm sure you can work something out." I laughed and shook my head. "That is definitely *not* how the song goes."

"And what would you like?" he breathed, trailing a tiny line of kisses across my collar bone. They were sensual and endearing, not rough or greedy like usual. I thought for a moment. "Just you. I want you."

"Just me?"

"Just you."

"Then can you promise me something?"

I leaned back to look the man in the eye. His question was a trick, I knew, but could I resist? "Promise you what…?"

"That you won't get me a gift."

I gave him an incredulous glare. "No gift? You've finally realized that your parents spoiled you rotten enough as a kid?" Kai only snickered and nodded. "Sure, if that's how you want to look at it. Just… please, don't get me a gift. I'm serious." His hopeful smirk

ANGEL

was another that could cure any disease. "So what are you getting me if I'm not allowed to get you anything?" I asked. "I'd give you my entire life, but I'll keep on giving after that, if that's what you'd like." I kissed his lips before my lips fell to burn a little soft trail across his cheek. Against his skin, I whispered, "I love you, Kaia Arche." I was satisfied with the answer I got—for now.

"I love you, too, Lucika Roggy."

....

Our bags were packed and we were almost prepared for the snowy alps of Switzerland. My birthday was today, or it would be 'today' when we arrived at our Christmas destination, and Kai had greeted me that morning with a platter of eggs and pancakes. They had probably been cooked by Rosa, since the meal was edible. "Are you sure we don't need to take our passports with us?" I asked as Mason drove us to the airport. Kai nodded. "It's all taken care of. All we need to do is relax." I huffed and deflated back into the soft leather seat. "A-And you're sure that everyone wants to spend Christmas with me?" He sighed and pinched the bridge of his nose as Mason caught my eye in the rearview mirror. "Luka, Kai's family likes you. A lot. I would be scared to be there if I were you. I bet Zach two-hundred bucks that someone will buy you a box of condoms. But... that's because they love you." He flashed a bright, pure smile as I rolled my eyes. I groaned and Kai glared at him. "We don't need condoms," he growled under his breath. I choked on saliva. "You both are freaking killing me," I exclaimed. They both smirked; the car fell quiet. Never silent, though. Mason's fingers tapped against the steering wheel. Kai hummed lowly, an incredibly soft version of one of his favourite headbanger tunes. As we pulled onto the pavement, I realized that the jet that Kai, his family, and his father's business partners had been using for the last few years was an incredible size. Mason motioned us out of the car with a grunt, knowing that he would be the one to grab our bags. That was what Kai was allowing him to live at the apartment rent-free for, after all.

The plane was spacious enough for a ring of recliners and couches in the back, the Gulfstream G280 named *The Tardigrade* was a beautiful aircraft with leather seats and hardwood accents. Towards the doorway sat a small table, two leather-bound chairs, a sofa, and-... I looked to Kai slowly.

"Really?"

He shrugged and set his duffle in the closest chair. "What? I promise it was there before I even *met* you."

My gaze travelled back to the white, forty-five millimetre dancing pole erected in front of the couch. "Take a seat, Luka. We'll be taking off soon," he said. He then left me to stand in his jet, in awe of his father's money. "Have fun at his house, Luka. It's pretty neat up there in the mountains," Mason popped his head inside the door. His smile was wide beneath his reflective sunglasses. "Um... well, you have fun, too, I guess. Take care of my mom, okay? She works too hard."

"Don't sweat it. She'll be fine," he replied. There was an extra layer of reassurance in his tone, a sincerity that was rare for him. "Thanks, Mason." Kai appeared to push his friend away from the doorway. After a few mumbled words to each other, they turned away and Mason disappeared. "You ready?" he asked.

"I've never been in a plane before, so... I guess?"

"It'll be fine. I-," but he was interrupted by a man who entered the plane, dressed in a crisp uniform and a sharp, comforting smile. Kai immediately stood to shake the man's hand. "Mr. Arche. It's a pleasure." Kai nodded. "Likewise. You're ready to take off?" I assumed he was the pilot, either him or the shorter, younger male who slipped into the cockpit behind them. "Yep. As always, take off can be a little rough, and the plan is to land in Interlaken, correct?"

"Yes. Thank you, Ben."

The pilot tilted his head respectfully to the both of us before strolling inside and closing the door to the cabin. "He's the pilot?" I asked as I stuffed my hands uncomfortably under my thighs. "Yeah. He's been working for Dad for almost five years now."

"That's a long time. I guess he uses this plane a lot, huh?" Kaia shrugged and shook his head. "Not particularly. But it's almost a twelve hour flight, so this is home for a while." I smiled stiffly and gripped the armrest much tighter than necessary as the engines revved and the plane jolted. I gripped the seat tightly as the wheels turned and we gained speed down the runway. Takeoff made my stomach drop and my teeth grind. Kai only watched me with an amused grin. Once we were actually flying, though, I felt better. It wasn't as rough as I thought it would be, and I was free to roam the cabin as I wished when turbulence wasn't an issue.

Kai grew bored quickly. A few hours after takeoff, Kai had begun some work on his laptop and I had completed a short nap. I rested my head against his hip, feeling the laptop adjust beside my hair when he typed.

I was bored, even with the music I had convinced him to play. The soft tunes hummed from speakers in the walls around us.

With a sigh, I stood and moved to the other end of the plane before grabbing my bathroom bag from one of the recliners. I rummaged through my belongings. Kai's curious gaze burnt holes in my shoulders. Inside the bag sat my necessities—a toothbrush, toothpaste, a little bit of shaving cream and a shaver—and some things that I thought we may-or-may-not need, like a box of condoms, the green dildo Kai gifted me, and, the item I desired in that moment, my cherry-red stilettos. Surely, Kai brought some toys of his own, so I probably didn't need to go overboard with those.

I slipped my shoes and socks off and put them on, smiling as they glittered in the bright sunlight that filtered through the plane's windows. With them, I trotted over to the pole and set a light hand on the cold metal. I executed an experimental circle around it. My actions had certainly caught Kai's attention. He stared up at me in shock.

"What? I'm just practicing some moves for later," I smirked. He raised a thick eyebrow as I did another twirl. My jeans and black quarter shirt were form-fitting, although I knew he preferred nudity; we both did, but he would have to wait for that. "Mhm," he hummed absently, watching my ass intently. "You brought toys, right?" I asked in a lusty hum. I dropped and stuck my ass out towards him while I licked my lips and batted my eyelashes. "I... I brought one or two... but I have toys there. Ones that I'm sure you'll love." Kai was mesmerized, his tone blank and distracted. The sharp bulge at his crotch was obvious and amusing. "Yeah?" I asked as I crossed the room and began a small strip-tease. I grabbed both sides of my shirt and whipped it over my head to land in a puddle beside me. I was half-nude and making extremely lewd expressions to the man gawking in front of me. My hands slid sensually up my sides, pushing at the thin layers of fat and the muscles underneath that pulled taut when I moved. When I was sure he was about to make a grab for me, I slid my fingers back to the hem of my jeans and toyed at the belt loops, dancing away from his touch.

He lunged forward to catch me in his tight, hungry embrace. I laughed and jumped away. His fingertips missed my ass by a centimetre. "Nah-ah, no touching." He could have made another try, but seemed to opt against it. He was having fun in the little game. "You got cuffs somewhere?" I breathed. He nodded toward a pocket on the side of his couch. "In there." I smirked and fished them from the cold leather before quickly strapping one around Kai's wrist. His eyes narrowed. The ones he had brought were dark leather, much more comfortable than the ones we had used in the past. "Can I?" I asked, my voice softening and my actions pausing. I hadn't even thought before dominating him. Was I allowed to do so? Maybe we could both find our inner switches for the day… He took a moment. Surely, it would bring memories. But I wasn't Cade, nor was I his and his wife's rapist. He knew that. Kai's jaw ticked.

"Okay," he whispered, gaze lowering. The man's reply seemed sincere.

My smirk returned, and in a blur I had his wrists hooked together behind his back.

CHAPTER
SIXTY-TWO

"I LIKE YOU IN chains," I told him while I stood to kick off my heels and push my jeans down my legs. They were discarded and forgotten in a second. "Really? You think you're cut out to be a dom, Angel?" Kaia was obviously trying to downplay his arousal. I breathed a chuckle while I put my heels back on my feet and returned to my post to straddle his hips, my arms around his neck and pulling at his hair. It was thick and soft, perfect.

"Maybe... we could switch for my birthday... why not take a peek at both sides of the spectrum?" I wiggled my eyebrows at him playfully. With a sigh, a smile, and a shake of his head, he burnt a trail of fresh slobbery spots up my neck. They gave new life to the yellowing ones that dotted my jugular. "We both know that you need someone to show you your place, Angel. What would you do without cuffs on your wrists or a paddle against that pretty little ass?"

His words sent chills through my spine. My groin grew tight; I stretched.

"Well, you obviously still have some submissive spirit in you. Big, tough man isn't so tough after all," I taunted in reply. His gaze darkened, telling me that I had successfully crossed lines. "How about you take these cuffs off and we can both see how loud I can make you scream."

ANGEL

I smirked. Neither of us wanted those cuffs off just yet, and we both knew it. "Please. You love this," I rolled my eyes. He laughed. "You're all talk, Luka. You'll never be able to live up to-," But I cut him off by stuffing a clean pair of my boxers into his mouth. His brows furrowed as his lips pulled above his teeth to sneer at me. I only cooed. "Aw... the big manly Dom can't talk anymore. Shame." Kai attempted to say something more, his eyes turning deadly, but all that reached my ears was a deep mumble. He knew what to do instead of saying his safe-word in this situation: I would routinely reach for his hands, and three short squeezes would mean a red signal. If his hands weren't cuffed behind his back, he would be able to hold up hand horns, a sign that held the same meaning. His mumble made me laugh, my nails digging into his shoulder as the other one palmed his erection through his pants. "You wait here—," I ordered, knowing he wouldn't be going anywhere, "—while I get the lube."

I found it in his bag, right beside a small paddle and a butt plug. Good choices, Kai. When I returned to him, he was subconsciously pulling at the handcuffs. So, with one hand on his shoulder and the other one shoving my boxers down my sides, I distracted him by pouring a generous amount of lube onto my fingers. Then, once straddling his hips again, I took one to the base, gasping against Kai's forehead. To voice his arousal, he shoved his face against my neck and gave a warning growl.

He didn't scare me, though.

I was having fun. I felt so powerful.

"Aw, you wanna see me make myself come? Anything for you, *slave*."

Kai visibly shuddered and thrust his hips up to gain any kind of friction he could. His instincts were making him desperate. I had been there before too. I released a deep groan against his ear as I added a second finger, wincing at the burn and laughing at his reaction. I wasn't sure what I expected. I had always voiced my discomfort with loud whines and moans, but he was very quiet, almost as if he had done something similar before. Or a few times.

Kai hadn't ever bottomed with me before. He was a sucker for prostate play, sure, but it was easier to focus on the care of one bottom, not two at the same time. I felt as though there was more to his excuse, but always took his "no" as definite.

"Oh, hush. You can wait. You've done that this long, haven't you?"

The bloodthirsty glare he shot me was priceless.

As I unsheathed my erection and began jerking it gently, two of my fingers pumping me much that same, Kai watched with anger and lust.

"Aw... poor man. Can't have his Angel like he wants."

....

"Wow," I breathed as I stepped off the plane, pulling my jacket tighter around my body to protect against the cold. Kai had made sure to have me dressed for winter weather, from my ski jacket to water-proof snow pants. I was tired after the long flight, but my excitement compensated. Kai wrapped his arm around my waist and pulled us toward the car that awaited our arrival on the tarmac. "Welcome to Switzerland, Mr. Arche," a man welcomed in a thick accent, holding the driver's door open as another man opened the passenger door. I slid into the car. The door was closed with a soft click. Soon, Kai was by my side inside the luxurious vehicle. I couldn't restrain the small giggle of excitement that blew past my lips when I stared up at the mountains.

The weather was cold, freezing, but that didn't impact the view. The breathtaking Swiss mountain ranges grew high above the town like snow-covered walls. The icy substance was everywhere.

ANGEL

It glittered like water in the bright sunlight, yet it didn't seem to be melting. "As pretty as you imagined it?" he asked after a moment. I licked my lips eagerly and shook my head. "Prettier." He seemed satisfied with my answer, and once the trunk had been filled with our bags and slammed shut, we were off.

Trees blanketed in snow sped past us in a blur as he drove us into the mountains on fading roads. "How far is it?" We were driving uphill... and hopefully to a place where we wouldn't be close to too many people. I was sure we would have our privacy since very few cars had passed us. "Not far, but once the car can't drive any further, we'll have to walk the rest of the way," he replied. I nodded and stayed silent for the rest of the drive. It wasn't uncomfortable, though. There was nothing needed to be said. We were both looking forward to our time together, and to be completely honest, I wanted to cry with joy. There would be no more maids or idiot best friends, or even doormen who wouldn't look up from their newspaper if you asked them to. The things Kai and I could get up to... my imagination was endless. Hiking, drying out in front of a fireplace after a snow day, sex until even Kai was spent, until neither of us could walk. We could listen to the wind blow and the snow fall while we came down from our highs...

"Well... I guess that's it," Kai said suddenly, pulling me from my daydream when the vehicle came to a stop. "Do we walk now?" I asked. I would have been lost by then. The road had disappeared and only snowy tire tracks remained. We were at a much higher altitude and it was even colder up there, if that was possible.

"Yep. It's a good thirty-minute walk to the house. I would carry you and the bags if I could, but...," he trailed off with a gleeful smile. I laughed and stepped out of the car. "Lets just go. I'm freezing." He smirked warmly and assisted with our bags before we set out towards his hideaway. We were heading towards the sun, which was just rising over the mountains, and I couldn't help but pause and adore it's beauty and the snow for a moment longer.

By the end of our small trip, I decided that Kaia was right. It was a very long hike to his second home, but was absolutely worth it, not only because of the stunning view he had over a gully between a few ranges, but also because of the home itself: two bedrooms, one-and-a-half bathrooms, no neighbors, and nearly one-point-five-million American dollars was all it took to build this private escape for a small family.

What a fucking birthday gift the place must have been.

I didn't enjoy too much at one time. Instead, I opted to take a rest and relax. My feet, sore and on the verge of blistering, begged me to remove my boots, and a shower didn't sound horrible at the time. "I'll be in in a little bit. Sleep for a while. Bedroom is on the right at the top of the stairs," Kai said quietly. I left him with a kiss and an adoring smile. Still, I found myself staring at the house.

As promised, at the top of the dark, elegant stairway, his bedroom welcomed me with open arms. I wouldn't even have to leave the bed, I decided. I would have everything I needed right there with the towel warmer in the corner and downy-feather comforter. Well, it was rather empty without him. The vacation house was built for more than one vacationer.

I woke around noon to the smell of meat frying in the kitchen. Kai's family had been there many times before, though. I could smell them, Kai's scent, in the sheets, stale and dusty, but embedded in the fibres. Bacon *and* Kai? I was in a dream.

I decided to take a quick shower and brush my teeth before I nearly slipped on my way back down the stairs and met him in front of the stove. His kitchen wasn't as big as the one in L.A., but it was certainly prettier with the cold rock accents and pale browns against grey countertops. It was modern and comfortable. A little bit cold, maybe, but it matched the stunning scenery outside perfectly. "Good afternoon," he smiled when I leaned my head against his shoulder. "Mhm... did I sleep for a long time?" I asked him. He chuckled and shook his head. "It's only five in the afternoon. You gave me plenty of time to complete a workout and take a nap." I jumped and gasped. "I slept for nine hours?!" Kai only nodded and laughed. "Dinner is almost ready. You're okay with bacon and scrambled eggs, right?"

"Wow, bacon, too? You should get a job with James for that. You're moving up the chef's pole one food at a time," I replied with a snort of laughter. Kai rolled his eyes and passed me a plate. "I don't know how the bacon will work out, by the way. The microwave wasn't cooking it very well, so I decided to fry it like Rosa does."

"Good choice." My laughter could be heard from the other side of the wall dividing the dining room and kitchen. Kai put my meal on the table before running back to the kitchen to grab one of his shakes. "Kennith was wondering how you're doing," he began once he had taken a seat across from me. I watched him fold his arms on the table, smiling around a bite of bacon. I pulled my foot up onto the wooden chair so I could wrap an arm around my knee. "Tell him I'm... doing okay. What's he doing these days?" Kaia shrugged. "Well, he takes a few classes, but he should be finished with that pretty soon. School never really worked out for him."

"Yeah. School can be tough, even when you're not blind. Kennith is straight, right?"

"Pan. Even though he acts like he'd be fine if the entire planet was destroyed by an asteroid tomorrow." My mouth formed into an 'O' shape as I nodded and shoveled eggs into my mouth. They were undercooked, but consuming them with the bacon helped with the gooey texture.

"I think maybe I should cook the meals while we're here."

"That bad, huh?" He wasn't offended, or I didn't think so, at least. He smiled at me guiltily. "No, no. It's not bad. But if I get salmonella I guess we know where I got it from." He erupted into laughter and shook his head. "Then you can definitely be the cook." For a few minutes, I allowed myself to sigh and stare out at the mountains. Kai did the same until we had both finished our food. I thanked him, of course, but he really could have done a better job. He cleaned our dishes and ordered me to familiarize myself with the house. Thankfully, it wasn't a huge residence.

The living room was large and cozy. Padded fabric seats kept us warm when we sat in them instead of leather. The fireplace against the wall wasn't lit, but I could imagine the bright warmth it would give off. Massive, floor-to-ceiling windows gave the viewer a stunning image of the snowy Alps. I could even see beneath the snow where it had been piled up against the window. Out back, accessible via the master bedroom or the kitchen, sat a massive, awe-inspiring hot tub that had been erected from a sleek, wooden deck and wrapped in a rock wall. An outdoor shower and wood benches sat beside it. The garage held two snowmobiles and a game room, complete with consoles and a pool table. The only thing left to see at the end of my trip was the door at the end of the hallway, the one that had been closed when we got here; it led to the basement, I assumed.

It opened to a staircase that went down. My assumptions were correct. I bit my lip and crept down the darkening steps. Once I had made it past the last step, I felt for the light switch, and the lights suddenly flipped on when I tapped it. They were dim and yellow, but they didn't remove from the room's beauty. A storage room of sorts, yet it was obviously a former living space. An antique fireplace sat in the corner, covered with items like empty photo frames and discarded papers. A box of toys and plushies sat in the corner.

ANGEL

Maybe Kai's when he was a child? Maybe... Cherry's?

There were boxes for paperwork and others for aged stuffed animals. A little box of sex toys sat at my feet beside the bright, expensive carpet. There wasn't any dust on that box. After deciding that my curiosity had been piqued, I crossed the room to the large frames that had been leaning against the wall, their images hidden behind mounds of dust and other photos. They stank like old memories and moths, but the scent was almost comforting. They weren't paintings. They were actually framed photographs, some almost as tall as myself. I flipped over a picture of Kai, his mother, and his father. There was one taken at his high school graduation. Kai was young then; he had a youth in his eyes. In the next photo, Kaia stood beside Mason in a bar, accompanied by erotic dancers. The lights made their angles exaggerated and their high spirits evident. I glared at Caden's face that hovered in the corner, watching the pair with what looked like a frown. I tried to decide if he was envious or loathing. Kai's gaze, although only slightly dilated with his alcohol intake and bright with his happy haze, was haunted. The photo was probably taken during the years he was with Caden.

The thought made me shiver.

Another frame held a photo of his siblings and him. Even Kennith was smiling a little. Maybe it was a Christmas or a family get-together? They didn't look *young*, but they were at least a few years younger. It made butterflies grow in my stomach, fluttering happily in my intestines. It was so... innocent. They looked happy. Like the perfect family. They all belonged together.

My brows furrowed when I found another one, having to pull it out from behind a pile of empty ones. It was as if this one had been hidden on purpose. It was a photo of Kaia and a beautiful girl. They were no older than seventeen, maybe fifteen. I instantly envied her beauty. She was too young to be the family's maid, and she wasn't a male, so it probably wasn't a partner. It dawned on me then that the girl was probably a photo of Kaia and Her. Cherry.

She was just as stunning as Kai. Long, wispy, black hair that fell to her thin waist and a smile that revealed pearl-white teeth. Cherry had large eyes and a narrow face. Her skin tone was dark, darker than Kai's, darker than Aja's. It was one of the darkest I had seen in a long time, even with L.A.'s diversity. The glints in their eyes were identical, joyful.

Maybe it had been taken at a party. The lighting was horrible and their faces were only lit by the flash of the camera, but I had never seen such a wide smile on my man. His arm was around her shoulder while she had hers around his waist, holding each other close. They looked like best friends; I finally understood what Kai meant when he said he was a different person before his life crumbled.

CHAPTER
SIXTY-THREE

"LUKA!" KAI CALLED from the kitchen. I nearly dropped the picture. "Coming!" I called back as I hurried to hide the picture and leave it as I found it. The image didn't leave me when I turned to dart up the stairs. I wasn't sure why I felt so guilty for finding it. I felt as if I was intruding on something, like I was suddenly crossing lines that shouldn't be crossed. Kai wouldn't want me to find it, I was sure. He didn't want to see those memories again. The pain would be overwhelming.

"Did you find my toy bin down there?" he asked once I had joined him in the living room. He relaxed on the sofa with a book in his lap and a steaming mug of hot chocolate beside him.

"Toy bin?" Dildos or plushies?

He chuckled and motioned me onto the couch with him. With a small smile, knowing the coast was finally clear and the subject had changed, I crossed the room and sat to straddle his stomach. "What are you reading?" I asked softly. There was no deviancy in my actions. No friction, no lewd expressions. I let my legs intertwine with his as I leaned down and pressed my ear to his chest just above his heart. It beat under my eardrum like a wild animal in a cage of bone. The slow rise and fall of his chest only added to the experience. "I don't really know. Rosa recommended it for Mason and I.

It's another cliche romance with some submissive and Dominant action, I guess. I kinda hate it. Mason barely made it to the second paragraph, but we both know that he can't read anyway."

I giggled and set my chin in the dip between his pecs. "So... about that submissive and Dominant action...."

He raised an eyebrow as one of his fingers drew an invisible line up my spine and back down to my tailbone. "I don't think we need the toy box. I have plenty in the bedroom," he told me gently. Our lips were close, so I didn't see any reason not to smash them together in that same moment. He smelt like coffee, bitter and tangy. The scent clouded my mind and made me thirsty for only one thing: Kai. His tongue did an infinitesimal dance against my bottom lip before I granted him access and he slipped between the gates.

"Wanna... do a... scene," I breathed around his tongue and the onslaught of kisses. Kai stood with my legs wrapped around his waist and my arms gripping his neck while he gave a low hum of approval. My mind was spinning. If it wasn't for my aching erection and hard muscles under my hands, I would have been completely lost in his scalding breath and intoxicating scent. I was dropped onto the bed and the sheets puffed up around me, giving Kai a moment to pull his t-shirt over his head. The lonely moment was short-lived because he didn't waste any time sliding my pants off my hips and down to my ankles. I kicked them off eagerly as he leaned back down to push our bodies together. "I want to do a tough scene, Angel," Kai told me in a low voice as he ground our cocks together through layers of blue jeans and boxers. "Can you do that?" He stopped moving. I placed a row of kisses along his jaw and gave a shaky breath, my spinning mind slowing to a halt. "Yes." He smiled and reached under my shirt to pinch at my nipples, rolling the stiff buds between his fingers and pulling on the piercings as he explored my mouth with his tongue. Eventually, I managed to remove my shirt altogether.

ANGEL

My back arched over the bed and my lungs grew hungry for new air when the sensations reached my brain and groin, making my mind turn to jello and my ears ring. He met my dazed gaze with his own. I was sure I looked like I had already been fucked into the sheets, my hair a mess, my cheeks glowing a deep pink, my chest heaving, and my eyes at half-mast with lust.

"Happy birthday, Luka," he breathed.

"Thank you," I whispered a reply.

With that, he reached under the bed to return with a spread bar. My excitement skyrocketed.

"Remember your safe-words tonight, Angel. You might need them... even hand horns if you need them," Kai warned as he removed my boxers and attached the spread bar's straps to my knees. We had talked about alternate safe-words before. We knew what we could use them if we needed to, especially with new scenes that could be tenser than others. When they were mentioned before a scene, I knew he had a kind of breath play in mind. Normally, it was safest to talk about the scene before anyone actually did anything, but we had done things like this before, I trusted him enough to know where my limit was, and he walked me through his work. He knew my hard limits. He knew what I could handle better than even I could. Once he had completed his first task, he moved on to my wrists, which he chained to the headboard with dark leather straps. I was exposed to him then, but he didn't give me time to absorb the sensation before he bowed his head to suck my left nipple between his lips. His tongue was rough on my sensitive flesh, scraping painfully. "Kai!" I moaned, my eyes closing and my teeth clamping over my bottom lip. He moved onto my right one as his hand pushed at the other lonely, pulsing bud. He sent bolts of pleasure straight to my groin with only a few, rough swipes of his tongue, let alone rolling them between his teeth and pushing them in against the metal. They were swollen and red, and I was writhing by the time he decided I had had enough.

"Tonight is about you. And you'll be able to come whenever you like...understand, Angel?"

His mouth had moved on to create a line of spots to my navel, sending my nerves into a whirlwind of over-sensitivity. My stomach quivered violently under his lips. "O-...Okay," I breathed. My eyelids fluttered and my back arched when he took my length into his mouth. I was suddenly surrounded by a wet, burning tongue and plush cheeks. He took me to the back of his throat without gagging. I was surprised to finally see his trained submissive side showing through, because I wasn't *that* small.

Soft moans and whines left my throat when a disgustingly cold object found my entrance. I felt liquid being squeezed into me, and I gasped. "It's f-freezing!" I exclaimed as my hands fisted and tore at the metal bed frame. He simply hummed, his mouth vibrating around my cock and adding to my elation. I felt the movement all the way to my eyes, where they jerked and closed. Soon, his fingers replaced the object—which I now assumed was a bottle of lube—and he curled them up towards my prostate immediately after that initial sting upon entry. My orgasm hit me harder than a freight train. My muscles spasmed and tensed as my toes curled and short moans and yelps fell from my dry lips. I licked them when my orgasm was through and the spinning had stopped. Thank god we didn't have neighbors, because they would undoubtedly have had people knocking on our front door.

But Kai continued after he had swallowed the last of my seed. I began to whimper, attempting to close my legs against the over-stimulation. He would have planned it beforehand; I should have guessed he had ill intentions. That was why he applied the spread bar. "K-Kai... no," I cried. It hurt so bad, yet I could feel another

ANGEL

climax approaching. It wasn't quick or blissful, it was slow and agonizing. I knew the safe-words, but did I really want to use them? That tiny scrap of pleasure, the invisible string that was dragging me to a new release was the only thing stopping me from whimpering 'yellow'. That would end the stimulation and possibly scare Kai away. If I couldn't handle this, then how was I supposed to withstand the rest of the scene?

But that was all before my mind had totally succumbed to his mouth. It blew me away like a tsunami, washing all thoughts into oblivion. Maybe it lasted a second. It felt like a good minute, but once my climax was through, I was spent. Thankfully, Kai stopped to give me air that time. "Good boy, Angel," he cooed gently. My eyes fluttered open at his words, and I was met with his gorgeous face hovering above mine. I gave a spaced-out, lopsided smile. "Can I suck you off?" I croaked.

He scoffed and kissed my forehead. "You've done well so far. I'm going to let you rest for-," but I cut him off. "Please?"

He hesitated with a confused frown. The cuffs were removed from the bed frame but reattached to my wrist when they rested on my belly.

"After all, Kai... a sub's greatest pleasure is pleasing their master...." I may have been exhausted, but knowing Kai had yet to get off would keep me awake all night. He was considering it, I could tell, with the way his brows created a sort of ditch down the center of his forehead. But, instead of finally approving, he flipped me onto my stomach, my knees bent and my ass exposed in the air. I yelped and struggled for only a moment before his fingers were at my entrance again, teasing and stretching it while he wrapped a firm hand around my erection. I whimpered. "I-I'm not ready... I need a few-," my objection ended in a soft moan as he pumped me slowly. His index finger pushed at my sensitive head, eliciting loud moans and panting from deep within my chest as it rose and fell erratically. He then rolled me onto my back and hovered over me with a mischievous glint in his eyes. Maybe I should have been scared of that...

The tip of the urethral plug was already half an inch inside me before I began to jolt and cry out. It was bigger than last time and ribbed.

"Sh... it's just like last time."

I quieted down after that, or at least until he began moving it again. He went slowly; Kai was trying to make it hurt more, draw it out. The way he was stroking me wasn't helping in the least. Overstimulated and having an object shoved up my dick was not the way I imagined my night to go. But maybe, in just a tiny little part of my mind, it was exactly how I wanted it to go. I couldn't come from it, though, could I? How does one come without the ability to ejaculate?

Kaia stopped eventually, though. He wasn't done; there were still a few inches left of the metal. A package opening drew my attention away from my discomfort.

"Kai...," I sobbed.

The object inside me had sunk and finally reached a point where it could go no further. My throat closed and my hips arched above the bed as he peppered kisses up my trembling thighs. Eventually, he engulfed my erection and bit the head lightly. My orgasm, which had been summoned by my desperation and pain, was overwhelming. "Just one or two more, Angel, you're doing so good. My angel." His words barely made it past my eardrums. Kai leaned across my chest with a hand that blocked the light. I expected him to grab my hair, but instead, his fingers wrapped around my throat.

My eyes opened wide. Then they landed on Kai. Then they rolled back.

The man choked me hard. With the hands on me and the

throbbing sting of the plug, my world was truly feeling like an acid trip. His thumb and forefinger put heavy pressure on my carotid artery, pressing just below my jaw with a kind of animalistic strength I hadn't seen in Kai in a long time. My hands shot up to wrap around his wrist.

If I thought the haze couldn't consume me further, I was very wrong. This time, my brain turned to a kind of black hole I would never be able to escape. The extra pressure added to my airway made my lungs burn. My hands around his arm lost their strength.

I was slipping. The next unexpected orgasm—if I could call it that—came slow and heavy. It made my lungs close up and my eyes open to the size of saucers as I seized on the bed. Colours and white noises surrounded me; sounds like crinkling sheets against my ear and my cries that sounded as if they were miles away. I was in magnificent, blissful agony, and Kai refused to let me rest until it was over. His hand didn't stop moving. They pumped and fingered me while he watched my face contort in torment. His other hand continued to apply pressure to my carotid. I was sure I would pass out any second.

Finally, once those minutes were over, I had nothing left. My body trembled after Kai pulled the plug and his hand away, strings of liquid oozing with it and running onto the bed. He released my wrists. I rolled to the side, my mind blank. No thoughts, worries, or pain bogged my mind. It was simply the feeling of floating, like I was high off sex. I couldn't feel Kai moving around me. I barely felt him pull me against his chest once he had removed the spread bar. Kai was speaking. He was mumbling short words, but they fell on deaf ears. My vision blurred and focused repeatedly when I had them open. When I closed them, I felt as if I had entered a different dimension, a world full of colour and silence, like a soundless movie.

After a moment, though, I felt sick. I was about to puke.

"Kai," I gave a low, painful moan as I curled my knees toward my chest and stuffed my head between them in an attempt to stop my spinning vision and scrambled thoughts. Words were finally beginning to break through the haze, disconnected, but they were words. It was Kai creating them, which helped me back to reality.

"Luka...relax... sh."

Only two words were comprehensible.

"My Angel."

I began to cry.

It wasn't just a few tears or a whimper. I began to sob, unable to stop the sudden, wild flow of water from my eyes. The utter depression hit me just as hard as my first climax had. My confusion and fear added to the dizzying emotions, and before I knew it, I was having a full-on breakdown. "Sh, Angel," Kai soothed. His voice was clearer then. We weren't underwater anymore. "It's okay. You'll be fine. Breathe." I did as he ordered, but once I had gotten my first gasp of air, my lungs ached for more. I began hyperventilating through my sobs, fueled by the burn in my crotch and sudden release from the awesome torture. At least I had Kai to cry against. My nails dug into his shoulder. He was obviously fighting the pain to comfort me. Kai held me, pulling my head into his chest. "It'll get easier in a moment. Just breathe. In for four, out for four." He exaggerated his movements and I was eventually able to copy them with only a little bit of difficulty.

"That was...," I sniffed and whimpered finally, "...really horrible and amazing and scary."

He smiled proudly. "It was goddamn beautiful." I was exhausted by the time our session was over, barely able to keep my eyes open. My body began to deflate after its breakdown. Sometimes, these emotions, what I knew as subspace, could last for far longer than a night, and I hoped that I would be able to keep myself occupied

ANGEL

while my brain balanced back out. "Don't sleep yet, Angel," Kai whispered as he jostled me slightly. My entire body was sore and tired. "Let me give you a bath first." I nodded and felt him lift me against his chest. He carried me to the bathroom where he set me on the closed toilet lid and turned on the water. It would take a few minutes for the soaking tub to fill. "Just stay awake for a little while. I know you're tired. But youre okay, right?" He squatted in front of me. I didn't fail to notice the large, wet patch at the front of his jeans. "Yes. I'm okay. D-Did you...?" He glanced down. A small blush lit up his features. "Yeah... I kinda did. I'll change them after your bath." I closed my eyes and nodded with a drowsy smile as my hands supported my upper body. The urge to cry was strong again. "Wanna sleep," I mumbled. Normally, sex didn't exhaust me *this* bad, but this really wasn't just normal sex, was it?

"You can sleep in the tub. Just let me get you there first."

My smile turned upside-down.

Once Kai had finished pouring bubbles and scents into the tub, he added me, and I shrank against the side of it like some kind of subspace sea creature. "That's better," Kai hummed. His fingers were then in my hair, massaging shampoo deep into the strands. Neither of us were surprised when my eyes closed and I began to drift.

CHAPTER
SIXTY-FOUR

I WASN'T SURE WHAT woke me that night. With our scene earlier, I expected to sleep for at least a day, but it only took me a moment of grimacing into my pillow to realize that Kai wasn't beside me. Had he already gotten up? What time was it? The glowing clock beside the bed read one-thirty. Why was he awake so early? Shuffling footsteps from the kitchen drew me from the bed. My muscles, still tight and sore, made my bones crack under the pressure. I grimaced at the noise. I only paused long enough to pull a pair of sweatpants over myself before making my way with haste out to the main living space. It was surprising how much light there was when the city couldn't offer it. The snow reflected the moon above us, too, making it almost seem like morning instead of the middle of the night. "Kai?" I whispered to the shadow that stood on the other side of the kitchen counter. He was only dressed in pyjama pants and a tank-top. "It's the middle of the night. What are you doing?"

But there was no reply. The man, who could clearly hear me, seemed to be ignoring me. "Kai," I groaned, crossing the room. Before I could grab his arm, though, he turned around to me with furrowed brows. "Why is... what are you doing with all that?" he asked. I froze in confusion. "...huh?" Kai looked around the room

ANGEL

with glazed eyes. "What are you going to do with all your...." he broke off into unintelligible mumbling. I only sighed and reached out to grab his hand.

Kai was sleepwalking.

"Come on, big guy, come back to be-," when my fingers made contact with his skin, the man immediately jumped and slapped it away as if I had burnt him. Something in his eyes changed then. He was scared and confused, and something in his gaze seemed as though he was torn between two ideas. My own eyes widened up at him, my heart rate picking up speed. The last of my drowsiness had disappeared in a second.

I watched, frozen, as he brought trembling fists to his face as if he was unable to uncurl his fingers.

If it was a night terror, he probably would have been quite a bit more agitated. Mason had told me once that he could usually get Kai back to bed easily during one of his sleepwalking episodes. Nightmares, not so much. If only he had told me *how* he got Kai back to bed. Leading him didn't seem to be working. Kai let out a half-mumble, half-moan as his body twitched. Clearly, he still wasn't awake. Was it safe to wake him up? Would loud noises do the trick?

"Kai?" I said quietly. Maybe I could talk him into going back to bed?

"No. I don't want it."

"Kai, let's go back to bed. Come on."

"I don't wanna sleep with your caterpillar legs."

His declaration had me giggling. It was mumble, and I wasn't sure if I had heard him right, but his sincerity was hilarious. "That's-," I laughed, smothering the noise with my hand, "-That's okay. You don't have to sleep with my caterpillar legs." That seemed to calm him considerably, because his hands no longer shielded his face. Instead, he pulled them against his chest and continued to curl and uncurl his fists. "Can I touch your hand?" I asked. He didn't reply, so I tried reaching for him again. That time, he grabbed onto it, his breathing slowing to match mine.

But, of course, when I began walking, he didn't like it very much. He gave a whimper and dropped my hand to put his hands back against his face and mumble unknown words to himself. He hadn't liked the movement at all. *You took one damn step. Come on.*

I sighed. It was going to be a long night.

....

The second time I woke, it was to the sounds of scratching.

"Cut it out, Kai," I mumbled into my pillow. I did not have that patience to do this again. Not after last night. As much as I loved the man, he certainly knew how to keep others awake. I was met by more scratching and another noise that was equally annoying: Kai's soft snores echoing in the room. My curious eyes were pried open slowly, and I glimpsed, through layers of lashes and sleepy residue, a lynx that had dug a large hole in the snow beside our floor-to-ceiling windows that made up one wall of the bedroom. "There's a cat at the window for you," I mumbled, already half asleep. "Mm...?" Kai groaned in response, his deep rumble vibrating my shoulder that touched his.

"He's asking for you. Leaving holes... by our window." By the time my sentence, a mixture of humor and exhaustion, was finished, I was asleep again.

"Tell him to leave," Kai grumbled into his blankets.

He was asleep then too. I didn't wake up for another hour, and when I did, Kai had turned me into a burrito, wrapped in arms, legs, and blankets. He snored in my ear, and I grimaced.

"Damn sack of potatoes... you're crushing me."

He didn't move, so I pushed his shoulders away from my chest

ANGEL

and sat up, stretching my arms out with a yawn. He mumbled an incoherent sentence and pulled my pillow against his chest instead. "I'm gonna make breakfast," I told him before giving him a peck on his cheek and moving to the bathroom to complete my morning duties like brushing my teeth and washing my face. That morning, when I stared in the mirror, I nearly jumped. A wild beast stared back at me, waves of hair matted up and down and sideways—it was a mess. I touched my hair. It snapped back up when I tried to brush the left side of it down. So, instead of running to Kai and asking him to give me a haircut that minute, I grabbed one of Kai's hair elastics from his bathroom bag sitting next to his sink and pulled my hair into a loose ponytail. It helped, although I knew that it wouldn't stay for long. I added a *Megadeth* t-shirt I had stolen from Kai's collection to my outfit.

It was Christmas morning, so why not go all out? I began to prepare an egg breakfast for Kai and I. Bacon was thrown over a skillet before I searched the fridge for eggs. Once they were frying, I made my way back to the bedroom. "Are you hungry?" I asked softly, taking a seat beside him and folding my legs under me. "Mm...," he replied groggily. I giggled and kissed his rosy lips. The action at least got his eyes open and a smile on his face. "Merry Christmas," he whispered. I gave him a toothy, bright smile. "I didn't know if you wanted eggs again. They're fried today."

Kaia sat up. "Can't go wrong with eggs, I guess." I nodded and leaned forward to kiss his cheek before standing to dart to the kitchen and save my bacon. It wasn't burnt, but it was close. "I have a present for you," he said, slowly following behind me and wrapping his arms around my waist. "Eat breakfast and then we can go to the living room." He smelt like coffee in the morning. It reminded me to turn on the coffee pot for myself. "Jesus, I could get used to this," he hummed against my ear. He began gyrating his crotch against the cleft of my ass, and I rolled my eyes as he bit down lightly on my neck. I wouldn't be ready to go again for weeks. He expected me to repeat last night after only a few hours of rest? "I'll be there. Go take a cold shower or something, you monster." He left me alone to finish his shake with a chuckle while I fried my eggs and pushed them onto a plate. I really wasn't all that hungry in the mornings, but, that day, I felt as if I could eat enough for an army. Maybe it was the lack of sleep. As I shovelled food onto a second plate, my thoughts began to drift to last night. I didn't remember a lot. I was too tired and aroused to put anything in memory. But I remembered the time before my high. The immense gratification, Kai's hands seeming to be on every part of my body at once. *Stop thinking about it. You're gonna want to do it again.*

"Just gimme a second," I hollered when the shower cut off and the towel rack banged against the wall. Kai replied with a loud hum before I slid the extra dishes into the sink and moved our breakfast into the living room where Kai had his feet up on the soft ottoman. His hair was still sopping wet.

There really were very few gifts I could give a man who had everything. That's why I was grateful that he had made me promise not to get him anything. "Merry Christmas," I said as I leapt onto the couch beside him. I handed him his shake and took a bite of over-easy egg. He chuckled and put an arm around my shoulders after snatching a piece of bacon from my plate and setting it on the arrest for later. "Merry Christmas, baby."

After we both took a few moments to eat and drink in silence, he reached to the floor beside the couch to grab my Christmas present: a sleek, black rectangular box with the name *'Luka'* printed on the corner of the lid in white letters.

"Open it... then I'll explain what it means." He handed it to me and I set it on my lap while he repositioned himself to face me.

ANGEL

My plate was forgotten on the coffee table. "Should I be scared?" I joked nervously.

"I don't want you to be."

My throat began to close with nerves instead of excitement, so I took a deep breath and mustered the courage to take the lid off the box. Kaia wasn't the kind of person to buy me a thoughtless gadget for Christmas. He would buy me something that would stick with me for the rest of my life. I wasn't sure what it was at first. It was wrapped in a thick layer of textured, expensive paper.

When my fingers finally found cold leather, I sucked my lip between my teeth. It was a collar, a beautiful one. A thin, rich brown leather band connected at each end by a short chain and lock with tiny metal rings, probably to tie restraints to, hung under the silver plaque that was nailed across the front, displaying a few cursive words: *'Owned and cherished by Kaia Arche'*

"Luka," Kai began slowly. I ran my fingers over the small words with wide eyes. Underneath the collar sat a folded leather leash to match. "This is a permanent collar." I met his gaze slowly, but I was unable to decipher his emotions. "Like... like forever?"

"As long as you have this collar on your neck, you will belong to me. Every part of you will be mine, and every part of me will be yours."

I released a shaky breath as my mind raced. It was the real deal. The collar was us forever. I instantly, without another thought, unhooked the lock, but Kai was quick to put a hand over mine. "Lucika, I need you to understand what this means." I didn't meet his gaze, as mine was fixed on the words over the front of the collar.

"Look at me."

He brought a finger to my chin and dragged it up, forcing my gaze to make contact with his.

"This collar is like a marriage. It's *permanent*."

My breath hitched as my stomach lurched. I wanted it so, so bad. "That's why I'm not letting you put it on now. You need to think about the fact that you could be my sub for what could be the rest of your life, or until you decide you want it removed. This is what I know I want. But it's your decision."

"I don't need to think about this," I whispered. "I know what I want here."

Kaia smiled so wide, I worried that his lips would snap. "That's okay. I still want you to wait. Just for a day or two. Then, if you still want this with all your heart, you'll have it."

CHAPTER
SIXTY-FIVE

AFTER OUR CHRISTMAS morning, we were still pondering what to do for the day. Kai wanted to take a hike through the mountains. I wanted to stay home and use the hot tub. So, we set out for a walk, deciding that the hot tub would still be there when we got back. The snow was fucking deep. I sunk with each step, and Kai sunk even deeper when he stepped into a snowbank. I laughed and watched him sink to his waist, getting stuck in the fluffy ice. He gasped and huffed, trying to wrench himself away. But, instead of getting angry after he had given up, he grabbed my wrist and plunged me into the snow beside him headfirst. I shrieked and laughed, ice thrown up around us as we found our inner child once again.

Naturally, we ended up giving each other a blowjob before we both headed back to the house to get warm. Kai made me hot chocolate while he heated some milk for himself. I met him in the hot tub, surrounded by mounds of snow and a stunning view of the white mountains that rose to touch the sky.

"We leave for Canada tomorrow," he told me as he stripped and slipped into the tub beside me. Both of us were then nude and comfortable among the bubbles and jets. I had brought a speaker with me and turned it down low. The sound got lost with the whisper of the trees, but I could just barely hear the hum of a drum solo. "I'm excited," I said. "But I didn't get anyone a present for Christmas. I hope that's okay."

"Honestly, we don't even really get presents for each other anymore. We just do it for the kids." Kai set his arms up on the back rest. "How are Jeremy and Kara?" I asked, sipping my steaming drink. It burnt my lips. I threw back a handful of snow to ease the pain. "Good. Really good. Lily is pregnant again, actually. She called me a few days ago and told me. She's only told Kennith and myself. Gonna wait until the whole family is there to tell everyone else."

"What?! That's awesome," I said. "Yeah," he replied, "I'm happy for her."

Both of us stared at the bubbles. "My mom is gonna be really uncomfortable there. She isn't used to that many people. She isn't used to a family like that," I told him.

"I think she'll be okay. Mason'll be there."

"True, I guess. Is his daughter coming?"

"I hope. I think she would get along with Jeremy and Kara really well."

"Yeah. I'm sure she would too."

I watched Kai sink into the water, his nose coming to hover above the little churning waves. His eyes, reflecting the lights below us like stars, snapped up to meet mine. He had caught me staring, but I didn't look away. I wasn't ashamed. I smiled seductively. He raised an eyebrow. Kaia suddenly surged forward, throwing up a small wave, and stopped just so he could run his hand over my crotch and cage me against the pool wall. His hands didn't stop there. They trailed up against my stomach; I shivered in the scalding water. He pulled at one of my piercings. I gasped.

I didn't want to be under him, though. I really didn't care about myself; after last night, I wanted to pleasure him instead. So, I

ANGEL

grabbed both of his shoulders and flipped us so he could sit against the wall of the hot tub. The man didn't protest. "Ah... good boy," Kai whispered as I sucked his flesh between my teeth. I was too far in headspace to pause and let his words register in my mind. Intoxicated by his scent and soft caresses, I found myself aching to touch every piece of his skin. I whimpered and ground our cocks together eagerly, my legs straddling his hips and squeezing often as my fingers pulled at his hair and massaged over darkening marks.

"What is my family gonna think when I get there and my neck is purple?" I simply hummed and dug my nails into his shoulder, eliciting a sharp hiss from his clenched teeth. "Watch it, Angel."

"Want... the collar on," I moaned between kisses. It would make me *whole*. His eyes rolled back slightly and he smiled when I found a sensitive spot on his neck. "Not yet. Suck me off, hm?" I paused and glanced down at the bubbling water with hooded eyes. *Yes*. My lungs filled with a large breath of oxygen before I plunged my body below the waves. It was quiet down there. No birds chirped and the wind didn't carry any chill, almost as if I had entered another world.

I didn't want to open my eyes underwater. So, instead, I reached out for him, and found him nearly instantly. To be completely honest, it was kind of a turn-off. I couldn't even hear his moans. I ignored that fact, knowing he would be in ecstasy soon, and took his length into my waiting mouth, sucking hard on the head before pushing it against my throat. His muscles tensed under my hands in reply.

That fact that I couldn't breathe sat at the edge of my consciousness for a moment before I rose to the top and took a gulp of air. Meanwhile, my hands worked him quickly, and for a split second, I could hear him gasping too.

Under the surface, I licked a ring around the head and dug my tongue into the sensitive little entrance at the top. I felt him jump.

I smiled. Eventually, just as I was about to rise for air, he put both hands on each side of my head. I almost worried that he wouldn't allow me to breathe again; my heart skipped a beat. But he *did* let me up. His firm hands held me there when I was prepared to resubmerge; he demanded a kiss. I gave him one.

Kai pushed me back into the water suddenly. Almost half of my precious oxygen was gone by the time I found his erection again. His hands never left my head. The panic was overwhelming. He was going to force my head forward, I knew. He did. I choked. He came. I could feel his thighs tighten under my clenched fists as I coughed. My lungs, threatened by the water I just couldn't keep out, began frantically moving for air, drawing in more water in the process.

When his hands were suddenly gone, I shot up, splashing him with water and gasping and choking for oxygen. His aroused smile made everything worth my effort, though, even if I couldn't really see him through my tears. "Thank you, sir," I coughed, not able to decipher if the heat on my face was saliva, tears, water, semen, or blush.

"Are you okay? That was rough." Suddenly, he was caring and worried, rubbing a thumb over my cheek and placing endearing kisses on my face. I coughed again, sinking against his chest. I nodded.

....

"I'm cold," I whimpered pathetically. Kai chuckled and removed one of his jackets to hang it over my shoulders. He was then left with only a wool sweater and a thick, knit long-sleeved shirt. "Now you're cold." I whimpered. We had landed at the Yellowknife airport around six-o'clock at night on the twenty-sixth of December and we were wandering the ten-below streets of the town. "I'll be okay. Come on, we have to meet mom and dad for coffee." I smiled and

ANGEL

took his hand in mine as we walked towards a small cafe on the corner, surrounded on two sides by mounds of built-up snow.

Inside, our breaths no longer pooled in the air around us. It was warm, and it smelt like Kai in there. Coffee. It was sweet, too, like hot chocolate and fresh-baked pastries. The smells and sounds of grinding coffee beans welcomed us to remove our jackets and find comfort in the place. "Luka!" Aja's voice exclaimed from across the nearly empty cafe. A couple sat in the corner while Mason, my mother, Micheal, and Aja sat against the wall opposite them. The woman tackled me into a hug despite her petite traits. I could feel tough, rippling muscles under her maroon sweater. It was a deadly reminder of her black belt. "Hey, Aja," I smiled. The woman leaned back and took my face in her warm, soft hands. "You're glowing!" I giggled and shrugged sheepishly. "Likewise."

"Come on, boys, sit down!" Micheal called, waving us over. The three of us crossed the weathered, wooden floor. Kai and I pulled chairs up. I almost instantly found my mother's hand and squeezed it under the table. She smiled at me. It was genuine, and I was happy that she was comfortable. We grew comfortable. A few of us nursed drinks.

"So... have they caught Cade yet?" Aja asked gently. What a wonderful conversation starter.

Suddenly, going back home didn't sound like a bad option. Kai shook his head and gave his mother a warning glare before he realized I had been watching. His frown turned into a warm smile. My gaze fell to land on the coffee-stained napkin underneath my mother's cup of steaming black coffee. "Merry Christmas, by the way. I hope you guys enjoyed your boring, lonely, stupid alone time," Aja said. Her voice, although her words were snarky, was playful. Kaia smirked. "Why, thank you. I didn't have to work for the first time in my life, unlike *you.*" Aja and Micheal obviously didn't like the fact that they had very busy lives, especially with a teenage, blind son still living at home. But they liked their money too. They sat defeated, glaring half-heartedly at their son. "It was a fine vacation," I sighed, smiling at Kai's parents and leaning against his shoulder. We exchanged a glance. *Very fine indeed.*

Back at the house, after our small meeting over coffee, we met the rest of Kai's family at Lily's spacious home. Lily was just barely showing, and her kids were excited to have a baby sibling. Aja and Micheal were close to tears at the news, overjoyed for their adopted daughter. Kai was quiet, though. He tried to smile, I saw, but it was hard for him to think of his sister having a child when he surely wanted a child of his own one day. Not with me, necessarily, but he had missed out on a lot since his wife's untimely death. I made a mental note to ask him about it sometime; I didn't want him sad during our stay.

The sixteen of us spent the night chatting over a beautiful dinner and around the living room fireplace before we resigned to our bedrooms for the night. Couples were granted bedrooms while others shared couches and recliners. As eleven-o'clock came around and the stars glowed over the home, Kai and I sat across from each other in complete silence, no footsteps, no voices. There was only the sound of our breathing, muffled by a jet-lagged film that hung over our senses. The bedroom was dark, only lit by the moon that shone through the balcony doors, the same way the moon had glowed the night Cade had visited.

"Sometimes it's tradition to have family oversee the official collaring of a sub," Kai told me, his voice only a deep mumble. His long fingers found mine and linked them together beside the black box on the sheets between us. "I'm glad we aren't doing that," I replied quietly. "You're sure you want to do this? I'm not going to be upset. I need to understand that this is truly what you want."

ANGEL

I nodded slowly. How could I be so calm? I felt as if I had been drugged; my body and mind were totally at ease. I wanted to be with him forever. Was that what marriage felt like? I was ready. Over half a year ago, I never would have believed I would want to be collared, something even more personal than marriage, but it was true.

"This is what I want."

Kaia didn't seem to want to unhook our fingers. It took him a moment, but eventually, he broke the contact and replaced it with my collar. "You'll belong to me after this. And I'll belong to you." His voice was so soft, my heart seemed to lull to a stop. I only sat in silence, entranced as he gently unhooked the collar and placed it around my neck. The cold leather sent shivers down my spine when it touched my flesh, lighting a fire inside me.

My eyes closed. The collar snapped together and it was locked by a tiny metal key.

CHAPTER
SIXTY-SIX

WHEN MY EYES opened, I could only sit and silently absorb his expression. He was happy, proud. Kai's fingers lingered on the words on the front.

"It's beautiful. You're beautiful."

"I wanna do a scene... to... finalize this," I whispered as I wrapped my arms around his neck. I smelled him, his coffee and chocolate, for what felt like the first time. The collar made everything *different*.

His eyes darkened. "In a house full of people? That sounds... fun." I giggled as he swept me off the bed and onto my feet. "Just one last thing...," he said suddenly. I had forgotten about the leash that came with the collar.

Kaia pushed the clasp around the leather, binding me as his pet. A slave. Our expressions didn't change for a minute; I was smiling widely and his smirk was one of playful joy. But then his face shifted. His eyes darkened and he straightened to his full height to tower above me. As he curled the leash tight in his fist, he pulled it taut until his breath tickled my cheeks and he stared hungrily into my eyes.

"Pretty boy," Kai smirked. My mouth watered.

"On your knees."

Without any choice or urge to object, I sank to the floor,

face-to-face with his bulging crotch. There was a moment of silence between us as he seemed to study—no, admire me. His hand cupped my cheek, and, unable to resist, I pushed against it and closed my eyes. I decided that being in that bedroom, sitting at Kai's feet, pleasing him with a collar around my neck, was heaven. Still, he gripped my leash tight and ran his thumb over my eyebrow. "Open your mouth, Angel. Now," he ordered. Not such a romantic order, but his command sent sparks straight to my cock that strained against my dark boxers. Immediately, he began working his belt open and his fly down. He was almost fully-hard and creating a tiny wet patch against the front of his underwear. It made me happy to see that he was probably aroused even during my collaring.

It would never get old. Pleasuring a dom? My dom? It was like a drug. Like a funhouse, full of surprises around every corner. New, exciting, leather-wrapped surprises with vibrating dildos and chains. Then, when we were out of the bedroom, I could still be his to command and teach. He was a gentle, kind man, and I knew he would take care of me. Then, I could take care of him. The thought made me wonder what it would be like to have him lay down stricter rules and harsher punishments. What fun *that* would be, to be chained and fucked for an entire afternoon after mouthing off towards him.

"Good boy, Angel," Kai praised as I pulled his underwear down his hips. My eyes widened with excitement as his length stood out towards my nose, begging me to take it as deep as possible. So that's what I did. There was no foreplay or taunting, I simply swallowed him. Instantly, the thick vein on the underside of his cock protruded against my tongue while my nostrils were engulfed by his small bush of pubic hairs. Once he reached the back of my throat and released a loud gasp, I pulled back, still connected to him by a string of saliva and milky liquid. Daring to test his limits, I pushed back onto him, dragging my teeth across the head in the process. This elicited a loud hiss as he jolted. His right hand gripped my hair tight, and I would be lying if I said that the sharp pain didn't turn me on even more.

But it wasn't exactly what I wanted.

I bit down against his base, hard enough to make both him and his erection jump. "Luka," he growled, pulling my head back roughly until I whimpered. He was angry. The realization made me feel victorious. "On the bed," he ordered. I did as I was told, prepared to take any punishment he gave me.

"I'm in charge, Angel," he growled against my ear, his voice hot and sultry. Kai was behind me, running a heavy hand against my ass and pushing against the fatty parts. Meanwhile, his words drove icy needles down my spine, causing a shiver to run through my quivering body. "Yes, sir," I answered. *Just stick it in already. Please. I need it. Make it hurt. Make me beg.*

"That isn't a bad idea, is it?" Kaia hummed. My eyes opened wide when I realized I had voiced my own thoughts, confused by the heavy haze that blanketed my senses. "Close your eyes. I'm giving you a blindfold." After he had adhered the leather strap around my head, I whimpered and turned around to feel for him. I needed him, his smell, his contact, to catch his hand in mine, or, if I was really lucky, find his chest and be able to slide my fingers down towards the prize. Kai didn't object when I reached for him. I caught one of his hands—or I grabbed the hand that came to rest against the centre of my chest—and instantly sucked two fingers into my mouth until my sweet, glossy lips felt the bases. Back and forth, I drove my tongue under, over, and between the digits, feeling the indent of fingernails and the soft flesh of cuticles. The pink, meaty muscle formed to the shape of his body like modeling clay. As I was occupied, he gently prodded and rolled each of my nipples. But his fingers grew bored quickly, so, with his free hand, the tip of his

ANGEL

index finger began to whisper over my skin, from my shoulders, to my pelvis, to my knees.

But never the spot I needed him to touch most.

"Please," I muttered around his fingers.

"What was that, pet?"

"P-Please!" I pulled his fingers out of my mouth.

"Please what?"

He was taunting me with those narrowed, hungry, humored eyes and a tiny, devious smile. I could *hear* it. "P... Please-," but I let out a loud yelp of surprise when he slapped the inside of my thigh—

"Shut your gay asses up!" Kennith's voice echoed through the still house. Zach's loud, rough laughter followed, before Lily's cheerful voice: "I'm tryna sleep in here, please just give us an hour or two before you get your freak on!"

We froze. Even Kai's face was panicked. *He should have been more careful what he wished for.*

Aja's ominous chuckle was then heard from the master bedroom, which had been given to Mr. and Mrs. Arche for the next few nights. "Oh, let them be. It's just boys being boys!"

....

The next morning, I woke with a small hand cupping my cheek. The palm was fucking hot—like it had been dipped in boiling water beforehand. It was also sweaty. I cringed, praying that it wasn't Kai's hand.

"I think he's dead."

"He's not dead, stupid. Look. He's breathing."

"Don't call me stupid! You're stupid!"

"Please leave," I groaned, swatting Kara and Jeremy away before pushing my face deeper into the pillows. Jeremy continued to squeeze my cheeks with his chubby little hand until my lips jutted out like a fish. "Please," I whined. "Ten more minutes. That's all I want."

"Guys, leave him be. Your mom is making pancakes in the kitchen, so you better get some before it's too late," Kai's cheerful and peppy voice interrupted the cheek-pinching. He corralled the children out the bedroom door. I deflated when it was closed behind them. "Just ten minutes," I begged. I hated mornings with a passion. It probably would have been better if I could wake with the sensation of Kai's breath against my neck, but that wasn't the case that day. Kai collapsed onto the bed, jostling me in the process. I swatted his arms away.

"No. I sleep."

Kai chuckled and kissed my neck just under my ear. "You're adorable when you're tired and grumpy."

"I'm not grumpy. You're grumpy."

But the man wasn't letting up any time soon. "Saskia's helping Lily make breakfast. We need to be up before they finish so we can actually get anything to eat." I was lifted—groaning with discomfort all the while—and the bed was quickly replaced by Kai's lap. But, with the extra movement and blood beginning to speed through my veins as I woke, my eyes widened. Memories of last night began to trickle into my mind. My hand instantly felt the collar, thick, smooth, and permanent. "Do you still like it?" He was watching me intently, waiting for any flash of hesitancy. My answer was almost instant. "Yes. I still love it. I still love you." The man pecked me on the cheek as a warm reply.

Twenty minutes later, I was cleaned, brushed, and ready for the day. I was looking forward to celebrating Christmas with my family. "Good morning, Luka," Aja greeted me with a smile as I entered the spacious dining room with Kai's hand wrapped around my own. They had just begun setting the table with plates of bacon and pancakes. Nothing gave light to the fact that we had been—very rudely, I must say—interrupted last night by Kai's family members.

"G'morning, Aja," I smiled stiffly. Lily put her hand on my shoulder as she set a tall pitcher of orange juice on the floral-printed table cloth. "Good morning, Lily." My voice was different, then, prepared for sly remarks and sex jokes. "How was your sleep last night?" she asked. I couldn't tell if there was some kind of hidden meaning in her question, so I took a deep breath and answered, "Great. Yours?"

Fuck, I had opened myself up to another realm of childish jokes.

"Not bad. At least, it was pretty good, until Jeremy came to ask me why you and Uncle Kai were making such weird noises."

"Did you tell him the truth? That Kai is a kinky bastard and they were getting their freak on?" Zacharia interrupted us with a wide smile. He had stuffed half a bagel between his cheeks. They puffed out like a hamster's. "Stop it, guys. They're...," Aja came to cut the two siblings off, but suddenly paused to think, her narrow eyes scrutinizing me. "...well, Kai is an adult. He knows that there will be repercussions to having sex in a house full of family, but...I'm not so sure about this one...." Finally, my savior, who had disappeared suddenly to leave me to the wolves, turned the corner carrying a bowl of sliced apples. The excitement that bubbled in my veins when I saw him never seemed to tire. It was obvious in his expression that he had overheard a majority of the conversation. "Oh, come on." His arm wrapped around my waist, firmly holding me against his side as if to protect me from his family. My smile was calm and amused, his was stiff. "He's twenty now. I'd say that's old enough to consent to a little fun."

"You mean fun like playing with toy cars at daycare or fun like taking a nap in the afternoon?" Zach was taunting his brother, playing with fire. His words widened the smile on my face. "I mean old enough to enjoy a little bit of whipping and chaining. Unlike you... wuss," was Kai's childish retort. I rolled my eyes and decided to busy myself by helping Saskia carry platters of pancakes into the dining room. Kai kept his hard gaze on his brother. Zach put a hand on his chest dramatically as his mouth gaped open. "Really? We'll see who the pussy is when I take off my leg and turn your head into a baseball."

"Fight me, bitch. Square up." Kai playfully pushed his chest out towards Zach, who mirrored his actions while Lily and I laughed.

"Hey, hey, that's enough. We haven't even sat down to have breakfast yet," Micheal said calmly. His sons calmed almost instantly, snickering and shaking their heads. Kai was different when he was with familiar people; I liked it.

My mother had been sitting in the damn corner of the room during the entire conversation, a small, content smile forming on her lips as Mason returned from the kitchen to hand her a steaming mug of mint tea. He added a kiss to her rosy cheek before taking a seat to watch with her.

Not only were his own wrists burning slightly from last night's handcuffs, which he decided weren't going to be padded, but he could still feel the sting of flogger lines across his spine. That was exactly why Mason had chosen a bedroom for Teressa and himself in the basement.

CHAPTER
SIXTY-SEVEN

BREAKFAST WAS UNEVENTFUL. Kennith was hidden away, and I assumed that he was sleeping. Kai's siblings droned on about 'the good old days' and I was left to laugh and quietly sip at my water—although Zach had decided that it was five-o'clock somewhere and that two or three glasses of wine wouldn't hurt before his morning shower. Kai was refusing to eat again; I watched him move his breakfast lazily around his plate. Then he cut his single pancake in half with the side of his fork. I stole a slice of fried potato. He gave me an expression of mock shock. I laughed and chewed, mocking him. Then, Kai snuck himself a piece of fruit, a chunk of crunchy apple, and popped it in his mouth. I had been victorious.

"So, how was your trip?" Kai and I were still laughing quietly between each other when his mother posed the question; my mother, who sat beside me, seemed just as interested. We looked between each other, unsure of where to start. "Um… it was pretty good," Kai told his suddenly quiet family as he nodded to himself. Both of us began anxiously tossing our food about our plates, refusing to make eye contact with anyone. We really didn't do anything other than have sex, so what could we say?

"Leave them alone. What the hell do you think they'd be doing if they were alone for a week in the middle of nowhere? I'm sure they weren't just sitting and enjoying the scenery," Zachary said, leaning back in his chair. Lily snorted, "True."

"What were they doing, then?" Jeremy asked before stuffing half a pancake into his mouth. His wide eyes flashed between Kai and I. Zachary elbowed his sister. "They were just having fun, kiddo," Aja sighed, tossing her napkin onto her plate. Then she laughed to herself; I wondered what was so funny to her. "Just having fun," she repeated through a snicker.

Micheal managed to coax Kennith from Lily's back home office after breakfast. He still refused to eat, but I was at least able to entertain him with some quiet conversation in the living room while Saskia, Aja, and Alex cleaned the dishes. He was glad that Kai had finally collared me, and he couldn't express his excitement enough. His milky, unfocused eyes opened wide when he touched the collar, unable to resist the cool leather. He knew that collaring was akin to marriage.

"Hey, Kennith," Kai interrupted us after returning from the kitchen. He had just finished his shake; I could smell it on his breath when he planted a kiss on the edge of my lips. "Hi," the boy replied flatly. He let his hand fall back into his folded lap. "What are we doing today?" I asked jovially. Kaia shrugged. "Whatever you want." I glanced at Kennith. His face was stretched long with boredom, and his dark hair was wild from a lack of sleep. He had been up reading again. "Do either of you mind if I borrow you for a minute?" the man leaning over my shoulder asked. Kennith shook his head. "No. Just stay quiet while you do whatever sinful things you end up doing," he hissed in reply, "I can hear everything that goes on in this fucking house." Kaia flinched. I put a comforting hand on his shoulder while I stood. Both of us watched Kennith leave, his hand guiding himself up the stairs.

"I mean, I wasn't talking about sex, but if that's what you want…,"

Kaia said. I dusted off my jeans and scoffed. "Shut up. We had half a week alone together and you still want to do it all over your sister's house? You're a perverted animal, Kaia Arche." Kaia laughed at my declaration, but he didn't object. I allowed him to lead me out of the room, his hand in mine, and out to the back porch after we had each put on a pair of heavy boots. Aja and Micheal were waiting out there; dishes had been done. Lily and her children were taking a brief trip into town to pick up one or two forgotten ingredients for that night's Christmas dinner. Laurent, Alex, Mason, and Zach were having a *Mario Kart* marathon in the basement. Saskia and Janet were sharing a smoke out front. My mother had decided to join them. She seemed to be getting along with everyone perfectly.

"Finally. Are we ready to go?" Aja huffed, tossing her head back on the lounge chair. Her puffy winter jacket protected her from the snow that had accumulated on the seat. Micheal stood as we stepped out onto the snow. I almost slipped. Kaia held me fast. "Go where?" I asked after I caught my balance. Surprisingly, the sun was shining brightly, and, for once, it wasn't negative-twenty, so I decided that my turtleneck sweater and many layers underneath would suffice. Kaia must have agreed, because he didn't turn back to grab a jacket when his parents stood and began walking silently around the house to the car. Still unsure of why we were leaving the festivities, I shot the man beside me a glance. He wasn't paying attention. I decided that I would know soon enough.

The snow was far too deep for any of the average cars that Aja and Micheal owned, so we were forced to borrow Lily's truck. Inside, I was surprised how comfortable it was. Of course, with the weather she lived in, the heated seats kicked on almost immediately, and the engine took only a minute to begin cycling hot air into the cab. "Where are we going?" I wondered aloud. I expected Kai to answer me softly and cheerfully like always, but the only answer I received was silence. My confusion was evident on my face until Micheal spoke up. "We're going to see Cherry. She was Kaia's wife."

For a moment, I was too shocked to speak. I looked between the two other men in the car for an explanation, although neither of them met my wide gaze. My breath left my lungs in a confused huff when Kai found my hand on the seat between us. He stared out the window, though, with a hard gaze that I was sure hid the pain that I would see if he were to turn. He squeezed my fingers tight; I could feel his torture in the grip. My surprise had been forgotten by then and replaced by grief for Kai and his parents.

The rest of our drive, which felt as if it went on for years, had my mind working overtime. We were visiting her grave, obviously, but why had Kai brought me with him? Did he do it regularly? He sure didn't look prepared for it, and I knew I wasn't. Our drive was short. It felt long, but when I looked at the clock on the dash, I realized we had only been driving for about twenty minutes. Kaia didn't wait for me when the car stopped. He hopped out first and walked around to the front so he could find his mother's hand. Instead of grabbing his back, she wrapped her arm around his shoulders and pulled him close. I felt as if I was interrupting something incredibly special.

"Come on. She's this way," Micheal waved me forward. I had been frozen beside the truck for a moment too long, watching the many snow-dusted trees around us sway. We had driven far from the city. I jogged to catch up with the trio, wanting to hold Kai's hand again. I missed it, and *I* wanted to be the one comforting him. I wanted to slap myself for thinking so selfishly. Under our feet, the snow crunched, but I could also feel the trail his parents were attempting to follow, worn bare by animal tracks and familiar visitors. Beyond the little ridge in front of us, I could see a clearing, and as we scaled the ridge, I could see a tombstone that stood out plainly in the sun. It was brighter, shinier, than the snow around it. A little mound of ice sat on the top. Kai wiped it away with a bare hand once we had reached the grave. It wasn't surrounded by flowers or gifts. Half the year, it was probably enveloped in snow too. I wondered what drove the family to put Cherry's grave in such a remote, unforgiving place.

"Hi, Cher," Kai said suddenly. The moment of silence that had come before seemed to pass in an instant. There was no reply from the tombstone; I didn't know why I expected one. Aja was the only person who didn't seem to be a statue. She knelt slowly, pulling a handful of cherry blossom branches, rife with bright, blooming flowers, out of her pocket and set them in the snow in front of the stone. I wondered where she could have gotten them.

Kai was breathing rather heavily, the air clouding around our heads in a haze. Aja slowly put her head against her son's shoulder, patted his arm gently, and whispered, "We'll be in the car." She didn't need to tell him to take his time. They had made the trip many times before, obviously. Micheal and Aja began making their way back over the ridge, their hands linked together. Their time with their daughter-in-law had only been a second… but it was enough.

Kaia remained silent. He had an exhausted glaze on his eyes, and it gave me a better idea of just how taxing the visit was.

He sank to his knees.

My heart lurched, but the sadness that radiated off him held me still. His jeans were getting soaked. His hands, which had landed in the snow in front of him, were submerged in freezing ice. He didn't seem to notice. I couldn't see his face from my height, but I could tell that the way his shoulders trembled and his breathing grew loud and labored wasn't because he was laughing.

I couldn't imagine losing someone I was planning to spend the rest of my life with. I couldn't imagine losing Kai, and Kai had lost his equivalent.

Slowly, I knelt beside him, grimacing at the sharp, almost painful, sting of water that soaked into my pants. "Hi, Cherry."

Kaia looked up at me in shock, surprised by my greeting. When I gave him a comforting smile, his furrowed brows relaxed, and he, although it may have taken all the strength he had left, smiled back. His eyes were red and watery; hot tracks ran down his face. The man sniffed and looked back down to the grave.

"I don't know if Kai has come to tell you before... but I'm Luka." Kaia leaned into me, his snow-dusted hair tickling my chin. "And I have... really, really fallen in love with your man." I couldn't help but chuckle, although I was unsure what I found so funny. It seemed unreal that I was having a conversation, even if it was one-sided, with a dead woman.

"I really like him, Cher. I love him like I love you." Kai's voice was hopeful, like he was trying to convince his dead wife that he deserved me, like he was begging to be able to keep me. My breath caught in my throat at his words. Would she support our relationship? Would she want Kai to be happy with me? Kai had been thinking the possibilities over since we started dating, I was sure, and I liked to think that Cherry wouldn't want her husband to be alone, whether he was re-married or not.

We sat in comfortable silence for another few minutes. Birds sang from the trees and the bright sun finally broke through to shine directly on us. Both of us lifted our heads to soak it in. Kaia's tear tracks sparkled in the light. He closed his eyes and smiled. I took Kai's hands in my own as I kissed the side of his head gently, but it was cut short when I felt the temperature of his flesh. "Jesus, your hands are freezing!"

"My hands are cold...," he replied lamely. He didn't open his eyes, but his face did drop away from the sun. I snorted and shook my head, rubbing them between my own and eventually bringing

ANGEL

them to my face so I could cup his hands and blow a deep huff of warm air against them. His eyes had cracked open by then, admiring my work. "Thank you," he smiled. I smiled back, flashing him teeth and continuing to rub my palms against his. "I think she'd really like you, you know. I really want her back, but... I'm really happy with you too. I know she's happy that you're here," he told me, ensuring that I met his gaze and understood. "Thank you for staying with me."

I replied with another kiss to his temple. "Please don't thank me."

"Can we get out of these clothes now? I'm really, really cold," the man said. The visit had been so brief, I wondered if he was there for permission of some sort. I could feel his body trembling, and I was sure he could feel mine doing the same. I nodded, eager to have a scalding bath with him. Kaia looked at his wife's tombstone with a brighter smile, one that wasn't weighted by grief, and said, "Goodbye, Cher."

CHAPTER
SIXTY-EIGHT

"I MISSED HER A lot. I'm glad you came with me to see her," Kai told me quietly as he dressed. I slipped on a pair of jeans. He did the same. We had finished our dinner of roast chicken, salad, and a plethora of fresh breads an hour ago. The Christmas tree that Lily had on display in the living room had been piled high with gifts for Jeremy and Kara. Although Kai's family wasn't religious in the least, the tradition had been carried on from Aja's side of the family. They didn't celebrate every year, he informed me, but they always did get together during the winter. While Jeremy and his sister worked away at the shining objects under the tree, I curled up against Kai with a glass of spiked eggnog. The lights had been dimmed, cinnamon-scented candles lit, and the dishes washed. Kaia smelt like cinnamon coffee. It was intoxicating. Around us, the family laughed, cracking jokes and recalling past Christmases. Alex struck up a game of go-fish with Zach and Laurent. My mother quietly shared a cup of tea and a lounge chair with Mason.

"I have a question for you two," Aja declared quietly, leaning in. "Since it's Christmas, are you going to propose or something?" Her question was mainly aimed at her son, but she also wondered what could be up my sleeve. His mouth fell open in shock, although we should have been expecting something of the like from her. I giggled

ANGEL

and touched the little collar on my neck. The family hadn't really taken much notice to it.

"Well... Well I kind of already did."

"What?" multiple family members replied. Zach's incredulous gaze was fixed on the two of us suddenly, as was Micheal's and Aja's. Lily looked up from her children to slap her brother on the shoulder. Kai flinched away from her. "What?! I mean, we're already kind of married...," he tried, unprepared for the onslaught of angry family members. My mother sat up to look me in the eye, her gaze unsure. By then, everyone in the room had their attention turned to us. I laughed and placed a hand on Kai's shoulder. "It isn't official," I explained in a calm manner, "We didn't go to a church, and we weren't wearing suits." We weren't wearing anything, really, but I decided to exclude that information. "But we made our vows, and we promised to stay together for a really long time, right?" I looked up at him. Maybe our bedroom relationship wouldn't stand when we're too old to walk, but that was a long time away. Until then, we were going to enjoy it. Kaia drew me into his side and nodded.

"Well when in the bloody hell was anyone going to tell us?!" Aja cried, rage seeping into her sneer. "Were you just not going to? Kaia Arche, you—you..." she struggled with her anger for a moment, her mouth working with an overload of words that hadn't yet formed. Micheal, accustomed to her outbursts, silently rubbed her back and waited for her brain to catch up with her mouth. Then she sighed—although it was more of a growl. "I'm so goddamn happy for you." She deflated, defeated. I laughed. Kaia was still breathing hard. "Thank you," I said to her, hugging Kaia's bicep in a playful attempt to calm him. He took my glass of eggnog, bitter with the last mouthful of sweetened rum, and threw it back. I scoffed. "You guys are *married?*" Lily asked as if we hadn't just had the conversation of the century. "You owe me ten," Zach declared, holding his hand out to his sister. She waved him away. He grimaced but retracted his hand, deciding to save their fight for another day.

That night was spent packing and we left early the next morning after a warm goodbye to Kai's family. Kennith, for the first time, came to greet me. He was quiet and reserved, but he seemed to be in a better mood than when I last saw him. His goodbye was quick and apologetic—I knew he liked being with his family, and he went to the reunions whether he wanted to or not, but something still made him feel alienated. All I could do was give him a tight hug and hope that one day he would be brave enough to experience the world with us instead of keeping himself locked in a bedroom. "Thank you for making him happy. He hasn't been for a long time," were the last words he mumbled to me. I smiled brightly and rubbed his shoulders. "Don't thank me. Makes me feel like I actually did something. He's happier because he wants to be," I replied. Kennith didn't object. Instead, he pursed his lips and shrugged, keeping his unseeing gaze on the ground.

We took a normal airline back to California. Using his father's company's plane had been a one-time thing. We flew coach the entire way, and the only thing I missed was the fact that I couldn't ride his thigh after I had jerked him off under the blanket. The frustration lasted for the full eight hour flight, even after we had both orgasmed. The plane's bathroom was looking mighty attractive. Mason and my mother sat behind us on the plane, giggling quietly together like schoolchildren. She didn't seem like the same person I had known just a few months ago.

When we landed, after the sexual frustration and tight muscles were over, Mason drove my mother home from the airport. He didn't expect to be home until at least ten-o'clock that night. It was only eight by the time we made it to Kai's apartment. I was eager to see Rosa again; I had missed her. I realized that I had missed everything, the garage, the cars, the quiet elevator to his floor. His world was mine, now, and I was more than happy to finally share it with him forever. The man removed his bags after mine and we took the elevator hand-in-hand. We were eager to change into sweatpants and sleep off our travelling after another hour of fun. "We're home!" I called out excitedly, expecting her to jump into our arms once the doors were open. The house was quiet, though. I sighed, my smile faltering. "Rosa?" Kai called. Still, no answer. He tossed his keys onto the kitchen counter and dropped his jacket over the back of one of the stools. "She's probably out getting herself dinner," he decided. "Hopefully she'll grab us something, too," I replied. I really didn't care what I was eating, all I knew was that I was famished.

"She'll be gone for a while."

Both of us whirled, our smiles falling. I recognized the voice before my gaze even met Cade's. He regarded us with a glare of enmity and hunger; the man was obviously there to even the score-board after my escape last time we had seen each other. Surprisingly, my stomach didn't drop when I recognized him. It only fell between my legs when I noticed the little handgun he pointed between us.

"Where is she?" Kai growled, unsure of whether Caden had hurt her or if she really was out shopping. I prayed it was the latter. "Don't worry. She's *fine*," was all Caden told us. He took a step forward. Both of us took a step back. We knew that Caden wasn't planning to hurt us. Sure, he had brought a gun, but unless we did something to upset him, he wouldn't use it. I wondered briefly if we could just pay him off, give him enough to get out of the country, maybe. But Cade was a mad man. He didn't want money.

"Luka, clothes off. Now. Kaia, on your knees." His command made me sick. I could see Kai turning green from the corner of my eye. He shot me a wary glance, knowing that we would both be pumped full of lead if we didn't obey. I was surprised by just how easily Kai seemed to be keeping his emotions under control.

"Now!" Cade's voice, which was once soft and firm, grew into an enraged roar that made both of us jump. Tears gathered in my eyes. Slowly, I lifted my shirt over my head. The gun was pointed towards Kai, but Caden's primal gaze was fixed on me, my body. My stomach rolled. My last meal threatened to come up when Kaia slowly sank to the ground, both knees hitting the wood softly. Caden seemed satisfied with his actions. "Cade, we can give you money—," Kai began. He was silenced by Cade cocking his firearm. Both their jaws ticked, one in fear and the other with impatience. I slipped my shoes off. As I hesitated with my pants, I glanced at Kai, wondering if Caden's motives were really worth it. Would he just shoot me and do whatever he was going to anyway? Kai's expression was agonized. It made my heart hurt to know that his wife and him had probably already experienced the exact same thing before she died.

"Keep going!" Caden ordered. His voice wasn't as loud or angry anymore; it didn't need to be. "How can this be better than money?!" I snapped finally, my hands balling into fists. My narrowed eyes were filled with fire. He, although initially surprised by my outburst, scoffed. "You think the embarrassment I experienced can be paid back with money? You should have just let me take you that night. That stupid bar tender shouldn't have fucking been there!" I wasn't sure how to reply, I just froze.

My fearful eyes found Kai's, and his expression matched mine. "You're so stupid for coming back here," Kai hissed at him. Caden laughed, "Revenge doesn't have a conscience."

Still, I was refusing to remove any more items of clothing. He took notice of it immediately. "You're not making this easy, Luka." Of course I wasn't. What was he expecting? The man flicked his gun towards the stairs, causing my heart to flutter. Both of them could see my lungs pushing up and down against my ribs. "Up the stairs.

ANGEL

Kai, you too. I can't—," Caden's order was cut short by the deafening sound of the elevator. It cut through his words like a knife and left us all reeling for a good second.

Someone was home, and by Caden's suddenly distracted and momentarily panicked expression, they hadn't been invited.

The lights blinked at the top of the metal doors. We watched it; one... two...

Cade moved fast, too fast for me. In a moment, my breath was gone, and his arm was wrapped around my shoulders, locking me tight against his front. I could feel his hot breath against one side of my neck and the cold end of his firearm on the other. It reminded me of the first few times I had met Kai.

The doors opened, and, with the loud, ringing *ding* of arrival, the entire room seemed to move at once. Cade straightened his arm and moved the gun away from me. Its sights fell on the figure exiting the elevator. Out of the corner of my eye, I could see Kai lurch just as quickly, seeking cover from any fire on the other side of the kitchen island. Rosa almost noticed the danger too late. I wasn't sure if she had even seen the firearm or sensed it; she was ducking so quickly. The bullet that should have hit her blew off a chunk of the drywall beside the elevator. Again, he pulled the trigger. She disappeared behind the island in a blur of black hair and red leather jacket. The air that once embraced the deafening cracks of sound instantly grew silent. Nothing moved, save for the gun still searching for a body part sticking out from the island. Cade kept his arm tight around me, squeezing my lungs even tighter than they already were.

"Why do you guys always insist on doing this shit right when I get home?" Rosa exclaimed, as if the timing was more of a hindrance than the bullet waiting for her. "If you hadn't come, one of them would already be dead, darling," Cade sneered. He wanted to get his show on the road. I could hear Rosa cocking a firearm from across the room. "Just let me go, we can pay you-," I began, hating myself for begging. He cut me off with the barrel of the gun pressing against my jugular, bruising the flesh. If he pulled the trigger, it would probably be sudden and painless, but then he wouldn't have a shield against Rosa. What options did he have? He was cornered, not having considered Rosa's early arrival, and he couldn't even his score with me when he had two living witnesses.

Rosa stood.

Her eyes were narrow and hard, and I wondered how she finally grew the balls to stand and point her gun at Caden. He was powerless against her. The man couldn't move fast enough to set his sights on her, nor was he willing to lose his leverage. If Rosa was to shoot, I would be the one going down first, and the realization turned my veins to icy little tubes, although I knew that Rosa would do her best to keep us all safe. Kaia was beside her in a moment, his gaze never leaving mine. I could see that he was scared; he knew that Cade wouldn't stop until one of us was dead. Rosa's shoulders and elbows were locked, her gaze steely. The action and the scent of fresh shots made her excited; she and Mason lived for it. That fact scared me. For a moment, we were all locked together at a standstill.

"What do you think is gonna be waiting for you if you pull that trigger?" Rosa asked. Cade scoffed. "Exactly what I've been wanting."

Rosa's jaw ticked and her gaze briefly met mine; she wasn't sure how to diffuse the hostage situation. She couldn't reason with a mad man. Despite the freezing little barrel against my neck, I managed to speak up with a little less difficulty, "You won't get away. You shoot me, Rosa is gonna shoot you. You won't survive." I did my best to make it sound like a promise, although my throat was raw and burnt with fear. "I'll kill you, anyway, Caden," Kai sneered, the threat ripping from his chest like a lion's roar.

I could tell that the man behind me was getting impatient. He rocked himself on his toes. I could feel his arm that caged my chest trembling. '*Don't do it,*' I prayed silently. Whatever he was about to do would not end well, especially when we all knew that if he emptied his firearm, Rosa wouldn't dare shoot hers until I was safely out of the way.

The gun left my neck. Cade aimed it, in a flash of black and flesh, and pulled the trigger.

"No!" I exclaimed, although it wasn't anything more than a short yelp. I had leaned forward just as fast and pushed his arm down with all the strength I could muster, knowing that he would respond with twice the force. I would have to trust Rosa to do *something;* shoot him or allow Kai to tackle the man and rip the cords from his neck. My eyes closed, my jaw locked, and my nails dug into Cade's arm.

Rosa pulled her trigger. My throat didn't even have time to close shut. I worried that I wouldn't be able to contain my scream.

I couldn't feel the bullet rip through the air, but I *could* feel Caden jerk and grunt at my side. As he fell, my shaking fingers tore his handgun from his grasp and flung it to the side, almost as if it burned me. Following the same ritual, I scrambled away myself, tripping into Kai's waiting arms. I didn't look back, but I could hear, above the ringing in my ears, Rosa's soft footsteps and Caden's soft gurgle. He was dying; Rosa's shot had hit its mark. The sound was distinct, and I couldn't manage to ignore it or pretend that I was anywhere but Kaia's kitchen at that moment.

Kai's grip on my shoulder was painful. His other hand was buried in my hair. It kept my head still, and I wondered if I would be able to keep my eyes shut and gaze away from the bloody scene behind me if his support wasn't there. The edge of my shirt sleeve had been splattered with the red liquid. I almost vomited at the sight.

"Kai, call 911," Rosa ordered. Although I was sure that she had just killed a man, she seemed to be the only one in the room with her brain still attached to her body. Mine was scattered, unsure. Knowing that I was safe made the urge to sneak a peek even stronger. Kai's mind was, well, probably not much better. Was he happy? I couldn't hear the gurgles anymore. Rosa was silent. Was Cade dead? Did I want to see?

"Kai!" Rosa exclaimed suddenly. Both of us jumped; I hadn't even realized that we had been frozen on the spot. He was quick to follow Rosa's instructions, but with my loss of support, I finally allowed my gaze to fall on Cade's body, almost eagerly. Surprisingly, it didn't evoke any new emotions. I was still scared and uncertain, but the relief I expected still hadn't arrived. He was motionless. I couldn't see his face. Rosa's stature wasn't as straight and rigid. Her firearm was in a still hand at her side. "You killed him," I whispered. It wasn't a question, but I certainly wanted to know the answer. Could he still haunt me? If he was gone, could I still remember his hands on my body like he was actually there? "You probably don't want to look, Luka. Stop it." My wide eyes snapped to hers. They were still hard and narrow. My body began to tremble. Blood was pooling on the floor beside the body.

When the bile bubbled up, I couldn't stop it. Kai's muffled voice faded behind me as he spoke to a dispatcher. One hand shot out to grab the counter edge before I was leaning to the side and vomiting loudly. It splashed my shoes. Tears welled in my eyes, obscuring my vision. Sirens sounded in the street below.

CHAPTER
SIXTY-NINE

THE OFFICER THAT arrived in Kai's apartment first was massive. He was a bodybuilder, quite obviously, and his scowl made me want to vomit again. Despite his gnarly appearance, he regarded the three of us with respect as his men worked. With his voice quiet and his actions slow, he led Kai and I into the corner of the kitchen. Kai turned me away from Cade. I gripped his hand tight. Across the room, Rosa had her arms crossed over her chest, looking two officers up and down as they spoke to her. Her posture was tense, but she didn't seem worried. "Sir," a new officer joined us, interrupting Officer Kent's explanation and position on the investigation they had already started. The four of us turned expectantly and watched the young woman hand a folded piece of paper to him. "It was left on their bed, sir." Kent's brows were furrowed. Kai and I exchanged fearful glances. Caden had left us a note. "So you've known this guy for a while," Kent said eventually, after the two of us watched him read it. His expression didn't change, which made me wonder what Cade left us. Whatever had been printed, I was sure that we probably didn't want to read it. "Longer than a long time," Kai replied. He seemed to be turning green too.

"Do you want to see it?" Kent asked. Kai and I exchanged fearful glances. We probably didn't, but the curiosity was overwhelming. "Can Rosa?" I decided before he could. Kent waved Rosa and her interrogator towards us. "Hello again, Rosa. I hoped to never see you again," officer Kent told her, shaking her hand. The fact that she wasn't in handcuffs finally made more sense. She returned the handshake with the same strength. "And you, Kent."

"A note was left. They want you to read it." The woman who immediately hardened her features held out her hand. Kent surrendered the note. We watched Rosa's brows furrow with concentration. She put her hand on her chin thoughtfully. The silence that crept by was angering as I watched her gaze flicker on the page. Was she going to release any information about it? Was she waiting for one of us to take it?

"They don't want to read it," she decided finally, thrusting it back into Kent's chest. Rosa's brows were pulled together in such a way that almost made her seem angry, but the woman was able to get her emotions in check quickly. He seemed slightly flustered, but understood, based on the contents of the letter. "Alright. Officer Holland here will bring you guys downstairs. I'm afraid this is officially a crime scene. It's on lockdown until we can get the information we need. Do you all have any place to stay for a while?"

"Yeah. We do," I answered. Surprisingly, my voice didn't crack or falter. The squeeze I felt in my hand that connected Kai and I fueled my confidence. Still, we didn't want to look at the men and women working efficiently around us, and I believed that that made us all stronger. If we did, the both of us would crumble.

The only place I could imagine staying was my mother's house. It certainly sounded better than a hotel, and I wanted to go *home*. No one objected to my answer. Kent nodded. Officer Holland, the woman who first gave us the letter, arrived to lead us away. We weren't allowed to pack any bags; I only grabbed one of Kai's jackets to wear instead of the shirt that was left bloodied. Rosa was moody during the entire ride through town, sulking in her seat like a child. As houses passed, they grew smaller and smaller, easing us into my world. We cruised past the basketball court I had once played in with old, forgotten friends. Then we passed the little back road that led up towards Mr Rhineback's haunted home. I had been beaten up in that alley. Mr. Rhineback welcomed me in for coffee afterwards, allowing me to clean my new cuts and teaching me that maybe his home wasn't so haunted.

The house we pulled up to looked distorted. I couldn't remember it being so small or so dark, and the apple tree on the side of the home was never that big and fruitless, looming over my window like an evil thing waiting to take me away. The outside was so misleading, though. Kai was grimacing at it. I almost wanted to laugh at him. Then I remembered why we were there.

"This is it?" Holland asked, her dark ponytail bobbing. "Yeah," I replied, unbuckling my seatbelt. The other two passengers did the same. "You'll each be getting calls soon. You'll be expected down at the station within the next few days," was all she told us. Rosa stayed a moment to thank her. It was obvious that her past with officer Kent and his department, whatever that past was, allowed us to make a quick escape from the scene. I wouldn't be surprised to learn that she had been sleeping with him—or at least something of the like. Whatever the reason, I was grateful. Kai was too.

Kai took my hand in his as we crossed the lawn, which had grown some over the winter months. His fingers were shaking; I knew that his mind would be reeling, even if our distance from Caden's body was growing. I could still see him on the ground and feel the gun against my neck. Far too many times have I had a metal barrel pressed into my flesh, and it was something I didn't plan on experiencing again. My own hand shook as I unlocked the door with the spare key hidden outside. Mason had heard the rattling and had the door open before I could touch the handle. His smile was bright. I was surprised to see that he wasn't naked after being alone with my mother for so long. His smile faltered when he recognized the toture and exhaustion in our eyes.

"What happened?" the man asked immediately. He looked between us, his heartbeat speeding. I clenched my teeth, tasting acid. "Do we have any alcohol?" was all I could think to reply with.

....

"So... So you'll be talking with the police again soon?" my mother asked. She set her mug of tea on the table and wrapped her sweater tighter around herself. Mason's eyes flickered between us. Rosa bounced to the music being fed from her headphones as she stirred macaroni and cheese in the kitchen. She didn't seem bothered by the series of events. I wondered if she was just relieved that no physical harm came to anyone she cared about. "Yeah," I replied. My nerves were calming. My home still smelled like musty cigarettes, although it was being replaced by fresh air and home cooking. It was more *home* than Kai's apartment. Kai was tense beside me. His grip on my hand was like iron. "Are you two having dinner, then? I'm not hungry anymore," Teressa said. She and Mason were planning on ordering pizza. The man put his hand on her back for support. I shook my head. I wanted to sleep forever, not eat.

Suddenly, Kai was on his feet, barreling past my legs. I barely had time to retract them, or I was sure he would have stepped on them. Three pairs of eyes watched him with concern while he disappeared around the corner and into the half bathroom that sat just beside the front entrance. The door slammed shut. We could hear him retching.

I closed my eyes and sighed. Rosa removed her headphones and

ANGEL

listened with an expression that wasn't exactly caring. My mother stared at the door with a gleam of horror in her gaze; she was just as concerned as I was. After a solid minute, once Kai's vomiting ceased and the air grew quiet again, Mason stood. He stepped over Teressa's legs, pursed his lips, and followed Kai's path slowly. The bathroom door opened and closed. Rosa shot me a glance. Despite her shield of disinterest, I could tell that Rosa was scarred by the night's events. She had known Caden even before Kai met him. She had seen everything from the beginning, and knowing that Caden's disgusting legacy wouldn't be forgotten enraged her. The people and relationships he had left in ruins made us all feel hopeless. How could we fix it?

"Tell them I'll be upstairs," I told my mother. I wasn't sure how long Kai would sit with Mason. Maybe they would only be a minute. Maybe Kai wouldn't see me for another hour. Whatever amount of time he needed, he knew that I would be waiting for him, no matter how damaged he was. Mom nodded and bowed her head when I leaned across the coffee table to kiss her hairline. My gaze didn't wander to the bathroom door handle like I expected it to. The home was still silent. Rosa's macaroni was burning.

In the attic, in the bedroom that had been my safe haven for so long, I was able to finally take a breath that seemed to reach my lungs. The air was warm up there; it cleared my head. My small collection of CDs was still untouched in the corner. I could hear the apple tree's leaves rustling outside the window. The branches scraped against the glass; I found it incredibly annoying. So, to block the noise, I pulled my curtains closed and collapsed on the bed that sat beneath them before tearing the crumpled blankets from the end of the bed up to my neck. They smelled stale. The familiar scent would return once Kai did, I knew.

I only had to wait, drifting between conscious and unconscious, for about twenty minutes. The footsteps were muffled by the comforter pulled over my ears, but my head snapped up when I recognized them as Kai's. His ruffled hair appeared at the top of the steps first. Then it bobbed and his long, agonized face grew over the top step. The man glanced around the room in dismay before his gaze landed on mine. He looked apologetic. I wondered why. I had vomited too. His mind had just taken longer to process that the man he had once both loved and hated madly was dead. "Can I lie with you?" Kai asked. His voice was raw, aged at least twenty years. I nodded silently, pulling back the covers to welcome him in. I had made it warm for him. Kaia crossed the room slowly, his legs shaking. I could see his hands trembling. His body, exhausted after vomiting for a good few minutes, needed the rest, and until he got a few hours of it, he would continue to look like he had been through hell. We *had* been through hell.

Once he was under the sheets, I realized just how small my bed was. There was barely room for Kai alone on the mattress that, for so many nights before, seemed as though it went on forever, leaving me alone in the cold. I was thankful to feel him align his body snuggly with mine, allowing no space between. He watched me with that black gaze, never leaving mine, and released a deep, hot breath. He had at least rinsed his mouth with mouthwash.

I studied his empty, beaten gaze for a long time. He looked *raw*. The man's eyes twitched. His breath grew uneven. In the sheets, the fabric that covered and cradled us, I could feel his hands moving. His fingers curled and uncurled against my belly. Still, they shook. I was about to grab them.

"I should be happy right now."

I blinked quickly at his sudden declaration, waited for him to elaborate.

"I feel sick. I know I hated him, but I loved him for longer. He hurt a lot of people. I'm sorry, I...," his voice trailed off. His eyes grew unfocused, landing on my collar bone. Without interrupting his working, aching thought process, I waited.

"Can you understand if I told you that I still wanted him to get better? To... To treat people right so I could forgive him? It's not fair that Rosa shot him. He made mistakes, he... he didn't deserve a bullet. He deserved a lot of things, but not that kind of death." Kai's gaze never wandered or focused. He was becoming increasingly agitated. With the last of my strength, I refrained from frowning at him. As much as I hated Caden, Kai had a different past with him. Then was the time for him to deal with that, even if he couldn't understand that his past love deserved what he got. Assuming it was something akin to Stockholm syndrome, I decided to leave the subject hanging in the air around our heads. Kaia would continue the conversation with James soon. Until then, I would hold him. He welcomed my embrace silently. Kaia closed his eyes against my chest.

"Yeah. I can understand."

Printed in Canada